SWEET SUNDAY

Also by John Lawton

SWEET SUNDAY

John Lawton

Grove Press
New York

First published in Great Britain in 2002 by Weidenfeld & Nicolson.

ISBN 978-0-8021-2423-4
eISBN 978-0-8021-9237-0

Grove Press
an imprint of Grove Atlantic
154 West 14th Street
New York, NY 10011

Distributed by Publishers Group West

groveatlantic.com

16 17 18 19   10 9 8 7 6 5 4 3 2 1

for

Nora York

who
blew in from Winnetka

SWEET SUNDAY

'A graceful generation that had to work for men wrapped up in their individual egos, a sin their flesh is not heir to.'

Joe Flaherty, *Managing Mailer*

'... the best of a generation were being lost—some among the hippies to drugs, some among the radicals to an almost hysterical frenzy of alienation.'

I.F. Stone

§

'It was fun to have that sense of engagement when you jumped on the earth and the earth jumped back.'

Abbie Hoffmann

'It takes a long time for sentiments to collect into action, and often they never do ... I wanted to make actions rather than effect sentiments.'

Norman Mailer, *Paris Review*

§

'Worst of all, expansion is eroding the precious and time honored values of community with neighbors and communion with nature. The loss of these values breeds loneliness and boredom and indifference ... once the battle is lost, once our natural splendor is destroyed, it can never be recaptured. And once man can no longer walk with beauty or wonder at nature his spirit will wither and his sustenance be wasted.'

Lyndon Baines Johnson

'You can't dig the moon
Until
You dig the earth.'
William Eastlake, from *Whitey's on the Moon Now*

§

'No one was saved.'
Paul McCartney

1994

'I have but one claim to fame.' Now, why do people say that? It doesn't mean what it says. They have no fame to lay claim to. What it really means is that they once met someone who was, or got, famous, which scrap of knowledge somehow enlightens their otherwise interminable obscurity—not even famous for fifteen minutes, just touching fame. OK, I have three 'claims to fame'. I was in high school with Buddy Holly, class of '55, in Lubbock, West Texas. I once, when I was fifteen and like Tom Sawyer thought senators must be ten feet tall, shook the hand of Lyndon Baines Johnson—I did not wash the hand for a week. And, I once met Norman Mailer. Well, twice really.

§

The first time I met Mel Kissing I asked him the question everyone asked him sooner or later. How does anyone come to be called Mel Kissing? Mel told the story I heard him tell a hundred times over the years that followed. Back on Ellis Island in the 1900s Immigration asked his grandfather what his name was. 'Last name first, then your Christian name.' The old guy spoke slowly, understood slowly, and maybe he was struggling with the idea that any part of him might be Christian and said 'Kissinger, Melchior' so slowly the Immigration guy took the 'er' for a pause and wrote down Kissing. Mel Kissing was really Melchior Kissinger IV.

§

I thought of Mel today. The day Tricky Dicky died, and TV went apeshit with a Nixathon. Wet April, waiting for spring. I was stuck indoors with the flu bug, hoping for the pleasures of channel surfing till my thumb ached. Instead I got Nixon. The nation got Nixon, and more Nixon, and it was like he'd never happened. The Nixon of the tele-obits was a statesman. Like there were two Richard Milhous Nixons. The dead statesman and the crook, and the dead statesman was somehow not connected to the crook. 'Only Nixon could go to China.' I heard that fifty times today. Old film of Tricky telling America there would have been no peace with Vietnam, no arms limitation deal with Russia, 'cept that he went to China. He's wrong. Only Nixon *went* to China. Anyone could have gone. Just so happened it was Tricky Dicky. And I defy anyone to point to a democratized China as a result of diplomatic recognition and 'most favored trading nation' status. That's just horsepucky. Why will we never have sanctions against China, whatever China does? Because in six weeks all those Wal-Marts the size of football stadiums that seem to fringe every American city would run out of stuff to sell as half their stock is made in China.

(Good God, am I preaching? Absofuckinlutely, darling—as my late wife would have said.)

§

Mel used to tell me it was people like me who would not vote for Humphrey who let in Nixon. I voted for Herbie 'Flim-Flam' McCoy, who ran on the United Fibbers of America ticket. 'All politicians are liars. The difference between me and them is I know it. Believe me, people. I'll never tell you the truth.' I voted for that. Me and about five thousand others. I wouldn't blame you if you said you'd never noticed

Flim-Flam McCoy. He polled less than Frank Zappa. And Flim-Flam didn't let Nixon in. That was George Wallace. A fraction of Wallace's southern millions would've saved Humphrey's skin. But fuckit, the man was not worth saving. Mel and I did not go up to New Hampshire in 1968 and root for Gene McCarthy just to see LBJ's stooge run in his stead. I'd sooner vote for ... well ... fuckit ... I'd've voted for Wavy Gravy if Wavy Gravy'd stood. Sheeit—wonder what happened to Wavy Gravy? Hi, Wavy, long time no ...

I thought of Mel today. I guess it's just Nixon—symbol of an era. Lots of things could make me think of Mel, but today it was the First Criminal. And I thought about the time in '69 when I was getting ready to call him and say, 'You know what today is? Today is exactly one year since LBJ said he wouldn't run again. March 31st. Let's go out and get skunk drunk!'

But he called me. Said, 'Can you come over to Brooklyn tonight? Norman Mailer's running for Mayor.'

Mel was a hotshot reporter on the *Village Voice*, Mailer was its founder and still owned a piece of the action. I'd done eighteen months at the *Voice* myself, and I'd never even set eyes on Mailer. But then, I wasn't a hotshot. It figured Mel would know Mailer. All the same, I said, 'What?'

And he said, 'Don't tell me you won't vote for Mailer. Dammit, Turner, I still blame you for Tricky Dicky!'

So that's why Nixon makes me think of Mel.

All former presidents will be at the funeral in California. Gerald Ford, Jimmy Carter, Ronald Reagan, George Bush. Slick Willie too. I hope they bury him with a stake though his heart. Just in case.

I buried Mel with a volume of Wallace Stevens. It was what he wanted.

§

It was the summer we went to the moon. The hottest, the sweatiest, the longest—the most American. 1969. The American year in the American century—whitey on the moon, our boy from Wapakoneta uttering the most rehearsed one-liner since Henry Morton Stanley trekked thousands

of miles across Africa with 'Dr Livingstone, I presume?' bursting on his lips
with every step. A small step for man and blahdey blah de blah. Before
that, before the Summer-we-went-to-the-Moon, it was the Spring-we-
went-to-Brooklyn.

I rode the subway out to Clark Street in Brooklyn Heights, and gave
myself enough time to walk down to the promenade and catch the last
of the sun going down over Manhattan. I have often thought that's the
best reason to live in Brooklyn. You can see Manhattan. You can stare
at Manhattan. You can ogle Manhattan, rising up on that narrow strip
of land like a castle with a hundred turrets and never get enough of it.
First time I saw it I thought of the Disney logo, Tinkerbell buzzing the
towers of a fantasy castle. The castle is largely Wall Street, but you can
suspend disbelief long enough to take in the finest skyline on earth. The
Statue of Liberty faces Brooklyn. The lady's a way off, but she's looking
right at you. I used to think this was odd. Give me your tired, your poor,
and she's looking at Brooklyn. Before I saw her I automatically assumed
the face and the slogan looked out to sea, to Europe where all those
huddled masses were teeming from. Now I'm glad she faces Brooklyn,
or I'd have to ride the tempest-tost Staten Island Ferry just to see her
face once in a while.

I went out to the promenade with Mel about a month after I first got
to the city—sometime in '63—just to be able to say 'Wow'. To be able
to send a postcard home and say I've seen the Statue of Liberty.

'What do you think I am? A fucking tourist? I live here. I was born
here. I don't have to look at New York, I live New York,' he said.

New Yorkers can be like that. I know an ex-cop who says things like
'I am New York', as though that goes with the round shoulders and the
beer-belly, and a look on his face that says 'hick' to you. They think all
out-of-towners are hicks. Mel used to call me a hayseed. Told me my
habit of chewing the end of a pencil was left over from chewing straw. So
often the people who see the beauty in New York City are people like
me, from out of town and out of state. New Yorkers can be blind to it.

That night I made a point of telling Mel I'd meet him at the end of
the block. There was no way I was going to ring on the bell and cold
call Norman Mailer, but there was also no way I was going to watch the
sun go down over Manhattan with a loudmouth New York Jew like Mel
whispering sweet cynicisms in my ear.

I walked back from the harbor to the corner of Pierrepont and Columbia. Mel was waiting. A little guy in a great fur ragbag of a coat, wrapped up against the winter with only hair and beard to show, and hair and beard filled most of his face, and if it weren't for the thick spectacles that magnified his eyes like the moon in a night sky you'd be hard put to find an opening in the fur. Then he smiled, a beaming grin of perfect teeth that had lived in the grip of braces most of his adolescence. The visible evidence of a childhood well-ordered and mapped out by his parents that had led to this urban gypsy and to their inevitable heartbreak—had they but lived to see it.

'For a gumshoe you make one hell of a noise,' he said.

I never apologize for the boots. I know he saw them as a clichéd symbol of the West, a symbol of everything I told him I'd left, but, dammit, once you break them in, a pair of Tony Lama's boots are the most comfortable thing on earth.

'Hi, hippie.'

'Hi, cowboy. Been out lookin' at your statue again?'

'Don't piss on it, Mel.'

'I wasn't.'

A hand shot from a furry pocket and pushed the bridge of his glasses back up his nose. His glasses always seemed to be slipping.

'I wasn't. I was about to say if you think it looks good from here you should see it from Norman's rear window.'

It was a short walk along the Heights to an old brownstone—up porch steps from the street and push at an unlocked door. Then the filtered, almost muted hubbub of whatever was happening up on the top floor filtering down to the lobby. A long climb. Five flights and Mel's little legs pounding away in front of me.

The room was full. The all American motley, gliding around under a curved ceiling, along the towering flights of books, in and out the hanging rope ladders. Rope ladders. Really. Made Mailer seem for the moment like a literary buccaneer. Rumour was he shinned up these ladders into the top of the house and wrote among the gods. Then, there he was in front of me. A good-looking little guy with an impish face and bright, bright blue eyes. Offering to shake hands except that he seemed to have a glass in each hand—one lot of bourbon swirling one way around the rocks, the other orbiting backwards like the tassels on a stripper's pasties as he gestured with each hand and set the booze in motion.

'Good to see you,' he said simply, and the necessity of a huddle passed over the pair of them as Mel said, 'A word if I may, Norman' and Norman put one arm across his back, bourbon in hand, and steered him into a corner.

I was left alone. Wondering who in this room I knew. I knew many of Mel's friends. But, given the kind of man he was, there were bound to be twice as many I'd never met or never even heard of. A good-looking—no downright beautiful—woman struck me as a face I knew, even if I could not put a name to it, blonde hair and big glasses, and I was picking my way across the room trying to think of an opener less corny than 'Haven't we met someplace?' when I saw a face I really did know. Jerry Rubin, leader of the Yippies, serene upon the sofa, a small body of calm in a sea of human turmoil. Another little Jewish guy all but lost in hair and beard. His hand shot up and beckoned me over.

'Raines. Last place I expected to see you.'

He had a point. I had long since ceased to be a joiner. There was no gathering in which I could not be made to feel unease unto surly silence. Mel had cajoled me onto the Pentagon March in '67, much as he had cajoled me into this room. I'd stuffed flowers down the barrels of National Guard rifles while Ed Sanders read the exorcism—'Out Demons out!'—and Rubin and Abbie Hoffman got us all to link hands and chant 'Ommmm' in an attempt to levitate the Pentagon. That was where we differed. Mel didn't think it would work. I knew it wouldn't work, and Hoffman thought it would. I'd no idea what Rubin thought. I'd spent a night in jail—hundreds of us had. Many got their heads cracked. I was not one of them. Last summer, the summer of '68, Rubin had called me up and told me I had to be in Chicago for the Democrats Convention. Absolutely had to be there. I took one look at it and headed for home. I wondered if I was about to be confronted with my cowardice.

'Last damn place *I* expected to find me. Who's the blonde?' I let him follow my look.

'Pussy power,' he said.

I always liked Rubin. He was against the grain—untypical. So many people at the forefront of sixties' protest struck me as being like Charlie Chaplin in *Modern Times*—unlucky enough to have picked up a red flag in the street just as a march turns the corner and makes him into an unwitting leader. Rubin was not like that. He wasn't the brightest guy I ever met, but he was born to lead. He loved to lead. He was, as he put it himself, a pretty mainstream kind of person. He never thought of himself as against the grain—as far as Jerry was concerned he *was* the grain. Whatever was happening in his generation he'd be at the heart of it. It did make me wonder what was happening here. Rubin and 'pussy power' did not sound like a natural combination. I almost pulled a muscle trying to raise an eyebrow at this.

'It's Gloria Steinem,' he added and before I could ask him any more a guy in thick black glasses—a beat's head on a jacket and tie torso—stood up at the back of the room and started calling the night to order. I got the slow Rolodex of the mind to flip a card. Yes. I knew the name. I'd just forgotten the face. A few years back she'd landed herself a job as a *Playboy* bunny and exposed it for the tits 'n' ass job that it was in a magazine. She and Mailer did not sound like the most natural combination either. I began to get the feeling that this was going to be the long night of the strange bedfellow—like me, everyone who'd made the climb to the top of the Mailer house was the unwilling partner in an odd couple combination. And then it hit me, as Norman took up a spot with his back to the harbor window, I saw Manhattan like I'd never seen it before. The greatest rear window in the world. I'd kill to be able to live with that sight. I found myself wondering how a writer ever got to write. Wouldn't you just waste your days looking out the window?

It was a reverie—the like of which I am prone to. Watching Wall Street go out, room by room, floor by floor. By the time I surfaced the night had changed and the mood of the room with it and if I'd paid any attention I might have known why. A mêlée of political chat and booze chat suddenly had focus—Mailer. What it didn't have was order. Everyone wanted a piece of Mailer. Somebody urged him not to run at all—sensitive if not good advice. I could tell from his look he was not wholly certain himself. Steinem said that Women's Liberation could not be ignored. A young black woman said he should step down, before he'd even stepped up, for Adam Clayton Powell, New York's best-known black politician, and Rubin threw a firecracker in the works with 'Why not a Black Panther?'

Why not? Mailer told him why not. Because they weren't running as a college boy prank, that's why not. And as I looked around it all seemed to me to split up into the kind of pranksterness that gave the lie to that statement. Only Ken Kesey's pranksters would have relished the anarchy into which we flung ourselves. Mailer wanted what he called a 'hip coalition of the left and right', to strike sparks off both and start the fire burning. It burned. A dozen people were yelling at him now. Who's left? What's right? These were not questions that needed to be asked. And they weren't going to get answers. A phrase sprang to my mind, from nowhere I thought at the time, now it seems like prophecy—you don't need a weatherman to know which way the wind blows. You just need half a dozen to blow up a Con Ed station. Whumpff goes Bank of America. Whumpff goes West 11th Street. Hot damn, hindsight.

A hip coalition? He was holding out a dream. Wasn't that what we'd been looking for since about 1952? What did it mean now? A fusion of differences into common cause between his generation and mine?

I have always admired Mailer. I think he was the first who told us what we were—White Negroes. Maybe his hipsters begat the beats, and the beats begat the hippies and the yippies, and maybe somewhere in all that unbiblical begatting I fitted and Mel fitted. All the disaffected. But Mailer was of an identifiable generation. The guys who fought World War Two. I could never see myself as one of them—that would be pretentious—and I don't know how to define my generation. I never fought in a war. Too young for Korea. Too old for Vietnam. Vietnam was being fought right now by a generation younger than me and Mel. I'm not sure they were represented in that room. I felt they should be. Whatever issue American politics could throw up—even at this level—Vietnam was the ghost in the machine.

People began to leave. Some walking out, some just drifting. Mel went back into a huddle with Mailer and a handful of the loyal. I waited. Ogled Manhattan. Stared at Steinem. And when Mel said, 'It's over. Let's go' I followed.

He was angry. He said nothing until we were in the elevator going down to the tracks at Clark Street.

'Chaos,' he said. 'Complete fuckin' chaos.'

There's a certain homogeneity to what I have learnt to call the Restofamerica. That is, what's left when you accept that New York is something else as well as someplace else. Restofamerica? Anywhere west of the New Jersey turnpike, east of the San Andreas fault. Capital? Chicago. The capital of everyplace else. I do not by this assertion mean to say that the Restofamerica cannot be factional, racial, whatever—look at Chicago itself for Chrissake, backdrop by Mies van der Rohe, accessories by Smith & Wesson. I mean that it doesn't seem to me to do it in that microscale, haunch-by-jowl fashion that New York does. Whittle it down to Lubbock, and yes, people find enough reasons to hate each other, but I've never felt that the diversity was so broad and so dense—and it's the combination of the two that makes the difference. The intensity is lacking. In New York every block can make a faction, every gathering of three people dissent.

I saw this difference—Restofamerica versus New York City—crudely illustrated the first time I climbed the steps inside the Statue of Liberty, playing the tourist—no Mel—hoping to dangle from the torch like Robert Cummings at the end of Hitchcock's *Saboteur*. Ahead of me, overdressed for the hike, an Hassidic family, Mom, two kids and a folding baby carriage and Dad—homburg, frock coat, string belt, beard. Behind me a 250-pound man in blue jeans and a windbreaker. He leans around me. Taps the Jew on the shoulder.

''Scuse me, sir,' all best Western manners, 'I'm from Colorado. And I ain't never seen anyone looks like you before, and I was wonderin'. What kind of a person would you be?'

Good manners counted for little. Dammit, if the guy had been wearing a hat he'd have doffed it. Instead he stood there smiling like a dumb hick and lit the blue touch paper.

'Whaddya mean what am I? I'm a Jew! You never seen a Jew before?'

'No, sir,' he said simply. And I believed him. There may be Jews in Mississippi, and there's a big community in Galveston—ship heading for Ellis Island, more teeming poor, blown way, way off course. But there are parts of this great country of ours where the nearest thing to a stranger is anyone to whom you are not kin, because the chances are that in your own briarpatch everyone you meet every day is someone to whom you are related. The Restofamerica binds by kin. Kin is a great Restofamerican notion.

I felt I'd seen New York at its most factional. Forget every block is a faction, forget every street—every single goddam New Yorker is a faction. Kinless in the head. I'd been to a typical New York political bash—I'd come out of it without a first idea of what the platform was. I was as wise now as when I went in. Mailer for Mayor. That's all I knew.

'What's the deal?' I asked Mel.

'The deal is statehood for New York City.'

I laughed. Just a little. A nervy kind of giggle, heading for an out and out roar, but the look on Mel's face told me it would be a mistake. He was deadly serious.

'That's not exactly an original idea,' I said. And it wasn't. I heard it kicked around from time to time ever since I arrived in the city. It slotted neatly into my Restofamerica spiel. It was the absurdist projection of that feeling.

'Maybe not,' he said. 'But it is *the* idea. And since when have we been slaves to novelty? I thought we were about being right not about being original. If the two pair off, all well and good. But to hammer us for a lack of originality sounds remarkably like the kind of thing my dad used to say whenever I argued with him. It's a generational thing. They said they wanted us to be original—we wanted to be right—when in reality they just wanted us to be them.'

It was a brief, pointless, adolescent speech—Mel could roll them out by the dozen if you accidentally invoked the spirit of the late Melchior Kissing III—and what it amounted to was another of the great clichés of the times. If you're not part of the solution you're part of the problem. He was calling me out. *High Noon* on a subway train. So I told him.

'Last year we were fighting for the soul of a nation. Now, suddenly we're whittled down to New York City. What're we doing? Reclaiming America borough by borough? Today New York, tomorrow Hoboken?'

'It's a start,' Mel said. 'It's this or nothing.'

'Last year we were united. We had common cause. Get rid of LBJ. Stop the war. Pull out of Vietnam. I couldn't see what the cause was tonight, let alone whether it was common. This Left-Right coalition strikes me as a fantasy. Dammit, Mel, the Left cannot agree with themselves—how are they going to find common ground with the right? On an issue as narrow as this? We've dissolved. We're into a feeding frenzy. The Liberals insult the Right, the Blacks insult the Liberals, the Right insult the Blacks, everybody insults the women and so it goes on. You think Rubin understands a damn thing Gloria Steinem says? You think she and Mailer are on the same wavelength?'

'As ever you are missing the point. You are getting stuck on matters of surface. Try and look deeper. There are battle lines being drawn, to quote Stephen Stills. This is the new battleground. If you think we fought for the soul of America then you're a bigger romantic than I thought—but if that's really what you think then we lost the soul of America when Bobby Kennedy got blown away . . .'

'Mel. We lost it when we let McCarthy get hijacked. Or maybe I should say hibobbied.'

'If your delivery weren't so laboured that would be funny. But . . . if we lost it on the national stage the only way back is this way. We can say who runs this city even if we can't say who runs America.'

'Hippies talk to feminists?'

'Yes.'

'Black bluestocking women talk to beer-belly Irish hustlers?'

'If you like, yes.'

'I don't believe it. And I can't do it.'

He took off his glasses, breathed on them. Pulled out a shirt tail, wiped 'em clean and shoved them back with that habitual Mel gesture—tip of his big finger pressed against the bridge. If people who wear glasses didn't wear glasses they'd have to smoke to know what to do with their hands.

'You can't walk away from everything, Turner.'

This was way below the belt. So I told him the truth.

'Mel, I didn't walk away, I ran.'

It was the best part of a month before I saw him again.

§

Mel had one thing in common with my brother Billy. Looked nothing like him (short, Jewish Mel versus tall, bony—rangy would be the word—brother Billy) but they could both talk the tail feathers off a buzzard. Until I met Mel I'd known no one with a gift for words like Billy. All through our childhood he dreamed out loud. I heard his version of *The Alamo* a thousand times—different every time, except that he was always cast as the hero in this dream. I got used to being a supporting player, Gabby Hayes to his Gary Cooper, Ward Bond to his John Wayne. But that dream was one the old man had thrust upon him. Billy, in full, was William Travis Raines, named for the commander of the Alamo. My dad, Sam, was Samuel Houston Raines, his father before him was Samuel Houston Raines, named for the first, the only President of the Republic of Texas. I've no idea who John Turner was. I was happy to be John Turner Raines, named for no one, carrying no burden of history. I could, after all, given the old man's tendency to memorialize, so easily have been David Crockett Raines. And the gags would never have stopped. Every kid in school would of wanted a piece of me for a name like that. I have enjoyed my anonymity. Billy reveled in reflected glory. He wanted the real thing, as big a piece as he could lift and carry, all to himself. I have never met anyone in such a hurry to grow up, no one with that rage to live. He made the six years between us into a generation. I was forever l'il brother. His deputy, sidekick and pupil. I was devastated when he left me. A light had not gone out of my life, a voice had gone silent, a voice that had whispered sweet mischief and adventure in my ear from the day I was born. He left me, took off into the dream and left me, stranded in the Restofamerica.

The Restofamerica we were born into was the Texas Panhandle, the *Llano Estacado*. The flat plains under the big sky, beyond the Red River, where John Wayne and Montgomery Clift raised a hundred thousand head of cattle. Plenty of people still raised cattle there.

My great-grandfather had settled on the high plains within a few years of the Commanches' last rout at Palo Duro. He'd set out from St Louis with two wagons, a Radiant Fairblast stove and four bales of Glidden's Patent Barb Wire, intending to fence himself a piece of California. This was as far as he got. The stove got installed in the cabin—I polished it once a week as a kid—the barbed wire stood out back and rusted. It's still there today. No one ever moved it. I'd guess there was just about enough to corral one jackass—maybe that's all he ever meant to fence in, about half an acre. The acreage he staked claim to he never fenced in, and it ran to thousands of acres, hundreds of thousands.

It was not yet a rich man's country. During the Depression plenty of people seemed no more than just dirt farmers scraping a living off scrubby fields of cotton. Maybe my father could have made money—after all we'd been there as a family since before Lubbock was even started as a township, and we'd gone on buying. We owned even more in 1940 than we'd owned in 1880. Grazing and arable as far as the eye could see and further. Sounds a lot, but there are ranches in the Panhandle closer to a million acres, and it was out beyond the point where any railroad would ever run or anyone else ever want to live. Wrong side of town and wrong side of tracks that never came. The Atchison, Topeka and Santa Fe (the second 'the' of the song title is entirely optional and strictly for purposes of metre), which quartered Lubbock like sliced pizza, passed us by. The interstate, when it finally arrived, passed us by. We were country—further out, thank God, than the reach of any country club. The town would never come out to meet us. Our development potential was zero. My father complicated his life. He'd commit to nothing fully. Some cattle, some cotton, never as much as the land would hold and never enough attention to either. If money came in it soon went out—cattle got bought and bred, then sold too cheap, crops got planted, then neglected in the fields. Got to the point where he'd hired and laid off the help so many times there was not a man in the county who'd work for Sam Raines anymore. That was my old man. Always struggling to make ends meet. Bound in chains to a crazy scheme of his own.

In the 1930s, when Billy and I were born, no one had found much oil around Lubbock. The first local strike had been in Yoakum County to the south around 1927 or '28, but there'd been strikes around Borger and Pampa, up near the Oklahoma line, as far back as 1920 or '21. As Lubbockians saw it the plain fact was that no one had struck oil as far north and as far west as Sam was looking. During the Depression, when the worst dust storms in living memory swept through, most people gave up looking. Not Sam. Sam said he'd hit it for sure. Everyone he knew said, 'That'll be the day' but that's Lubbockians for you.

By the end of the war Dallas and Galveston had grown rich on the oil trade, and there'd been drilling aplenty and new fortunes made all around Midland and Odessa—and a couple of counties north in Hutchinson County, or south in Gaines, the plains were forest-thick with derricks. But my old man was a crank, mocked by his neighbors for daring to think he might strike it lucky, mocked for the time he'd wasted, the money he'd lost looking for a gusher on his farm. I often think it was that made Billy as bold as he was. Standing up for the old man's failures. Outtalking, outshouting anyone who thought Sam Raines' twenty-third or thirty-third borehole a fit subject for a joke. I just got used to it. Said nothing. My old man was my old man. Drilling for oil on an empty plain of scrub northwest of Lubbock was by no means the crankiest thing about him.

I was not embarrassed by our father. I liked where we lived. I loved our farm. In the shadow of the one feature that broke that endless horizon—a vast shale plug that sat out on the plains less as though it had risen from the earth, more as though it had tumbled from the sky. You could see it from miles around. It meant you could always see home. You could see home before you even cleared the city limits. There was no such thing as a skyscraper to get in the way—although there was sky to scrape aplenty. I loved the four room wooden shack my great-grandfather had built in 1881. He'd built there because the plug of rock cast a shadow that kept the heat of the day off the house. It was, it still is, called Bald Eagle Rock because nothing grows on it, but I never once saw a bald eagle there. I could stand up there and dream. It's a family trait. Billy would stand up there and dream into words, and if I'd heard enough that day I'd just turn off to him and watch the sails on the windmill turn.

When I was seven my mother took sick and died. It was the day Japan surrendered. Left with two boys my father was lost. Widowed at forty-two, he had no idea how to handle it or us. I remember my first day back at school after the funeral—he'd made up my lunchbox for the first time. A bar of chocolate and an unripe apple hard as a bullet. Vitamins, proteins, nutrition meant nothing to him. Kids just grew. All you had to do was stoke 'em. It should not have surprised either of us that day in 1948 when he came back from a trip to Tucumcari and brought with him his new wife—Lois, nineteen years old, tall and tan and beautiful, without a doubt part Indian, and a shock to the system. She knelt down and hugged me. At ten years old I was still a runt of a child. She could wrap me up and smother me in her arms and breasts. Billy was sixteen, and a tad under six feet tall. He forestalled the embrace, stuck out a hand for her to shake. Lois smiled and took the hand. Told Billy how Sam never stopped talking about him.

That evening, halfway up the mountain, watching the sunset, Billy had stopped talking.

How to describe a West Texas sunset? Well, first off you will run out of vocabulary down the pink to red to purple end of the spectrum. You will find yourself splitting words like frog hairs—pinky-red, reddish-blue, magenta drifting to maroon (not that I ever met a Texan who described anything as magenta) and so on. Let me say as simply as I saw it that the evening sky just glowed, soft and slow, it glowed until the sun vanished over the far, far horizon.

After an hour or so I had to ask.

And Billy said, 'What's wrong? What the hell do you think is wrong? The old man comes home with a store-bought wife, tells us she's our new mom and you ask what's wrong.'

The old man had not said that. It would have been the cliché from every other Western if he had, but he hadn't. Hadn't even called her 'Mom'. Introduced her as Lois and told us how they'd fallen in love and married in three days. He hadn't been looking for a wife. But I was baffled by the notion that you could buy a wife in a store. I asked how much Lois had cost. Ever the educator, Billy explained the phrase. Didn't talk to me like I was an idiot. And lapsed back into that untypical, unimaginable silence. The old man called to us in the darkness, voice booming out below us, bouncing back off the rock to echo across the plains. We climbed down, Billy still not speaking. Lois had milk and cookies laid out for us. I got used to Lois. Never called her Mom, never had to. I'd gotten another best friend. After Billy Lois was my best friend. After he went my only friend for a while. I liked Lois, immediately. But Billy loved her. Took days for him to realize this, and years for me to notice.

§

1969. Mel rang me at my office on Lafayette and Spring. A voice to whisper mischief.

'You busy?'

'Kind of.'

'You working?'

'Er . . . I'm in the middle of a case.'

A lie. I was twiddling my thumbs waiting on anything to happen.

'Can you come to a couple of meetings?'

'A couple?'

'There's one out in Queens . . .'

'Mel. I am not going to Queens. Not for you, not for Norman Mailer, not for anyone.'

'Upper West Side?'

'Maybe.'

'Brooklyn.'

'Where in Brooklyn?'

'Menora Temple in Borough Park.'

I dearly wanted to be able to say no. That was worse than Queens— halfway to Coney Island. The coward in me won hands down.

'OK,' I said.

'Fine. Meet me at Michel's on Flatbush Avenue. I'll buy you dinner.'

He hung up. Should have smelled a rat. Mel is the kind of guy who waits for you to buy dinner. When I got there I found an entire entourage in the restaurant. Mel hanging on Mailer's every word. I guess I should of written it all down. If I'd known it was part of history I'd of written it down. Norman said hi and shook hands like he remembered me. I can't remember a tenth of what he said. Just the moment when he was knocking 'fuckin' phony Manhattan liberals' and Mel looked at me and I looked at Mel. A 'does he mean me?' look. Both of us wondering if he included us in the put-down.

But he played the temple like an old pro. If politics is show biz—and Menora Temple is surely a theater with its plastic palm trees and red-flocked wallpaper—then Mailer deserved to win. On the way over Mel said, 'You may not recover the soul of America, but you are about to see the great beating heart of New York. And it is named Mailer.' I would have to concede that he was right—on that night if on no other.

I had picked up fragments of the manifesto. You had only to read the campaign buttons to get the gist. Mel had pinned a cute one on me the minute I arrived. It said, plainly, 'No More Bullshit'—I wondered how long they'd go on giving that one out before someone complained. I saw other people wearing 'Mailer/Breslin/Vote the Rascals In' and 'Power to the Neighborhood'. I liked that—it was the anarchist core of Mailer's message—'property is power, we have none, Washington and Albany own us'. Ditch Washington, quit Albany and devolve power to the most fundamental level, the boroughs. Let Queens be a city, let Staten Island rule itself. And there was the absurdist, the near-poetic 'I Would Sleep Better

Knowing Norman Mailer Were Mayor', probably the longest campaign button slogan in history. The message could get quirky to the point of eccentric—someone asked Mailer if he were in favor of legal abortion. He replied, 'Only if you let me outlaw the pill.' Was that a yes or a no? And quirky to the sharp point of truth—crime will persist as long as it's the most interesting thing to do.

But, that night—after he had stomped the stump of declaring the 51st State and throwing down the gauntlet to Albany—out of this rag bag of ideas he pulled a notion so off-the-wall, so sane and so original he had New York, and me, eating out of his hand. Let us, he said, keep Sunday sweet.

It's fifty years since T-Bone Walker gave us "Stormy Monday" (and I've lost count of the number of Black Tuesdays and Thursdays in that time) and a couple of years before this some guys down at the University of Texas had had themselves a Gentle Thursday—which speaks for itself—but nothing, nothing compared to the sublime idea of Sweet Sunday.

When Mailer was Mayor, one Sunday each month in New York City would be 'sweet'—that is no cars would run, no buses, no ships would dock, no planes would land. The subway, which any other time ran round the clock day and night, would be silent. So would the apartments, because Norman meant to cut off the electricity too, so no radio, no TV, no washers washing, no driers tumbling . . . and, as Mel cynically whispered in my ear, no refrigerators freezing, no elevators elevating and no air conditioners doing whatever it was they did.

I didn't care. Let the ice in my icebox melt. For once I shared Mailer's vision. Shut down the city. Who knows maybe people would talk to each other again? Suddenly I could see a life worth living, if only for one day a month. I had a vision of a peaceful populace, playing chess in Washington Square, walking the dog up a 5th Avenue free of traffic . . . sitting in Battery Park watching Liberty to see if she winked . . . whatever. It was a redundant religious idea pushed into the secular and boosted back to meaning. I cheered Mailer for this. So did a couple of dozen freaks. But not Mel. Mel said, 'Are you nuts? This'll never work. This is just word-spinning. He's thinking on his toes and talking through his ass. Wait till he sits down.'

Norman did not sit down, he took questions from the floor.

What will happen if you get elected?

'Washington would fall to its knees.'

What will happen if you really put Sweet Sunday into practice?

'On the first hot day the populace would impeach me.'

Always leave 'em wanting more.

Always leave 'em laughing.

I got the joke. Sure it *could* be a joke, but it had that hint of . . . there is no other word for it so I say again . . . the sublime. And I could not remember when I last felt the cool hand of sublimity on my brow. Sunday, Sweet Sunday. And just a whisper of mischief.

§

1966. I was a failure as a journalist—gently fired by the *Village Voice* with 'Sorry Turner, but you are crap'—and it bothered me not one bit, but all the same I had a living to make. I was a law-school dropout who'd never practiced. I had oddjobbed my way into a dead end in less than three years. I'd worked for the *East Village Other* (looking back, was it news or pornography? Hindsight will not tell me), for Liberty House over on Bleecker, selling Deep South goods in the Deep North—which was where I first came across Abbie Hoffman, long before he invented the Yippie (Q: what's a Yippie? A: a hippie who's had his head busted by a cop), both of us then just former civil rights workers alienated by the shift to "Blacks Only". And I'd worked for the War Resisters League and the Peace Eye Bookstore over on Avenue A and blahdey blah . . . but all of that put together hardly amounted to an income. Half those places were volunteer stuff, paid nothing. To go back to the law was not exactly my preference, but I had rent to pay, a landlady dropping unsubtle hints such as 'You're five months behind, why don't you get qualified and earn some real money?', a block on asking my father for more money, and a block on my imagination that led me inexorably to the easy option. I was yawning my way through it one day in the fall, when my sharer and landlady Rose asked, 'Would you do me a favor?'

'Sure?'

'Remember that woman used to clean for us. Mrs Kosciuscko? She rang me at work yesterday. Her son's being drafted. He won't go. The old man won't speak to him and she's terrified.'

'Why'd she call you?'

'I'm a professional. Probably the only one she knows. It hardly matters to her that I'm not a lawyer. I use long words and go to work in an office—that's all she sees.'

'What is she? Polish? Why doesn't she talk to her priest?'

'The Catholic Church has but one line on the war—duty.'

'And?'

'I thought you might have a better line. You know the law. And you've been in jail. Maybe you could talk some sense to her. Perhaps reassure her.'

I saw Mr and Mrs Kosciuscko. It set a pattern for the way I worked for the next four or five years. They came round to the apartment. A short, fat woman in her forties who could hardly keep from weeping and a short fat man in his forties who maintained a near-total silence. Would I just talk to Mikey Jr? I was an educated man, she could see that. At the mention of his son's name Mikey Sr grunted. With each repetition he seemed to push nearer the point where that angry silence might explode.

Mikey Jr gave me two minutes of his time in a diner out in Queens the next night.

'The old man got shot up on Omaha Beach on D-Day. He keeps his medals in a velvet box on the dresser next to the bed. He expects the same of me. I say, fuck 'im. No fuckin' medal's gonna make me feel any better about losing one of my balls. I got better uses for 'em.'

Mikey was no college student—he stacked pickle jars in a warehouse in Essex Street, a block off Delancey on the Lower East Side. Smelled of vinegar at fifteen feet. I doubted he was any kind of conscientious objector—and if he were it took brains to prove it to the draft board and somehow 'fuck my old man' didn't strike me as the most constructive argument ever assembled. This kid was going to get inducted. If he'd been middle-class, brains, money and a slick lawyer could all be factors in an exemption, but this was an acned, greasy-haired, blue-collar punk who smelled of vinegar. He was perfect cannon fodder.

'So. Mikey. What's your plan?'

He looked at me as though I was a mind-reader. Real surprise on his pocky face. But he told me all the same.

'Canada, man, I'm goin' to Canada. I was wonderin' how to tell the old woman. I was going to mail her this.'

He took an envelope out of his trousers pocket. The handwriting looked more like that of a ten-year-old than an eighteen-year-old. It said 'Mrs M. Kosciuscko' in pencil.

'But I was wonderin'—maybe they could trace me from a postmark. Would you give it to her? Not now, not today. Like in two or three days?'

I could have said no. I didn't. I kept my word to the kid. Mrs Kosciuscko wept when she read it. Through the tears I could see that it part was relief part new-worry. Mikey Sr tore the note into a thousand pieces, put on his purple heart and declared that he no longer had a son. A month or so later she called me. As long as he was safe. She could live with it, she could talk her husband round, as long as she knew Mikey was safe. Would I go to Canada and just check on him? She'd pay—she had a legacy from an aunt they'd never touched.

I could have said no then—I didn't. It wouldn't be hard to find him. Odds were he was in Toronto and if he was in Toronto he'd gravitate to where all the other draft dodgers were. Took me less than three days to find him. I brought home a long letter from Mikey, a promise that he'd keep in touch, and best of all, a note to his father saying he was sorry but he had to do it and hoped his dad could find it in his heart to forgive him. I did not tell them how I dictated the note to Mikey and threatened to break his arm if he didn't sign.

I waived the fee—but out of it I got the beginnings of a job. I applied for a PI's license. I'd been arrested more times than I could count, but never in New York state, and out of all those nights in jail I had only one charge and one conviction—from a civil disobedience sit-in in South Carolina in the spring of 1961. I was clean, I would pass muster, and tracking down the Mikeys was something I had discovered an aptitude for. And the word went out. If your kid goes missing Turner Raines can find him. I had clients coming to me from all over the tri-state area. I brought no kids home—that was stated up front, it was not the business I was in—but I brought peace of mind to worried women and warring families for fifty dollars a day plus expenses. Between times I spied on cheating husbands and trailed petty embezzlers and all the other shoe-leather wearing tasks that went with the job.

My landlady Rose said, 'Who would ever have thought there was a living in it? I mean, darling—anyone with a bit of clout and a good lawyer doesn't have to fuck off to Canada, now do they?'

Maybe she was right. Most of my 'clients' were blue-collar people defeated by the system, not knowing how to manipulate it for their own ends. The best scam I ever heard was a guy who took on the draft board by confusing their bureaucracy. They wrote to him. He wrote back, and every time they replied to him he replied more quickly than they did. Endless obfuscations and queries, anything to keep his file afloat, going from one desk to another, from one poor damned clerk to another—until, inevitably, one of them lost it. It worked. Came the day they stopped writing to him. He'd beaten the system. That took brains and patience. Not something I saw much of across the other side of my desk.

By 1967 the trade was booming—all thanks to LBJ's Selective (such an understatement) Service System aka the draft—and I was something of an authority on draft law. I even bought a suit just for court appearances— all neat in neutral colors and my hair slicked back with greasy kid stuff. I'd finally found my niche by becoming a private eye. If LBJ kept up the escalation (another understatement) I figured I could be the second self-made millionaire in the family by about 1982. I had enough business to open an office on Lafayette Street over the East River Savings Bank, twelve floors up with a view of the Williamsburg Bridge—not bad, better than facing a brick wall, pretty at night with the lights twinkling, but nobody's favorite—at the end of a long corridor of frosted glass doors and black-stenciled lettering that never ceased to remind me of a scene in any Raymond Chandler novel. Down these mean corridors a man must go, so I went. I made it home from home. Coffee pot, kettle, an ancient, gurgling icebox, a brand new ice pick and a shelf of books for all those days when trade was slack.

That May, the 'Brooklyn spring' of '69, trade was slacker than usual and I was killing a morning. Eleven o'clock and the heat of the day was already up. Looked to be set for a blazing summer. Mel wanted me over in Greenwich Village in the evening for another shot of Mailer on the campaign trail. Nothing till then. Cup of coffee and a battered copy of Hemingway's stories—the clean, well-lighted place. *Nada y nada.* A tap at the glass door brought me a Mr and Mrs DiMarco from Mott Street,

around the corner and a block over. More often than not couples came
as couples. Sometimes just the mother, never the father on his own. Joey
DiMarco, aged nineteen, had burned his draft card and vanished two
weeks ago. A script so routine I could have held it up as idiot boards and
cued them. You really don't need a weatherman.

'He's a good boy,' Mrs D told me.

'Yeah,' Mr D chipped in. 'Good for nothin'.'

Cue the next board. Mr D was like a younger version of Ed Begley
in *12 Angry Men*. All the fathers were variations on Begley or Lee J.
Cobb. The Cobbs could be angry. Big men rising up out of their seats
to stab fingers at me. The Begleys mixed the angry and the pathetic
in equal measure. If they ever got out of the seat I could blow them
back down.

Joey had been working in his old man's restaurant. I can't remember
its real name. It was smack in the middle of Little Italy at a time when
Little Italy was a lot bigger than it is now and Chinatown hadn't begun
the inexorable creep north with Houston in its sights. I'd been there a few
times myself—great *aglio e olio*, spaghetti swimming in the most pungent
broth this side of Naples, you sweated garlic for four days after—and we
all called the place Holy Joe's. It was inadvertently accurate. The old man
was holier than thou in all his attitudes. The kid had failed to graduate
high school and the old man had stuck him in the cellar of the restaurant for the last three years, chopping onions, shredding lettuce, turning cabbage into coleslaw. He did this six days a week until nine in the
evening. Where he went after that or on Sundays they didn't know. That
summed up a lot of the people I faced across the desk. They didn't know
their own kids. They couldn't tell me the names of any of his current
friends—those Mrs DiMarco named were the teen versions of the little
boys who'd played in the street with her son eight or nine years back. If
I were nineteen and spent my days and nights in a cellar, well aware that
this was 1969, and that the world over my head had exploded into full
colour with stereo two or three years ago, I'd've cut and run too. And I
wouldn't have waited on the Draft Board for my cue.

I found Leonardo Lerici, childhood friend of the miscreant. He worked
in an electrical goods store on 14th Street and studied double entry book-
keeping at night. A kid out of his time. Determined to make good through
the system—not that he would ever have called it that. His concession to

his own generation was that his hair lapped his collar and the tie and shirt were in matching paisley swirls, the regular guy's version of flower power.

'Joey and I don't see so much of each other any more,' he said in answer to my enquiry. 'You should tell Mrs DiMarco I'm sorry Joey's gone. And what you shouldn't tell her is she should pray he never comes back.'

'That bad, eh?'

'Joey was my best friend. We known each other since I don't know when. We were christened the same day in the same church. Went to our first communion together. Difference being Joey's first was also his last. You can't keep a friend who lives like Joey does.'

'Like how?'

Leonardo looked at me as though he were weighing up the worth of telling me any more.

'Like drugs?'

He shook his head.

'Not Joey's thing. He was happier with a bottle of Bud.'

'And ...'

'Things ... like ... you have to tell me this won't go any further ... like it won't get back to Joey.'

'It won't. Talking to me is like talking to a lawyer. I couldn't tell even if the cops asked me to.'

'Joey ran with a mean crowd. They were dealing in stolen stuff. I know this on account of he came in here once or twice offering me color TVs and stereos at a few dollars a pop. I blew him out. I haven't seen him since Easter. Truth is Joey's a punk. That's what his old man made him.'

Thank you, Dr Spock.

'Were the cops onto him?'

'Not that I heard. All I heard is he laughed off his draft notice. That was Joey all over. Reality didn't apply to him. He'd've forgotten all about it until they issued the next one and told him to report for induction. Then I heard he'd split for Canada.'

I spent that afternoon asking a few more kids the same questions—a quick tour of Italian–American youth in the age of Aquarius. The NYU student, brighter than all the rest, working his way through college, economics, pol sci and 'You want fries with that?'—the young married, working double shifts, living in two rooms on Hester Street with an irresistibly fuckable wife and the inevitable, irresistible babe in arms, prisoner of his own cock—and the dope-smoking, effortlessly laid back hippie selling Afghan jackets, posters, Fugs albums and City Lights anthologies in a head shop on Tompkins Square. They all said the same thing. Joey had lit out for Canada. They hadn't seen him. It was just what they'd heard in the old neighborhood, twixt Mott and Mulberry. And it was logical. It was what you'd do if you knew no better or no other. Of all the ways to dodge the draft it was the most drastic and the most simple. Kids like Joey DiMarco weren't going to get college deferments, get commissioned in the Air Reserve, find a smart lawyer, cop a Rhodes Scholarship or land a non-combat posting in photography or information. They were always going to shout, cut and run or give in, grunt and die.

The next stage in this all too familiar process could have been designed to bring out the worst in a man and something approaching the best in a woman. I could not just light out for Canada without spelling out the cost, the circumstances and the rules to the parents. Cue the next card. Look out, kid, dunno what ya did.

I went over to Mott Street around six in the evening. Mr DiMarco went nuke. I knew he would. He would bluster.

'You think I got thousands of dollars to throw away on that no good kid?'

Mrs DiMarco played the voice of reason.

'That's not what Mr Raines said, Louie. He said hundreds, that's all, just a few hundred.'

'Hundreds, thousands. What does it matter? It'll all be wasted. Get it through your head, Gina. The boy has been a disaster. I mean. Is this what we raised him to be? A coward? A kid who runs away from his country when there's a war on?'

'He's not a kid anymore, Louie. He's nineteen. He's got ideas of his own. Principles maybe.'

'Principles my ass. He can't even spell the word. You want principles I'll give you principles ...'

Above the TV, given pride of place, between the Pope—not the current guy, the one before, John XXIII—and the Madonna, was a framed photograph of the President. Not the current guy, not even the one before, but the guy before him—JFK. Mr DiMarco snatched it off the wall and held it up like an orthodox priest in procession clutching an icon, nestling it on his chest opposite his heart.

'I'll give you principles. John Fitzgerald Kennedy, the Catholics' President . . . "Ask not what you can do for your country, but what your country can do for you." Now that's a principle!'

Mrs DiMarco looked from her husband to me. I wasn't going to tell him, but clearly she was.

'Louie, you got it the wrong way round. It's "ask not what your country can do for you but what you can do for your country".'

'So? It means the same goddam thing, don't it?'

'No,' she said quiet and firm. 'It doesn't.'

He exploded. It sounded like 'Sheeeeiiiiiitttttt!' but I couldn't be sure. It didn't much matter. I'd heard this fifty times already. 'His country needs him', 'My son is a coward,' which would give way to 'I have no son', 'We raised an ungrateful sonuvabitch', 'Where did we go wrong?' A variation on this was 'Better Dead than Red' which, rarely, could lead to a half-baked discourse on the Red Peril, but that was not most men. Most men did not believe in ideology. In that generation most men had scarcely got their head above the parapet of 'work, family, more work', the quick quick slow working man's shuffle from cradle to grave, to have an ideology. As his 'the Catholics' President' made clear even the tissue thin ideology of Republican versus Democrat meant very little to Mr DiMarco. He was an American, after that an Italian hyphenate and a Catholic, and that's about as far as it went.

After this, and it could last fifteen minutes or more, they either stormed out, banging the door fit to shake down the building, or they got to sobbing, and an understanding wife would wave me away with a whispered 'tomorrow'. Every so often, like one in ten, the husband—those who fancied themselves more Robert Mitchum than either Lee J. Cobb or Ed Begley—would try to throw me out. DiMarco opted for a practiced display of door slamming.

Mrs DiMarco sat down as soon as she heard the outer door bang.

'You have to understand,' she said. 'Louie is . . . Louie is . . . offended, yes that's the word, offended by Joey. He was at Anzio. Did I tell you that? Imagine, a second generation Italian having to invade Italy. He takes all this too personally. You young people, you're different, aren't you?'

Rhetoric or question? I risked an answer.

'I guess so, but I never got asked to fight in a war. Too young for Korea, too old for this one.'

'Then you're lucky. I waited for Louie to get back from Europe. I'm not going to wait for Joey to come back from Vietnam, wondering all the time if he's going to step off the plane or be carried off in a body bag. I lost two brothers in the World War, that's enough for any woman. If you think my boy's in Canada you go there. All I want to know is that he's safe, and he knows he can come to me or his sisters any time. I'll handle his father. God knows I've done that since 1943. Just find out what he means to do with himself, and if there's anything he needs.'

I asked a tricky one.

'Mrs DiMarco. I'm pretty certain Joey is in Canada, but I'm curious. Why would someone like Joey have a passport?'

I'd known New Yorkers who'd never been out of the state, no further than the public beaches on Long Island, people for whom Penn Station was the gateway to a foreign country, let alone out of America.

'A kid like what, Mr Raines? No, don't answer. You mean a blue-collar kid with no college education and a Three Stooges accent who reeks of garlic all day. What would he be doing with a passport?'

'I guess I phrased myself badly.'

'I'm sorry. This is getting to me. I apologize. But the answer to your question is his grandmother, my mother that is, died two years ago and left Joey some money on condition it was used to send him to the old country. That's how come Joey has a passport.'

'Like I said, I'm sorry.'

'Don't be.'

§

I kept my appointment with Mel that evening. If nothing else I had to tell him I wouldn't be around for a few days. Let him know to keep an eye on my office. I walked across town to PS 41, the Greenwich Village School, at the corner of West 11th and 6th. A prime example of the modern–shabby school of public architecture. Built to rot. All toughened glass and steel panels. Ashes to ashes, rust to rust. I was late. The meeting was already under way. I stepped into the lobby and found myself up against a set of locked glass doors. I'm sure if I'd tried I could have found the way in, but what I saw and heard through the glass doors made me bide my time.

Mel reckoned this was the night Mailer would pull his irons out of the fire. This was to be the most prepared, well-argued address of the campaign so far. Tonight the numbers would be rolled out. Statistics tripping from the tongue. What had we spent on defense since 1960? Apparently 551 billion dollars. As much, if not more, than had been spent nationwide on housing and education. That was America at the end of the decade of riches. And then Norman would paint a picture of the powder keg and tinder that were the cities of America. I had queried whether anyone needed to be told this anymore. It was only just a year since the death of Martin Luther King. The flint that struck the tinder in Detroit, Washington, Baltimore and a hundred other powder kegs the breadth of the country. 'Just be there,' Mel had said.

What I saw was a circus. A bunch of hairies seemed to have hijacked the meeting. Balloons were batted back and forth across the aisles by skinny, bearded guys, like a weightless basketball game. Fine—Abbie Hoffman always said revolution should be fun, that this was America's contribution to the revolution; something so American it could happen only in America. Fun, revolution as the great put-on. The great game. Hairy clowns in hippie garb for whom nothing should be sacred. The motley denim, tie-dye crew for whom the three-piece suit was just a walking prison.

I could only just make out Mailer on the stage, for all the guys surrounding him. Bobbing up and down and gibbering. Then a Viet Cong flag was unfurled onstage. Predictably, Norman asked for it to be removed or he'd leave. Then the even more predictable cry went up: 'Fuck you!' And as if by prior consent it began to turn from sporadic 'Fuck you's' to rhythmic, concerted, mantra-like 'Kill! Kill! Kill!' Twelve or twenty voices chanting in unison. And 'Kill! Kill! Kill!' elided, slid effortlessly, into a chilling, a blood-can-run-cold 'Kill for Peace!'

How many turning points can one life have? I had seen Chicago in '68. A turning point. To hear this again was to live a piece of it all again. A momentary flash of the worst we could offer. The worst I had seen. I was debating with myself whether I should just walk away without

finding Mel, when Mailer's voice roared out over the PA. He named the
hairies as 'the Motherfuckers', a group he was prepared to say had been
infiltrated by the CIA.

He was wrong. On both counts I am sure. They weren't the Motherfuckers, a Lower East Side bunch simply named for the slogan 'Up Against
the Wall Motherfuckers', that I'd seen around for a couple of years. They
were the Crazies. A fine difference you might say. And I would agree
with you. And I would add that maybe Mailer got off lightly. I had
known the Crazies to do a bare-ass routine, in which whatever 'phony
fuckin' liberal' they were targeting would be presented with a pig's head
on a silver platter. And whatever Mailer really thought of 'fuckin' phony
Manhattan liberals', to the Crazies we were all fuckin' liberals and all legit
targets—just made to eat our own words.

The room emptied. A sudden surge towards the back, a hundred and
more people heading for the street. A little guy with a button of a face
was pressed up against the glass, shaking the doors and yelling at me. He
looked for an instant like the central figure in a Francis Bacon painting,
one of those popes in glass booths or whatever, where rage seems red and
muted, the body rigid and the mouth and throat exaggeratedly, silently
animate. I pointed to the side, to where the open doors were flooding
with people. Then I looked again. This little guy, round of face, shiny of
cheek, angry of mien, was wearing Mel's clothes. It was Mel. Mel without
a beard. As the tail end of the crowd followed Mailer across 6th Avenue,
he emerged, the last straggler from the ruins of the meeting.

'Jesus Christ! Did you see that? Did you see that? The fuckers just
shouted us down!'

'You mean you didn't expect it?'

'Of course I didn't expect it.'

'Let me guess . . . you're the good guys, right? So all the Crazies and
the Motherfuckers and the God Knows Who should just leave you alone.'

'Fuck you, Turner.'

Fuck solves a lot of things. There should be a dictionary devoted solely
to the word.

'When did you shave off the beard?'

'What?'

'I hear Norman does not like beards. I hear he's against dope too. You
going to give up the weed next?'

'You think I shaved off my beard for Mailer?'

'Well, did you?'

'Of course not. Why would I do a thing like that?'

None of this quite had the toothpaste ring of confidence. He'd had that beard as long as I'd known him. He'd shaved it off just once.

'Last time you shaved it off was when we were in Philadelphia. Some horny sophomore got you to do it.'

Good God, he was blushing. I'd hit home.

'You shaved your beard off for a woman? Who is she?'

'Nobody you know.'

'Somebody who doesn't like beards?'

'Look—stop raggin' me and come with us.'

'Where?'

'We're moving the meeting to Union Square.'

'Well, that's traditional if nothing else. But I need an early night. Canada in the morning.'

'Naw. Come with us. We might just shake off this bunch of crazy motherfuckers. Now, you coming?'

'Absolutely not.'

I should have. I really should have. I never saw him again.

§

The date I drove north has stuck in my mind for lots of reasons. What happened when I got there. What happened when I got back. But, simplest of all I remember it because I picked up a paper at a corner newsstand on 7th Avenue as I drove out of the city. May 28. The news had broken that we'd given up Hamburger Hill. It became the Iwo Jima for our times. Iwo Jima, whatever the truth behind that flag hoisting, had been a symbol of American courage since 1945. Hamburger Hill's been what? A symbol of waste and stupidity. Fifty dead and five hundred wounded and nobody knew why. Hill taken, hill given up and fifty body bags get sent back to Mom and Pop Averageamerica.

I took a slightly eccentric route north. As the crow flies, and as long as you didn't mind blacktops that dodged and weaved, it would pay to head out towards Scranton and wind your way along the banks of the Susquehanna and head for a crossing into Canada at Niagara. That was how I'd done it the first few times. Ever since, well almost ever since I'd taken the Hudson Valley route, north out of the city, across the George Washington Bridge into New Jersey and up the interstate and over the Catskills to follow the railroad track from Albany to Niagara. It enabled me to call in on an old friend from Georgetown.

As soon as I heard the name I knew it had to be the same woman. Mel and I had gone through College with a Tsu-Lin Shin—mostly Chinese, part German—damn missionaries get everywhere—and part Vietnamese. I doubt she was ever going to practise law, any more than Mel or me. The third or fourth time I had to drive up to Toronto I checked with the War Resisters League down on Beekman Street, not a block from Rose's apartment, and they said, 'You might save yourself half the journey. Look in on Tsu-Lin in Palenville. She gives the runners a halfway house for a while. The kids seem to know about her the way the moms and pops know about you.' Had to be the same woman. Had to go see.

Palenville? Never heard of it, but it wasn't hard to find. A short hop off Interstate 87, which runs all the way up the valley to the Quebec line, a small village nestled in the Blackhead range of the Catskills. First sight of it, the kind of one store and a gas-station place (make that one store, gas station and video rental today) most likely to be populated by Irish and English from way back, made me wonder what the locals made of a hybrid like Tsu-Lin.

'Johnnie, what brings you to this neck of the woods?'

She sat on a wicker chair in front a vast, crumbling turn-of-the-century mansion, something probably built by a New York tycoon in the days when steamships ploughed all the way upriver to Rome or Athens for the convenience of Vanderbilts or Rockefellers.

'I just drove up from New York.'

'Well, John Turner Raines, you don't look like a big city lawyer to me. Too hairy by far.'

'I'm not. I'm a private eye.'

'No shit?'

'God's truth.'

'What exactly are you detecting up here, Johnnie?'

'Draft-dodgers?'

'Uh uh?'

'It's not what you think. I don't chase kids and bring 'em back. I find 'em and I try to keep families in touch. I'm legit—check me out with the War Resisters League if you don't believe me.'

She got up, stretched to the tips of her toes and kissed me on the cheeks.

'I already did. They called and told me you might be dropping in. Of course I believe you—but you have to admit at first hearing it's a pretty unbelievable story. You must have had to work to establish yourself with those kids.'

'I did. Took months.'

'Me too. They come here wanting God knows what from me and suspicious as sin. Now which of my waifs are you hoping to reunite with his loving parents?'

I named whichever kid it was that week—Tommy this, Ricky that . . . whatever.

She led me indoors, pointed to a cork board on the studio wall—six feet across and almost as high—plastered with Polaroids and stuck her finger on a mug shot.

The kid's parents had given me a high school yearbook print of the runaway—white shirt, tie, lots of teeth. I could just discern the man beneath the mask, a waif in hippie's clothing.

'This guy?'

I stared just to be certain. When I turned back to her the camera was aimed at me—a quick flash and I was part of her portfolio.

'Yep. That's him.'

'Went north two days ago.'

'Tell me,' I said. 'Don't you think this collection might be somehow incriminating?'

'How so? Is what I do illegal? Is what you do illegal? You tell me, lawyer man.'

'No—but there are men in suits who can stand on your doorstep and ask a lot of questions.'

'Let 'em. Do I give a fuck? Besides do we either of us think any of these kids are ever coming back? Do we think LBJ's Amerika is going to amnesty them? Every last damn one of them is safe in Canada, tucked up in Toronto, marooned in Montreal . . . and I can't think of an alliteration for Quebec.'

'Coralled in Quebec?'

'That'll do.'

'Why do you take them? Why do you keep them?'

'Work in progress. What does every painter need? Brush fodder. Better brush fodder than cannon fodder.'

'You paint?'

She looked at me with that eye-roll that meant I'd just stated the all-too-obvious, threw the dust cover off her easel. A small canvas was maybe half finished—twenty or thirty heads in juxtaposition, in unnatural colors. A touch of Bosch about them. It seemed to me that heads were either devouring or disgorging one another.

'I've ground to a halt on this. Something that wasn't quite right about it. Something just not working out. I think maybe it's the scale. Too small.'

I looked. I turned my head this way and that, but I hadn't a clue. What I knew about art you could jot down on the back of a map of Rhode Island. Nor, to screw up a cliché, did I know what I liked.

'I leave meaning to the critics, but if you figure it out, let me know. Meantime, I'll fix supper.'

One reason I do not eat Chinese food is that after college and countless improvised meals by Tsu-Lin, when Mel and I were too drunk or too stoned to do anything smarter than phone out for pizza, I could never face the monosodium-glutamate rich goo of commercial Chinese food again.

Over dinner I watched her hands move over half a dozen dishes like fluttering hummingbirds—a little of this, a dash of that—ate my fill, nostalgic to the last noodle, and answered her questions about the lives Mel and I had led since we last met the best part of seven years ago. She was deeply curious about Mel. Everybody always was. He seemed to fix himself in people's minds. I had gotten used to it. I was well over six feet tall, and if I say so myself, a looker and a bigger hit by far with women. Mel was short, pudgy and nothing to write home about. But the combination of wit and aggression, energy and commitment made him a force. I was always Tonto to his Lone Ranger. I called him Kemosabe in college. He didn't even think it was funny. Just accepted it at face value.

'Mel's been at the *Voice* since 1963. He's turned out to be a first rate investigative reporter. Tried to make me into one. Got me up from

Washington, stuck me behind a desk and tried to teach me. Couldn't be done. He goes his own way, takes as long as it takes to come up with a story, and every so often they scream, "Where the fuck is Mel Kissing?" and every so often lets himself get as far as the talking stage when bigger papers want to headhunt him. Lets the *Voice* know they can't take him for granted. He's turned down a lot of money to stay with them. It was Mel exposed that illegal garbage dumping racket about six months back.'

Another roll of the eyes and flat utterance of 'Fascinating.'

It was—but only to New Yorkers.

'And is the Tom Wolfe of the East Village married?'

'Nope.'

'Girlfriend?'

'Not as many as he'd like.'

'But more than you?'

'No comment.'

Nothing I said seemed to surprise her. Perhaps we had all gone similar ways for all our differences. We were none of us part of the Amerika for which our education had been designed to prepare us.

I asked her why she had got involved in war resistance.

'Why do I do it? Simple enough if you think about it. My family has moved on each generation for almost a hundred years. China, Hong Kong, Macao, Saigon. I was born in Macao, but the first country I can remember is Vietnam. We left when I was three and the Japanese invaded. We went back and the French invaded—we left again. Finally washed up in America. Turner, I know what it's like to leave home, to turn your back on everything that mattered and everything that made you. I was sixteen when I got to America—almost grown. These kids who run to Canada may well be making the biggest decision of their lives. Sure anyone can get to Canada in a day—makes it too easy. I give them time to pause. I don't put up any argument. I just let it be known that if they want to lay low for a couple of days or a couple of weeks they can do it here. Whether they go on or go back is no matter to me—I'm not out to make or un-make the army that's raging across my country. I gave up my country—I'd just like them to have a chance to think about it before they do the same thing. My father died with China on his lips like Orson Welles with Rosebud. It shouldn't have to be that way.'

'What do the locals make of all this?'

'God, Johnnie, they don't know. They think they know everything that goes on, but that's just village life. No different here from Vietnam or Gascony or Yorkshire. They think they know—they hardly ever do. No, there's six ways in and out of here. Nobody sees a thing. If they did I might well have had a visit from the Feds by now, but I haven't and I don't think I ever will.'

That had been three years ago. The Feds never had come—the waifs, as she always called them, seemed endless. It seemed sensible to ask about Joey DiMarco—he was far from being the usual runaway. Thief or not he seemed from all I'd heard to be more mainstream than anyone I'd chased after so far. But there was nothing to lose by asking.

I arrived at Tsu-Lin's late morning, after a couple of hours' drive in my beat-up VW. She wasn't at the door to meet me. I found her up a ladder, at work with brush and palette on another of her vast canvases. She slipped down quickly, offered me one cheek instead of the usual Gallic kiss on both. I caught her chin in one hand and said, 'What are you hiding?'

'Just another purple heart,' she said and squirmed from my grip. I could see now, a fading bruise on her left cheek, fading but big. Big as a man's fist.

'Who did this?'

'One of the waifs. Who else would it be?'

'Did he tell you his name?'

'Joey. He didn't have a surname. Most of them don't,' she said.

I said, 'It's DiMarco.'

She wiped the paint off her hands on a rag, looked me up and down and said, 'He the one you're after? If he is, be careful. He's a mean son of a bitch.'

'When was he here?'

'Just over a week ago. Spent a night here, casing the place, then he grabbed me, socked me when I said I'd no money and took $229. Cleaned out the stash I keep in the kitchen drawer.'

'You were alone.'

'Yes. I guess it was always a risk so I won't be needing any lecture you might be thinking of giving me.'

'You gonna stop now?'

'Of course not. Are you?'

'No.'

I stayed two or three hours, more to reassure myself than her. At last she said, 'You staying the night?'

'No.'

As I got back in the car she said, 'Turner. I want the money back. I can afford to lose it. But I can't think of a single reason why I should.'

Nor could I. Then I thought and said, 'Did you take your usual mug-shot of the guy?'

'No. Wouldn't let me. If I'd been smart I should have smelled a rat at that point. Like I said, Turner, be careful.'

§

I hit Toronto just after midnight. No matter—the guy I stayed with usually studied late. I could count on him being up till two or three. He opened the door with an economics text book in his hand.

'Hi, Mikey.'

'Hi, Raines.'

Mikey Kosciuscko had become a good friend. He had found a freedom in Canada, a direction, less from escaping America and the draft than from escaping his family. There is an old adage—you never know what you can do until you don't have to explain it to your dad. Well, if there isn't there should be. Mikey'd finished high school in two years of evening study and was now a college freshman, University of Toronto. He worked mornings and evenings, went to college in the afternoons and studied halfway into the night. Had to admire the kid. I'd had it easy. Everything paid for. I'd never waited table or pumped gas in my life. Oh—and he dropped the 'y' from his name. Part of growing up I guess.

He yawned a lot, made coffee and asked me his usual, 'So, who you after this time?'

I told him.

'I was over at the Rochdale two nights back,' Mike said. 'The Frisbee brothers were there ... '

I'd met the Frisbee brothers. Doug and Bob Frisbee. Two kids from Minneapolis, so named because they did little else but play frisbee. They were Canadian National Champions. And they were earnest advocates of Nixon, or whoever came after Nixon, granting amnesty, but only so they could go home, become All-America champions and take on the world.

'... they have a new place now. They said this really weird guy had turned up on them. Could be the kid you're looking for.'

'How so weird?'

'You know Doug and Bob—not great with words. They just said he was straight, but straight in a weird kind of way. Like they pass him a joint to take a toke and he doesn't pass it on, like he doesn't know what to do with it. Sucks it down to the roach. Then he rolls over and barfs. It's like he doesn't know the rules. Like he's ... straight. Straight and heavy at the same time. That was their phrase—straight and heavy.'

Straight and heavy? That could be Joey DiMarco.

I said I'd look first thing in the morning. Check out the Frisbees' new commune.

In those days it was possible to drift from commune to commune— always a place to untie your bedroll, always a vegetarian pot on the hob, and few—if any—questions asked. Rochdale—which Mike had mentioned—was a high-rise warren that had become a mecca for drop-out kids across Ontario—I'd bump into kids who'd driven all the way from Sault Ste Marie on Lake Superior just to hang out at the Rochdale and score some dope—and for dodgers from across the border. I had daydreams of dodgers and deserters going in there and emerging thirty years later like Jap soldiers from the jungle. I say dodgers and deserters. Not a good idea to roll the two together. Same motive maybe, but the deserters had nothing left to imagine. They'd seen it. They were hard, took what they wanted from anyone and shit from no one. The kind of kids who gave ready shelter to draft-dodgers soon found deserters too much to handle.

I found the Frisbee brothers' commune. Down one of those endless leafy avenues off Bloor in the Annex district—a two-block walk from Honest Ed Mirvish's store. You know the place. No two houses quite the same. No two houses quite different enough. Doug and Bob's house stood out—zap colors on the picket fence, a mess of reds and yellows, peeling door and window frames, sheets tacked up for curtains and a front lawn surrendered to the predations of squirrels, not a blade of grass or a flower to be seen.

No one answered at the front. I went around back. Hammered on the door. Heard nothing. A chain-link fence, playing host to a few dried out trailing plants, separated this garden from the one next door. A small, bald, wispy old man was moving down the fence to the end of the garden away from me.

'Excuse me, sir. You wouldn't happen to have . . .'

He scurried on, glaring back at me a couple of times. I caught up with him by a gap in the fence. He was clutching a dustpan and brush and he was looking up at me still glaring.

'Excuse me, sir. Have you by any chance seen . . .'

He drew a line in the dust to complete the sense of the missing chain-link fence, like a kid in some baked dirt schoolyard daring me to step over it.

'This,' he said, 'is what you people do to Canada.'

He threw the contents of the dustpan at me, quite possibly aiming at my face—the crud bounced off my chest instead.

'This is what you do to Canada. Filth, scum, crap.'

I looked down at my feet—I was standing among the shards of a couple of dozen used hypodermics.

'Send us your bums, send us your junkies, send us your scum!'

In the years in which I'd been coming up to Canada I had not encountered this kind of resentment at the tide of disaffected youth we had unleashed upon our nearest neighbor—but I'd not doubted for one second that it existed.

'You can't control these kids. So you send 'em here. You can't win your goddam war so you export it to us. Scum! Nothin' but scum and bums and junkies.'

I'd said nothing. The old guy seemed to run out of steam and glide gently to the side, the dustpan in one hand, the brush in the other, hanging at arm's length, pulling him into a round-shouldered stoop. Maybe he thought I'd hit him? Who knows? He ran for his back door, yelled

'God bless America' over his shoulder with as much irony as he could muster, and locked himself in.

Was I going to search every commune in Toronto or was I going to get tactical? I looked down at the needles again—drugs did not seem like Joey D's scene at all. The tactical move would be to track him down to the Toronto equivalent of his New York scene—that is, wait until dark and hit the clubs in Yorkville. I was never sure whether Yorkville was a Lower East Side or a Greenwich Village, maybe it was the former aiming to become the latter. Half the clubs weren't even licensed—run by potheads for potheads. That whittled down the task some. Beer 'n' rock 'n' roll 'n' girls. That was Joey D ... and if he had to put up with a few hippies along the way, so be it. Suddenly I could see a place for Joey in all this—for a small time New York thief always in search of a 'mark'. I could imagine Joey in a few years' time—dealing dope to the hairy tribe he despised and occasionally asking, 'What does this stuff do for you guys? I tried it once and barfed.'

§

He seemed to know me at once. That kind of second sense some crooks have in the presence of the man. I was scouring The Technicolor Orange about ten the same evening, propping up the bar and trying, as unobtrusively as I could, to look at every face at every table. Looking for someone who might be Joey D with a new haircut, or Joey D in a hat or Joey D growing a beard. He'd changed nothing. The photograph I had of him could have been pulled from the back of a Polaroid minutes ago. The out-of-date greasy quiff. The sharp, imported suit. The narrow, shiny tie. The fistful of rings. The unrufflable arrogance of a punk looking to be a made man.

I was wrong about the beer. He was nursing a large scotch on the rocks. When I got to him he said, 'Don't tell me—the old man sent you?'

'Right,' I said.

He was sitting in a booth—he waved me into the seat opposite with a kind of 'hail-fellow-well-met' bonhomie that he probably learnt from his father—the little man's assumption of the role of big spender. Every guinea a godfather.

'I'll buy you a drink, tell you I'm doing OK, and then you can head off back to Pops.'

Circumstances there were under which I would have accepted this. An address, a letter, some sense—and here I was not so insistent on the truth—of how they meant to support themselves, and I could and had gone back to New York and calmed the heaving breast of parent-hood. But—fuckit—there was Tsu-Lin and the $229 the little bastard had ripped off.

'Ain't gonna be that easy, Joey.'

'Uh?'

He was looking around for a waitress—trying hard for the effect of me being of no particular importance to him.

'Two hundred and twenty-nine dollars, Joey.'

'What?'

'That's what you took from Tsu-Lin Shin in Palenville. I'd like it back.'

'She a friend o' yours?'

'Yes.'

'No problem.'

He pulled a fat roll from his inside pocket, peeled off three big ones and said, 'Keep the change.'

The cocky little shit. I was fit to kill him now. Where had he gotten hold of a stash like that? Throws me $300 and thinks nothing of it because he's got two or three thousand riding on his hip? I never did get to know.

At last a waitress passed us, topless, young, shy and carrying a round of drinks to another table. Joey grabbed her by the arm.

'Hey, a beer for the man here. And another Chivas for me.'

She said, 'Just a moment, sir,' and Joey slapped her across the tits—slapped her hard. The drinks tray toppled and tears welled in her eyes. The next thing I knew Joey and I were on our feet—face to face but for the fact that his face was not much higher than my chest. I was getting ready to adopt the placatory 'now just a cotton-pickin' minute, son' tone of voice I had surely learnt from my father, but he poked me in the chest with a stubby middle finger.

'Butt out—butt out—go home and get out of my face.'

That made four times he'd prodded me—enough to let me know that, little or not, the kid was built like a log-cabin. Didn't stop me. I prodded him back and out of nowhere a switchblade sliced through my shirtfront and sank into my belly. He'd stabbed me. The little bastard had stabbed me.

§

I spent the best part of the next month in hospital. The wound took infection. I narrowly escaped peritonitis, and lay there pumped full of antibiotics with a drain in my side to let unspeakable goo run off.

The cops talked to me. I would not press charges. I gave up on Joey D. If I ever got back to New York in one piece, I'd invent something palatable for his parents. I owed it to the client to lie.

Mike said, 'You're an idiot. I known guys like that all my life. Typical Wop hellraisers. Always wanting to be bigger than they are. He'll never amount to anything.'

'That's what your old man used to say about you.'

'Sooner or later someone will send him to jail.'

'Then let it be later and let it be someone else. I have a reputation to think of. How many kids in this town will talk to me if it's known I call the cops on them? Mike, forget it.'

Mike shrugged it off. He was angrier than I was, partly I suspected because he could see a little 'there but for the grace of God go I' when I described Joey D to him.

'Is there like anything you want?'

'A newspaper would be good. I feel like the world has stopped turning while I'm in here.'

'It's only been three days, Raines. You could be here a while.'

'Fine. Get me an American paper. *New York Times* would be good. *Boston Globe* maybe. And a packet of Reese's Peanut Butter Cups.'

I watched a lot of TV. More Rowan and Martin than could be good for a man. Failing to find the *Times* on a regular basis, Mike brought

me the *Daily News* every so often as a kind of consolation prize. Eight
cents in New York, a half dollar in Canada. It was kind of him. Kept me
in touch with the burgeoning madness of home without the effort of
having to read long sentences. Hardly a day passed without some pro-
nouncement from Tricky Dicky, some new lie about his peace program.
That's the neatness of having a 'secret' program, you can say what the
hell you like. Troops in, troops out—and a lottery for the draft. That last
was no lie. Bastard meant every word of that. John F. Kennedy's final
dream orbited the moon as Apollo 10—'Moon Summer' was under
way. The papers hashed over the abandonment of Hamburger Hill—the
Pentagon had deemed it an indefensible site, because of 'the difficulty
of supply'—so what if we mangled the lives of five hundred and fifty
Americans kids taking the damn thing? I missed Charlie Mingus at the
Village Vanguard and . . . and . . . Leo Gorcey died and a piece of my
childhood died with him.

Leo . . . the most rascally, streetwise, sneering, wisecracking of the Dead
End Kids, as Bowery-brash as Mel Kissing. I'd spent hours in movie
theaters watching him and Huntz Hall play the fool. I'll never forget
the episode where they inadvertently volunteer to be rookies and take
the army's induction test—banging square pegs into round holes. If you
succeed the army won't accept you as this is held to be the definition of
a moron. If only we had that today.

And . . . I saw the New York campaign ads for Mailer and Breslin—
'The Other Guys are the Joke'. But the other guys won. Mailer lost the
Democratic primary. Fourth in a five horse race—so it wasn't just my
missing vote that did it. Maybe now it would be possible to talk to Mel
about something else.

When Dan and Dick had said goodnight, when Goldie Hawn had
shrieked her last shriek, when Arte Johnson's 'interesting' had ceased to
be just that, when I'd read the papers and the books Mike had got me, I
still had plenty of time to think. And reading about Leo Gorcey's death
plunged me back into childhood and thinking of my childhood I thought
of brother Billy.

§

1950. Billy had the most remarkable mind of anyone I've met. Minds like Billy's might be more commonplace now in an age that has over-reached for thirty years or more, but 1950 was not a year in which anyone overreached. It was a year, and for that matter a decade, in which we played safe. We did right and we thought right. Billy thought pure left-field. A man born to come off the wall before the damn thing fell on us.

By the time he was twelve he had outread his teachers. He'd come home from the library with an elementary textbook of physics or chem-istry or astronomy and a week or two later would be reading a college level text. But he was not content with theory, in any matter—Billy's was above all a practical mind. In those days there were vast areas of rural Texas that had homes lit by kerosene and water wound up from wells in buckets. This was the way we grew up, the way Sam had grown up and most likely the way Lyndon Johnson grew up. A world without gadgets, because a world without electricity. Billy fixed that.

A feature of the Texas plains is windmills, pumping water for irrigation. Billy told Sam he could rig one to generate electricity. All he needed was a couple of trips to a scrap yard. I was six at the time, but I can still remember the conversation that took place, the three of us standing on the patch of footworn dirt in front of the porch.

'Son, are you sure about this?'

'Sure I'm sure.'

'It's just that it seems an awful lot for . . .'

Sam could not finish but it was obvious, even to me, how the sentence had to end.

'You mean it's an awful lot for a kid to come up with,' Billy said.

'I mean it's an awful lot for a kid to be asking.'

'Trust me, Dad, I can see.'

'I'm not so old I'm blind myself.'

'No, Dad. I mean I can see.'

Billy tapped his forehead just above the bridge of his nose.

'I can see see. I mean I can *see.*'

Sam looked foxed. Our mother appeared on the porch, shook a table-cloth free of crumbs and Sam looked at her as if to say, 'He's your kid, he sure as hell doesn't get any of this from me', but she folded the cloth, said nothing and went back inside. She knew no more of Billy's schemes than Sam, but unlike him she expected her kids to put on seven league boots and stride past her. That's what kids did. She no more understood Billy than Sam did, but she wasn't baffled by him.

'Billy, how much is this going to cost?'

'Nickels and dimes, Dad.'

Nickels and dimes was all Sam had—over in Europe and across the Pacific the Second World War was generating a boom economy for those back home. Lubbock was growing—reaching its adolescence as a town—as airbases and manufacturing moved in and brought new labor with them. As ever Raineses were not benefiting from this. All the same, Sam drove him into Lubbock and Billy came back clutching a box load of automobile innards. Bits I didn't know the name or purpose of and I'm damn sure Sam didn't either. For about a week Billy labored with yards and yards of electrical cable, with Sam doing just what the kid told him. At the end of the week Billy gathered the four of us into the cabin and threw the switch. Half a dozen twelve volt bulbs lit up the room. Hardly Times Square but five times brighter than kerosene, and as Billy reminded the old man, it was free. It was a glimmer in that house, a light that scarcely penetrated the corners of the room, but looking back it seems to me now to be the blinding light of the beginning of a dream.

Billy did not, probably could not stop. The water that one mill had pumped into a tank from which it was bucketed for household use he next piped into faucets. For the first time in her life my mother had running water—cold only—at the sink.

By the following summer Billy had added hot. A machine on a colos-sal scale that had the two of us digging old bottles out of every dump in town. We unearthed the archaeological strata of Lubbock, dug right back to the turn of the century I should think, and came home with around fifteen hundred glass bottles. He went to the old man and said, 'I need a thousand feet of black rubber hose pipe and a small industrial diamond.' The old man protested the cost, but didn't argue for long. Our mother blackmailed him, said if he didn't buy the boy a diamond she'd prise one out of her engagement ring. Then Billy made a device that looked

a lot like a giant geometry compass, with the diamond set in the sharp
end, that neatly lopped the bottoms off all the bottles by inscribing a
perfect circle in the glass. One tap with a wooden mallet and the bottle
broke in two without shattering. Then Billy threaded the hose through
the bottles and made a glass snake in three high rising coils next to the
house. Then he went to Sam again and said, 'I need three 100 gallon steel
drums—used won't do, they have to be new 'cause they have to be clean.'
The old man demurred, thinking this was it, but then Billy came back
and said, 'I want twenty bales of hay.' He got them too. Hay cost Sam
nothing—I think he was relieved that his son had finally asked him for
something he didn't have to go out and buy. Billy built a hay box two
feet thick around each barrel. Last of all, he hooked up the whole thing
and plumbed it into a cold water feed. It wasn't pretty. It rose up the side
of the house like a series of cockamamey pyramids, each barrel higher
than the last till they reached the roof, the glass coils leaping between
them reflecting the light back at you in a blaze of sunshine. Each barrel
fed a separate faucet—lukewarm from the first, near enough boiling from
the last. It worked. Like a dream. Sam scratched his head and wondered
about the mystery of genetics—or he would have done if he knew the
term. Billy baffled him.

It was about 1949 when Billy's reading of geology started to pay off. He
had now turned his mind to Sam's great obsession. Oil. Sam set down his
rig and drilled at random. Pointless, if you think about it. The man had no
system whatsoever. Billy grasped strata and sedimentary layers—he could
recognize an anticline when he saw one—Billy could read stone like it
was text. As far as Sam was concerned it might be stone but the text was
hieroglyphic. All the same he let Billy steer him across the plain, let him
choose the spot, let him read the geological samples the drill brought up.

'What exactly are we looking for, son?'

I watched Billy crumble a handful of red earth to dust between his
fingertips. I wonder if he'd already seen how close we had come. Already
he rationed what he told the old man, he'd learnt to give him no more
than he could comprehend in a single grasp.

'Salt, Dad. We're looking for salt.'

Sam looked blank. Billy might as well have said shinola as salt.

'It's often the crust over an oil deposit. The first sign you get that you're
approaching a gusher is salt. Pays to slow up when you see it.'

When he was eighteen he won a scholarship to UT at Austin. All tuition, room and board paid for—wouldn't cost Sam a cent. As reward Sam let him take me on a holiday to Arizona. Billy had long wanted to see the red rocks of Sedona. Sam even agreed to swap vehicles with him, just for the week. We got the pickup—only a year or two old—Sam got Billy's renovated, string and elastic band, rust and cowgum 1928 Oldsmobile flatbed. I liked the flatbed. Billy had rescued it from ruin, all it needed to be complete was a mattress tied to the back with Grandma Joad on it. Nobody thought it would make Arizona and back. It was a mark of Sam's faith in the two of us that he lent us his most prized possession. I was twelve. I'd never been out of the county let alone out of the state. My excitement was limitless. I did everything Billy told me—I carried the books he wanted me to read, even read some of them, a basic geology, a history of the settlement of the West—fine by me, it was full of characters like Wyatt Earp and the Ringo Kid—and a couple of English novels. The summer of 1950 was the first big summer of a short life lived under a big sky. We drove Route 66—so long ago I doubt there was even a song about it.

Towns rolled by just like they do in the song, Albuquerque, Gallup, Flagstaff. It took us a day and a half to get to Flagstaff. Ike hadn't built the interstate yet and you slowed through every small town you passed. We ate in truckstops most of which advertised 'the best cup of coffee on Route 66', and when night fell we just pulled up the first dirt road we saw and pitched our tent. Nobody hassled us. Nobody appeared out of the gloom toting a shotgun and the stereotypical look of an inbred halfwit. It was still the Restofamerica but it was Anotheramerica. Remember, we'd just fought the last good fight of the Twentieth Century. We'd won the century—the rest of it was ours to do with as we pleased. We still had fifty years to build New Eden. Even God had only seven days—or was it six? America was a kinder, gentler place, because it was a more optimistic place.

On the evening of the second day we stood in the mainstreet of Jerome, AZ—a town that seemed to be made of matchwood and perched on a cliffside to spit in the face of gravity—and stared at the red and purple streaks that tore across the mountainside above Sedona. Billy could read strata like the plot of a novel. He reeled them off to me, the congealed story of the earth's crust writ large on the face of Arizona. I wish I could remember a word of what he said, but science has always been a foreign language to me. Permian, Mesozoic, Eocene, Pre-Cambrian—if he'd said Martian I'd of believed him. I was in awe of my big brother, in thrall to the magic of his words. He was young Copernicus to me. We trailed around among the sandstone mountains for three or four days. Billy chipped away with his rock hammer and filled a sack with lumps of stone and each evening he'd set them out in a row and give me the history of each one. Sandstone—that's about all I can recall. Sandstone. Every hue from salty white to veinous puce.

The night before we were due to turn around we were camped three or four miles from the truck. We were on the Mogollan Rim that cuts across the north east corner of the state, and had walked, backpacks and all, along a narrow, winding, perilous path high above Wet Beaver Creek to a rocky outcrop set above a clear, clean pool of water. A slice of the old Eden. As the campfire burned low Billy set to musing, just like he did on nights when we sat on the side of Bald Eagle and looked out across the plains. Only now we looked up through a cloudless sky to the stars.

'You read those books I gave you?'

'Sure,' I lied. I'd skimped through the geology primer, read all the history of the West, but I'd got halfway through one of the English novels—*The First Men in the Moon*—and switched to Zane Grey's *Riders of the Purple Sage*. It had seemed the more appropriate.

'*First Men in the Moon*, right?'

'Right.'

It was shining down on us, full, faintly blue and bouncing off the pool below us.

'We're going there.'

'What? You and me?'

'No, stupid. America. Man. Man is going to the moon.'

I don't know when NASA got started, but if anyone had thought of it in 1950 I'll be amazed.

'When?' I asked, knowing that what could sound fanciful with Billy was often merely literal.

'Oh . . . 1965 . . . 1970. No later than that.'

'In a gravityless iron ball?'

(That was how H.G. Wells had done it, and I think Jules Verne had fired his guys out of a big gun.)

'No,' said Billy very matter-of-fact, eyes still fixed on heaven, not looking at me. 'That won't work. Nice idea, but it won't work. No, it'll be rockets, rockets as big as skyscrapers.'

There was a long silence. At the end of it Billy said, 'I have a dream.' I had no idea what to say to this. The kid was a dreamer. But it did not sound to me as though he was simply stating what was obvious.

'I have a dream of America.'

Another long silence followed. We stared at the moon. I could feel my teeth begin to chatter. Billy broke reverie, ducked back inside the tent, emerged with a blanket, wrapped it around me, and took up exactly where he had left off.

'I have a dream.'

'Is that like the American Dream?'

'No. No. In fact I'd say it's almost the exact opposite of the American Dream. What is the American Dream? A dream of easy money, of get-rich-quick? Of making it anew in the newest country?'

'I guess so.' I hadn't a clue what it was. He made a fundamental concept of being American sound plainly vulgar.

'Fine. In its place, fine. But I have a dream of America, not an American Dream. And that's different. The founding fathers dreamt America.'

'They did?'

'Sure they did. No other country had ever sprung into being overnight. Somebody had to dream it. Thomas Jefferson and George Mason had to dream it first. They invented America. That's what we all have to do. We have to dream America so we can invent it. America is ours to reinvent.'

I struggled towards meaning, straining for a spark of anything big brother might take as a sign of intelligence.

'But America's already invented—the Constitution and that.'

'We'll reinvent that too.'

'Why?'

'Because if we do not we cannot reinvent ourselves. We have to dream America anew to reinvent it, and then we dream ourselves and reinvent ourselves. All this will happen in our lifetime as surely as man will go to the moon.'

Another long silence. I was falling asleep, but I dared not. I knew he wasn't through yet.

'I have a dream. I shall invent myself. I shall become.'

'Become who?'

'There was no word missing there, Johnnie. That's the whole damn sentence. I shall become.'

I asked the perplexing question. Had to.

'Will I "become"?'

'Only if you dare to dream.'

I awoke under the blankets inside the tent. He must have picked me up and put me to bed. Sunlight filtered through the canvas. I could hear the crackle of a wood fire, smell the sweet aroma of woodsmoke. I threw back the flap and found Billy sitting more or less where I'd last seen him. On the flat rock, above the edge of the pool, his back to me, still looking up.

'Did I fall asleep?'

'You always do. There's coffee in the pot. Eat and pack. We have to go soon.'

'What's the hurry?'

'Nothing. Don't worry, you'll be fine.'

'Why wouldn't I be fine?'

'I have to drop you at the bus depot.'

'The bus depot?'

'I'm not coming back with you.'

I took a couple of steps toward him, meaning to spin him round and get a look at his face. It was a gag, right? I had to know it was a gag. But he dived off the rock, a butterfly arc, to slice the water. When he bobbed up again he said what he'd just said. 'Don't worry, you'll be fine.'

All the way into Flagstaff I kept asking why and he'd say, 'I told you last night.'

In the Greyhound station he stuffed a one way ticket to Amarillo in my hand, about fifteen dollars in notes and change and said, 'Call the old man when you get to Amarillo. Don't worry, he'll come and get you.'

'What do I tell him?'

'Nothing.'

'When will you be back?'

But he hugged me and never said another word. Walked back to the truck, pulled out of the terminal and headed west. Never looked back. Never waved.

§

I rode Route 66 east in a Greyhound bus seated next to an old cowhand who clearly thought me beneath his attention or his words. He just chewed tobacco, occasionally slurping back a river of black spittle from his chin, and stared out the window. I got to Amarillo and called Sam collect. I sat three and a half hours in the depot, ate chocolate bars from an automat and waited.

Lois was first to tumble out of the Olds. Threw her arms around me and kissed me and cried. Sam had questions. Lois would not let him ask them. All he knew was what I'd told him over the phone. Billy was gone. And the truck was gone with him. I guess Sam wanted to ask the question I'd asked, 'When will he be back?' But if he'd been able to ask I would not have been able to answer.

It was a bumpy, slow, silent ride home. Sam seemed more sad than angry. Every so often Lois would squeeze my hand, but she'd no more speak than the old man. Me in the middle, Lois slipping one arm around me. I can smell her perfume to this day. And Sam gripping the wheel like it was a lifesaver thrown to a drowning man, eyes fixed on the road ahead.

A few miles from Bald Eagle he spoke. The sum total of all that he'd been holding back for the last six hours.

'He's ruined me. The goddam kid has ruined me.'

But he hadn't. Billy had made Sam. Made all of us.

The next couple of weeks of summer went by with Sam working furiously, burying himself in any activity by day, and by evening watching the track for any sign of Billy—looking for the tell tale trail of dust whipped up by the wheels of a pickup.

Then Lois announced she was expecting. My father whooped with joy and added two rooms to the house in anticipation—thrown up with his usual mixture of enthusiasm and carelessness. Six months later my brother Huey was born—Samuel Houston Raines Jr. But two months before that the old man drilled right through a salt crust and struck oil. Like I said, Billy made us.

It was a character-forming moment. Sam had been a feckless dreamer all his life. I'd already worked out that if we ever struck it rich he'd find

a way to fuck it up. He didn't. He came home plastered in oil, hugged
Lois—must be traditional to ruin your wife's clothes at a moment like
this—sat down without any 'Yippee! We're rich!' and said, 'This is going
to be tricky. We need money now. Lots of it. Backing, financial backing—
or this could slip right through our fingers.' It was calm, a precision of
mind I had not expected. I had never admired the old man more—he
took success exactly as Billy would have done, in his stride, with a pragmatism that made him rich. He took samples for evaluation, hawked
the samples round every bank in the Panhandle till he found one that
believed in him, took out a loan and took off for Pennsylvania and
West Virginia. He came back with seasoned oil crews—complete pros,
guys who'd spent a lifetime drilling oil back East. Within a year he was
back in credit, and then the oilmen in slick suits, cowboy hats and shiny
boots came up from Midland and started to talk temptation money to
this hick in blue jeans and a check shirt who lived in a wooden shack.
Sam refused all offers of a buy-out and managed the whole damn thing
himself. Within eighteen months he was a millionaire. Billy made us and
what Sam learnt from Billy made us rich as Croesus. The dream come
true. Not my brother's dream, you will understand, but the other dream,
the American Dream.

§

You ever dreamt of being rich? Seems un-American, almost indictable
not to. Most Americans would think a man without that dream a fool. As
I was saying, Sam had been a dreamer all his life, tumbleweed between
the ears, and windblown to the point where the man was a hazard to his
own well-being. But he got seriously rich and I began to wonder which
of his dreams he would summon up first. Took a while, the financing of
the company meant he could take little out of it for the first year. All he
did for himself and the family was buy a new pickup and tack the two
extra rooms onto the shack. But after eighteen months or so he was ready
to spend. The dream he chose surprised us all.

We stood on the porch of the shack, me and Sam and Lois, and Lois holding young Huey. And Sam pointed up to the bald mountain and said, 'That's where the new house'll be.'

I looked at Lois seeking some reassurance, but she just smiled, so obviously pleased for her man. Build a house on the mountain, where Billy and I had stood to watch the universe turn above our heads and corkscrew off into infinity, and looked down on Texas stretching off into the lesser infinity below us? It was pretty well sacrilege. It was the stupidest thing I'd ever heard.

He did it. He embraced modernity with a fervor I had not imagined he could possess for a concept I did not think he knew. If I say the house looked a little Frank Lloyd Wright then I am gracing it too much from my own paucity of comparison. It was a glass and concrete monstrosity, about fifty feet up the shady side of Bald Eagle, overlooking our shack. He did not demolish the shack. The shack stayed in the sight line of the huge plate glass window on the dawn side of the mountain. A memento of our humble beginnings? He'd of laughed out loud if I suggested that. Nor was it a lasting reminder of his first marriage, to my mother. If it were he might have kept it as it was, left the old chairs and table, and the iron bedstead, like museum pieces. He didn't. He cleared it and used it to keep tools and tack in. I used to sit in there, the way I'd used to sit up the mountain staring at the stars, now just gazing out through the coating of dust on the windows, swimming in the smell of oil and leather that had replaced the smell of cooking and the waft of Lois' scent. It wasn't life on the mountainside with Billy. No one whispered the secrets of the universe in my ear anymore, I was alone with my own thoughts, but it wasn't all bad. The occasional burst of rain on the roof could bring my skin up in goose bumps. I would sit through a rainstorm as though it were the most erotic experience known to a boy until Lois came out with a flashlight and an umbrella, insisting I should come 'home', and I knew then it wasn't.

It was years before I could see the new house for what it was. Must have been the early seventies. The Sam Shepard/Antonioni film, *Zabriskie Point*. There's this house, all glass and steel and concrete, that gets blown to pieces over and over again as the film repeats itself. That's what my father's house looked like, *Zabriskie Point*. Don't know how many times I sat in the shack and mentally blew up the new house. Enough for a movie to strike a chord in me the best part of twenty years later. Into that house Sam packed all his dreams, his wife, his sons, his memories, his frustrations, his deep-felt satisfaction that he had made his mark on the world, etched himself into it as bold as canyon. I could have anything I wanted. I never knew what to ask for. I could rip through the consumer world like I was taking scissors to a mail order catalogue. But I never did. I would have liked the impossible, I would have liked my brother back, but Sam's firstborn was never mentioned in his presence. Only Lois and I ever talked of Billy. And after a while not even that. If she thought of him at all she ceased to tell me. I guess there was safety in silence. And as Huey grew there was another brother to entertain and be entertained by us. Young Huey looked a lot like Sam. But, then, so he should. Billy too looked a lot like Sam. Everyone said he was the spittin' image of his daddy. Could be it was just a cliché, but I could see it in every movement the child made. Few things could disappoint me more than that as he grew older I saw so little affinity in the operation of their minds. In that respect Huey was Sam to the T.

§

It must have been '52 or '53, the Senate elections looming up, when Sam decided it was time to play politics. We'd had a new senator last time around in '48. Scraped home with an eighty-seven vote majority, a ballot no more or less crooked than any other in Texas, and earned a nickname that wouldn't stick, 'Landslide'. Sam decided he'd like to see 'Old Landslide' re-elected and gave $20,000 to his campaign fund—a sum so large it merited a personal visit from the man.

He came out to Bald Eagle, the down-home weekend senator, starchy-looking Levi's, chunky belt buckle, pearl-buttoned cowboy shirt and Stetson. He swept off his hat with one hand and shook Sam's hand with the other, telling him how much pride and pleasure he felt in finally meeting such a loyal Democrat. For loyal read rich.

Lois emerged with young Huey in her arms. Sam gave the full intro for the boy, 'This is my youngest, Samuel Houston Raines.' The senator ruffled the kid's blond curls and said, 'Would you believe it, them's my brother's Christian names—Samuel Houston. My great-granpappy fought alongside old Sam at San Jacinto.'

And then he spotted me, spindly and shy and shot through with all the inhibitions of adolescence. I didn't speak and Sam didn't speak for me.

'And you young man, you would be . . . ?'

I muttered my name, thinking to myself that the guy had the biggest ears I'd seen this side of a jackass. He dropped the Stetson on a chair, grabbed my right hand in both of his and said, 'And I'm Lyndon Baines Johnson. LBJ to my friends and I hope all the Raines family will look upon me as their friend.'

Still clutching my hand he looked directly at Sam and made a bullshit line sound a hundred percent sincere. 'I want you to know, Sam, that you have a friend in Washington.' Bullshit, pure bullshit straight from the critter's ass. But, truth is, he meant it.

§

At age eighteen I'd reached the same point Billy had. College. I could go down to Austin. Several kids I'd grown up with were going down to Austin. But I had to get away from Texas. If I did not get away from Texas I did not know how to 'become'. I didn't know in the first place but that was neither here nor there. Stay home and I'd never know. Where home was didn't much matter, it could have been Tuscaloosa or Tallahassee, I would still have felt the same.

There was only one problem. Sam.

'I've gotten into college, Dad. I've been accepted to Georgetown.'

Sam mulled this over a while. He could hardly be surprised. He wanted all his boys to be college boys. I'd kept it a secret. But all the same he must have known.

'Would that be the Georgetown over to Waco or the Georgetown over to Denver?'

'Neither Dad, it's the Georgetown over to Washington.'

'DC?'

'Yep.'

'You're going east?'

No Raines had gone east, not since the first Raines had gone west—and even then he'd only set off from Missouri.

'Why Washington?'

'It's a good place for Law.'

He'd known for a year or so that I wanted to be a lawyer. That he didn't mind. He thought a lawyer in the family was a good idea. He hated lawyers. To breed his own seemed like the obvious solution. He'd never have to deal with one outside his own family again. But Washington he had to wrestle with.

It was a day or so before he got back to me about this. Picked up the conversation right where he'd left off.

'It's what you want, son?'

'Of course.'

He slapped me on the back.

'Well, if you're headed east we'd better go pick you out some wheels.'

It was acceptance of a kind. He wasn't happy, but he wasn't going to argue. But it was clear as moonlight he expected me to come back.

If I'd of let him the old man would of packed me off to college in a brand new Cadillac. He drove me down to the dealer's and told me to pick one out. I said no, I couldn't let him. And I certainly couldn't tell him I thought it was a car for a middle-aged man. So middle-aged he wouldn't drive one himself. In the end he gave in and bought me what I wanted, a sound, solid Chevy pickup—the gleam of newness gone but less than three thousand miles on the clock—from a sprawling used car lot on the edge of town.

He said, 'Why d'you want to show up at your fancy eastern college looking like a good ole boy? All you need now is a shotgun in an overhead rack and a dead 'coon jammed in the radiator grill.'

I said, 'You want them to think I'm a Yankee?'

First laugh I'd managed to get out of him in ages.

I passed my last summer at Bald Eagle. Working on the ranch. Cattle, pigs and hay. Like we weren't rich. Like, as Sam was wont to say, 'we wuz just folks'. I would not have had it any other way.

The day before I left Sam said, 'I'll give Lyndon a call. Let him know you're coming. Washington's a big place. You'll need somebody you know.'

I didn't know Landslide Lyndon. He was a man I'd met once. A man who'd scared me shitless with his ears.

'You don't have to do that, Dad.'

'Yes I do. You never know when you might need a friend.'

And I could not talk him out of it. I figured it didn't matter. LBJ would just say sure, pocket the next donation and forget about me. I was wrong.

I'd been less than a week in Washington—still green to city life, still a hick from the sticks to my fellow students. A guy from the floor below knocked on my door.

'Raines. Lobby phone's ringing for you. A woman.'

I took the stairs three at a time. Lois. Had to be Lois. Then a voice said, 'Mr Raines? Please hold one moment. I have Senator Johnson for you.'

Oh God, no. But I held.

'Johnnie Raines?' A Texan drawl, a ham version of my own voice. Had to be real.

'Yessir.'

'Yore daddy told me you was here. Son, you have a friend in Washington. Let me show you round the Capitol. Just call my seccretary and fix a time. Be a pleasure to see one of Sam Raines's boys again. Now tell me. How was Texas when you left her?'

'Big, sir.'

He roared with laughter and rung off. I never called him. I never looked round the Capitol. Years later, when I stood outside the Pentagon and yelled, 'LBJ LBJ how many kids did you kill today?' I told no one I had a friend in Washington.

§

1969. It was a hot June evening. Sticky with the humidity of sunshine and rain. Summer had burst and blossomed while I'd been in Toronto—a low lilac light in the sky, tinting the side windows, occasionally glinting in the rear-view mirror as I followed the highway south and east down the New Jersey bank of the Hudson. It was going to be a strange summer, it was written in the sky. Texas had lilac sunsets, as well as magenta, purple and plain old bloodshot. It was the first time I'd seen one over the grimy haze that was New Jersey. I parked the car in a high-rise stacker in Hoboken—I have never seen the sense of keeping a car in Manhattan, it's a walker's city—the price of which was the occasional broken window and the accumulated dents in the hood where the local kids stomped on it. It was almost dark by the time I emerged from the PATH station in Manhattan. I walked from Cortlandt Street up Broadway to my office. I had a vision of a month's unopened mail piling up behind the door. I'd fish out what mattered and take it home with me. Maybe Rose would be home. I'd fling the mail in another pile, open a bottle and listen while she digested a month's gossip into two hours' straight talking. After that I'd probably fall asleep. She might not even notice.

The door opened smoothly. No mail, no mess. Just a pair of leather brogues resting on my desk, attached to feet that belonged to Donald Speke, Detective First Grade, working out of the 5th Precinct at Elizabeth Street.

'Donny? What brings you out of a Sunday night?'

Speke didn't answer. Just swung his feet to the floor, looked past me and said, 'Cuff him, Jack.'

I had no idea who Jack was. I didn't even see his face. I just dropped the bag and stuck out my hands behind me, as years of passive resistance had taught me to do, and felt the metal snap onto my wrists.

Into the elevator, down to the street. Bundled into the back of their car. Jack at the wheel, Speke sitting next to me, not looking at me, all of six blocks to the Precinct House.

'Donny. Could you tell me what this is about?'

'Lieutenant wants to see you.'

'Fine—has Nate forgotten how to use a phone?'

Speke turned to look at me. It came home to me that the man had never liked me.

'To you, Raines, it's Lieutenant or Mr Truegood. I don't know where you're coming from talking like you were one of us. You're not. You private guys are all the same. You think you're cops. Well, sit on the cuffs, feel steel under your ass and get the message.'

I got it. I shut up. I was used to being arrested, although it was a good few years since this had happened to me, and never in New York. I knew the procedure and I knew to roll with it. This could not be much. I'd been gone a month. I could not even have a moving violation or a ticket. It was some sort of foul up and I'd be on the streets again as soon as I'd seen Nate. Nate and I got along surprisingly well. I think he regarded me as a rare specimen. The total New Yorker regarding the total outsider.

They whisked me past the front desk to where Nate's name and rank in flaking black stencil on a frosted glass door faced me. Speke knocked once and pushed me through the door ahead of him.

Nate was feeling the heat. He was cursing and fiddling with the electrical outlet that seemed to be powering a big fourteen-inch blade fan somewhat erratically. It purred and stalled and purred again. His jacket was slung across the back of his chair, his collar was popped, and all the buttons on his fancy vest undone. Nate was not the easiest of men. He had a reputation as a hard man. There was a rumour that the big dent in the top of his battered metal desk was caused by him pounding the head of a perp into the surface. This was not true. I'd been there when he'd done it. The fancy dresser cohabited with the slob in Nate. Not being able to find an ashtray one day he'd simply taken a hammer out of his drawer and beaten a hollow into which he could drop the ash from his cigar. But this begged a question—he hadn't used a perp's head, but what was he doing with a hammer in his desk drawer in the first place? I'd never ask. He liked me. That was the straw I clung to.

Nate looked angry, but he wasn't looking at me.

'What's with the cuffs? Did I tell you to cuff him? All I said was go get him.'

Speke said, 'Sorry, Lieutenant. I just . . .'

'Just what? For fuck's sake take 'em off.'

Speke unlocked me. I rubbed at my wrists. Nate stared at Speke until he backed out and closed the door behind him.

'Take a seat, Raines.'

'Nate—what is all this about?'

Nate got back behind his desk.

'This is serious, Raines. I had to pull you, I didn't tell Donny to cuff you, that comes of him thinking when he should be doing. But I had to pull you. I've had guys in your office and down by Front Street since yesterday.'

'And?'

Nate pulled a file from the top drawer of his desk, missing eye contact as he said, 'It's murder, Raines.'

I knew enough law to say nothing to this.

'You know a guy named Melchior Kissing?'

Oh Jesus no—not Mel.

'Yes. I know Mel.'

'This Kissing feller was killed Friday night, in your office, with an ice pick in his head.'

Oh Jesus—not Mel. Oh Sweet Jesus spare me Mel.

'Since when nobody's been able to find you. The Captain told me two and two was four. I said this wasn't you. Don't prove me wrong. Tell me where were you between ten p.m. Friday and about four a.m. Saturday morning?'

'Asleep. In Toronto.'

'You can prove this?'

'A dozen witnesses. I've been in Toronto most of the last four weeks. More than three of them in the hospital. You want names?'

'Probably not—all the same it ain't gonna be that simple.'

Simple? In a couple of copspeak sentences Nate had just ripped out a piece of my heart and flung it bleeding on the floor. I wanted to faint, throw up and die all at once. I turned my face into the blast from the fan. Let it blow me back from the brink. Cool this searing pain in my heart.

'Passport,' I said, and I could hear my voice begin to break up. 'I have my passport in my pocket. In and out stamps from the Canadians at Niagara.'

I took it out of my inside pocket. Pushed it across the desk to Nate.

'Well—whaddya know? Two little blue maple leaves. In May 28, out June 22. I'm gonna have to keep this for a while. You understand?'

I nodded.

'Now,' he changed tack. 'To the nitty. The ice pick. You do own an ice pick?'

'Yes. Goes with that near-antique icebox in my office. You have to hack it clean sometimes. It's . . . it's a necessity.'

Killed with an object I'd picked up a thousand times in three summers. I could feel it on the palm of my hand even as Nate spoke. Cool and smooth. A black handle, heavy in the hand, a short, shining, stainless steel spike. The means of Mel's death. I touched it. How could I touch it and not know? Was it not cast into the form and structure of the thing as inevitable as the ordained day of death. Was it not written? How could I not know? How could I touch it and not know?

'The ice pick that killed Kissing was covered in prints. Prints match those on the typewriter, the door handle, the icebox. You name it, they match.'

I knew what was coming, so I said, 'They probably are mine. You want to fingerprint me?'

'Sure, why not? Let's get Speke back in here. Let him do something useful.' Nate roared for Speke, told him to come back with an ink pad.

The look on Speke's face was copsatisfaction—if they were 'printing me I was going down. He rolled the fingers of my right hand across a sheet of white paper. I saw the image of my fingertips appear like Rorschach patterns upon the paper—that unmistakable scar on the tip of my index finger—a bulbous line like the swirling red storm of Jupiter. Speke handed the sheet to Nate. Nate picked up his reading glasses, held them away from the page and used them to magnify the image. Then he picked up a forensic photograph of an index fingerprint, weighed up the similarity and said, 'Yep. It's you.'

Speke smiled at me in a fuck you sort of way. It was me. I had not doubted it.

'Let's hear it. How did your prints get to be on a murder weapon? And Donny—get out.'

Speke vanished with his smile.

I said, 'It's my ice pick. Anyone could have picked it up in my office. Anyone in gloves.'

'What was Kissing doing in your office if you been gone a month?'

'He had keys. His office could get to be hectic. He used mine from time to time when I wasn't around. Same with his apartment. He lived just north of Houston. If he wanted to work of an evening he could just walk five blocks and get away from it all. He must have just let himself in.'

'Ah uh? And when we asked this broad you live with where you were, how come she said she didn't know?'

'You talked to Rose? You told Rose?'

How had she taken it? She and Mel had had a cat and dog relationship for years. They could fight fit to spit and draw blood, but she was bound to be hit hard by this.

'I don't live with Miss Diment, Nate. We just share an apartment. If you ask me I could have sworn I told her I was going up to Canada. But maybe I didn't. It would have made no difference if I didn't.'

Nate pondered this one.

'A month you say? Hospital you say? What kept you a month?'

'Kid stabbed me. Wound got infected. Needed to be drained. I got pumped full of antibiotics. Reacted badly to them. That's about all there is to it.'

'By kid you mean one of your draft-dodging punks?'

'Yes.'

I could not deny it. Joey D was a punk.

'And lots of people knew you were there? And you got out of hospital when?'

'Friday about five in the afternoon. I spent the night with friends, thought better of leaping into a car on Saturday so I drove down today. I can account for all of my time since I got discharged.'

'I don't doubt it, Turner. I don't believe you did this. I also don't believe you'd be so dumb as to walk back into your own office two days later as though nothing had happened with an "oh gosh" ready on your lips.'

'When did they find him?'

'Morning after. Yesterday. Blood had seeped through the floor into the office below. It being a Saturday the cleaner was in. She dialled 911. We slipped the lock on your door and found the guy.'

'Where is he now?'

'Downtown morgue.'

'Can I see him?'

'Later. There are more pressing matters. I checked with the NoHo cops at the 9th Precinct. It appears Kissing hung out with a weird crowd. Did you know he lived in the same block as that fuckin' lunatic Jerry

Rubin? The NoHos know that place, they busted it a while back. They say it's regular trouble.'

'Of course I know. Mel and I go way back. Nate—*I* hang out with a pretty weird crowd. They're none of them murderers!'

The NoHo cops were plenty weird themselves. They'd patrol St Mark's Place in packs of ten or twenty—was that paranoia or terrorism?—but they'd take a live and let live approach to a little dope. And that ended up emphasizing the deliberate targeting when they did bust someone. It had been a year almost to the day since they busted Mel's building— they didn't bother with a warrant, they said they were investigating a murder up in the Bronx—all they caught was four ounces of cannabis, but they looked for the killer in Rubin's letters and files. I also heard they took away some grotesque sex toy Rubin had dreamt up, but God knows this could be pure Yippie fiction, I never saw the damn thing. And Rubin got a busted coccyx from the beating they gave him. What was that—law or politics? Mel and I raised his $1,000 bail overnight by hustling everyone we knew.

'Yeah . . . sure,' Nate was saying, '. . . but that's just your job, right? Chasing dodgers and runaways. I tell you this guy was A1 weird. Hippies, Yippies . . . all of 'em potheads.'

Just my job? Well, believe that if you want.

'Nate—when did you last pull a reefer-smoking, crazed killer? Sure, Mel was a hippie. But he paid rent and taxes and held down a regular job just like you.'

'Yeah—his job. I was coming to that. I understand from Miss Diment that Kissing worked on the *Voice*. We talked to the guys there. Nobody seems to know what he was working on. Do you know?'

'No. He'd never tell me things like that till he was good and ready. He'd spent most of the last three months campaigning for Mailer.'

Nate held out his hands, turned his palms up and looked incredulous.

'Mailer lost on Wednesday! What the fuck was so important in Mailer running for mayor that it was worthwhile knocking off one of his guys *after* he quits?'

'Nothing,' I said, feeble and confident at the same time. 'Mel getting killed has nothing at all to do with that.'

'Then why kill him?'

'Nate, I'm as clueless as you are. But, if you don't mind, I've just been told my best friend is dead. I'd rather like to go home and think about him for while before I have to talk about him.'

Nate stood up. Yanked his tie back into place, swept my prints off the top of his desk into the open drawer. He seemed to want a few seconds to weigh this one up.

'OK. I don't see why not. But . . . the usual applies. Do not leave town without telling me. Report back here tomorrow noon . . . and . . . I gotta ask you for your piece.'

'My piece? I don't own a gun, Nate.'

'Whaddya mean you don't own a gun? I endorsed your application for a permit myself.'

'I got the permit. I guess I thought it went with the job. I just never got the gun. When it came to it I just couldn't see me with a gun.'

'You know, Raines. There are worse things could happen to you than some draft-dodger stabs you. You go after these crazies without a gun, and believe me some of them are very crazy, and you're going to wind up shot.'

It was good advice. I was not about to take it.

I found myself back on the street. Warm rain again. I held out my hands and watched the black smudges on my fingertips dissolve eerily in the green light from the precinct house lamps. Identity washed away. Anonymous once more. What now? Where now? Alone again. I wanted to go home and I could scarcely make myself move. Life seemed suddenly both bare and complicated. My house keys were in my bag. The bag was where I'd dropped it. On the office floor. The keys to the office were in Donny Speke's pocket. I looked back up the steps. Speke was watching me through the doorway. Flipping a silver half-dollar over and over again pretending he was George Raft when he wouldn't even make Elisha Cook Jr. I didn't want to speak to Speke.

I hooked a dime out of my pocket, walked down the street to a payphone and called Rose.

'Where the fuck have you been, you bastard?' was the first thing she said, then she broke down crying before I could get another word in. When her breathing slowed and I could hear the roar in the earpiece diminish, I said, 'I'll be home in ten.'

§

Rose was on the sofa in her robe. Stripped of make-up. Greasy streaks of cold cream bouncing back the light from her face. Thick eyeglasses instead of contacts, making her look like an overgrown adolescent. I always knew when Rose was hell-bent on getting drunk. She'd take out her lenses and put on the glasses, anticipating the point when she'd be too stinko to do it. She was nursing a large glass of gin. Ninety-nine percent stumblin' drunk already. She looked dreadful. I didn't ask what I looked like.

'Have you been crying all weekend?'

I fell into the chair opposite her. Scraped off my boots heel to toe.

'Pretty much. Those coppers who came looking for you gave me the hard time they couldn't give you. Turner, where the fuck have you been?'

'Canada. And I'm sorry.'

'You know, I've never adopted the current vogue for calling them pigs. Perhaps it's because I was brought up on the notion of "if you want to know the time ask a policeman" and village bobbies with big boots and black bicycles, but that Speke chap really is a pig. Talked to me as though I had committed a crime in not knowing where you were. Had one of his mates follow me if I so much as went out to get a pint of milk. And then the bugger sat on the doorstep all day, just waiting.'

'They won't do that anymore. I told them all I know, and like I said I'm sorry.'

She swigged gin. I decided it was just what I needed. I just didn't want it neat. I went to the icebox and rooted around for a tray of ice cubes. It was frosting up badly. There, on the top shelf, was a black-handled ice pick just like the one that killed Mel. God knows they're common enough, a couple of dollars in any hardware store, but it stopped me cold. It was stuck there like something I'd have to spend the rest of my life avoiding. Like passing a gibbet. A permanent symbol of Mel's death. I plunged one hand to the back of the icebox, grabbed a tray and just pulled. The force of it tore the tray free from the frost, spun me round, scattered ice cubes across the floor and flung me straight into the arms of Rose. Her head upon my chest, drunken, heaving sobs, mumbled words I could not understand.

I watched the ice melt into puddles on the kitchen floor, heard Rose run through a mantra of 'Bastards, bastards' and 'What're we going to do?' When she stopped and I felt her go limp I was pretty certain she'd passed out. So many evenings had ended this way. I carried her to her bedroom, flipped the quilt over her, and turned out the light. I went back to my own. A room scarcely bigger than the bed. Rose had dumped all the mail addressed to me here on the bed. Everything in me said 'mañana', so I tipped it off, lay down and fell asleep with my clothes on.

§

The first thing I knew was the scent of hot coffee wafting under my nose. I opened my eyes. Bright, bright light of morning. Rose bending over me. Dressed, made-up, lenses in, not a trace of chenille or cold cream. A vision for the working day. Sunlight turning the mop of red hair gold. One hand held the cup, the other fiddled with my shirt buttons.

'So?' she said looking down at the strip of tape and bandage on my belly.

'I . . . I . . . er . . . got stabbed. Nothin' serious.'

'Nothing serious? God, Johnnie, you're such a fool.'

I got up when I heard the door slam, grabbed the pile of mail, and decided to face reality. I tossed the first two. I did not want a subscription to the *Reader's Digest* and I honestly didn't care how much I owed American Express. The third stopped me cold. Mel's handwriting. A Friday night postmark. I tore it open. A single sheet of paper and another envelope. 'Turner—just keep this till I ask you for it. M.'

I tore open the second envelope. His address book, an audio cassette, a slip of paper torn from a telephone message pad—the same kind I kept in the office—with one address on it. Someone called Marty Fawcett of West Rogers Park, Chicago. And a couple of pages of gobbledegook I knew to be shorthand. I did not read shorthand.

This was an old if neat trick. How to hide something where no one can find it for twenty-four hours? Let the United States Post Office do it for you . . . neither rain nor snow nor gloom of night and all that jazz.

Mail it to yourself, mail it to a friend, but while it's in transit it's safe—federal offense to interfere with the mail, after all. Mel had wanted this hidden, at least till Saturday. I could not help but wonder from whom.

I stuck the cassette in Rose's player and listened. A lot of echo, a lot of engine noise and a surging background of human voices, then—

'You're not wired, are you, kid?'

'Of course not. I'm a professional journalist.'

I could almost see Mel flourishing his shorthand notepad and ballpoint pen even as the lie left his lips.

A horn honked. A voice coming from the loudspeaker cut in—'all aboard for the six-thirty for New Palz, Kingston and Albany'—and drowned out the next sentence. At least it told me where they were. Underground, at the Port Authority Bus Terminal on 8th Avenue. Then the other voice was saying, 'Did I say I was going to make it easy for you?'

And Mel, 'You gotta give me more than this. There's no story here, just a rumor. And I can tell you—I hear rumors like this all the time.'

'Oh, there's a story here all right. You just have to find it. Or maybe I should say you have to earn it?'

'Please—I'll earn it. It's my job. But you gotta point me in the right direction at least. I can't just place a classified saying were you present when—'

A bus honked again. A deep bass reverb, bouncing off the walls smothering what Mel was saying. I wound back the tape. 'When ... blew away ...' Was it 'blew away'? Meaning what—the common euphemism for killed, for killed almost casually? I couldn't be at all certain. When the honking stopped, the other man was speaking.

'You find the New Nineveh Nine and you'll find your story.'

'The what?'

'The New Nineveh Nine,' the voice now dropped to a stagy whisper, inadvertently close to where Mel had his microphone hidden. 'And that's the last time I'll say it.'

'A name,' Mel was saying. 'Just give me a name. An individual.'

The loudspeaker made the last call for the six-thirty Albany bus.

'Fawcett. Find Corporal Fawcett. Marty Fawcett.'

'And you?'

'That's all you're getting, kid.'

'But what do I call you?'

'You need to call me anything? OK. Call me . . . call me . . . Broken Arrow.'

I heard the man's footsteps walk away. Heard Mel mutter 'Oh shit' to himself. Then the tape clicked off.

I played it again. It was like getting late to the theater. I felt I'd missed the first act, caught the second. It was impossible to know what they were talking about. When might help. I called the Port Authority, asked if there was a six-thirty Albany bound bus every evening. No, I was told, it was Thursdays only. Weekday buses were on the hour. They put on an extra bus on Thursdays on the half hour and two extra buses on Fridays at twenty minute intervals to cope with the increased human traffic out of the city in summer.

I was impressed. The postmark on the envelope read 10.30 p.m. Friday. In a little over twenty-four hours Mel had tracked down this Marty Fawcett. I don't know how he did it. He was a better detective than I was. How much had he been able to deduce from the clues this Broken Arrow had left him. 'Corporal'—a soldier. A former soldier? I knew what Nineveh meant. Maybe Mel had too. Fort Nineveh in Georgia was a boot camp for the army. Just outside of the township of New Nineveh, not twenty miles from the Alabama line. I'd passed through it a couple of times in the early sixties on my way to civil rights actions in Albany, GA. Quite without in-cident. It was where they licked the grunts into shape before they shipped them out to 'Nam. But I still hadn't a clue what Mel had blundered into. All the same, I was certain it had killed him. Knew it in my bones.

It was getting close to noon. Time to clock in with Nate Truegood.

§

I checked in at the front desk. Nate saw me at once. He had conceded to the summer, abandoned the vest in favor of a sleeveless, white cotton shirt, and installed a brand new fan on top of his desk.

'Would you believe technology?' he said. 'I went out and bought it from a Chinee on Canal this morning. This sucker comes with five settings,

Whisper, Breeze, Zephyr—now what the fuck is a zephyr?—Cooler and Powerblast. It's like trying to use my wife's blender—do I want to chop or frap or fuckin' fricassee? I usually give up on account I can't decide. Right now we're on Cooler. Great, eh?'

Then he slapped a clear Ziploc bag in front of me—must have sat there holding it on his lap all the time he was, literally, shooting the breeze—ready to catch me off guard.

'You recognize this?'

The ice pick was inside. Handle dusted for my prints, spike crusted in brown bloodstains. If he wanted a shock effect, he got one—but to no purpose. I guess it was worth a try, I'd already done cliché number one in the cop's book of clichés by returning to the scene of the crime.

'Of course. I thought we already agreed. My prints were all over it. Though now you come to ask, I kind of thought I'd lost it a few weeks back.'

'What do you mean "lost"?'

'Just in the office. About the time the hot days started up. I needed it . . . and one day I just couldn't find it. There's a dozen places I could have mislaid it. Gap between the icebox and the wall, slipped off the top of a filing cabinet—I don't know.'

Nate put the ice pick back into a drawer.

'Well, it was handy when Kissing came to be killed. Now, I got your keys here. You can go back into your office. We're through with it for the time being.'

He threw the keys, I caught them.

'That's it?'

'More or less—except to say, and Raines I mean this, don't hold out on me. I know you, you'll pick this up, and gumshoe your way through it, so far out of your depth your nose won't be above the shitline—but it's murder, it's cop business so you tell me everything single damn thing you find out.'

'Of course,' I lied. 'And what have you got?'

'What have I got? What the fuck have *I* got?'

I thought for a second I might have pushed him too far. Nate could go nuke if you hit the right button.

'Raines, I don't have diddley. I don't have even the shadow of a witness. Nobody saw a damn thing. That building of yours has no doorman, no signing in or out, and anyone can come and go even at ten o'clock of a Friday night.'

'Midnight even,' I said.

'Yeah, right. Midnight.'

His frustration vented itself in silence. I decided to wait until he surfaced. Usually he'd snap pencils—he bought them by the gross just for that purpose, or crumple up paper coffee cups to throw at someone, usually Speke.

'And forensic. What do the clowns in white coats give me? You. They give me you, the guy with the iron-clad alibi. You know, if you cleaned that office of yours once in a while there might be the possibility of fresh dirt. Right now the killer could have trailed in horse-shit and we'd be no wiser.'

I changed the subject.

'Can I see Mel?'

'You don't have to do that. Guy from the *Voice*—name of Jephcott—ID'd him already.'

'I still want to see.'

'Not a pretty sight.'

'Nate, let me see him, please.'

'OK. You want to see—we'll go downtown. But, you don't have to do it. I just wanted you to know. I look at stiffs all the time. Wouldn't do it, myself, unless I had to.'

Driving down to the morgue, Nate said, 'When d'you last see a body?'

I'd never seen a body and told him so. Sam hadn't wanted any of us kids to see our mother dead, and since then I could not recall that I'd known anyone who'd died—not friends, not kin. Good God, that now seems an age of innocence. How could I ever have been so young?

It was like film noir—in bleached-out color. A black man in a white outfit rolled the tray out of the wall, peeled back a plastic sheet and there was Mel pale and bloodless. I'd forgotten he'd shaved off his beard—I almost turned to Nate to say this wasn't Mel Kissing before memory of that last night at the Village School clicked in. He was neater by far in death than I'd seen him in life.

They'd cut him some. A butcher line right down the middle.

'Did they have to?'

'We always have to. I once had a victim who'd been shot, stabbed and then they backed a truck over him. Had to know which it was killed him.'

The wound in Mel's forehead was high up almost in the hairline. Bone and flesh had caved in around the blade with the force of the blow.

'What did you learn?'

'One blow, pierced the skull and buried the blade almost to the hilt in his brain. That took some strength.'

'So he died instantly?'

Nate didn't answer. I had to tear my eyes off Mel and look at him before he'd speak.

'No ... no he didn't. Frontal lobe isn't vital to the motor functions. It's not like breaking a guy's neck when everything goes at once. It's got more to do with sensation.'

I waited for what he was not telling me.

'He appears to have got up, spike still in his brain, made an effort to get to the door, maybe with his assailant still in the room, who knows? Then we figure he lost consciousness, hit the floor and bled to death. That's why we got such a wide span for the time of death. Blow could have been struck several hours before he actually died. Now—you seen enough?'

I'd seen enough to last me, to stay with me, to run rampant through my waking dreams for the rest of my life. I took a last look at Mel, so un-Mel-like without the beard and glasses, wishing I could think of a parting gesture, wanting to do right what I could not even begin to imagine. I did nothing, let the attendant pull the sheet back over him. Impotent in the cage of my own emotions.

'We couldn't find a next of kin.'

We were out on the sidewalk. Nate dragging me back to the here and the now.

'His parents are long gone. He's got a brother—burned out on scag years ago. I've never met him or even heard mention of where he lives.'

'We can release the body, but who to?'

'As long as I'm not under suspicion anymore it had better be me.'

'You know how to set up a Jewish funeral? I wouldn't know where to start.'

'Me neither.'

§

It occurred to me to go and check out Mel's apartment. He lived in two and a half rooms on East 3rd, a little way off the Bowery. A dozen impulses told me to go, three good reasons warned me not to. First, anything Mel thought mattered would be in the envelope he mailed to me. Twos, if whoever had killed Mel was watching I could end up dead. And threes, if Speke was watching then he'd fink to Nate and Nate would know for sure I was holding out on him. Instead I went to my office.

The office was a mess. Speke's doing I was sure. My books knocked off the shelf, splayed out on the floor, spines bent back, pages falling out, lying where Speke had shaken and dropped them. Every drawer in my desk emptied out and stuffed back. Fingerprint powder on every surface and every handle. My typewriter looked like a chunk of wedding cake dusted with icing sugar. It meant nothing. I'd been turned over before. I spent the afternoon creating order and walking around the dry patch of Mel's blood on the floor halfway between my desk and the door. I am not a squeamish man—a coward maybe—but the shitty stuff of life has never made me cringe. Eventually I had to touch the stain, to feel the dust of Mel's life between my fingertips. What did I expect? Epiphany? The soul of the slaughtered crying out for justice? A voice from the afterlife answering all my questions—who would do this, who would do this to a loudmouth, smart-ass, irritating Jewish runt of a man who never hurt anybody in his entire life? Dust I saw, dust I touched and dust was what I got. I'd've left it there—what else did I have of the man?—but I had clients to think about. Even if the news didn't spread and kill off my business I'd hate to have to explain it away every time someone asked the obvious question. I'd get on my knees and scrub Mel away. A brush, a bucket and tip him down the sink. Not today. Maybe tomorrow.

§

It was one of Rose's sober nights. I was glad. I didn't know how much to tell her, but there was something I needed. A stinking night, somewhere in the high nineties. She threw open all the windows and served up a salad, with black olives and spring water. We sat on the fire escape gulping in air, spitting pits into the street. She pulled off her top, sat there in her bra and skirt and tipped a glass of water over her chest.

'If this goes on I'm going to take my hols and go home for a couple of weeks. It's Wimbledon fortnight—you can always bank on it absolutely pissing it down for Wimbledon.'

'I thought it was Manchester was famous for its rain?'

You will note—small talk is not my forte.

'England—darling—all of it—is famous for its rain. Why do you think A.A. Milne always depicted Christopher Robin in wellies and Pooh in a sou'wester? Why do you think a gentleman always carries an umbrella even in summer?'

'To hail a cab?'

'Quite right. Touché, darling. Daddy carries his everywhere and never uses it. First sign of rain and his arm shoots up for a taxi.'

'Do you miss . . . all that?'

'Not for a fucking moment. Now, why don't you tell me what's on your mind? You've been itching about something since I got home.'

I retrieved the two sheets of shorthand notes from my room.

'Ah . . . I see. Mel. I'd know that scrawl anywhere.'

'I don't know what it means.'

She gazed at it for few seconds, tucked a strand of hair behind her ear. 'I rather think he had his own methods. His shorthand had sort of evolved. I can read about half of this. He's been ringing round old friends—or something like that—old school chums who went into the army or government. Mostly he's drawn blanks but . . . see, near the bottom of page two he's written down the name "Barclay Fulton" . . . one of those names that you'd only find on a British bank or an upper class American.'

'We were in Law School with him.'

'Well—he's done rather well for himself. He's at the Pentagon now. According to Mel a member of Tricky Dicky's defense team.'

That made sense. Barclay had been born to that. I could never figure out what Mel and he had in common—Barclay, a New Hampshire Ivy League Republican with 'Live Free or Die' for a bumper sticker, and Mel, bred in New York's immigrant, street-corner Socialist tradition—except that they both lived for politics, albeit from opposing ranks.

'Mel called him Friday morning. Looks as though he called Mel back round about—gosh, it's a mess—looks like seven in the evening. Then there's a word looks like "West" something. I can't read the rest.'

'West Rogers Park?'

'Could be. Like I said Mel's shorthand had evolved and that's putting it politely. Are you going to tell me what this is about?'

Not if I could help it.

Rose grabbed me by the shirtfront.

'Turner, do not go after this! Read my lips! Leave this one to the fuzz—it's what the bastards are paid for.'

Nose to nose I whispered, 'Rosie, they haven't got a clue.'

'Not one?'

'Not one. Nobody saw a damn thing.'

'Then turn this over to them.'

'I can't do that.'

'Because it's Mel?'

'Exactly.'

She let me go, sucked on another olive, spat, pinged the pit off a trash can and said, 'Well, that clinches it. I'm definitely going to England. I'm not sitting around in this armpit of a city waiting for you to get killed too.'

There was no connection between the two, but it was a waste of time asking Rose to be that logical. Two days later I drove her out to Kennedy to catch the early evening Pan Am flight to London. I felt better on my own, felt, for no good reason, as though I could get somewhere, do something. Besides I had a funeral to arrange and what was a funeral to Rose? Just another excuse to get shit-faced.

§

Of course Mel had lied to me. He did what we all did, all us Mailer kids, his 'White Negroes', we disowned our families and rewrote our histories to satiate the nagging images of ourselves that existed only in our minds. The hot pursuit of the cool. Of course Mel had family. How had I ever been able to kid myself he hadn't?

I found two maiden aunts out at Brighton Beach. The Misses Lippmann—Gloria and Barbara—living in one of those box houses on a lot not three feet wider than the house. House after house, row after row, all neat behind little chain-link fences, on street after street stretching out at right angles to the sea. I understood at first sight. If this was where Mel had grown up, no wonder he represented himself as pure Manhattan, the original Bowery Boy, and uttered nothing but contempt for the burbs and the boroughs.

And yes—his parents were dead, but not as he told me when he was eighteen but less than two years ago, when they had both passed away within six months of each other of pneumonia.

The aunts wept when I told them Mel was dead. They wailed like Trojan women when I told them his death was not of natural causes. Who would ever want to kill young Melchior? The light of his family, the brightest kid on the block, the scholarship boy?

I had to ask. There was the matter of the funeral arrangements. Did they know how to bury someone? A purpose in life with death seemed to shake them back together.

'Sure, we'll call Jack. He's the Rabbi in a shul over in Sunset Park. He'll want to do it in person.'

They said they'd call me and I should come over and meet Rabbi Jack. They did, so I went. The prospect made me nervous. In my entire life I do not think I had ever had a business conversation with a priest. There were priests aplenty in the civil rights movement—Methodists and Episcopalians—and I'd discussed God and death and Jesus with not one of them.

In contrast to two tiny women in their late sixties, Rabbi Jack was a black bear of man of about forty or so, all beard and belly. He heard me out in silence, just nodding occasionally.

'Must have been hard on you,' he said at last.

I was feeling sentimentally honest. The remark, shall I say, touched me.

'He was like a brother to me,' I heard myself say.

'He was my brother,' Jack intoned, with an all-men-are-brothers solemnity.

'Sure,' I said.

'No,' Jack came back. 'I mean he really was my brother. I'm Jack Kissing. Mel was my kid brother.'

A phrase of Rose's came quickly to mind—'the two-faced, lying bastard.'

By now I had Nate Truegood ringing me every day.

'When are you gonna bury this guy? It's a hundred and five in Central Park. The morgue is overflowing. Ice cubes cost more than diamonds! Will you organize this fuckin' funeral or do I have to come down and do it for you?'

By the time we got it together—oh the aptness of that hippie phrase—Mel had been on ice for three weeks, quite, I was told, against the tradition. I drove out to the New Montefiore cemetery in Farmingdale. Rabbi Jack read Kaddish over him. I went along feeling about as out of place as a redwood in the desert. As the first clods of earth got shoveled onto Mel I threw in the Complete Poems of Wallace Stevens. Rabbi Jack looked at me, kind of quizzically, so I told him.

'Years ago, when we were in school together, he made me promise I'd put a copy of Wallace Stevens in the grave with him—if he went first.'

'A reciprocal arrangement?'

'Of course,' I lied. I didn't tell him Mel and I had been smoking dope for the first time in our lives, and that dope made him emotional and me stupid. I hadn't been able to think of anything I wanted in the grave with me. Not a damn thing. I'd told him I wanted to float to Valhalla on a burning boat like a Viking. Like I said, dope makes me stupid. Good job he went first, it was a damn sight easier finding a copy of Wallace Stevens than it would have been to find a longship.

Afterwards, among the baked meats and the second cousins, Jack came up to me in the house at Brighton Beach and said, 'I saw very little of Mel after he got out of college. We none of us did. Distressed my parents, but as the kids say nowadays he had his own thing to do. But, I'm glad to know he had friends like you.'

Oh fuck, I thought, do I really have to live up to that?

§

No doubt about it. I did not need to be anointed by Rabbi Jack Kissing—but, yes, I had to live up to every word of it. I got a haircut from a Polish barber on East Broadway (no point in looking any more like a hippie than I had to—just made asking awkward questions and getting straight answers that bit the harder), closed up the office, weighed up the significance of Nate's 'Don't leave town without telling me' and concluded it had had its day, got the girl next door to feed Rose's cat (there being still no sign of Rose—how long does a tennis match last?) and got myself on a plane to Chicago. It was all I had by way of a lead. Already a month had gone by.

I'd called Barclay Fulton. It went sort of . . .

'Barclay. It's Turner Raines. Remember me?'

'Raines. Yes. Of course. How have you been?'

'I'm fine. It's Mel Kissing who's not so good.'

'Not so good?'

'Well . . . actually he's dead.'

And so was the line. He hung up on me. I kept trying for two days and got the busy signal, and then on the third I got the discontinued. But by then I'd got the message. Barclay never was going to talk to me and dearly wished he had not talked to Mel. Chicago it was. LaGuardia to O'Hare, one blistering day in July. Once more into the Restofamerica. If I'd had to draw up a list of places I'd been to that I never wanted to see again, I think that toddlin' town would be number two or three on that list. It was less than a year since I'd been there.

§

Summer 1968. I had Mel on the phone. 'Don't duck out on me, man. This is important.'

It wasn't and I told him so. Going to the Democratic Convention in Chicago was a waste of time. It wasn't a convention, it was a coronation. Hubert Humphrey was LBJ's chosen one. And that was that. The Hump was his vengeance on us all. We'd thrown him out and to pay us back he'd sicced a total loser onto us.

'Mel, I didn't spend a freezing winter in New Hampshire just to watch the Hump get elected. We've lost. Bobby Kennedy's dead, McCarthy hasn't got the delegates. If you want to see it stay home and watch it on the tube.'

'See it, see it. Raines, you are so goddam passive. See it—I want to touch it, feel it—I want to fuck it!'

He set Rubin onto me. I got the Yipster standard line from him.

'Look at it this way. It's going to be fun. Who wants a revolution that isn't fun?'

'Jerry, that is complete nonsense.'

'And . . . there are the inherent possibilities.'

'The what?'

'Chicago is Daley's town. Mr Mayor is a predictable man. We have only to push him so far and he will turn his pigs loose upon us.'

'You're nuts. You really want that? There'll be a bloodbath!'

'It's exactly what I want. I want every TV camera in Chicago to record what happens. The pigs will go crazy—Mom and Pop back home on the couches of Amerika will see it. Maybe then they'll say—if this is what Amerika is doing to our kids in Chicago what are we doing to kids elsewhere, what *is* happening in Vietnam? If we can do this—at home—to our own . . . what can we not do overseas to gooks and slopes?'

'You'd push the cops to that just to get a reaction?'

'Damn right I would.'

'You could end up reaping the wind.'

'I know that.'

'Maybe Amerika doesn't react. Maybe Amerika just changes channels?'

'It'll be on all of them—CBS, NBC, ABC. They won't dare miss it.'

'Jerry, this really isn't me.'

'Johnnie, do it for me. We're running a pig for president.'

'What?'

'I mean. A real pig. Four legs. Goes oink. Shits everywhere. You could mind the pig while we start the revolution.'

God help me, I gave in to the bastard. His 'do it for me' had been a sly paraphrase of 'you owe me'. Mel and I had campaigned for McCarthy in the New Hampshire primary when the Yippies were writing him off as just another suit and his left-wing and hippie supporters as people who'd 'stripped clean for Gene'. Rubin told me McCarthy was the real enemy—Nixon was an upfront villain, you knew where you were with Tricky, McCarthy's liberalism could not but be a mask for the bad things we did not yet know about him. We did not agree. We went to New Hampshire. Us and several thousand others. And Rubin gave us shit for weeks after—Mel had even signed his damn Yippie Manifesto back in '67—'Amerika is a Death Machine'; repetitive stuff, not a spark of poetry to it—could there be a bigger turncoat? I hadn't. I never believed the Yippies amounted to more than half a dozen people, but then that was part of the joke, the big put-on. A mass movement that existed only in its own press releases. I gave in because I didn't want Rubin calling me chicken for the next six months. I went to Chicago as the most reluctant Yippie in that crazy little Yippie world.

When I said I'd taken one look at Chicago and ran, I was speaking metaphorically of how I'd felt. I arrived well after the vanguard of Mel, Rubin and Hoffman to find they had gotten themselves rooms and had not bothered to save a room for me. A hotel was out of the question. Chicago was full.

'You'll be with the pig, man. They won't let a pig into the house.'

'Have you got the pig?'

'Not yet.'

'Fine, I'll sleep on your floor.'

'No, man, we think it would be better if you found a place in the park where we could stash the pig.'

I should have walked out there and then. In fact I spent a night in Lincoln Park dodging club-happy Daley cops and eventually fell asleep around dawn with my back to a tree while the generation gap raged about me. I woke exhausted and grubby to find two bits of jailbait sitting at my feet, solemnly passing a joint between them, T-shirted, bra-less, sporting Yippie buttons, and no more than fifteen years old to look at. One of them passed the joint to me. I said no. I couldn't start the day stoned. I could not get through the day without thinking Rubin had initiated a latter-day Children's Crusade.

'Do you girls know anything about pigs?'

'Man, this is Chicago. Pig city.'

I spent much of that day bewitched, bothered and bewildered, wondering just why I'd come. They were predicting half a million—the big Yip-In (or was it the big Yip-Out?) anarchy on the sidewalk, fucking in the streets, LSD in the water supply. I'd seen just a few hundred so far—I think the cops outnumbered us about two to one.

Rubin and Abbie Hoffman fell out over the pig almost at once. Rubin said, 'Raines grew up on a farm. He knows about pigs.' It had been fifteen years or more since I'd last had anything to do with pigs, but what the heck. Hoffman drove out to Belvedere, Illinois and came back with this cute little pinky-white sow. Rubin said she was not hefty enough—he wanted a piggier pig, a grunting, rooting hog, not this cool character who looked more likely to say 'howdy doody' than take a piece out of you. Hoffman handed me the pig leash, said, 'a pig is a pig is a pig' and vanished.

Rubin drove back into Illinois, found another hog farm, persuaded the singer Phil Ochs to part with the money and returned with a two-hundred pound boar, white with a black rump patch. He didn't act mean, but he sure looked the part. I was now a two pig pigman. For the 'nomination', I left the little sow with the jailbait sisters and we took 'Pigasus'—yes, 'Pigasus'—to the Picasso statue in the downtown Civic Center. We sang the national anthem, 'Pigasus' got pignapped by the cops—which I felt relieved me of any responsibility for him—and heads got cracked. I heard a rumor that the cops told the guys they busted along with the pig, 'Got you now, boys—the pig squealed.' Who says they don't have a sense of humor?

I got back to Lincoln Park—managed to outrun the cop who tagged me—and found the sisters of mercy high as the rafters and no sign of the sow.

'What happened?'

'The pig lit out, man.'

'You mean you let her escape.'

'No man, we liberated her. Free the pigs!'

Suddenly I was the official Yippie pigman with not a pig to my name. I thought of going home there and then. The younger, smaller of the sisters came on to me, her breasts pressed against my belly, head on my chest, a hand between my legs.

'Loosen up, man. Let's make out. Fuck for peace. I could blow your balls and sis could blow your mind.'

Not while I was still sane we couldn't.

The cops were hard to insult. You called 'em pig and they wore it like a medal—they adopted 'Pigasus' as a mascot. Hard to insult, but there was one bunch found a way. We'd reached another of those endless Mexican stand-offs outside the Hilton Hotel. Cops holding us back, delegates and newsmen and hangers-on trying to get inside.

It seemed to me they came out of nowhere, sidestepped and sucker-punched the cops and ran for the building lickety-split—a dozen hairy guys with buckets. Buckets of what? I didn't need to ask. They threw them every-where—at the cops, the TV crew, the delegates—a dapper man wearing a Brooks Brothers suit and a Gene McCarthy button, one hand plastered to the crud on his suit, his lips voicing 'what the . . . ?'—and they threw 'em at us. Shit. Not manure, not animal shit, but human shit, a stinking mess of human shit and piss so rancid they must have been crapping in those buckets for a week. The cops broke rank and started beating the hell out of those guys. I watched 'em go down fighting. I had to admire their guts. They were giving Rubin exactly what he wanted. I watched a TV cameraman wipe the shit off his lens and point the camera at the carnage. Let Mom and Pop Couch get an eyeful of this. Everything Jerry had asked for and more.

The last thing I heard as the battle cry went up was the cop chant of 'Kill kill kill!'—exactly what the Crazies would chant one year later in the Greenwich Village School, the last time I saw Mel.

I turned around. Walked away. And then ran. Found the nearest CTA station and caught the L-train. I was caked in shit. A bum on the train—the kind of guy you just know reeked of cheesy rot—held his nose and got out at the next stop. I'd had enough. I rode all the way to O'Hare, cleaned myself up and got on a plane back to New York.

'Why does it bother you so much?' Mel called me when he got out of jail again. 'We just made the mothers do on camera what they've been doing to us for years.'

'No, Mel. It was worse than that.'

'Worse? They damn near killed you in Mississippi in '61!'

'It's not what the cops are doing. It's what we're doing. I don't know where we're going anymore. In fact I think some of us may be as crazy as they are.'

'What? You mean the shit? It was a stunt, that's all. Some corny piece of street theater. We been doing street theater for years. Ask me what our decade's been about and I'll tell you—street theater, send up what you can't pull down.'

'I don't know where it's leading. We were going to take back Amerika— now I don't even think I recognize Amerika and I don't see where we are in it. Mel, is this what we fought for?'

'Maybe not, but it's a means to an end. "By any means necessary", remember?'

'Six or seven years ago you would have said that was the logic of a fascist.'

'Fuck you, Turner. Fuckyoufuckyoufuckyoufuckyoufuckyou!'

He went on saying it till I hung up on him.

Hoffman called me.

'Y'OK, man?'

'Sure, I'll be fine,' I lied.

'I hear pain in your voice.'

'Pain? No. I got away without a scratch.'

'I meant like spiritual pain, man.'

'I don't do spiritual, Abbie.'

You ever wonder when the sixties—I mean the concept not the calendar—ended? Like a party game? Like 'Where were you in '63?' 'JFK blown away?' 'How did we get from surfin' safari with the Beach Boys to buckets of shit?' Did it end right there, on the streets of Chicago in August 1968? Probably. But everyone will have a different day. Personally, the sixties ended when I put down the phone on Mel the week after. The day I told him the revolution had died. I'd tasted shit. Everything since has had the taste of ash.

About three days after I hung up on Mel, a newspaper clipping arrived in the post. *Chicago Daily News*, showing Mr and Mrs Pigasus reunited 'in pokey' and smiling their pig smiles across the top of a sty door. The signature at the torn edge read simply 'MK'. I took it as cloture. Like I said, I never wanted to hear the word Chicago again.

§

1969. I'd a rough idea of what Mel had dropped on me. I had the feeling that it was no big deal. But that competed with the sure knowledge that whatever it was it had got him killed. The whatever was the stuff of rumor—rumor but you knew it happened. Had to happen. Fragging. Platoons, whole platoons or lone lunatics had been known to turn on their officers. A fragmentation grenade lobbed into a tent in the night and some greenhorn second lieutenant gets taken out. I'd even heard of one guy who'd surrounded his billet with Claymores and blown the hell out of half his own platoon. Paranoia strikes deep in the heartland, just like the man said. Strikes a damn sight deeper when you're in the other guy's heartland.

I picked up a rental car at O'Hare airport. I may not have been the smartest gumshoe in the world, and I may not have had years of experience under my belt, but I had the feeling—must have been my day for 'feelings'—that I was being followed. Now if I read that in a book I'd think 'bullshit' just like you're thinking now, but I seemed to keep seeing the same car in the rear-view as I picked my way from the highway to the suburbs of the North Side. Never right behind me, one or two cars away. If I'd been more certain than that I'd've tried to lose it, but by the time I got to West Rogers Park I seemed to have lost it without trying. Maybe my 'feelings' were my paranoia. Back in Chicago. Richard J. Daley's heartland. Bound to put me on edge. Besides, I'd never been a great believer in detective's instinct. What did a 'feeling' matter? The job was all about shoe-leather. I'd been at it long enough to know that.

West Rogers Park was not Brighton Beach. A 'burb—that was undeniable, the lots were as regular as tablecloths, green grass stripes for gingham check—but the houses were bigger and no two looked alike. Each one custom built it seemed by a different builder, the lots probably filled in at different times, sometimes years apart, as the twentieth century crept slowly up the side of Lake Michigan from Chicago. It was a place apart from the city, a place, I would guess, of homeowners and families. Each house with a garage, each garage with a basketball hoop over the door, and a kid's bicycle abandoned in the drive. I had an Andy Hardy moment, one of those visions of childhood that probably never existed this side of a Hollywood backlot—a boy on a bike, zipping along the street aiming folded newspapers at every porch, missing as often as not. 'G'mornin', Mrs Jones. G'mornin', Mrs Riley.' I didn't have a childhood that remotely resembled Andy Hardy's but I could never resist wondering who did if I ever thought I'd stumbled into the right set.

Maybe it wasn't Marty Fawcett either. The Fawcett house stood alone at the very end of a north–south street, on three times the land, with a two-car garage. No basket ball hoop, no bike. Every other house spoke stability and respectability to me, this one said 'hell no, we got money'.

It was deathly quiet. Not a whisper of a radio, not a hum nor rattle of a domestic appliance. Even the doorbell seemed to ring sotto voce at the other end of the house, and then I could hear footsteps, tapping softly towards me.

A short, black woman in a black dress and a white apron opened the door.

'C'n I he'p you?'

The elisions—the missing 'l' in help—spoke Mississippi to me. Another Southern Black who'd made the long ride north up Highway 55 to Chicago. Been a while since I'd heard that accent.

'I was wondering if Mr Fawcett was at home.'

'Mr Fawcett's at his office, sir.'

A woman's voice called out from within the house. 'Alice? Alice? Who is it?'

Alice turned to answer the woman who stood shadowed in a big arch at the end of the lobby. 'Ge'man wants to see Mr Fawcett.'

I called across her.

'I was just hoping for word with your—'

The woman came towards me. I'd been about to say 'husband', but this woman was a slender, good-looking fifty-year-old. I managed to say 'your son' without sounding as though I'd changed direction mid-sentence. All the same the word seemed to galvanise her.

'My son? Come inside, please. Alice, close the door.'

Mrs Fawcett led off through the arch with me and Alice trailing. A big room, with chunky cream-colored furniture, an electric punkah fan twirling slowly in the center of the ceiling. She stopped by a huge, white marble fireplace, its mantelpiece packed with photographs, its cold hearth stuffed with dried flowers, and turned to face us.

'I think summer's finally arrived, don't you? Perhaps some iced tea?'

I said yes. Alice disappeared to the back of the house without waiting to be asked. Mrs Fawcett held out her hand to me.

'Carrie Fawcett,' she said. 'You knew my son, Mr ...?'

'Raines, ma'am. Turner Raines. And no, I don't know your son.'

She turned her back on me again. Picked up a table lighter from the mantelpiece, struck the flint a couple of times and when she turned back she was Bette Davis in I forget what movie, a king size cigarette between her fingers, a long trail of smoke curling from her nostrils.

She sat down. I followed suit. I began to get the feeling that I was here on false pretences. The sooner I spat it out the better.

'Mrs Fawcett, I'm a Private Investigator, working out of New York City. I have ID if you care to see it.'

She shook her head.

'Why would I doubt it? How do you think Marty could help you, Mr Raines?'

'I ... I'm investigating a murder, ma'am. I think it's possible the man who was murdered might have met or talked to your son.'

'Murdered? Who's been murdered?'

'A journalist. Name of Mel Kissing.'

'No,' she said without the need to think about it. 'Marty never mentioned anyone of that name to me.'

'All the same. I would like to ask him myself.'

'Of course, you're only doing your job. But ... Mr Raines, my son died six weeks ago.'

I felt stupid. It had been implicit in her question—'You knew my son?'—and I'd not noticed till now. My reaction must have been written on my face as plain as a punctuated sentence.

'No, Mr Raines. Not what you're thinking. No one murdered Marty.'

'Natural causes, then?'

'If you can call cancer induced by Agent Orange, and all the other filth we're tipping onto the jungle over there, natural—then yes, Marty died of natural causes. He was diagnosed with a brain tumor at Christmas. Our doctors gave him three months. He lived six. I suppose I should be grateful for that. No, Marty wasn't murdered, but he was killed all the same. Vietnam killed him as surely as if he'd stepped on a land mine.'

And I felt as if I'd just walked into a field of them. The maid let me off the hook. Brought the two of us iced tea. I strung out a few sips for a minute or more and then played my hunch.

'It may well be Vietnam that brings me here, Mrs Fawcett.'

'Vietnam? You were in Vietnam?'

'No I wasn't . . .'

'Of course. You're not that generation, are you? Marty was twenty-one. You're nearer thirty I suppose. When you were draft age it was all so low-key, wasn't it? Something odd going on in Laos that I could never quite understand or the President could never quite explain.'

'I'm thirty-one as it happens. I'm guessing that this has something to do with the war. I don't know what. And all I'm doing is following clues.'

'You have a clue?' she said as though she thought I hadn't.

'The only lead I have is a man who calls himself Broken Arrow. I don't even know his real name. I don't know the first thing about him.'

'*Broken Arrow*,' she mused. 'As in the Jeff Chandler film?'

My turn to feel stupid again. I'd made nothing of the name. I could see it now, even as she said it.

'I'd say that that was a film about a warrior who wanted peace, wouldn't you? Jeff Chandler as Cochise. He looked gorgeous, didn't he? Hardly believable as an Indian, though.'

Of course I'd seen the film. Lois and me. A night out while the old man babysat in '51 or '52. Jimmy Stewart and Chandler trying for peace between the white man and the Apache.

'This man—'

'You mean Broken Arrow?'

'Yes. He met with Mel Kissing shortly before he was killed. He mentioned two names. Your son's was one and the other was the New Nineveh Nine. Does the New Nineveh Nine mean anything to you, Mrs Fawcett?'

She got up again, went to the mantelpiece and took a plain black-framed photograph off the end. It was tiny, about as small as a postcard. Seemed almost odd to have framed it at all. It was group of men. A formal, posed shot of ten guys in uniform. Beyond that almost impossible to tell.

'It's the only photograph of Marty and his friends I have. He sent me nothing once he'd got to Vietnam. Letters at first, but no photographs.

And then the letters stopped. And then suddenly he was home. It all happened so fast. These are the New Nineveh Nine, Mr Raines. Marty and his friends in training at boot camp. Marty is third from the left, front row.'

I'd guessed right. So far, so good.

'Did Marty ever tell you their names?'

She shook her head.

'No. As I said it's all I've got. I know Marty emerged as team leader, that was his nature after all, and they made him up to corporal when they shipped out. But, again as I said, he was gone only to be back. His tour was over so quickly. I'd expected him to be gone a year. It was a matter of months. Don't ask me how many. He went back to work—he'd worked briefly in my husband's business after college and before the draft—and it was as though he'd never been gone. He no more talked about his war than my father talked about his time in France in 1918. Life went back to normal. Until he got ill. Then nothing was the same.'

'Could I get this copied?'

She lit up another cigarette, blew another ponderous trail of smoke.

'Why not? And as tomorrow's Saturday if you drop the photograph off my husband will be home. He and Marty were close. Who knows. Perhaps there are things he could tell you that only a father would know?'

I slipped the photograph into my pocket.

'Do take good care of it, Mr Raines. It's all I've got of Marty now. A part of all I've got. If you see what I mean.'

I drove into downtown Chicago. I found a small photographic shop in the Loop, a two-room shop nestling right under the L tracks. A window full of dusty adverts for Kodak, and carefully dusted, lovingly cared-for cameras, all the way from tripod and bellows to 35 mm. Inside a man of seventy or so was replacing the hood on a pre-war Rolleiflex. A small array of tiny screwdrivers laid out on a sheet of baize, a magnifying glass lodged in one eye like a monocle. I put Carrie Fawcett's group shot in front of him.

'Can you copy this postcard for me? I don't have the negative.'

He picked it up. Didn't look at the image, turned over the frame and looked at the back.

'Sure. I can make an inter-neg. But I'd have to break the seal on the frame. You want it good as new?'

'Yes—and if possible I'd like the copy enlarged.'

'Sure, a little time, a little money. Be tomorrow morning—that OK?'

I told him it was, drove straight around the corner to the Bismarck Hotel and checked in for the night. I sat in my room, ordered room service and flipped through the TV channels and ordered more room service. Nothing would have induced me to venture out into downtown Chicago on foot. It was too soon. It was less than a year. As far as I was concerned Chicago still burned. I wondered if Chicago felt the same about me.

In the morning I called in the photoshop around eleven. The old man came out of the back room clutching a ten by eight blow-up of Carrie Fawcett's postcard.

'We got lucky, son. Your "postcard" turned out to be a contact print. You know what that is?'

'Sure.'

'Whoever took this worked on an old plate camera—five by four negative. Normally, if I tried to copy and enlarge from thirty-five millimetre you'd get a kind of grainy finish—kind of what happens when you photograph a photograph. But you can see the buttons on these boys' jackets.'

He turned the picture to me. There was Marty, third from the left and the features of all his buddies resolved into focus.

'Speakin' of whoever took it. The man is in shot. You see that black line snaking out of the foreground?'

He traced a line up the shot with his finger.

'It's a remote trigger for the shutter. Leads right to our photographer. The black guy on the far right.'

I followed the snake. It led to a grinning—they were all grinning— huge black face, set on a thick neck, on a chest three feet across. He was several years older than the other boys in this picture but that explained why there were ten in the New Nineveh Nine. This guy was wearing sergeant's stripes. It was easy to imagine the scene in Georgia, a day or two before they were all shipped out—Sarge lines 'em up in front of the camera, and the kids get sentimental: C'mon Sarge, we want you in this shot too.' So Sarge rigs up his remote, steps into shot and becomes one of the boys. But, then that was his nature. He'd been no different when I knew him as plain Maurice 'Mouse' Kylie back in Lubbock. Two hundred and fifty pounds of fun, and one of less than half a dozen black kids I'd grown up with. I'd not seen Mouse in more than ten years. Not since his going away party in 1958, the day before he enlisted in the army. It was hardly believable then. Mouse just didn't seem the type, but from everything I'd heard from Lois and Huey over the years he'd made a go of it. Sergeant Mouse.

'Y'OK, son? You looked to be miles away.'

I was. I paid the man and left.

I was sitting in the car in West Rogers Park for about five minutes, listening to rain pour down on the roof. One of those sudden, torrential summer storms. At ten I gave up and dashed for the Fawcetts' front door, hunched over my bag, wanting to keep the photograph dry at all costs.

I was expecting to see Alice, the Fawcetts' maid, but when the door opened there stood a big guy, my height and a lot heavier, aged about fifty and wearing a suit and tie. Saturday morning and the guy was in a suit and tie.

He stepped across the threshold, indifferent to the rain, stuck out his right hand, palm up.

'The photograph,' was all he said.

'Mr Fawcett, I'm—'

'The photograph.'

I fumbled around with my bag, rain rolling off me in rivulets, and found the framed postcard. He snatched it off me with one hand, stuck the other, finger first, into my chest.

'You ever come here again, you ever bother my wife again, you ever call, you ever write and I will have you run out of town on a rail. You understand me, Mr Raines?'

'Mr Fawcett, I'm—'

Never could get to the end of that sentence. He swapped the prodding finger for the flat of his hand and shoved me down his drive, blow by blow, foot by foot, phrase by phrase, me staggering backwards fighting to keep my balance.

'Leave. Leave now. Go back to where you came from and do not bother us again. My son died for his country, Mr Raines. Leave us in peace!'

It was turn and run or let him push me over. I ran. I sat in the car and dripped puddles onto the floor. I wiped the wet hair from my forehead and reached for the ignition. Before I could turn the key, the passenger door was yanked open and a slim body in a transparent plastic rain cape slipped in beside me. Her mascara was running and I had the romantic notion that it was only the rain that hid her tears.

'Drive around the block,' she said. 'My husband thinks I'm taking a nap. We'll have a few minutes that's all.'

I glanced in the rear-view as we rounded the first corner, half-expecting to see a fat man running after us and ruining a good suit in the process. He wasn't.

'George got very angry,' Carrie Fawcett began. 'I thought he'd welcome anything that shed light on what Marty went through over there. But he just exploded. "What were you thinking of?" and "Good God, woman, what have you done, what have you done?" Called me stupid. Married twenty-five years and he's never called me that before.'

'I'm sorry.'

'Don't be. He'll pay for it. Did you copy the photo?'

'Yes.'

'You keep it. You do what you have to do. But when you find out what happened, I don't think I want to know. George is right about that. Marty died for his country. Maybe not much of a hero, but a hero all the same. My hero. I'd like to hang onto that. I'd like to hang onto as much of my son as I can. I don't want to know—whatever happened.'

'Whatever happened?'

'Whatever. All I know is . . . *something happened.*'

It was a considered phrase, she'd put a lot of power into two words. Eyes not looking at me, both hands chopping down in the air toward her lap as though she was taking the measure of some invisible object.

'Something happened?'

'I know. It sounds meaningless. But that's what I know, something happened. That's all I know. Something happened. I heard George saying to Marty, last spring, not long after Marty came home, "These things happen, these things happen in war".'

'But you don't know what they were talking about?'

'Mr Raines, if I knew I wouldn't be sitting here talking to you in the middle of a thunderstorm while my husband pushes my marriage to the edge of divorce. Of course I don't know.'

§

I had more than a 'feeling' this time. Something that soon coalesced. Could not help thinking that a '69 tan Ford I'd caught sight of in the rear-view had been there on and off for a while, and that, while I wasn't sure of the make or year, the car that been behind me for a spell on the way in had been tan too. It was too obvious where I was going—back out to O'Hare. Who would be driving a rental out to the swamps of Wisconsin? O'Hare in all likelihood was where they'd picked me up in the first place—if they had. It was impossible to lose them, and, besides, I'd never had to do this sort of thing before. The most amateurish thing about this whole amateurish set-up was me.

I got lucky. I pulled out past an eighteen-wheel oil tanker on the freeway, expecting the tan Ford follow, only to see the tanker go into a skid that jack-knifed it. The noise was deathly. A gut-wrenching screech of brakes and rubber. The guy in front braked so hard at the sound of it I had to swing past him to avoid rear-ending. I looked in the mirror. The tanker was sliding towards the guy I'd just overtaken. It bumped him right off the road, spun through one hundred and eighty degrees and skewed to a halt. The road was blocked. The tanker sprawled full width on the highway with two of its tires blown out.

I didn't know how long I'd have. I roared into O'Hare with my foot on the floor, annoyed the shit out of the rental guy by rushing him through the paperwork, and ran for the terminal. I went to two airline desks and booked tickets for Atlanta and Seattle on my American Express. Then I went to a third and bought a ticket to Lubbock via Dallas for cash. This left me about twenty minutes before boarding. Maybe enough time for whoever to find me, maybe not.

I stood in a payphone booth, my back to the concourse, called Lubbock collect and got Huey.

'Do you still see anything of Gabriel Kylie?'

'Sometimes. He works in a body shop out near the airport. He's waiting on the draft, just like me.'

Huey laughed, trying to take the sting out of what we both knew was true. Eighteen years old and life and death were a government-run lottery.

'Could you go see him, ask him if he knows where his cousin Mouse is stationed now?'

'No need. I saw Mouse only a couple of days ago. You can ask him yourself.'

'I don't get it.'

'Mouse is out of the Army. He got home last year. I think it was March or April. If you'd been back you'd know. He took his discharge and opened a studio downtown.'

I didn't ask what kind of studio. I was more interested in why Mouse was out of the forces. I thought he was in for life. A twenty-year man. Then a pension at forty-something. Then endless years of sitting around reminiscing like a cracker-barrel philosopher. Job done, money earned, glory gone.

'We all did,' Huey said, when I'd rambled out my thoughts. 'But he's home. I know his mom was surprised. Mouse just got off the bus one night, right in front of their old house, gave her a hug and said he'd never leave her alone again. No letter, no phone call. Just turned up with everything he owned in the bag over his shoulder. Way Gabe tells it, he and Mouse spent the next night out back with a bottle of whiskey and a can of gas and drank themselves stupid and burned Mouse's uniform. Gabe told me 'cause he was scared. He's none too smart if you recall. Got it into his head they'd done something illegal, that maybe burning a soldier's uniform was like burning the flag. Y'know?'

For all I knew it probably was illegal.

I gave Huey the flight time and told him to meet me at the airport.

'Sure,' he said. 'What are brothers for?'

Six hours and several packets of peanuts later I found myself looking around for the unreliable little runt, and for a moment or two completely missing my stepmother.

She was parked across from the exit. Station wagon pulled up in 'dropoff/pickup only'. Shoulders back, one foot pressed against the car, arms folded, a billowing red blouse, stretch jeans, neat little two-tone cowboy boots and billowing red hair. She was forty, and looked younger than me. Thank God, for all her jeans and boots she was not one of those Western women who aped the men to the point of wearing over-large Stetsons so they looked like Calamity Jane. She knew her assets and only the fiercest sun would make her hide the hair.

'Damn that kid,' I said.

She draped both arms around my neck and kissed me.

'Aw—he's got his own life to lead.'

Kissed me again.

'Now, say "hello Lois" and "you sure are a sight for sore eyes".'

I did. She was. From the day she entered our lives I doubt that I had seen a woman as beautiful as Lois this side of the silver screen.

She sashayed round to the driver's side, walking like she'd got oil wells in her backyard—well, she had—yanked open the door and revved the engine.

Lois never thought I came 'home' often enough. Never said so. But I knew it. It was implicit in the almost earnest way she brought me up to date on family and town gossip. By the time we got out to Bald Eagle I knew not who was screwing who—that was not Lois's idea of small talk—but whose cattle were thriving, whose were sick, who'd just bought a state-of-the-art John Deere, how the price of beef and oil and cotton and sorghum were holding up, and how most of my school friends were faring. Most of them, needless to say, were married, had kids, and were working locally. Some, the ambitious or the feckless, were on their second marriages before I'd gotten around to my first.

We pulled up in the shadow of the mountain. I have never been able to see what my father did to it as anything but monstrous. A great glass zitty on the face of Mother Nature. He'd even given us a choice. You could climb forty-eight steps to the lobby or take a glass and chrome elevator. As a kid wild horses would not have dragged me into the elevator. It was, not that I would have known to use the term, vulgar. Today I was bushed. Flying had drained me. I let Lois lead me up the mountain, out onto the deck, and stick a cold beer in my hand.

'Where is Huey, by the bye?'

Lois settled herself back in a recliner. It must have been around eight in the evening. A heat-hazy July evening and not a hint of a breeze. If we sat long enough I'd catch a West Texas sunset for the first time in a very long while.

'Out. I wouldn't rightly know where. Anywhere out of your father's way, I guess.'

'Are things that bad between them?'

'No. Put it like that and they're not. Sam is mostly well-disposed towards the boy. Truth to tell he's had an easier upbringing than you had.

I don't mean money neither. Sam had . . . kinda mellowed by the time Huey came along. There's nothing he wouldn't do for Huey, but Huey won't let him. However, there is one issue on which Sam is a stickler.'

'Is it anything special?'

'Huey got drafted. How special is that?'

Suddenly we were on my patch again. What didn't I know about things that special?

'It's mundane. Happens to most families. It's special. It rips them all apart in a different way.'

'You know what it's coming down to, Johnnie? It's like a war between the generations. That's got to be the worst kind.'

I knew what she meant. Of course it was war. I had been a believer in and on occasion a user of a particular guerrilla slogan of that war myself—'Never trust anyone over thirty.' The fact that I was over thirty did not diminish my belief in the words. But at the level Lois meant, this level, father to son, I had been a non-combatant. There was tension enough between me and the old man, but a war it wasn't. I think things were eased for us. He'd lost Billy to something he'd never be able to figure out and it's possible it made him back away from any confrontation with me. And neither he nor I had fought in the foreign wars that were on offer to our generations. We were both oblique to them. Sam was too young for the First World War and near-enough forty when the Second started. I might have scraped into Korea if I'd been a year older, but I was an asthmatic kid. The near-desert air around the farm was great for my lungs—the gasoline and lead air of cities wasn't. I had no problem getting registered 4-F—exempt from all military service. Whatever skirmish we got ourselves into before Vietnam we got ourselves out of without my help. By the time Vietnam came along and we abandoned the fiction that our boys were 'military advisors'—25,000 advisors, how much advice does one country need?—I was too old anyway. War was not an issue between me and Sam. He could not have, and never would have, pointed to his own service and urged the same on me. But he was picking a fight with Huey. And I had a deal of trouble figuring out why.

'Huey makes it as hard as he can,' Lois said as though she'd read my mind. 'He doesn't talk enough sense for Sam. It all begins calmly enough, then Huey will start spouting slogans at Sam, Sam'll get mad, Huey'll get madder and by then he's just yelling at Sam that he won't go and nothing

Sam or anyone can do will make him. It's not that Sam wants him to go. He wants what he calls an "honourable solution". Accepting the draft is only one way to get it. He'd be happy if Huey would just consider the alternatives. But he won't. Sam told him he could volunteer for the Navy or the Air Force. Stay out of the action. Huey just screamed at him. Sam told him he could join the National Guard and serve his time as a part-timer for however long it took. Huey laughed in his face. But worst of all—he could just take up his college place and see what happens when he graduates. Who knows, the war could be over by then?'

I doubted that. And I doubted that Huey would have the patience to serve six years in the National Guard.

'So tell me about Huey and college. I'm not caught up.'

'Well, Johnnie, maybe the two of you aren't as close as you were. God knows, I'm his mother and I never felt more remote from him. Yep—he's been accepted at U.T. Physical Sciences. He can start in the Fall. But to hear him talk you'd think it was a poor choice between Vietnam and college. They're both "straight"—that's another of his slogans, along with "Hell no, Huey won't go".'

'There are other ways.'

'Uh-huh?'

'In fact there are how-to books written on how to dodge the draft. If I've seen one I've seen a dozen. Everything from faking a sports injury to french-kissing the recruiting officer.'

'No kidding? What dodge would you suggest for your little brother? I don't see him french-kissing nobody.'

'Essential agricultural worker?'

'No,' she said. 'That wouldn't work. That would mean Sam lying. Huey doesn't lift a finger on the ranch. And it's not as if the ranch's been our livelihood these last eighteen years. Sam wouldn't tell that lie.'

'Conscientious Objector?'

'On what grounds? It's not as if he's a Mennonite or a Quaker. I should know. I brought him up in a religious nothin', a vacuum. Blame me for that one.'

'Principle. I deal a lot with kids who'd sooner burn their draft cards than go.'

'Huey already did that. Round here there's boys servin' time for just that. Some boys burn 'em in front of the draft board or City Hall. Huey burned his at the dining table in front of my sister, her husband, their two little girls. Table cloth went up like brushwood, Sam threw coffee on the flames and threw Huey out the house. Makes you wonder what kind of a gesture it was. Against war or family? I'd have a hard time finding a principle in that, Johnnie.'

'But all the same there is a principle. These kids believe in something. These kids believe in non-violence.'

'I don't doubt it. But we'd have a helluva time proving that with Huey's record.'

One more thing no one had bothered to tell me.

'He got busted when he was sixteen—smashed up a store, beat up on some kid and resisted arrest. If he'd not been Sam Raines's boy he'd of been sent to reformatory. Sam made him pay for it all out of his own money. The damage, the fine. Didn't help the father-son thing any—Huey being flat broke for a whole year while he works it off. And remember, Huey didn't have the same childhood as you, just the same dad. Huey's a rich kid. He's used to having money.'

'Or,' I was nothing if not persistent, 'he could see a sympathetic psychiatrist.'

'A psychiatrist? Johnnie, you been away too long. A psychiatrist in West Texas? God knows there might even be such a critter—you look hard enough among the rocks and rattlers you might find one sympathetic or not—but the only recognisable psychiatric disorders in West Texas are being vegetarian or queer. Not liking beef or girls is about as crazy as it gets!'

'OK. I give up. You've beaten me. I submit.'

She smiled. The pretense of the outraged cowgirl faded from her face. She got something close to wistful, that funny half-giggle creeping into her voice. She leant closer to me, a mock-confidential whisper no one else should hear.

'Y'know, when Sam started asking "What is *wrong* with that boy?" I told him he should blame me. I was one of those mothers who read Dr Spock's baby book. Sam said "sure" and changed the subject. He'd never heard of Spock—he didn't know enough even to make the *Star Trek* gag everybody else makes. God, how Sam would blow his stack if Huey didn't like beef 'n girls.'

'What's that about beef? I sure could use some.'

My father appeared in the doorway. I'd been so intent on Lois I had not heard him pull up. He kissed his wife, dutifully, a peck on the cheek. Hugged me, then held me at arm's length with a silent 'let me look at you'. I looked at him. I suppose he must have been sixty-five or so at that time. He was a few inches shorter than me. He had a beer belly rising, but most of him was still muscle, and while his hair was gray it was still thick and waved across his head the way my brother Billy's used to.

He put an arm around Lois. Lois, smiling like she was really happy. Part of her adopted family put back together for however short a span.

'How long d'you reckon on stayin', son?'

'I don't know, Dad. Not more than a couple of days.'

Lois said, 'I ate hours ago, why don't you two come on in my kitchen and I'll fix you something.'

We ate beef sandwiches. Drank more beer. And Sam ran through his roster of questions. How's-business-son-Fine-Dad-You-know-there's-always-a-place-for-you-here-Sure-Dad. It never varied. He'd always ask, and I never knew if the routine mechanics of it all was in any way an acceptance of the fact that I had gone for good or if he thought I might one day just say yes and come home.

We burned quickly down to sporadic exchanges and then silence. It was OK. I was relaxed and he seemed to be too. I caught my sunset. The three of us on the west-side deck watching heaven roll purple into puce, magenta into pink. Sam slunk off soon after ten.

'What time does Huey get in?' I asked Lois.

'Often not at all. I've heard him roll in lately around dawn. But there's times he's gone two or three days.'

I went to bed without seeing him. 'Bed' was virtually a separate apartment. Sam's millions had bought privacy. I'd grown up in a room with Billy. My mother and father on the other side of a planed timber wall three-quarters of an inch thick. As a teenager I had a room the size of a barn, my own bathroom. I still had. All my kidstuff still in place simply because there was no need ever to pack it away. The house had all the guest rooms a man could ever want. That said, my kidstuff was sparse. No team pennants, no old uniforms, no yearbooks. I had never played games. Baseball bored me—I'd never been able to see the flow—it was all stop and start. Basketball was strictly for the over-tall, and I'd blossomed—Good God, is that the word?—late. Football? Well, that was just guys in body

armour crashing into each other. My kidstuff was books and records and
torn Levi's. The Wells and Verne books Billy had given me, Carl Sandburg's
Life of Lincoln and Vachel Lindsay's poems—all about Johnny Appleseed.
Old 78s of T-Bone Walker and Lightnin' Hopkins. And early, great Little
Richard (Sam: 'Are you skinnin' a cat up there, boy?') And the Levi's I
had come on when Carolyn Tucker gave me my first hand-job when I
was thirteen. I am nothing if not sentimental.

$$\S$$

I slept in till past ten. A fitful night. Awake for hours wondering just
who those guys in the tan Ford could be. I shuffled into the kitchen. Lois
stuck black coffee, granola, and fresh fruit in front of me. It was a major
concession. My father had started the day with ham 'n' eggs ever since
he was weaned. Lois gave me what I wanted. Sam usually just pulled a
face and muttered. The one time Mel had come back to Texas with me,
we—Sam, Lois, me, Mel and an eight-year-old Huey—had gone out
to eat, Mel had ordered a vegetarian meal in a catfish bar. The waitress
slapped down an undressed plain green salad in front of him with, 'Here's
yore bowl of grass, boy.' I thought Lois would die laughing. Now she
just sat opposite me and talked while I ate what she probably took to
be mule fodder.

'When you've done . . .'

'When I've done?'

'Sam's been up since six, just poking around the stables. He'd love it
if you saddled up and went riding with him.'

So I did. There was no sign of Huey, and while I was out with Sam not
a mention of him either. I am not a good horseman. And it had been so
long since the last time that I was aching along the inner thigh muscles
by the time we got back. In between we rode Raines country. We could
have ridden all day and not seen the end of Raines country. And I got
the male version of Lois's hometown gossip. I learnt a lot about tractors
and the endlessly fascinating life of the Texas longhorn—eat, shit, breed,

riveting stuff—but Sam didn't know who was screwing who either. And
I watched windmills turn, derricks pump, and cattle roam. I saw not a
glimpse of the deer and buffalo, but it was home, it was on the range, and
if I ached it was all my own fault. I would not have missed it for the world.

Back at the house I put my feet up, stretched out and told myself I
should find a stable in upstate New York and go riding more often or
give it up for good. Lois appeared. I looked at her upside down.

'Huey got back around noon,' she said.

'Good. We got things to talk about.'

'Would you talk to him for me?'

'What about?'

'Just get him to see sense. Cool things a little between him and Sam.'

'He won't listen to me.'

'You're his brother. You could try.'

Of course I could.

Huey did not appear for dinner. I let him sleep and turned the handle
of his door quietly about seven just to see if he was awake. He was. He
was standing on a chair painting the back wall. One image was already
complete. The logo of the Atlantic record company, right down to the
45rpm wording and the title, 'Respect'—Aretha Franklin. The other
one he was still at work on, deftly adding little white brush strokes to a
five-foot portrait of the Track record label. Track was the English label
Jimi Hendrix used to record for. It had mattered to Huey to have the
authentic English singles, 'Hey Joe', 'Purple Haze' and the Bob Dylan
number 'All Along the Watchtower'. Rose had brought them back from
England specially. I understood this. There were Elvis freaks for whom
only the Sun singles would do. Forget RCA, forget reissues or compila-
tion albums—only Sam Phillips' one horse label was the McCoy.

'Which will it be?' I asked.

He turned sharply. A little look of surprise on his face.

'Oh . . . I guess I haven't made up my mind. "Hey Joe" would be simplest, but I'd really like "Watchtower" . . . but y'know, all those letters to do.'

I sat on the bed, a kingsize with the British flag as a counterpane, and
looked at the contents of his bookcase while he inched in a long thin
white line in silence. Huey's reading was bang up to date, the bedside
literature of your average American hippie, at least of the average American
hippie who is fresh out of high school with a college place tucked under

his belt and who still lives with his parents and has pocket money. Shiny paperbacks by Alan Watts, Allen Ginsberg, Norman O. Brown, Herbert Marcuse, Lenny Bruce, *The Tibetan Book of the Dead*—all looking unread. Not a crack on the spine of any of them. *The Whole Earth Catalogue*—to me one of those books I saw ever after in used book stores that made me wonder, 'What the fuck was that about?' A book full of ads for things no teenager could possibly want. I had concluded it was some sort of McLuhanesque image explosion. Like take the pictures from *The Mechanical Bride* and forget the text. But I could be wrong. That and a couple of Herman Hesse novels were the only books that looked as though Huey might have read them. At the very least he should have read Bruce's *How to Talk Dirty and Influence People*, not just because I gave it to him but because everybody should.

He leapt down from the chair, near-shoulder length hair flopping across his face. A small kid, by family standards. Eighteen and scarcely full-grown. Not really past that pocky stage kids get into at thirteen or fourteen.

'You're a hard man to find,' I said.

'I got my own shit to do, y'know. Besides, I hang around here I get hassled.'

'So I heard.'

'They been on at you too?'

'They?'

'OK. I mean the old man. It's not Mom. It's old Leatherbritches. You want a beer?'

'Nah—let's stay here a while.'

'It's OK. I got beer.'

He pulled open a closet door. It masked a big white icebox.

'You have your own icebox?'

'Sure—my own color TV and stereo. I got at least five stereos. I upgrade every time a new gadget comes along. You got Dolby yet?'

He stuck a beer in my hand. A cold, cold Rolling Rock. Stuck Hendrix on one of his stereos. 'Purple Haze' all in *my* mind, and way too loud. I realized I was talking to a rich kid, exactly as Lois had warned me. Maybe I was out of touch. Maybe every kid in America had his own closetful of chilled beer, a new stereo every six months and a kingsize bed.

'Or I could roll up some dope. I got some Acapulco gold. Really good shit. This guy comes up from Juarez a couple of times a month.'

I sipped at the beer by way of answer and said, dogged and stupid to the last, 'Your mother just wants you to be civil to Sam. Give the old guy a hearing.'

'Sure. I know that. She says that all the time. But there's no talking to him. He just wants me to go to 'Nam and get my cojones shot off.'

Regardless of my gesture Huey stuck a hand under the mattress and pulled out a packet of honey-brown dope, tore open a cigarette, and proceeded to roll himself a joint. It occurred to me to remind him of the old axiom that smoking dope and drinking beer together is like pissing into the wind, but I didn't.

I said, 'Look, can we just talk about this? I kind of feel I haven't quite got your attention.'

I got up and turned Hendrix down a notch, hoping to make my point.

'What's to talk about? If Dad just sent you here as his messenger then fuck you, Johnnie. That's what I'd say to him. Fuck you.'

'Jesus Christ, Huey. For once in your life will you just listen! Sam doesn't want you to go ...'

'Good! 'cause I ain't going.'

'Huey—you got your papers, right? You got a draft card, a number and you've been asked to take a medical, right?'

Huey blew smoke at me. Sipped beer. Sneered. Looked like an asshole.

'I can help you. This is my subject. My job. I'm hot on this. I can help you. It doesn't compromise your moral stance just to think about ways around all this, does it?'

'My "moral stance"? Are you for real, Johnnie?'

He laughed out loud at me.

'Morals—morals are for the straights. There's only one issue here. They want me to go. I ain't going. That is that. Finito.'

'They?'

'They. Not just Mom and Dad. They. They ... out there. The system. Fuck 'em.'

'Huey. They can make you go. Believe me, they have the power. But if you'll just think about it now, and decide on a course of action you won't have to. Anyone with a modicum of sense and money can get out if it. The system, as you call it, is *that* unfair. Why else do you think 'Nam is full of poor white trash and black guys? The only people who go now are those who can't get out of it.'

'I don't have to think about it. Fuckit. I won't go because I don't want to go. I won't go because they can't make me. They don't have that right.'

'Yes they do.'

'The fuck they do!'

'Huey—a right is not something natural like sunshine or cattle shit. It's something the system grants you or doesn't grant you. And it hasn't granted you the right to duck out of military service just because you want to.'

'Jesus Christ, Johnnie. Screw that shit. What about the Declaration of Independence? We hold these truths to be self-evident . . .'

He was thrashing around for the words, arms waving in the air, beer in one hand, joint in the other, as though trying to conjure them up like Mickey Mouse bringing the broomstick to life. When I was a kid every last one of us could have recited at least the first ten lines of it without having to think about it.

'. . . That all men are endowed by God . . .'

'By their creator.'

'With inalienable rights.'

'UN-alienable.'

He'd got to the bit you could sing along to, poetry by George Mason, publicity by Thomas Jefferson.

'Life, Liberty and the Pursuit of Happiness.'

We chimed neatly on that one. Almost raised a smile on Huey's face. What trace there was of it I wiped away.

'That's not in the Constitution. Nor in the Bill of Rights. Nor in any amendment since.'

'It's not? Then fuck the Constitution, fuck the system, fuck Amerika!'

We had gotten, in so few words, to the heart of the matter. Fuck the system, and fuck Amerika with it if needs must. If this was how he talked to my father, then the old man must be bursting blood vessels on a regular basis. You didn't fuck Amerika while my dad was around.

'Huey. I didn't come here to fight with you.'

'Oh yeah? Why did you come here?'

I saw the opportunity to pull the fuse out and took it.

'As a matter of fact I came to see Mouse Kylie.'

Huey thought for a second, the redness of anger beginning to drain from his face.

'Yeah. Right. It's all set up. Mouse'll be in Chucky's bar tomorrow night. I said you, me and Gabe would meet him there.'

'Chucky's. I don't know Chucky's, do I?'

'I guess not but you know Chucky, Sweet Chucky Bunker. You were in high school with him. He has a bar downtown on Avenue H now. Just a block away from the old railroad depot. "Pig Heaven" he calls it. Beer an' pizza. He'll have a good night tomorrow. He has this tape recorder thing that records right off of the TV. I'm thinking of getting one myself.'

'Tomorrow. What's happening tomorrow?'

'God, you are out of sight. It's moon night. *Apollo 11* lands tomorrow sometime in the afternoon. Chucky has this gadget set up to play it back to the guys in his bar in the evening, just before the moonwalk. Those assholes love that kind of shit.'

He was right. I was out of it. I had completely forgotten. Moon night. Men on the moon.

'Why do you need to see Mouse?'

I told him. I had this odd notion that letting him see how 'real' things could get beyond the limitations of his own bedroom and his shallow, callow imagination. I was wrong. He said, 'Guys following you? Like in the movies? Cool.'

§

It was more time than I wanted to kill. I rode again with my father in the morning. He opened up a little, my muscles stretched some. If I'd stayed a week he might have told me everything that was on his mind. He told me how he felt about Huey. Lois had it right. He loved the kid and just wanted him to do something and not let events roll over him. If he could do the decent something, all the better, but he wasn't about to force him in one direction or the other.

We ate lunch—again without Huey stirring from his room—and Sam took his siesta. About three in the afternoon, Sam reappeared, banged on Huey's door, called me and Lois in from the deck and flicked on the

TV set. Huey stayed put. Sam watched *Apollo 11's* lunar module touch down on the moon, and I watched Sam. Watched him wipe tears of pride from his eyes, so quickly he was hoping neither his son nor his wife would notice.

In the evening Huey got up and got out his shiny 1969 red Jeep—roller bars, floodlights, eight-track stereo—like I said, rich kid—and drove me into town.

Now, Sweet Chucky is not called Sweet Chucky on account of his disposition. He is, truth to tell, a sonuvabitch. He got called Sweet Chucky when we were in high school and Chucky's idea of a mid-morning snack was a two pound bag of sugar, and a hefty slab of white butter, sliced into strips. He'd dip the butter in the sugar and suck till both were gone. Used to make you want to puke just to watch him do it, but plenty of us did—stood around in the schoolyard and watched Chucky swell from one hundred to three hundred pounds over a couple of years. At twenty he'd been a colossal oaf of a man—for Chucky to be running his own bar and grill was like an alcoholic getting his own distillery. Pig heaven.

We got there mid-evening. Still light, still hot and still sticky. The blast of Chucky's air-conditioning hit me like icy mountain air—if mountain air could ever smell of stale tobacco and unwashed denim. It was all too low, too dark and too much fake knotty pine. Sawdust was real though. It was a guys' hangout, the only women in the place were behind the bar, and according to the sign they went topless on Fridays and Saturdays. Missed it by a day, thank God. Never could see why tits and beer went together.

A skinny black kid waved at Huey and he led me across to a table in the middle of the room. I would not have known Gabriel Kylie. He was skinnier than Huey and as tall as me, and he was stuffing his face from a pizza the size of a cartwheel.

Huey offered no introduction. Gabe just struck out an oily, cheesy hand and said, 'John? We ain't met since Cousin Mouse went into th' army.'

'And how old were you then?'

'Eight. I sat on Aunt Lula's stairs and watched you and Mouse get out of your heads.'

So we did, so we did.

Huey went up to the bar for beer. There was a half-empty Lone Star on the table next to Huey's bottle of Bud.

'Mouse about?' I asked.

'Sure, he's just getting me some more pizza.'

'More?'

'I know what you're thinkin'. But I hear they don't draft the fat guys. Like there's kind of a medical limit for bein' fat and if you're over it they can't get you. I aim to beat it. They didn't get Chucky. And Chucky says it's bein' fat did it for him.'

'Gabe, Chucky was three hundred pounds the last time I saw him. You've a ways to go.'

'You ain't seen him lately then. He's bigger'n that now.'

He pointed to the bar. Two young women were pouring beer, and between them, scarcely hidden by the cash register, was the biggest human butter mountain I'd ever seen. Sweet Chucky ten years on. Not a pretty sight. But ahead of him, weaving his way between the tables, with a pizza held aloft like a magician's spinning plate, was another man-mountain, but this one was black, six feet four at least, but there wasn't an ounce to spare on him, and every one of his two hundred and fifty pounds was solid muscle. Mouse.

He slapped the pizza in front of Gabe. I stood up, meaning to shake him by the hand, and got bear-hugged instead.

He held me off, just the way my dad did, at let-me-get-a-look-at-you length.

'Man, you is one skinny motherfucker. Don't folks eat out East?'

'Aw, Mouse, we's too polite. We don't fart neither.'

Mouse hooted.

Huey brought beer.

We reminisced.

Gabe ate.

When the small talk got whittled down to nothing—and I'd already declined several offers of him driving me over to Carolyn Tucker's house—Mouse said, 'Gabe says you was askin' for me, Johnnie.'

I reached into my bag and put the blow up of the New Nineveh Nine on the table in front of him. Mouse picked it up, angled it to the light and said, 'Yeah, me and my boys. What was it botherin' you then, Johnnie?'

I used Carrie Fawcett's words, 'Something happened, Mouse. I just wondered if you knew what? If like maybe they'd written to you, or you'd see any of these guys on leave or whatever.'

'No. I ain't seen none of them. Where d'you get the photo?'

'Marty Fawcett's mother.'

'And how is ole Marty?'

'He died, Mouse.'

Whatever front it was that Mouse had thrown up since I first put the picture in front of him cracked a shade. This hit him. I knew he was holding it all in, but there was a flicker.

'How?'

'Cancer. About six weeks back. His mother blames it on the chemicals they use over there.'

'She could be right,' Mouse said, soft as a whisper.

'So you don't know what it was that happened?'

'Of course I know. I was there.'

I thought he must have misheard me.

'No. Mouse. I meant what happened over in 'Nam. Not back in Georgia.'

'I went to 'Nam with the Nine.'

My turn to crack a little. He'd surprised me now.

'So you do know?'

'I just told you I did.'

'And?'

'I can't talk to you about this because you weren't there. If you'd been there then it would be different. But Johnnie, you weren't. Don't blame you for that, but that's the way it is. You were there or you weren't.'

He said it in exactly the way I'd heard people say 'you're either on the bus or off it.'

'Why were you there, Mouse? You were a training sergeant at Nineveh. Why were you in 'Nam at all?'

Mouse put the bottle to his lips and drained it.

'Volunteered,' he said at last.

'Can you tell me why—or did I have to be there to know that too?'

'Goddammit, Johnnie, you got no right to get snippy with me. But yes, I'll tell you that. I'd been in the forces best part of ten years. I'd seen action just once, in the Dominican Republic. Another of LBJ's excursions. By December '67 I'd been a weapons instructor for close on a year straight. I'd sent God knows how many platoons of boys out to 'Nam. I realized I couldn't go on doing it. It wasn't any desire for more action. What I'd seen was enough for any man, and my momma didn't raise no fools. But there seemed to me to be a moral dilemma here. I was sending boys out to die. Seemed wrong to me. I was asking them to do what no one was asking me to do. So when the last bunch got shipped I asked to go with 'em. They were a bunch of kids I got along with fine. The brass told me they'd already assigned a company sergeant, and for a while I figured I'd see out my time teaching more kids in Georgia how to shoot straight, but a couple of days later they said there was room for an Information Specialist and as I was qualified the job was mine.

Well, you can imagine how I felt. Information Specialist is armyspeak for photographer. I'd owned a camera since the day your brother Billy taught me how to make a pinhole camera with a cookie box and a sheet of baking paper. If there'd been a college a black man could of gone to and learned the trade when I was a kid, I might've done it. If I'd graduated high school I might've done it. But there wasn't and I didn't. Enlisting was a way of earning a living for me and my momma and beating the draft. If I joined they couldn't hardly draft me. Wasn't the life I'd of chosen, but when did a black kid ever get his druthers? But I made what I could of it. Made sergeant and 'cause I was deadeye dick with a rifle, I made weapons instructor and marksman too. And along the way I took the US Army Information Specialist's course. Never thought I'd get to use it. So—there was no way I'd turn this down. I wanted to be there, and if the army wanted me toting a Kodak rather than an M16 then that was OK too. That's how I came to be in 'Nam.'

'And?'

'And nothing. That's all you're getting.'

'Mouse. You signed on for twenty years. Three months in Vietnam and you're out? What happened?'

Mouse got up. Two hundred and fifty pounds of army-fit black man towering over me. But it was still Mouse, as likely to hit me as kick a lame dog. He just put a hand on my shoulder, shook it gently and said, 'Good night, Johnnie.'

The bar-room reappeared to me out of the self-contained world that had been me and Mouse for the last twenty minutes. Above the bar-room burble I could hear Gabe chomping on his pizza. He had melted cheese running down his chin and flecks of bell pepper spattered across his T-shirt. I was beginning to think dodging the draft might be turning into a labor of love.

'You winning there, Gabe?'

'Sure am.'

I looked at Huey. He was grinning, holding in a laugh like he was fit to bust.

'He'll either get 4-F or a heart attack.'

'Heart attack be damned. I mean to win this one. I ain't get my ass shot off by no little yeller man. What I ever do to him?'

I saw a flicker of light across the room. The TV came on over the bar. And Sweet Chucky roared above the hubbub.

'Mah felluh 'Merikins. Are yoooooooo ready? Ten, nine, eight, seven, six . . .'

At five there was a rush to the front.

'Four, Three, Two, One.'

Chucky hit a switch on his VCR and grainy blips rippled across the screen and settled into an image. I got up and moved forward.

'Hey,' Huey said. 'I thought you watched the landing with the old man?'

'I did. I just want to watch it again. Don't you want to see a man walk on the moon? I do.'

'Me too,' said Gabe, scooping up enough pizza to last him ten minutes away from the table.

'What's to see?'

To answer Huey would have been to play his game. I was in two minds about the whole thing. I remembered, as anyone of my generation would, Jack Kennedy pledging to take us to the moon. And I saw it happen as one of the most uneasy, self-conscious pieces of myth-making imaginable. It was irresistible. Irresistible because it was complete kitsch.

Huey preferred an audience when he wanted to grouch. We slyly inched into putting elbows on the bar. Huey stood between me and Gabe. Chucky slapped a beer in front of me.

'Ah thought it was yew,' he said without pleasure. Then he turned his back on us and craned his neck to see the screen.

'We copy you down. Eagle.'

'Houston, Tranquillity Base here. The Eagle has landed.'

The eagle had landed. The whole bar cheered. A national ambition found its steel feet in the moon dust. Huey looked surly. I put a few dollars on the bar and ordered in more drinks. Chucky and his girls rushed around serving everyone, Chucky's eyes darting between his cash register, his watch and the TV screen.

'OK. Everybody stop. We goin' live.'

Chucky hit the volume just as the hatch came off the Lunar Module. It seemed to be dawn up there—a searing, horizontal light. We watched Neil Armstrong emerge in an outfit that looked clumsy till he started to move—big moon boots and that backpack kind of thing that kept him living and breathing. We watched him come down the ladder to stand on one of the big round pads resting in the dust. It took, I guess, no more than ten or fifteen minutes, but it seemed like an hour. How often can you go into a bar, anywhere in America, and hear yourself breathe?

Armstrong stepped out, left foot first, half-walked half-floated to the surface and said the line. Now, it's as famous as the Zapruder film and the grassy knoll. Then it was new, as old as it took for a signal to get from the moon to Houston and into the world's TV sets. And still it was corny. I thought so. God knows, maybe half the guys in that room did, but it had to be my little brother who said so.

'Aw, this is just crap, man. Whitey's on the moon. So fuckin' what?'

A dozen heads turned, Chucky too. Lookin' straight at Gabe. Gabe did his 'Rochester' impression, wide-eyed and innocent.

'Weren't me, man,' he said to them all.

'Whitey's on the moon. Big fuckin' deal.'

They knew now who was speaking, and he had not enough sense to shut up.

'I mean, man . . .'

To whom was he speaking? Was I 'man'?

'I mean. Space is like shit. I mean there's nothin' out there. Just rocks an' shit. I mean, it's not like there was little green men or Buck fuckin' Rogers. It's just crap. This is what matters.'

Huey tapped his forehead, right where the third eye would be, and failed to use the two he'd got.

'This is what matters . . . inner space. That . . . it's just shit. Whitey on the moon. A zillion dollars to send three guys up in a tin can. Well, shit to it.'

Chucky leaned in to me.

'I hate to say this, after all, we ain't met but a few times in a dozen years, but if this long-haired hippie kid you call your brother don't start showin' some respect real soon, I'm going to throw the three of yewz out. And if he calls me "whitey" one more time I'll punch the little shit's lights out.'

That was good enough for me. It was good enough for Gabe. Gabe was gone fast as chicken fried lightning.

'Come on. We're leaving.'

I pulled Huey away from the bar, but he shook me off and turned back to push his luck one more time.

'You gonna let this sack o' shit shove us around.'

'Yes,' I said, cowardice being the better part of discretion.

He turned to Chucky and he bellowed.

'Ain't no lardasses on the moon neither, fat boy!'

For a fat boy Chucky was agile. He was over the bar with a baseball bat in his hands in seconds. But in less than seconds I'd hustled Huey to the door, and all but thrown him through it. We'd parked a few blocks away. I hoped the walk would cool Huey off.

A block from the car, right outside the Cactus Theater, three or four guys jumped us. I got suckerpunched and went down feeling as though half my teeth had been knocked loose. Huey came down on top of me and six or eight (or was it ten?) boots began to kick the living shit out of us. Silent guys, grunting some, but letting their feet do the talking. I was on the verge of spewing, when it suddenly stopped. I heard a few thwacks of wood on flesh, and then I could see just one pair of boots standing there. I looked up, my neck shot sparks into my skull, but I could just make out Mouse standing over us. An ax handle in his fist. I leaned over the curb and threw up.

Mouse must have tucked one of us under each arm. The next thing I remember is being in the men's room of the Cisco Bar on the other side of the street, hunched over the basins washing the blood from my mouth. Huey was next to me, bruised, battered, but unvanquished. Arrogant and snotty as he'd been ten minutes ago. Not one flicker of recognition on his face that we'd just escaped broken ribs, ruptured spleens, maybe even death.

'Who are these guys you think are following you?'

'What?'

'You said something about guys you thought were following you. You know, in Chicago. Looks like they found you.'

'Huey, you can be one stupid sonuvabitch. Those guys weren't after me. They were after you. They're just a bunch of Lubbock barflies, with some shred of national pride. You insulted them. You insulted everyone in that room, dammit. They just slipped out of Chucky's ahead of us and waited. You and your big mouth. And where do you get all this jive talk? "Whitey's on the moon"? What the fuck was that about? Whitey? Do you know what those guys would have done to Gabe if they'd caught him instead of us? Godammit, Huey!'

'Aw—they all know Gabe. Gabe is one of the guys.'

'No, Huey. In there Gabe was a target. You made him a target with your bullshit. Why do you think he cut and run? Do you think he wants to get his head kicked in just because some white kid decides to pull a jive-brother number on him?'

Huey ran wet fingers through his hair, pulled it back from his face and loomed at the mirror as though he were looking for zits. He let his moptop fall back and blew himself a kiss. Just a tad, I was beginning to think my little brother was a punk.

'We could of taken 'em.'

Right.

I emerged from the can still spitting blood. Mouse was waiting, idling the motor on his pickup. He called out to me.

'Get in. Sure my momma'd be glad to see you.'

It was not what I expected. I looked at Huey. Blood on his shirt split lip and shiner of a black eye coming, but a cocky little shit of kid all the same.

'Go ahead,' he said, 'I'll be OK.'

He threw the car keys high in the air, reached out a hand and snatched them back at arm's length. The brazen certainty of youth. I climbed in next to Mouse.

§

In a couple of blocks we bumped across the railroad tracks—that was where the Kylies had always lived, between the Fort Worth and Denver Railway and Dunbar High School, east of Avenue A, in a red shingle house from which you could hear freight trains hoot the whole night through. Mouse and I had met here just before the end of World War 2. Billy and I were down at the depot, trying out his home-made pinhole camera—he had to photograph a steam engine, nothing else would do—and this big, eight-year-old black kid had come up to us, all questions: 'What's that?' 'What you got there?' That was fine by Billy, he was all answers. I knew Mouse from that day until the day he joined the army.

Every house we passed was lurid with the flicker of TV screens, the glimmering water-green light bouncing off the walls into the windows. Mouse's house was dark. If Mrs Kylie was home, she'd already gone to bed. Moon or no moon. Mouse's father, Ed Kylie, had come back to this house from Germany in 1945, clutching his Congressional Medal of Honor. Lubbock hadn't much wanted to honor its local hero, nor did Ed much want to be honored. There was no parade—he just nailed his medal to the front door and let the world see. After he died Mrs Kylie prised the medal off and put it back in its velvet case. The nail head remained. I could see it as Mouse slipped the catch on the screen door—now is that symbolic or what?

The two of us tiptoed to the back of the house. No sooner had he pulled on the refrigerator door than a voice from upstairs yelled, 'That you Mo'reece?'

'What'd I tell you? That woman can hear a icebox open at a hundred yards, and the flipping of a beer cap at a mile.'

He handed me a bottle of Lone Star.

'Yeah, Momma. S'me. I brung back a face you ain't seen in a whiles.'

A light went on. Mrs Kylie appeared at the top of the stairs, staring down at us. A graying woman in her sixties, wrapped in a blue robe.

'Hoozat?'

''Member Johnnie Raines, don't you, Momma? We was buddies back in my high school days.'

'Step into the light, son.'

I stepped. She peered.

'You walk into a tree, son?'

'Something like, Mrs Kylie.'

'Well, you sure do have a look of your momma 'bout you. How long is it now? How long's she been gone? Must be a while.'

'Twenty-four years come August,' I told her.

'My, my. And where you been all this time?'

'I live in New York City. Mostly.'

I added the mostly out of pure cowardice. I lived in New York period, and I was trying to diminish if not negate the inevitable response.

'My, oh my. No good ever came of livin' in New York.'

She bade us both goodnight, told Mouse not to drink too much beer and my-myed herself back to bed.

Mouse flipped the caps on the beers and led the way out to the back porch, a flaking whitewashed porch onto which he had, mercifully for the night and the chiggers, fixed a brand new screen. It looked out onto the scrubby backyard, baked dry and plantless by the sun. Mouse had built a barbecue. I found myself wondering if that was where he'd burned his uniform.

It was past ten, dark and still blistering hot out there. Mouse seemed to have created the only cool spot in West Texas. He stared at his beer. Sat a while. Stared some more, and I began to wonder if he was ever going to speak.

'You were asking,' he began in a tone and style utterly different from that in which he addressed his mother, 'about the New Nineveh Nine.'

I said nothing, decided to let him cue himself.

'Like I said, I trained those boys. Taught every one of them to shoot. Every last damn one. You got that picture you were toting at Chucky's?'

I took it out of my pocket, more battered and creased than it had been an hour ago.

'You know these boys by name?'

'Just Marty Fawcett.'

Mouse pointed to each one in turn.

'Front row. Pete Chambers, college boy from private schools and Harvard. Came from Connecticut. Stanley Mishkoff. Brooklyn Jewish. They kinda made him the squad mascot—too short to be anything else. Marty. Notley Chapin. From San Diego. Man, Notley was weird to begin with. I used to wonder how he ever managed to get hisself conscripted in the first place. But I guess it got so the board saw so many dodgers pretending to be weird they couldn't tell if he was faking it or not. He wasn't. Notley was off the wall. Question is, what planet was the wall on? Back row. Al Braga, another New Yorker. Had his good side I guess, but mostly a mean son of a bitch, a hoodlum in the making. Grew up in the Italian myth—all his uncles were Mafia. At least that's what he said. Sort of thing I wouldn't have boasted about. Truth is, the kid was a car thief who got told it was prison or 'Nam by the judge. Fool chose 'Nam. Marcellus Gore—Gus we called him. Only black kid in the squad. Nice kid, but lost. Never been out of the county in his life before let alone out of the state. Tod

Foster, from Arkansas, one of the two comedians—the other's standing next to him. Bob Connor from south Boston. Never figured out what Boston Irish had in common with an Arkie, but they were inseparable and the gags never stopped coming. Curtis Lee Puckett, from Kentucky. As mean as Braga when he wanted to be, but hellbent on becoming a soldier. Took orders and discipline like they were milk and honey. That boy could drill till he wore a hole in the parade ground. And then there's me. On the end there, looking like a beached whale. That was the New Nineveh Nine. Now I know what you're asking. Thing is, Johnnie, you don't, do you?'

'No. If I did I wouldn't be here.'

'So what do you think you've found. A fragging? A platoon that ran amok and killed a few gooks too many?'

'Something like that. Is that what it is?'

'First, you tell me why you're asking.'

'Friend of mine back East, my best friend as it happens, was working on this when he was killed.'

'Killed?'

'Murdered.'

'What was he? Some kind of cop?'

'A reporter, for a New York paper. He'd traced Marty. I don't think he got a chance to speak to him though.'

'And that's it? That's why you're poking around here for the first time in more'n ten years asking me questions?'

'Yes. And I'm sorry.'

'Sorry to be asking me questions?'

'Sorry it's the first time in ten years.'

Mouse waved this away with a hand.

'S'OK. We got this far. I'll tell you what you came to learn.'

He picked up his bottle of beer. He wasn't drinking any more than I was. I left mine sitting on the table. I still felt too close to blood and nausea for beer. I think he needed it just to have something to do with his hands. Mouse began his tale, and I could not begin to imagine how precisely he had chosen the word 'learn'.

'They got to 'Nam Christmas '67. I got lucky. I had Christmas back here with Momma and Gabe and flew out from Seattle in the New Year. I got to Da Nang on a wet Thursday in January. But any day would have been a wet day. That was the season. It just rained all the time. I picked up a 35mm Kodak, a Rolleiflex and a Colt .45 from stores and followed them out across Quang Nam province in a Chinook. Three quarters of the way to the Laos border and a hell-hole called LZ Mighty Joe Young. LZ's armyspeak for Landing Zone and Mighty Joe Young was pretty well what the Vietnamese name for the place sounded like to American ears. I never heard it called anything else by anyone under the rank of Colonel. Joe Young was nothing more than a big bunch of Quonset huts surrounded by jungle and swimming in mud. The front line in a war that didn't have a front line. CeeBees made it with a thing called a Rome plow— an earth mover the size of a house, just tore through anything and flattened it. Ripped down trees till they got a space, threw up huts and watched it all turn to mud. Mud got so bad you couldn't dig a hole and call it a latrine. You shit in pots, tipped out the pots into an oil drum and twice a week the Vietnamese gophers'd douse it all in diesel and set fire to it. Smell of burning shit used to hang over the place all the time.

'The battalion had spread the Nine out across a couple of companies. Not many kids get to go through basic and then serve shoulder to shoulder. They were luckier then most. Five of 'em went into the same squad in Alpha company, three, Pete, Stanley and Gus, into the same squad in Charley and strangest of all, Al Braga got kept back in Da Nang because they needed a skilled mechanic at base. Car thief, mechanic—same thing as far as the army was concerned. Braga was already protesting about it when I passed through. Said he didn't come to 'Nam to grease engines, he came to kill gooks, and if he didn't get to kill gooks he'd look for somebody else to kill. They eventually let him go, gave him what he asked for, a front line posting. When most men were asking for the opposite. He got to Joe Young about ten days after me, but by then they'd all changed. I knew it as soon as I set eyes on them. They'd been three weeks in 'Nam and they'd aged three years. They'd patrolled some. They were all still alive, but they'd seen men wounded by sniper fire, watched some poor guy lose a foot to a booby trap and maybe they'd figured out it was only a matter of time and statistics before it was their turn. Nine of 'em. You could count for sure on one getting killed, another two crippled and another three wounded before the year was out. Four or five might make it back. Which four or five? God knows. They'd all changed. Marty got made a corporal almost at once, put in charge of the squad, but then he'd been pretty much their leader from the start. Notley got weirder than ever. Stopped cutting his hair, grew one of those tiny beards you get just in the dimple of your chin and one of those stringy hippie moustaches. And the dope that man could get through. I suppose you think we all got stoned? Man, I never touched the stuff till I got back here and Gabe turned me on to it. But that's what people want to believe. Let 'em. Was true of Notley. But I guess you could say the change in them all was visible in the names they'd painted on their helmets. Like they wanted to be even more different then they really were. Like they were changing personas by changing names. Saying "I am not the kid you knew back home." Only Marty still used his real name. Stanley, they called Sputnik, on account of that's what he looked like. A round-faced little guy. All he needed was spikes and he got those when they made him a radio operator with one of them long, whippy aerials waving out above his head. Bob Connor was One-Line—after all the one-liners never stopped coming. Tod was Arkie—nobody seemed to exercise much imagination where that was concerned. Nor with Pete—he just got stuck with Ivy League. Braga was Hotwire—claimed he could boost any automobile without a key, so why not? Notley was Zappa, after Frank. Gus was Floyd, 'cause he looked a lot like Floyd Paterson. And Puckett was Shack, 'cause he was forever telling you how he grew up in one. Must have felt right at home in 'Nam. No drop in his standard of living whatsoever.

'Whatever—they won their point with me. It was almost as though I didn't know them. As though they'd got their war now, and it wasn't my war. And the war I'd seen was nothing like this. Nothing was as hot, wet, dirty, rotten as Vietnam. They hardened up in a way I'd escaped. I thought back to all the bullshit those kids had taken in basic from drill sergeants who'd cut their war teeth in Korea or like me spent most of their service time on home postings, and I realized nothing had prepared them for this, and that if one of those bastards was flown out and dropped in now he'd have to learn from them. I followed. I was still "Sarge" but I followed. I did my job, not that anyone could define it for me. Information officer in a war of misinformation. I took pictures. I built myself a darkroom and I printed photographs no one wanted to look at.'

It seemed a moment to stop his flow. A risk but I took it.

'I would like to see them.'

Mouse looked back at me in the gloom, said nothing.

'Really. I would. I mean. You still have them, don't you?'

He was gone several minutes. I began to wonder if I might not have shattered the spell, the mirror crack'd. But I heard him lightfooting down the stairs in his socks and he reappeared on the porch with a big red album under his arm and a glowing joint wedged between his fingers. He passed both to me.

'My momma warned me not to drink so much beer. Like I said, Gabe introduced me to one of the finer things in life.'

I drew on the J and felt the smoke curl around the back of my throat and the familiar, unholy joy uncurl in my head. Like the man said, you can have quite enough of beer. I flipped open the album. Leafed through Mouse's back pages. Treading through it on my fingertips as gingerly as a faithless husband sneaking in after midnight. A shot of a painted woman outside a bamboo and timber shack. A Vietnamese whore trying to look like a skinny, pouty version of Jane Russell, toning down her otherness with the ubiquitousness of Western make-up, Western poise and Western know-how. It was parodic. I did not know how any man could find this attractive, but then I'd never been that man to whom she was appealing. Two dogs caught tussling over something in the road, who'd stopped to look down the lens at Mouse the way only dogs do. A burned-out jeep. A Chinook taking off, the grass all around it flattened like Kansas in a tornado. Three guys in fatigues, arms wrapped around shoulders, bonding and grinning.

Mouse read my mind. 'Pretty basic stuff, huh?'

'Something like that.'

'You'll be glad of something ordinary. Now, shut the book and pass the joint.'

Mouse took up his story again with the first exhalation, his voice smoky and dope-croaky, gaining depth and volume with every sentence uttered.

'About a week after Al Braga rejoined Tet hit. The biggest, the bloodiest uprising so far. Could have been worse for the Nine. But it was a baptism of fire all the same. Could have been worse—they could have been in Hué or Saigon—it was cities saw the worst fighting. Probably lasted only a matter of days all told, but when it was over it was like a tidal wave had washed over Vietnam. Hué had been a nightmare. Cong occupied for a month, fought over street by street, house by house. There were companies in Hué I heard got wiped out to the last man. Got so the life expectancy of a front-line grunt was down to seventy-two hours. I saw a little of Hué when it was all over and Charlie had pulled back. They flew me and my cameras up there for a few days to put it on record and they flew me back again. I've never seen devastation like it. I found myself wondering what did the most damage—the attack or the counter-attack? Hard to believe what we did in Hué helped any. And by "we" I mean the United States not just the guys in uniform. Charlie took a ville or a suburb or a town—we pounded the shit out of it. Hué, Cholon, Ben Tre. You ever hear the line about Ben Tre? The one that made the papers?'

Of course. I thought everybody had.

'It's anonymous . . . nobody's layin' claim to it, but after we flattened Ben Tre into matchsticks someone on our side says, "We had to destroy the town in order to save it." That goes for Hué too. Could be before this war's over that'll be the key phrase for the whole of Vietnam. Had to destroy it to save it.'

Mouse took a toke and passed the joint back to me, momentarily lost in his narrative.

'But—like I was sayin', the Nine came through all that. The Army really worked those kids. By the middle of March they looked and sounded like veterans. I'd been out with each squad once, easy missions in each case, and I'd been back and forth to Da Nang, often for no better reason than a colonel wanted a mess photo of the senior staff all together or a picture to send home to the wife and kids. One idiot even had me flown across a battleline with flak bursting all around the chopper just to photograph some damn Vietnamese pig he'd adopted as a mascot. Another wanted a picture of his dog. God knows 'Nam has enough dogs and pigs to go round. There were times I thought we'd invented napalm just as a glaze for roast pork. But the Nine, they patrolled hard, almost non-stop, met Charlie head on more'n half a dozen times. They say it's a war in which you cannot see your enemy. I met guys served whole tours in 'Nam and never set eyes on Charlie. They did. They'd seen action. Watched guys shot up and blown apart. Tried to stop open arteries with pressure bandages. Gathered up dead grunts and loaded the bits into body bags. They were no longer FNG . . . Fucking New Guys—the guys who came after the guys who came after them, they were the FNG now. I finally figured out what it was about them . . . it was childhood's end. I'd known them

as boys. I suppose this is where I have to say they were now men—but
what the fuck does that mean? What's "a man"? Someone who's finally
worked out he's mortal just like everybody else? That's manhood? Having
to see someone else blown apart just so you can realize it could happen
to you? Horsepucky. If that's the definition, then the point of war is to
wise up the unimaginative. I heard idiots tell me crap like "war makes
men"—all war does is make dead boys. Best I can say about the Nine is
they'd seen enough to take off the shine and maybe not yet enough to
get bitter or numb about it. Maybe wised up to war, but not broken by
it. You could see that in the eyes of the short-timers. Guys who knew
exactly how many days they had left to serve and were counting down
to it. They'd been to the limit. They'd been broken—shot up, patched up
and sent back to the line, and they'd watched their buddies die week after
week and they'd killed Cong and they'd got past the point where they
cared one way or the other about killing Cong. The Nine had just tasted
it. Three months in the field. No one hurt, no one really sure if in all the
rounds he'd fired he'd ever hit Charlie. But . . . they were still alive—not
one of 'em had gotten a scratch yet. Every now and then they'd get back
to base, find a chance to meet up, take the rise out of Stanley, listen to
Bob's string of gags and get shitfaced.

   'It was then the Colonel showed up. The day after I got back from Hué.
Now, Johnnie, you flip that book open again about the halfway point.'

   Mouse leaned over to me, put his hand flat on the page when I hit
the right one.

   'Yeah, that's the feller. Jack Feaver. Colonel. United States Special
Forces.'

   It was a small color snap, another square contact print, not big enough
for detail and slightly out of focus. A big, strutting kind of white man,
almost as big as Mouse himself, leaner, sleeker, loaded down with weapons, a green blur at the top of his head.

   'A Green Beret?'

   'That ain't no cabbage leaf on his head. Yeah. That's him. John Wayne
for real. He turned up around the third week of March. Alpha and
Charlie were both back at Mighty Joe Young. He flew in looking like a
one-man arsenal. Y'see that thing looks like a sawed-off shotgun in his
hand? It's a grenade launcher, an M79. You see that thing in the holster
on his belt? That *is* a sawed-off shotgun. I knew the first time I saw him

what it meant. Man who carries a sawed-off means to kill, means to kill not like raining down shells or napalm, or loosing off every round in an M16 at shadows, but up close, to kill a man when you can see his face. Shotgun ain't much use over fifty feet away anyways, so a man with a sawed-off means to kill you when he's looking you right in the eye. I had him tagged for a crazy from the start. He shows up with written authorization to recruit for a ten-man patrol to go a week out towards the border. Volunteers only, and he's askin' for 'em. None of the short-sticks would go. Any man who's counting down to the end of his time means to live through it. The new guys just looked baffled. They didn't know what to volunteer meant. They'd always followed orders, and here was this guy not giving orders. Maybe it was only guys like the Nine who would ever volunteer. Guys with one foot in the swamp. Just wised-up enough, just green enough. Marty upped and spoke. I'm with you, he said, and then the others were bound to follow. The comedians, Notley, Puckett. Where Marty led they followed. I was standing by Walter Hollis, Platoon Sergeant. He just grit his teeth and muttered "Shit" and got in line. That left the lieutenant in a fix. Second Lieutenant Norman Gurvitz. He could hardly stand by and let his men go without him. He followed Hollis no more happy about it than Hollis was. "I need ten men," Feaver says and Marty asks for the other four to be brought over from Charlie Company. Feaver's back in less than thirty minutes with them all in tow. Al Braga, Pete Chambers, Gus Gore, and little Stanley. And the other eight are happy as hogs in a peach orchard, 'cause they all got Stanley back. Whatever they were now they were still young enough, superstitious enough to believe in things like the power of having your own mascot. Stanley loved every minute of it. When else does a short, fat, Jewish kid get to be the center of attention? They wore that kid like a cap badge.'

As if on cue, I could not but think of Mel Kissing, of Jerry Rubin, of Abbie Hoffman—all the short, Jewish guys I'd known, desperate to be the center of attention.

'Next morning they were setting off at first light. I showed up, toting my cameras, just the .45 on my belt for defense. Braga had an M60 machine gun across his shoulders, Stanley was RTO, Radio Telephone Operator, with the radio strapped to his back, Gus Gore had a lightweight mortar and it looked to me as though everyone was carrying double ammo, maybe five, six hundred rounds apiece. I didn't say nothing. Feaver just looks at me and says, "Those stripes won't count for nothing here. I got all the sergeants I need."

"Fine by me," I says. "I'll just be one of the men."

"Why the hell not?" he says. "I said I wanted ten, didn't I? Nine green-horns and a weegeeman. Why the hell not? Just keep that shutter clicking."

'I was the one who lacked imagination, I was the greenest horn of them all. Walter Hollis was an old buddy. We'd done boot camp together back in the fifties. He was in the Army same reason I was—unless you could sing do-wop, the only chance for a black man to get out and get up. But he said to me first day out, "Why d'you do this, man? I got no choice. These boys is my boys, but you? Why, man?" I had no real answer to give him. There was no necessity for me to be there. I could be back in Da Nang snapping hookers and pot-bellied pigs. It was tougher than anything I'd done on patrol. Made route marches in Georgia seem like picnics. By the end of that day you could of dragged me to a hammock and sewn me up, I felt as though every vine and every thorn in the whole of Vietnam had tried to choke me or slash me. I had blisters the size of half dollars and skeeter bites like teenage zits. Feaver says to me, how do I like life as a foot soldier? I told him I'd been there before, just not lately. Got a smile out of him, so I cut in quick and said, "What exactly are we after, sir?"

"After? We have a mission, weegeeman. We have a mission."

'And that told me diddley squat.

'I was doing what the Nine had done for the best part of three months, slogging through swamp and jungle loaded down with seventy pounds of gear—two cameras, twenty rolls of film, trenching tool, poncho, ammunition, flares, tin hat, knife, malaria pills, iodine tablets, C rations, clean socks . . . you can get to love clean socks. You know what the American infantryman is? A factory workshop on legs, a human Swiss Army knife with a blade for everything, a mobile unit that works till exhausted and beyond.

'Jungle got so thick by the next afternoon you could hardly tell it was day. Sun just didn't make it down to the bottom. It was like hacking through jello—jello, slime, green slime that grew. We seemed to cover a matter of only a few hundred yards in an hour. Must've been more but it sure felt that way.

'We dug in—not literally, couldn't dig a hole in the jungle floor for roots, made skeeter tents out of our ponchos—we looked like an Indian camp of midget teepees—posted guards, cooked up C-rations—and then they all did their own thing. Did things just like they'd do at home in the privacy of their own rooms. Braga took out his collection of fuck shots, women doing it with God knows who in God knows what position, and I'll swear that punk beat his meat. Marty flossed—didn't matter where we were, what we'd eaten, Marty would floss. Chambers wrote letters to his girlfriend, Stanley to his mother, Connor told dirty jokes half the night, and Notley—man he was weird—Notley did his latest thing, he'd sit in the lotus position and meditate. He was in the middle of the goddam jungle doing a hippie number on a hard-case like Feaver. Feaver just ignored him.

Stanley says, "Do I get on the radio and report our position, sir?"

Feaver says, "What is our position, Private?"

Stanley says, "I don't know."

"Then you can't report it, can you? Just maintain radio silence."

'On the third day we came out into elephant grass—that's kinda like razor blades on stalks high as your head. And where the grass ended we found ourselves looking down on a village—a dozen hooches, no more than that, a flat-bottomed little valley, a stream no more than six feet wide and long narrow rice paddies either side of it. It was bizarre. They'd built their hooches out of garbage—crates, boxes, cans, all the stuff that gets thrown away on an American base. Through binoculars I could even read the labels on the side—Budweiser, Brillo, Coke, Campbell's, Heinz, Pepsi, Marlboro, Reese's, Camel, Hershey. Reading the side of one of those hooches was like watching the ads between two bits of *Bonanza* on the TV. I hadn't a clue where we were, Feaver did all the navigating himself. We were in the middle of nowhere, and it looked like an out-take of back home. America in a straw hat, America toting a rice bowl.

I heard the lieutenant say, "Do we go in, sir?"

Feaver said no, we go round it.

"But they might be VC, sir."

"Might? They sure as hell are."

'He wasn't a great one for explaining. Frustrated the hell out of Lieutenant Gurvitz. A couple of days later, we're taking a break, he comes up to Feaver, I'm a few yards off, rubbing my feet, Hollis is next to me, cleaning the condensation out of his rifle, and he says, "Sir. I've been following the map with my compass." And he unfolds the map between us, so Hollis can see as well. "Here is where I think we are, and here is where we encountered Charlie the last two times out. It seems to me that we're swinging south, almost as though we were coming up behind them.'

"You could be right," says Feaver.

'But Gurvitz ain't through. He points to a river, for all I knew one we'd waded across, I'd lost track of them, three or four, I wasn't sure, and he says, "If we're here, on the west bank of this river, and this is where we are, isn't it, sir?"

"So?" says Feaver.

"Then I'm afraid we'll have to go back, sir. We're in Laos. We're not in Vietnam anymore, not these last five miles. We're in Laos."

'Feaver laughed out loud at this.

"You don't say," he says. "And what do you think the Laotians will do about us?"

"Well, sir. Technically it is an act of war, an invasion."

"Then let 'em fight back. What're they gonna do? Nuke Washington? Lieutenant, it's just a line on a fucking map, probably not even an accurate line. Do you think Charlie bothers about lines on maps, do you think the Ho Chi Minh trail carefully toes a line down the Vietnamese side of the border? Haven't you learnt yet? It's all Vietnam—don't matter what they call it. It's all Charlie. We're just taking the war to them, 'stead of waiting for it to come to us. Why do you think we bomb Laos every day?"

"We bomb Laos?"

"We bomb Laos every goddam day."

"I didn't know that."

"Gimme a break, Mr Gurvitz."

'Gurvitz had nothing more to say. I looked at the map. It seemed to me we were skirting a big hill numbered Hill 77. The village we'd passed wasn't even marked on the map.

'Next day it was uphill and downhill. Foothills below Hill 77, which we kept to our right. My feet were hardening off. I wasn't finding it so bad. We had another river to wade, wider than most, thirty or forty feet. Made us vulnerable, strung out like that with no cover. Sniper on the far side got off a couple of rounds. We all turned on his fire flash, pumped a hundred rounds and a couple of grenades into the trees and he went silent. When we looked back Stanley Mishkoff was lying on his back under the water. The obvious target, the guy with the wavy aerial over his head. Foster pulled him up, but there was a hole clean through his helmet and clean through his head. The Nine had lost their first man. Lost their mascot. Two or three guys ran up the other bank. Found Charlie, looked to be a kid of fifteen or so, wounded, badly shot up and not like to live, dragged him to the edge. They kicked him and they stomped on him and they cursed him. Then Al Braga racks up the M60 and cuts the kid into pieces with it. Till Feaver stops him.

"You're wasting ammunition. You'll need it, when your chance comes."

"Motherfucker killed Sputnik!" Braga screams at him.

"You'll get your chance," says Feaver. Then he looks at all of us. "You'll all get your chance," he says, "every last one of you." And Walter Hollis just whispers, "Oh shit" so only I can hear him. "This fucker's gonna get us all killed."

'We lost a couple of hours burying Stanley. Usually you call in a chopper to take out the dead, but Stanley had fallen on the RT and smashed it, so we dug a hole, Hollis said a few words and then we were on our way again. Nine were eight, but they weren't the same. They were blooded now.

'It was next morning, midday sun not quite on high, when we came to the next village. Gurvitz got out his map again, tells Feaver this one is marked but not named.

"Call it what you like," says Feaver. "We're gonna put it on the only map that matters."

'I watched Gurvitz scribble in "Village 77." Just had time to stuff it in his pouch before Feaver says, "Fan out, we're going in. Everybody watch for trip-wires."

'It was bigger than the last, maybe thirty hooches in all. Packed in tight to a broad clearing, wide paddies all around it, water buffalo grazing or whatever it is water buffalo do in water. Pigs and chickens and kids roaming around in the dirt.

'There was an old woman. Could've been eighty or more. Hard to tell with Vietnamese women. They start out looking so good and then age so fast. I say eighty. God knows she could have been fifty. She watched us all come into the ville, like men stepping on broken glass. Lightfoot and silent. She had this big calabash type thing over an open fire. She was stirring it with a wooden spoon three feet long. She looked up and she just watched. She said nothing and her expression didn't change. Wasn't blank nor indifferent, or stuff like that. Seemed to me like nothing could surprise her, as though she saw us as some sort of inevitability.

'I took her photograph. First of many. Full on staring at me without a flicker.

'We turned out the hooches. Mostly women, some old men, lotsa kids. Not a man under sixty among them. We searched the place, looking for weapons, hidey holes, bunkers, ammo dumps—all the usual evidence of VC being there. We found nothing. If the VC had been there it was a while back, they'd left no trace. If it was a VC village—and there was a theory most of us held to that everyone was VC—then they'd covered it well. To me they were just peasants.

'Gurvitz reports to Feaver, "Nothing, sir. They're clean."

"Clean," Feaver says. "How can they be clean? Where do you think the guy who shot Sputnik came from?"

"Sir, there's no evidence they're VC."

'But the Lieutenant is trying to fold the flood, 'cause mostly the Nine are all fired up about Stanley. Whatever happens now they want to get even. They'll do whatever Feaver tells them. And Feaver tells them.

"If it walks kill it. If it crawls kill it. If it grows kill it."

'Braga opens up on half a dozen women straightaway. Blasts them to bits.

'Gurvitz yells for him to stop, tries to argue one more time, but by now Feaver has a pistol to his head, tells him to shut up or he'll blow his brains out. And then he moves out the men at the top of his voice.

"KILL THEM ALL!"

'And they did, they wasted everyone, old men, women, kids. They lobbed grenades into hooches, they gunned them down when they ran, they blew them away as they pleaded for mercy. I watched a woman wrap her baby in her arms and try to shield it. Puckett shot the kid at point blank range. Blew the kid out of her arms. She was spattered in the blood and guts of her baby, then Puckett shot her too. Connor and Foster rounded 'em up like cattle, maybe fifty in a crowd, herded them into an irrigation ditch and shot 'em like they was popping at fish in a barrel.

'Hollis froze. Gurvitz wandered around weeping. Then Hollis unfroze, started firing off single rounds, while everybody else was set to rock 'n' roll. Picking off the men, as though this somehow was more acceptable to him, as though Walter couldn't bring himself to shoot a woman, but couldn't bring himself to disobey an order either. But Notley—Notley just laid down his rifle, sat cross-legged and let it all happen around him. Feaver seemed like ten men, a killing machine, a man gone berserk, yet still he didn't let Gurvitz out of his sight. Seemed to regard him as the one threat to him. He ignored Notley. It was as though he couldn't even see him.

'Notley sat at the center of it all, like he was out of it, but like he was the hub at the same time. Notley and that old woman with the calabash. Stillness in the eye of the hurricane. Till Al Braga realized she was there and blew the top of her head off, that is.

'I don't know how long the firing lasted. You could tell me it was ten minutes or an hour, and the only reason I'd say it was less than an hour was I don't think our ammo would have lasted that long. But go quiet it did. It dropped on us like a blanket. Silence. Not a bird, not a squealing pig—after all we'd killed the pigs too.

'Then the air began to fill—it filled with the sound of Gurvitz crying and it filled with the smell of blood and open guts—a stinking gory, shitty smell that gradually overtook the stink of cordite.

'Then—the men came running, up from the fields downriver. Little wiry, peasant guys in wooden hats, clutching nothing more lethal than hoes. Feaver grabbed Gurvitz by the arm, slung a couple of bandoliers over his shoulder and said, "You load"—dragged the kid out toward the men and opened up with his shotgun and his M79. At close range, a sawed-off shotgun is a messy weapon. But that's nothing compared to a grenade launcher. Shotgun can pulp a man's face and chest. Grenade just dissolves him into a bloody mist. Maybe twenty or thirty men came running. Feaver stood his ground, like some old gunfighter in a Western—like *The Magnificent Seven*—took 'em one at a time, blasting away with first one gun and then the other, one hand then the other. Gurvitz crouched behind him loading each gun as he threw it down. He didn't miss once. One guy got within three feet of him. Feaver cut him in two with a machete.

'The only living thing left was a big, old water buffalo, standing a ways off, up to its knees in water, not seeming to mind the noise. Feaver loaded one last grenade, took aim. It looked like an impossible shot. Just too damn far for such an erratic weapon. We watched the critter explode like a bag of water a couple of high school kids had dropped off the roof.

'It was over, there was nothing to kill anymore. Feaver had us drag all the bodies to the irrigation ditch and pile 'em up. I counted as the Nine did it. He saw me counting and asked me how many. I told him. Give or take half a dozen I made it one hundred and thirty-four. One hundred and thirty-four. Everyone that lived in Village 77.'

Mouse stopped. He'd talked so long I felt it was akin to the silence after the gunfire he'd described. It came down and left a void. The unholy joy of dope had evaporated like morning mist. I was back with blood and vomit. I felt like I'd been cased in glass, a brittle, transparent skin between me and Mouse and everything he'd said. The night was pitch dark now. The table lamp cut an arc across the room, I could see my own hands, splayed across the photo album, Mouse's huge hands resting on his legs. I could scarcely see Mouse at all.

'Mouse?'

'Sure.'

'Mouse. What were you doing all this time?'

'Following orders. What did Feaver tell me? Keep clicking. So I clicked. I got it all on film.'

'But ... but ...'

'Why didn't I try to stop it? Is that what you tryin' to say, Johnnie? Why not? Because Feaver would have killed me. He'd made it perfectly clear he'd kill Gurvitz. Believe me he'd of done it if Gurvitz hadn't backed down. And the way the Nine opened up on those gooks I had little doubt any one of them would have killed me if I got in the way. Only one not blasting away for Stanley Mishkoff was Notley, but he didn't get in their way either. It was all for Stanley. Nothing I could have said would have made a nickel's worth of difference.'

'Mouse ... it was ... it was a massacre,' I bleated.

'Sure it was. A massacre. A gookshoot. Happens all the time.'

'You can't mean that?'

'Johnnie. I never saw another killing on that scale, but if you're there—and like I said an hour or two back "you had to be there"—you hear stories like this all the time.'

'Innocent people cut down without a second thought?'

'Yes. What the hell else is a free fire zone? Oh, you never heard of that? Means what it says. Brass draw a circle round a district, and say any Vietnamese found inside is presumed to be VC and killed if encountered. Even without that they're fair game. I was being flown back to Da Nang one time in a gunship. We fly low over a garbage dump, and there are twenty or so gooks scrabbling over it looking for the good stuff Uncle Sam throws away. So the guy in charge tells the pilot to come round again. He drops a load of C-rations and candy bars, so the gooks all converge on 'em, we hover while they do and he drops a white phosphorous shell and cooks the lot of 'em. He and the pilot laugh all the way back to base. That's what it's like. Things like that happen all the time. And not just to the gooks. There was one guy at Mighty Joe Young got paranoid about getting some peace and privacy, so he rigged claymore mines all around his dugout. Took out half his own platoon when they got drunk and decided to roust him.'

I realized I'd bumbled into the source of an urban myth—a much told tale, the mad grunt with the claymores.

I said, 'But this is different.'

'So you keep saying. You gonna tell me why?'

'Because it got you discharged from the army and pensioned off. That's why.'

Mouse sighed. 'Let me finish. There was more. There was more. We got ourselves together. Nobody was cheering. Braga and Puckett were grinning, Gurvitz looked to be in shock, the rest were silent. Nobody's got nothin' to say. Then Feaver says, "Torch it."

Hollis says, "It'll be visible for miles around."

"Right," says Feaver. So we torch the place and move out, back the way we came. First break we take for food Lieutenant Gurvitz sits down, puts his .45 in his mouth and pulls the trigger. We didn't even bury the kid, just took his dogtags, kicked earth over him and moved on.

'Walter Hollis was walking behind me, telling me again that "this guy is gonna get us all killed". VC stepped out of the trees, put a gun to his neck and damn near blew his head off. I couldn't turn quick enough. I got off one shot and missed. Marty Fawcett dropped him. Then all hell breaks loose and we hit the floor as the bullets start flying. We return fire and start crawling out of there. Feaver tells Braga to blast 'em as soon as we're clear and he cuts up the jungle with a burst of fire. I don't know if he got any of them. We got sniped at every so often the rest of the day, and all the next, but they didn't score. We'd return fire and the sniping would stop for an hour or two, but it seemed pretty clear to me they were dogging us.

'When we came to the first village again, the one made out of crates, Feaver led us in, marked a couple of mines on the way and took us right into the ville. It was empty. Fire still glowing, food in the pot, but empty. They'd heard, and they'd run. It was close to dark. All the rules say you don't overnight in a ville, too easy a target, but Feaver says, "Demolish this place, fill the crates with dirt and dig in."

Marty says, "Supposing they have mortars?"

Feaver says, "If they had mortars they'd have used them. They wouldn't be trying to pick us off one by one. We're the ones with the mortar."

'And he tells Gus to get his mortar set up and ready.

'By the time we were in position we looked like a wagon train circled and waiting on the Injuns to attack. Attack they did. Feaver says to ignore rifle fire, and wait for movement. They couldn't scratch us with AK47s. Just gave away their own positions. Reckon there must have been more 'n fifty of 'em. Feaver has Gus lob a mortar shell at the flashes, and that does the trick. They come at us like Englishmen going over the top. Feaver launches flares, lights up the clearing like daylight, yells "Fire" and we cut 'em down. Then a second wave comes at us, and in among them, dodging bullets like a linebacker, is this little guy with a really weird looking jacket. Takes me a second or two to realize what it is. He's wearing a chestful of explosives—the guy is a human bomb. All the other guys are dying just as his cover. He means to leap the Hershey Bar stockade and blow himself up and us with him. And nobody can hit him. Braga is changing belts. Marty keeps missing him. I have Stanley's M16 and the damn thing jams on me. But—shit—I'm deadeye dick, aren't I? I taught these guys to shoot. I stand up. Pray to God nothing hits me. Take my .45 in both hands, draw a bead on the little fucker and squeeze. Blast lifted me right off my feet. Knocked me cold for a minute. By the time I come to, Gus Gore is checking me for wounds and saying, "It's all over, you got him." I sit up, look out as the last flare dies off, and there in front of our stockade is a crater, ten feet across and two deep and no sign of the little fucker.

Feaver claps me on the shoulder and says to me, "Nice shooting, wee-geeman. That bastard would have done for us for sure. Welcome to 'Nam."

'Welcome to 'Nam. I'd finally killed somebody. Ten years in the US Army and I'd finally killed somebody. Welcome to 'Nam.

'We lit out at first light. I remember picking my way through the bodies, the bits of Cong scattered around from the night before. Like wading into the dead. Later that day we're back in thick jungle. Foster is walking point, Connor has the compass and is a few steps behind. Good point man needs second sight, intuition like a dog. We put the company clowns on it. Second sight didn't get a look in. You know what a Bouncing Betty is? It's a small mine with three prongs, you have only to brush one as you pass it. But there's two charges inside it, and detonation isn't instant. Damn thing leaps out of the ground on the first charge, makes a sound like a popgun going off. Shoots up to about waist height. By now, if you're the poor motherfucker that's tripped it, you're a step or so ahead, and the guy behind you becomes a target as well. Foster tripped one. When the second charge went off it blew him in two and put a hole in Connor's belly the size of a football. One piece passed right through him traveling so fast it shimmied up the side of my forearm ...'

Mouse shoved his right arm into the light. There was a shiny scar with puckered edges, about ten inches long. A shallow, gouging wound, as though some thoughtless child had scraped a quarter along the side of a shiny new automobile.

'I figure you won't want to see the Purple Heart, but I got one. So did Notley. Same chunk of metal finally spent itself in his helmet. When I wheeled round with my arm burning there he was with a wash of blood flowing down over his face. Everybody else had hit the floor. But there were no more bangs, no bullets. I didn't turn round. I'd seen what had happened. I didn't need to look again. Nine was Six. We didn't even kick earth over them this time. We collected up the bits, wrapped 'em in ponchos and left 'em. Gus Gore bandaged us up, Feaver got us together and said chances were Charlie had mined the trail in several places, so we were going off-trail. So we did. Took us about five days out I reckon, took us eight to get back. Slashin' and cuttin' and crawlin' our way back to Mighty Joe Young. Braga just threw the M60 away when he used up his last belt, Gus dumped the mortar, and Feaver said nothing. So we got back. No machine gun, no mortar, no radio, out of C-Rations, all but out of ammunition, fifty percent casualties.

'We were coming up the slope to our perimeter, sunset on the thirteenth day, guards had sounded the alert, there were guns trained on us—waiting for us to ID ourselves. Feaver sends Marty up the slope, then he walks next to me a while. I'm dog tired. Man, I'm tireder than I've ever been my whole life, and he kinda makes out he's giving me a hand, then he slips his knife under my camera strap and the 35mm drops into his hand like an apple from the tree.

'I just looked at him.

He says, "I have more use for this than you do. And I'll take the other films. I know you shot more than one."

'I had my 35mm tins in a cartridge belt, like ammo. I unhooked it and let him have it. He says, "Believe me, Sergeant Mouse, you've done the right thing, and if you got the right shots you did a good job."

'I said nothing. I just let him walk on past me right into the compound. I had the Rolleiflex slung at the back. Maybe he didn't notice it. Maybe he didn't realize that kinda square leather box held a camera. Those old two lens reflexes look nothing like modern cameras. I'd used it. I had a roll of twenty-four in it and I'd shot 'em all off at Village 77. He thinks he got it all. He hasn't. I got twenty-four color shots of what happened there. Now—turn to the back of the book. There's a small folder, like an envelope, tucked into the sleeve.'

I looked but once and I never looked again. Even when those photographs became public property I never looked again. There is a myth—and I do not mean by that that it is a lie—that the Vietnam war was the first television war, and took place in the living rooms of America night after night. The truth in that is that it was night after night—but it wasn't live, it was often days old and as such controlled and mediated. The first war that wasn't was the Gulf War, happened here and now, in your face. What I saw on Rose's black and white portable TV in the comfort of our downtown Manhattan apartment in the late 1960s could be bloody, but nothing in the nightly news could prepare me for the color carnage in Mouse's twenty-four shots of Village 77. The euphemisms suddenly took on a literal quality—blown away, wasted. People literally being blown away by our fire power. We huffed and we puffed and we blew their house in.

In a curious way the bloodiest shots, the action shots—Foster and Connor mowing down a dozen women in a crossfire, a tide of blood lapping at their feet—Al Braga, hatless and locked in a permanent and silent cry of triumph, mouth wide, eyes wide, arms wide, holding up the severed head of an old man—the ditch full of children riddled with bullets—the moment the water buffalo exploded—made less impact than the more passive, the recorded moments Mouse had snatched between the action. Notley, still sitting crosslegged, expressionless, bits of someone's brain spattered in his hair like death's own confetti—a woman putting her body between her unseen assailant and her children, a photo that left me trying to count the seconds till she died—Walter Hollis looking sideways at the camera, his pistol hanging loose at his side, his face far from expressionless, the eyes telling you he is in hell . . . and the old woman with the calabash just staring back at the camera.

I flipped over the last photograph. Mouse had scrawled the date and place on the back. 'Village 77. March 31st, 1968.'

A lot happened that day.

'I don't know what happened next. I slept the whole night and most of the next day. Then a second lieutenant I'd never seen before wakes me up and says, "Get your shit together, you're outa here." I didn't get to shit or shave even. Next thing I know there's this big Chinook on the edge of the base whirling away. Two sergeants scream at me that I'm the last and throw me and my kit into the 'copter, and there inside are the six survivors of the Nine, all lookin' as rough as me and askin', "Whasshappenin', Sarge?" Like I should know.

'At Da Nang we finally get to clean up and the next morning we parade in front of a half-colonel who says something like, "You've done sterling service, men." Yeah—I'm sure that was it. Sterling service. "And your government is happy to inform you all of your discharge from the United States Armed Forces at the end of your tour of duty. Your tour ends, 1300 hours today." He looks at his watch, like every one of those guys hasn't already worked out that it is exactly five hours and forty minutes away. They're looking at one another in pure disbelief. Then he says, "Sergeant Kylie, PFC Chapin? There'll be purple hearts for the both of you. Men, my congratulations." Then we all salute like puppets jerking our arms up and down. A corporal come round, hands each of us written orders. Four of the six are flying out today—all on different flights. Me, Notley and Pete Chambers are flying down the coast to Saigon, to wait for a flight the next day or the day after.

'So, the guys get shitfaced over lunch—ripped between the happiness of knowing they come through alive and the knowledge of what they had to do to come through alive. Nobody mentions what happened over the last couple of weeks. But I can almost smell it. That mildewed, rotting cotton smell that hung over everything in 'Nam. I could swear I smelled it, wafting our way every so often, blown in with a joke or a beer. The taste of jungle in a Da Nang bar, the lick of death that'd never leave us.

'That afternoon, the three of us say goodbye to the other four and I haven't seen any of them since. I heard from Marty once, but he didn't tell me he was ill. And Gus writes to me. I figure Puckett and Braga went back to their own briarpatches—they were the kind that weren't happy anywhere else. The rest of us get into Saigon in time to have an evening out. But we all have different ideas of what that should be. All I want is a bar and a whiskey while I wait for some little guy in a photoshop to develop my roll for me. I have to know what I've got. If I don't know I don't think I'll ever relax again. Notley goes in search of a hooker and a pipe of opium. Pete Chambers wants to do what he always did if there was light enough. Read and write. When he wasn't writing letters he was reading. Read that *Madame Bovary* by the beam of his flashlight completely encased in his poncho while we were out there. Now he has this thing, *The Quiet American* by some English guy called Greene. All he wants is a good café, a cup of coffee and to read. We all arrange to meet up with him at ten. At twenty of ten some kid rides a bike packed with plastic explosive into the café and blows up himself and half the people in there. By the time I get there, the medics have Pete's body under a sheet and Notley is standing there quiet, with tears rolling down his face, clutching the bloody, ripped up book Pete had been reading.

"Now we are five," he says, and I knew he meant like the ten little Indians, being knocked off one by one by one.

'Next day I flew out to Honolulu. Day after that I landed back at Seattle. The real world. There's this banner says "Welcome Home Returnees". Not soldiers, not men. Returnees. Is that word even in the English language? Some other second lieutenant collars me for a "debrief". I show him my papers. Honorable Discharge dated three days back, April 15. Purple heart, full pension. The Presidential "thank you". I tell him to fuck off. Catch the next plane back here. Spring the biggest surprise you can imagine on my Momma. I spent a week or two just thinkin'.

Like I'm Dana Andrews or Fredric March in *The Best Years of Our Lives*. But, I'm due a cash payment as well as the pension, and I know what to do with the money. Always did. I bought the lease on a little studio and set up Mouse Photo. That's the way it's been for more'n a year now. I tell nobody what happened. Nobody asks, least nobody you can't satisfy with a standard answer. "You had to be there." Works on most. Then you show up. I guess I always knew somebody would. Never thought it would be you. I thought one day it might be Jack Feaver himself. Hard to believe men like Feaver can just breeze into your life with a mission and then breeze out. You know, I never did find out what the "mission" was.'

I slept on the couch. The light woke me early. I lay an hour or more watching the sun bleach out the day. I pulled on my jeans and wandered out to the yard. There was the clumsily built brick barbecue, something glinting dully in the ash. I picked up a piece of charred cloth. It crumbled in my fingers and a brass uniform button dropped back into the pit. I poked around, found a couple of strips of colored ribbon. The last vestiges of whatever medals Mouse had had pinned to his chest. He called to me from an upstairs window, 'Come in and get some eats. Momma's got coffee on the go. After, I could take you down the studio.'

I sat at breakfast feeling like a faithless child as Mrs Kylie asked me a couple of dozen questions about my family to which, largely, I did not have answers. In the end she said what Lois would not, 'You should get home more often, son.'

Mouse drove me downtown to a concrete strip of modern lock-up shops on the south side of 19th. 'Mouse Photo', and a caricature fat mouse, on the shingle. He rattled through a big bundle of keys, thrust back the door and flicked on the overhead lights. It was the opposite of the photoshop I'd been in in Chicago only a couple of days before. It was spotless and minimal. Uncluttered by design, white beyond white, and with one of those infinity curves along the side wall so he could photograph people or things without lines or corners. A couple of light boxes, a workbench, a door marked Keep Out, which I assumed led to his darkroom, and on the back wall a blow-up, bigger than you'd think photos could ever be, bigger than life, of the old woman from Village 77. Staring that blank stare back at the camera, minutes away from death, knowing it and not flinching or moving.

'Mouse. Why?'

'It's what I do. I take photos. I snap life, make it smaller, sometimes make it bigger.'

The sheer size of it served to bring home the magnitude of what had been done. There wasn't a mark on this woman, but plastered across the wall, eight foot high, I could not help but see the mark of death. After all Mouse had told me it would have been a man of little imagination who did not imagine it however unwillingly.

'How ... how did you ever expect this to stay a secret?'

'Johnnie, this is 'Nam—way out in the jungle—not some town in Kansas half a mile off the interstate. Who was ever going to know? Wasn't the first time the United States Army shot up a bunch of gooks for no reason. Of course I expected it to stay secret. Who would tell? I wasn't going to tell. What do you think I'd say? That I did nothing while a squad I'd help train killed a hundred or more unarmed women, old men and kids?'

'These things have a way of getting out,' I said, hearing Carrie Fawcett's voice in my head saying 'these things happen' even as I said it.

'These things? These things! Johnnie have you any idea what "these things" are? Have you any idea what goes on in war? The guy you pass on Main Street on his way from the drug store to grocery, with two kids trailing behind and a shopping list his wife give him—what do you think a man like that does in combat? He does what the fuck he's told, that's what. And after a while it gets so he'll do what he was told like it was just a shopping list. A bottle of aspirin, a new toothbrush, a gallon of root beer and a box of Cheerios—and while you're out kill every goddam slope you see. Soldiers are no different from you or me. They just kill when they're told to and most of 'em get not to mind. You been there, you'd have done the same. You want to know why I told no one? 'Cause doin' nothin' don't make me one ounce less guilty than the guys who pulled the trigger or lobbed in the frag grenade. This didn't come out—"these things" don't come out because they're done by regular guys and when regular guys get home they just want to put their heads in the sand and pretend it didn't happen, 'cause once they're home they can scarcely believe it did happen. Johnnie, I don't tell no one cause I was guilty as sin. Believe me, nobody told nobody nothin'.'

'Somebody did.'

'Yeah. Right. Else you wouldn't be here.'

'And you're telling me.'

'More than that. I'm giving you all the proof you need and saying do your worst.'

'What?'

He reached under his workbench, slapped a big buff envelope into my hand.

'Keep the photos, Johnnie. I got copies, I got the negs. Just do what you gotta do.'

'Mouse, I don't get it.'

'It's out. You come all the way home to find me and you got what you wanted. Now tell who you gotta tell, show 'em the photos and let's see what breaks loose.'

'Mouse?'

'I'm ready. I'll take what's coming to me.'

I tipped the photos out onto the bench. Seeing is believing, but I couldn't look again. They lay there white side up. Mouse flipped the top off a Coke bottle and stared at me as he put it to his lips. I scooped up the photos and put them back in their little folder, put the folder back into the envelope. The man felt so brittle I was actually scared to say what had to be said.

'I need a name, Mouse. I have to talk to one of the others.'

'What?'

'Look, I'd just like to have corroboration, to hear it from someone else.'

'Those photos ought be all the co-robberation you need.'

'Doesn't work that way. Just give me a name. Doesn't matter who.'

'Yes it does. I wouldn't urge you to talk to Braga or Puckett. They're as likely as not to answer you with a bullet. Shit—if you'd gotten to Marty Fawcett he'd as likely shot you himself. If I send you to Braga he'll kill you without blinking. In fact—if Al even hears that you're askin' questions about Village 77 he'll come lookin' and you better not be around. Hell, if you have to talk to someone, then it had better be Gus. I kept in touch with Gus. I kept track of one other guy—leastways he drops me a line from time to time—but Gus is your best bet. Just don't go steamin' in there—remember you might as well be asking him to commit suicide.'

'That's Marcellus Gore, right?'

'Right. Good kid.'

'And he took part?'

'Yeah—he did what he was told. Johnnie, I can't pretend I know how Gus'll react. But if he blows you off, you go with what I give you and you don't mention him 'cept as a member of the squad. I don't want to see Gus singled out. You get me?'

'Yeah, I get you. Now—where does Gus live?'

'He went home. Jus' like me.'

'And where's home?'

'Mississippi. Lazarus, Mississippi.'

If I had to draw up a list of places I never wanted to see again—Mississippi, anywhere in Mississippi, would be top.

§

1960. I wanted Sam to understand. I would have liked him to understand. I had made the journey home from Washington at least twice a year while I was in school. Driving halfway across the nation. The obvious line from DC to Memphis to Fort Smith, Oklahoma City, Lawton and Lubbock was something I liked to vary. I'd swung South, Deep South, a few times, to Atlanta, Montgomery, Natchez and home through Dallas. I do not know that I was surprised by what I saw—the 'whites only' rest rooms, the 'colored' drinking taps—but I was shocked. The bare fact of segregation so much sharper than the abstract notion embodied in 'separate but equal'. Now, I'd grown up in a segregated Lubbock—and I doubt my hometown was any better from the black point-of-view. We had a place that was 'across the tracks' that was strictly black—call it the 'hood—I used to drive over just to hear the music, saw Little Richard and Ike Turner rip it up when I was seventeen. And I do not doubt my family *was* better—I never saw my father abuse a black man or heard him speak ill of one just for the sake of it—but my hometown, the fact of its segregation notwithstanding, had never achieved the numbers and proportions to make race the threat it seemed to be in Alabama or Mississippi—or Washington. It was in-your-face. It was the rot eating the heart of America. So easy to ignore.

Washington itself was a city that would have surprised my father—the nation's capital, as laden with symbolism as you wish to make it, was a southern, black town, much, much more so than Lubbock—a reclaimed swamp as hot as Cairo—in which southern Blacks counted for nothing, a town that was clearing its black people out of the center under the guise of urban renewal and making the Anacostia River the boundary of another country—call it the ghetto.

Sam said, 'But it's not your fight.'

'Yes it is.'

'What have we ever done to the nigras? I hire and fire men without looking at the color of their skin. I never told you not to play with the nigra kids. Wasn't me segregated your school. That's just the way the town was.'

Indeed it was. I was 'bussed' (no—not *that* sense of the word) to school. The school bus began and ended its route at Bald Eagle. I was the first kid on it in the morning and the last off in the afternoon. All the way to Lubbock High on 19th Street—an all-white school in which I was not happy—though I doubt the two matters are related—until the bell rang. Like I said, Lubbock having no skyscrapers I could see Bald Eagle from miles off on the way back, and given the family propensity to daydreaming my head and heart would reach home long before my feet. When, at the age of nine or ten, I had asked Sam why Mouse and I could not go to the same school he had not ducked or dived, but had explained as simply as he could the plain, brutal facts of segregation. That Mouse and I had struck up a friendship was against the odds, but Sam did not discourage us—indeed he was never less than welcoming and pretty soon Mouse's mother came out to meet my mother, checking her out as surely as she was being checked, and they swapped recipes over the kitchen stove. And when, years later, the advent of 'bussing' (yes—*that* sense of the word) meant that Huey and Cousin Gabe could and did go to the same school Sam would pass no comment.

Whereas now he had something to say. Not much but he was saying it.

'Dad—nothing you say is wrong. But the question is what did we ever do *for* them?'

'What do you want to do?'

'I want . . . I want to change America. I want . . .'

As ever Billy's words came back to me.

'I want to invent an America. I want an American revolution.'

'Son, I think you'll find we had that back in 1776.'

'No, Dad. That wasn't a revolution, that was just a change of ownership.'

He didn't understand me. If he had, I think that last remark would have provoked him to fury. My dad, like many a Texan, flew the stars and stripes as proudly as the Lone Star of Texas or the flag of the Confederacy and saw no contradiction.

'Son, you can't change the world.'

He'd been telling me that for years. I suppose three-quarters of the dads in America had said that to their kids at one time or another. It was the adopted slogan of the parents of the baby-boomers.

'I'm not trying to change the world, just my part of it.'

Billy, out in Arizona, quoting me one of his heroes, 'You read the H.G. Wells I gave you, right? *The First Men in the Moon?* Well, he used to say, "If you don't like the world change it."' I could not have quoted that to Sam. The very mention of Billy's name would have numbed him into silence. He'd have found something that needed doing out of the house, mumbled his excuses and left the argument hanging—Billy's ghost translucent in the air between us. I had made a hash of it. All Sam could see was that I wasn't coming back. I was leaving him. Mel might have put it better, but I'd not been able to persuade Mel to make the journey. And if I had? Mel would like as not have convinced my father that changing America was little more than a euphemism for blasting our way through it. Mel was not so much into inventing America as tipping her upside down and shaking her.

Sam did mutter excuses. I found him an hour or so later down on the plain splitting wood. It was one of the tasks he'd saved himself when wealth had relieved him of every task but managing and counting his money. I'd no longer find him sprawled under a truck with a set of wrenches but he did those things that gave him not so much simple pleasure as a centre of gravity. He'd keep the stove fed, he'd do any task involving a horse.

He'd achieved a rhythm close to metrical. Stick a log on the stump, whack it twice across the compass, boot it onto the pile. The longer he chopped wood the more he had to think about.

'Will you need money?' he said at last.

'I have a job. The Student Nonviolent Coordinating Committee.'

'The what?'

'SNCC—most people just call it Snick. They're the guys who pioneered the Sit-Ins. You heard about the sit-ins, didn't you, Dad? Y'know. Desegregating the diners and the lunch-counters and things. I volunteered. So did Mel.'

'Is it a real job?'

'It's a real job.'

'A real job that pays?'

'Ten dollars a week.'

'That real, huh?'

'I'll be OK. I can teach. I won't starve. Look at this way. It's the unknown. Full of possibilities. Who knows what opportunities are there?'

Sam split a log with about twice the force he needed to use on it, then he swung the axe one last time and buried its blade in the block.

He stuck out his hand, shook mine fit to crack bone, and said, 'You just call if you need anything. Anything at all. It's what Western Union's for.'

He looked at me—him, the greatest opportunist of all time—as though he did not believe in the possibility of anything so casual as chance.

It wasn't long before opportunity arose. I knew something would. I had felt for about four years, ever since Elvis broke nationally, although that is another symptom rather than a cause, that we were a nation about to break. This was the way the pieces fell. Interstate travel had been officially desegregated in the 1950s. Like a lot of federal laws it counted for little in the South. Schools had been desegregated in 1954—by '57 Ike was sending troops into Little Rock, Ark., to enforce it. But, late in 1960 the Supreme Court desegregated the bus terminals. It was a gauntlet thrown down. Just what Mel and I and thousands of others had been looking for. The Congress for Racial Equality, a black organisation twenty or so years old now, decided to test the law. They would put riders on the long-haul buses out of DC, bound for New Orleans, black and white, side by side, who would try to ride together—that was the easy part—and when the buses stopped try to eat and piss together in towns where lunch counters and toilets more often than not bore 'whites only' signs if they felt themselves to be civilised and plain 'no niggers' if they didn't. CORE would organize but kids like us, SNCC and so forth would mostly do the riding.

Mel and I volunteered and went into training. We were schooled in the disciplines of non-violence and passive resistance—the techniques that had helped Mahatma Gandhi shut down the British Empire. There was more to it than just letting your body go limp and offering no resistance. It was, our instructors, told us, a discipline of the mind as much as the body—not even to think of wanting to retaliate. I had no trouble with this. Mel did. Even the going limp would just result in a rigid little man, feeling, as the people playing the cops told him, like a washboard. Mel kept saying 'fuckit' but wouldn't quit. He achieved the semblance of passivity, but I knew he was itching to hit back. We trained three days—cover the back of your head over the brain-stem with your hands, guard your genitals with your knees, and re-paper your mind. Even had a reading list—Thoreau, that was pretty predictable, Tolstoy, and Gandhi himself. I think it fair to say that Mel did better on the texts than on the practical.

A guy came in to tell us what could happen to us, not the legal penalties, but the illegal ones—the beatings and the kickings that might be just around the corner. Scared me. I could not see that it did anything for Mel but feed his anger, but then, as it came, anger so often masked fear. I'd lived in the South, he hadn't—I was scared and complacent at the same time. I spoke the language, felt that I had lived with the beast and looked it in the eye. I hadn't.

A woman came to impress upon us the philosophy of the Movement. Althea Harris Burke. A short, muscle-bound black woman with a strong Arkansas accent looking for all the world as though she had come to teach us self-defense.

'You're not fighting any individual. You're not fighting any group of people. You're not fighting any one man ...'

Mel chipped in quick as a snake, 'You are fightin' *the* man.'

She could not help smiling at this. Mel wiped that from her face.

'You are fightin' Amerika.'

Could she hear that 'k'? I could. She took back the high ground, standing over the two of us as we sat on the floor.

'You are fightin' the system! The white racist shoutin' in your face is not your enemy. He is another victim. The system makes him what he is. The system is your enemy not the individual. The victory is not the defeat of any man, the victory is in justice being done.'

Mel's attitude cost us.

The day before the first bus left Althea said to me, 'Your friend ain't ready.'

I knew exactly what she meant and played dumb.

'He got too much aggression pent up inside a' him.'

'Well,' I said. 'He's a New Yorker. Kind of goes with the territory.'

'No, Mr Raines, clichés won't do. He ain't gettin' on that bus, nor the one after. Thing is. Are you on or off? Are you stayin' with him or do you want to ride?'

Of course I wanted to ride.

'Look,' I said, 'we both know what the non-violent movement stands for—we joined it with our eyes open. When it gets tough you can count on Mel.'

'So what do you actually do?'

'We advise on voter registration and on actions to secure voter registration. Mostly we write nagging letters to Bobby Kennedy.'

'Where? Where do you do all this advisin' an' writin'? Here in Washington?'

'Mostly, some in Atlanta, sometimes in Philadelphia.'

'Philadelphia? That's a long way from the front line, Mr Raines. Have either of you been out onto the back roads of Alabama or Mississippi?'

'No.'

'Then you don't know you can count on your li'l buddy, and you ain't gonna put him to the test till I say so. Now, I ask you again—you on or off?'

'I could leave him, but we came into this together and we'll see it through together.'

Two buses left without us.

It wasn't long before the Freedom Ride saw first blood. A violent confrontation in Rock Falls, South Carolina. Only when it made the papers, not just our papers, but national papers, did I realise what we were into. Only America's first man in space eclipsed what was happening to that first Freedom Ride—it was an opportune distraction. Certainly distracted me for a while—I had one thought leading off into tangents of memory, but starting with 'Billy Raines, can you see this? Billy Raines, can you see this, wherever you are?' Did he see the arc Alan Shepard cut through space?

Just outside of Anniston, Alabama the lead bus got firebombed—riders got hospitalised—and when the rest made it to Birmingham, the bus terminal turned into a near-massacre, riders beaten to the ground and not a cop to be seen. Then Montgomery became a place of siege, Martin Luther King all but barricaded into a church, surrounded by the national guard, an escort to the state line, and finally in the terminal at Jackson, Mississippi, an orderly procession right through the colored lounge, right through the whites only, into the paddy wagon, into the court and into the state penitentiary.

Things changed after Birmingham. CORE wanted to stop, SNCC to carry on. No justice in quitting. So SNCC took over from CORE with their blessing. The word went forth, the torch got passed to a new generation, blahdey blahdey blah—now they needed all the riders they could get and it mattered less what Althea Burke thought of Mel's self-control.

Mel and I got picked to ride the bus back the other way—maybe we were the only people with the air fare?—New Orleans to Washington. I figured that gave us about five hours to make our statement to the world. In Jackson we would surely be locked up and thrown in the slammer, just like the others. But at least the threat of violence had receded. The world was watching, we would hardly get the chance to pass through Alabama, and the deal in Mississippi seemed to be tacit between the state and the federal government. The cops would protect us—but they had to lock us all up to do it. How convenient that Althea had defined victory for us before we set off. Just in case we couldn't recognize it when it came.

We were paired off. Twelve of us. All men. Black with white. Mel with an Alabama kid as short and garrulous as he was himself. I could hear them, mile after mile, chatting, arguing, placing pointless bets on who would be the first to see what out of the window—two points for an Olds, five for a Caddy, lose five for a Ford, score ten for a truckload of beer—and me with a lean, dapper young lawyer from Boston, all neat in a black two-piece suit despite the rising June heat. Just a white lapel with 'Freedom Now' stamped on it to break the monotony. A quiet, perfectly self-contained man, Harlan Finch, who had learned a knack I never could, how to read on a moving bus without throwing up. We talked little. I slept a lot.

Some of us peaceniks relished the power of song—I have heard 'We Shall Overcome' sung more times than I could ever count, that or 'Blowin' In The Wind'. Nobody sang on our bus. Maybe too many northerners. Too many men. Maybe nobody could sing. The only time I ever heard Mel sing it was an earplugs only version of 'All Shook Up'. We pulled into Jackson Terminal in near-silence. Tensed for the bust that we all knew would swiftly follow. The door swung open. A cop leapt up the steps, nightstick out, yelling at the driver.

'Y'cain't stop here.'

'I gots to piss. Mos' likely they all gots to piss.'

The driver waved a hand towards the back of the bus, where we sat in pairs like pieces thoughtfully placed around a chessboard. It was as though the cop saw us for the first time.

'Oh Jesus Christ. No.'

He pushed the driver back into his seat with the end of his stick. No real force, but the threat of it.

'Drive on!'

I got up. Walked towards him.

'Excuse me, sir. We all have tickets for Washington via Birmingham.'

The cop ignored me.

'Drive on. We got two busloads of these beatnik Yankee militants backed up in there already. We're running out of paddy-wagons. Drive on. I don't care where you dump 'em so long as it's outside city limits.'

He looked at me now.

'Where do you people come from?'

He wasn't talking geography. He leapt off, the door closed behind him. The driver slammed the bus into reverse. I lost my footing and fell to the floor. By the time I got up again he was spinning the bus around, jerking it through the gears and gathering speed.

I crawled to the front and tried to get him to pull over.

'You wanna die for black folks that's your choice. Me? I'd sooner live.'

I staggered down the swaying bus towards Harlan.

'Does it matter where?' he asked as I dropped beside him.

'Does what matter?'

'We came to ride desegregated or get arrested doing it. We will surely be arrested. Does it matter where?'

I didn't answer. I watched the suburbs roll by, wondering when the driver might risk stopping for gas or a piss. Would we reach the Alabama line on reserve fuel with bursting bladders?

Forty miles on—I never did know where—the driver pulled onto a broken blacktop in front of two hand-cranked pumps that looked as though they had stood there since the discovery of gasoline. It was close

to dusk. Evening cool. I looked around. Where we were was more of a
pit stop than a town, with just two houses, the gas station, a Coke machine, and a store.

The driver got out of his seat.

'I gots to refuel. If you gots to piss, then there's cans round the back.
I wouldn't worry none about desegregatin' 'em. They've been marked
white and colored since God was a boy. You ain't gonna change 'em now.'

I heard Mel say, 'There's nothing like a challenge.'

The driver opened the door and vanished into the falling darkness.

I stood in the aisle, Harlan behind me, Mel behind him. All hesitating.
No one quite knowing why. Then Mel said, 'What gives? We forgotten
how to do it?'

I looked out. If there were toilets, they were round the back where I
couldn't see them, but I didn't need to see them to know what was written on them and that we would burst before they let us in there. They
seemed to me to have come out of nowhere. A dozen pickups had slewed
all around us, we could neither go on nor go back. Then they gathered, a
bunch of rednecks bristling with the self-righteousness of the poor white
man who has nothing going for him but his belief in his superiority to
the black man. They smiled. One guy slowly slapped a baseball bat into
the palm of his hand. I have never understood why violence smiles as it
waits for you. It must be a pleasure. Only conclusion I have ever been able
to reach on it, but one I hardly grasp.

I had to get off the bus ahead of Mel. Whatever happened I did not
want him to be the one to start it, but as I reached the door Harlan Finch
stepped between me and the rail and said, 'I should go first.'

I whispered my answer, 'Harlan, these could be some mean customers.
Let me go first. I speak their language.'

'Time they learnt mine,' Harlan said and stepped off the bus. Crossed
the ground between us and the mob in a few long strides and despite
what he had said to me stopped at a regulation passive-resistant, non-
provocative distance, avoiding excessive eye contact, letting his body
language, a term we knew not, say as much as it could about him being
non-confrontational. He believed in that. I believed in that, all of it. I'd
bought the whole package.

'Gentlemen,' was his first word in that corny Kennedy-esque accent
of his. He never got out a second. One baseball-hatted bubba looked at

the next, grinned like an idiot, said, 'Now, what in hell do we have here? A nigger with a fancy twang in his voice?' He leapt forward, punched Harlan in the face and Harlan went down under a rain of blows. They'd hit him six or seven times before I could get to him. One bubba stood with what I took to be a wooden beer crate raised over Harlan's head when I shoved myself between them.

'Please stop,' I said. 'He means you no harm and he can't hurt you now he's down.'

'If 'n' ere's one thing I hate more 'n a uppitynigger it's got to be a uppitynigger-lover.'

And he brought the crate down hard aiming for my head. I blocked him with a forearm, heard a bone crack in my left hand, and then I hit him with my right. The pathetic triumph of instinct over intellect. A force so visceral and blind, welled up from places of the heart I had never been before, so deep I could not feel the pain of my broken bones or my fist connect with his jaw. The last thing I can remember seeing was the Essolube logo on his cap as I decked him. The last thing I heard as they pounded me into the ground with that damn crate was Mel yelling 'Turner, no!'

And I thought I was there to restrain him.

I woke. A hospital ward. Took me half a minute to remember where I was and why I'd come. Was it the jail ward, bars at the end of the line of beds? I turned my head to see and found I couldn't. I was fixed in some way. Then I realised. My head was bolted to some sort of stabilizer, there was a cast on my left arm and my jaw was wired up. What the fuck? I slept some more.

When I came to again a near-silent doctor stripped the apparatus off my head, muttered something about a hair-line fracture and left me to suck sweet goo through a tube. I could look now—hurt like hell but could just about manage it. Yep—I was pretty sure I was in jail again. It did not yet occur to me to wonder where.

A bluish-skinned black man was pushing a broom three feet wide along the middle of the ward—gathering dust and fluff into a moraine ahead of him. He stopped by me, wheeled the line of dirt my way, leaned in to me.

'You de guy got beat up out on the de highway?'

'Uh-huh.'

'So you're whitey come to set all us niggers free?'

What could I say to that?

'Where you f 'om?'

'Tuxush.'

'Texas! Whassmadder wit you, man? You know what you gonna do? You gonna get us all killt. Texas? Ain't you got niggers o'yo' own you could get killt in Texas 'stead o' comin' to Miss'ssipp?'

He pushed away, broomed out into the corridor and from down the ward I heard Harlan's voice.

'Well, Mr Raines, shall we do that? Shall we liberate Texas next?'

He laughed. I damn near pulled a muscle trying to turn my head and get a look at him. Had to be a jail ward—any civil hospital would have put Harlan in 'Coloreds'. Until he spoke I'd thought I was there alone—alone of all the Freedom Riders.

Oh Althea Harris Burke—did you write the irony into those words yourself? Freedom to get every nigger in Mississippi killed and me along with them?

It must have been the third or fourth day when my fingertips found the scar at the back of my head. A shaved patch the size of a silver dollar, a small, scabby wound, as though it covered a hole. I tried asking what but nobody seemed willing to talk to me.

The day after that I woke to find Mel shaking me gently by the good arm.

'Wake up, wake up, Turner. We have to go now.'

Mel was bruised and plastered with Band-Aids, and accompanied by a uniformed deputy sheriff.

'Go? Go where? Are we on trial?'

I must have sounded like an idiot to Mel, but it seemed logical to me. We'd been busted. We were always going to get busted. We were in jail. We'd be put up in front of the bench, fined God knows what, the gavel would pound and we'd be driven to the edge of town and told to fuck off—or else we'd be bussed to the pen for sixty days. I'd heard it all before.

Mel helped me into my clothes. I caught a glimpse of Harlan dressing a few beds away from me, a bandage wrapping his head like a turban. He was quicker than me, came across and helped Mel thread my unruly legs into trousers. The deputy didn't lift a finger, didn't speak to us until we were in the back of a patrol car speeding out to an airfield.

I watched the streets of Jackson pass by in a blur. I tried the easy questions like where and why, uttered through teeth clenched shut with brass surgical wire.

'We're going home,' Mel said softly, but he wouldn't tell me why. I looked at Harlan, wedged between me and the door. I could see he knew no more than I did.

'Did I miss the trial?' I bleated, and the deputy twisted in his seat and said, 'You got some powerful friends, boy. You jus' got pulled from the fiery furnace of burnin' hell. Don't let it fool you. Y'don't come back now. Y'don't come back to Mississippi. Next time we'll let 'em kill ya.'

They got me up the steps and into a plane. I was walking in the middle of a dream. I fell asleep again, and woke to find we were airborne and my senses somewhat clearer than they had been. I was still seated between Mel and Harlan, the bookends to stop me tumbling back into the dream.

'Mel, what the fuck is going on?'

'You fractured your skull.'

'I know that.'

'And you got a blood clot on the brain. They had to drill through your skull to let it out.'

My fingers found the scar again. I knew now why it felt so neat and round.

'And?'

'And I thought you were dying and I called your old man.'

'You called my father?!'

Harlan chipped in quietly from the other side.

'We had good reason, Turner. You did nearly die.'

'You-called-my-father?' I said emphasizing every word so hard I thought I'd chew through the wire.

'Had to,' Mel replied.

I knew the rest. He didn't need to tell me. The deputy's words rang in my head now with all the sonorous clarity of meaning. Mel had called Sam. Sam had called LBJ, that 'powerful friend', and the Vice-President of the United States had called the sheriff of a one-horse town in Mississippi, told him how much he'd appreciate the charges being dropped against his ole friend Sam Raines's boy and those two guys with him, and he'd found something the bastard wanted and horse-traded our freedom—Johnson was nothing if not the greatest horse-trader in Washington—and with it traded our dignity and our honor.

God, what a mess. What a way to end. I could not forgive Mel for this. I meant to get back on that bus as soon as I was fit, and when we stopped I meant to eat and drink in a desegregated diner and piss in a desegregated can and if I couldn't I'd get arrested and stand trial. Good God, what had he done?

I passed a couple of weeks in hospital in Washington. Sam and Lois phoned. I had enough mental energy to convince them not to fly out. Harlan came and told me he was riding again. Washington to New Orleans that afternoon. Mel came. Surprisingly little to say. Most surprisingly of all, Althea Harris Burke came.

'If you came to say I told you so, get it over with.'

'OK. I told you so.'

'You feel better for that?'

'Whatever. I sure as hell bet I feel better 'n you.'

'Not difficult,' I said. 'Miss Burke, what exactly is it you want?'

'Do I have to want something?'

'You want something. I can see it in your eyes.'

'You have a great way with words, Mr Raines. Maybe I just came because I like you.'

'You don't know me.'

'Maybe I came because I think you might be my kind of guy.'

Good fucking grief, was I blushing?

'Miss Burke. There are things you don't know.'

'Sure. You lived twenty-something years. There's lots I don't know.'

'I mean. Things about the Freedom Ride. You think Mel started that fight in Mississippi that got us all beat up, don't you? It wasn't Mel. I punched the lights out on some pork-bellied redneck. It was me.'

'It was you?'

'Yes. Now—do you still think I might be your kind of guy?'

'No—but you might be my kind of idiot.'

I have never been so coyly or so easily pulled. Ms Harris moved herself in on me. I never did get to finish my Freedom Ride. I never did go back to Mississippi, but truth to tell that was fine by me.

When Mel flung all this in my face in '68 I was not at all surprised. Of course we'd gone in there expecting violence—but we'd also gone in hoping to avoid it. It was that rare thing, a clear-cut black and white situation. White men were beating up on black men. In a world made up of the shifting shades of gray it was about as simple as that, and we'd gone to Mississippi to tackle the forces of night in the firm belief that we could expose and destroy them. Seven years later it seemed a lot different. It seemed to me that in the mind of Amerika we had legitimized the export of the forces of night. The violence of Jackson and Montgomery was now to be found everywhere in Amerika. We had taken on the beast in its lair and turned it loose on the nation. I could not see how this had happened. But a line was crossed—choose your war, choose your line. Mine was August '68 in Chicago. We had internalised the beast—taken a piece of the night into ourselves. The beast dwelt in night and the night was us. The only black and white thing about Chicago was the pig.

§

1969. Early the next morning Lois drove me back to the airport.

'When will you be back?' she asked.

'Not long,' I lied.

And then I made a big mistake. I was in need of clothes. I needed to sort out money. I needed to touch base. So I flew to New York.

There was no sign of Rose. I checked my mail. Stuffed a bag with clean clothes. Called the *Voice.* Some woman told me Rose was spending an extra week in England. I left a note for her. Got myself out on a night flight the same day to Jackson, Mississippi. In and out of New York in less than eight hours. Big mistake.

I left the airport at Jackson looking for a car rental. It wasn't like Kennedy or O'Hare. There were two to choose from, one of which had nothing—'we don't have but six vehicles'—and the other had only a fat gas-guzzling Chrysler in powder blue. A car about as subtle as a giant zit in the middle of your forehead. It was a take it or leave situation. I took it. I could not manage without. Lazarus was fifty miles or more up the Delta. And it was dark. Dark, hot and humid. Mississippi had a way of falling on you like a wet wool blanket. All I wanted now was to shower and to sleep. I drove into Jackson in a car that was all but luminous and found a hotel. I felt better about myself in the morning. I could not feel better about the car. What more could a private detective want than a car that said 'here I am' in blue paint nineteen feet long?

I got to Lazarus late in the morning. It was what I'd thought it would be. The highway ripped right by, the railroad tracks ripped right through. It was one of those small southern towns untouched by money, a backwater where white was likely to be as poor as black, and the divide spelt out by the phrase 'across the tracks' was literal. Lazarus was cut in two— whites on one side, blacks on the other. I drove slowly through the white side of town, curious, blank faces staring at me from the sidewalks, past boarded up shops and patched up wooden houses, to the point where the road humped over the tracks, and I passed into another land, one unimaginably poorer than the one I had just left. Just when you think you've touched bottom, another layer gets peeled away and you realise you've been bobbing well above the line.

The change was instant. Most of the houses weren't even houses. They were trailers with porches and steps tacked on. That ubiquitous symbol of poverty visible on the porch of almost every dwelling—a busted, rusting icebox next to the broken-down couch. I'd been careful not to meet the gaze of any man who'd looked out at me in this powder blue nightmare as I passed through whitetown. In darktown I was twice as cautious. I looked out for traffic—there was none, the only cars were up on blocks at the roadside—and I looked out for the street name Mouse had given me, Raintree Row. Home to Marcellus Gore.

I found it, directly opposite the church. A trailer well-looked after, freshly painted up, the garden planted with squash and corn, a young pecan tree, a white picket fence marking off a neat square. But the church was a showstopper. Four trailers welded together and topped off with a steel spire. I had never seen a trailer with a spire before. I could not help but stare. I parked the Chrysler in front and crossed the street. Considering I hadn't passed a moving car since I crossed the tracks, there seemed to be an awful lot outside the Gore home—everything from pickups to shiny black sedans. Should have told me something. Didn't.

I pushed open the gate and followed a brick path—yellow, was that appropriate?—to the door of the trailer, and knocked.

A tiny, old black woman opened the door. All in black, a dress that reached the floor, a bushy head of white curls.

'Mrs Gore? My name's . . .'

A voice from inside cut me off.

'Hoozat, Gramma?'

And the old lady turned to look back. A lean-looking young black man in a tight, stylish black suit appeared at her shoulder, another man just behind him. The two stepped past her. The one with the pencil line moustache spoke.

'Y'go back inside, Gramma. Momma needs you. We be takin' care o' this.'

All three of us observed a deferential silence as she shuffled back inside. I could hear the clink of china and cutlery, the sound of a woman weeping somewhere. And it finally came to me. The black clothes, all those cars, the out-of-state plates. I'd blundered into a funeral. The Gores gathered to bury one of their number.

I said, 'I'm sorry, I shouldn't have come' and turned to leave, but the young guy had me by the shirt and was yelling, 'What you want, man? What you want?'

'I made a mistake. I'm sorry.'

'Mistake! Mistake?'

Then the guy behind, black suit, lean and fit, no moustache, stopped him and pointed past us to where I'd left the car on the far side of the street.

'Lucius. Look.'

Lucius let go of my shirt and looked. Then he hit me. A poorly aimed right to the side of my head. I rolled with it and made a dash for the gate. I made it to the car before they grabbed me again. The other one punched me in the mouth and I tasted blood. Then they got me to the ground and started kicking. How long does training have to last before you call it an instinct? I rolled into a fetal ball just like I'd been taught for the Freedom Rides all those years ago.

'Motherfuckaah! Motherfuckaah! You got some nerve showin' up here. You killt my brother!'

Lucius pulled me halfway upright, banged my head against the car. He wanted me to hear what he had to say. I found myself looking up into the eyes of a city sophisticate. These two might have started out as po' country boys, for all I knew sharecropper's kids, but some northern city had put a five- or ten-year veneer of sophistication and self-assertion on them. They weren't scared of whitey anymore.

'I didn't kill anyone,' I said through blood and spittle.

'White man in a blue Chrysler chased my little brother on his motorsiccle and ran him into the ground. You killt him same as if you put a gun to his head and shot him. Antony!'

On cue Antony stuck an automatic in Lucius's hand. He put the barrel under my chin and dug it into the flesh.

'Say your prayers, motherfuckah.'

I couldn't. I had said not a prayer since my mother died. There was not a word could have come to me. I could not even close my eyes to avoid looking at the man who was going to blow me away. And I saw a black hand grip Lucius's shoulder. The pink of her fingernails level with my eyes. Saw a black head lean into his. Heard a woman's voice say, 'You gwine be stupid all your life, boy? Put the gun down or you'll fry in the chair, and the rest of us likely as not get burned out an' lynched.'

'It was him. I know it was him. Look at the goddam car for fuck's sake. Look at the goddam car!'

'Give me the gun.'

Lucius strung it out as long as he could. He banged my head against the roof of the car one last time, then he let me go and held out the gun to the woman. She took it in her left hand. He tried to avoid looking at her. A recalcitrant child caught in the peach orchard rather than a grown man restrained from murder.

She said, 'Look at me.'

He looked and she slapped him hard across the face with her right.

'Y'ever say "fuck" to me again I'll hit you twice as bad. Now get home where your momma needs you and start acting like grown men not a couple of punks.'

She yanked me to my feet, thrust me through the open door of the church and slammed it shut behind me. I could still hear her yelling at them through the panels. I moved away, and found myself alone in a place almost unimaginable. It was a low, flat rectangle of a room, the point where the four trailers met making a cross, appropriately in the center of the aisle. The ramshackle exterior had done nothing to prepare me for what I now saw on the inside. Three of the four walls carried a wraparound mural. A version of Da Vinci's Last Supper. That every disciple and the man himself should be black should not have been surprising. It was. But what was more surprising that they were black faces I knew. Christ was Sidney Poitier, and if I'd known the painting or the Bible well enough to tell one disciple from another, I would now be able to say who played James or who played John or Simon-called-Peter in this black triptych on formica and plywood, but all I can say is that Paul Robeson, Martin Luther King, Joe Louis, A. Philip Randolph, Cassius Clay (why do I assume it was painted before he took up Islam?), Louis Armstrong, Medgar Evers, a man I thought might be W.E.B. du Bois, and another I was damn sure was Malcolm X, all figured among the eleven that went to heaven. Judas had a look of Richard Nixon about him but I couldn't be sure. I think all that mattered was that he was white. In fact my first reaction was white. I sat there thinking . . . Am I the first white man ever to see this? What would whitey say? Would he think this a violation? And I knew damn well he would. Because I knew that I, a non-believing, right-thinking white liberal, was wide-eyed about it. Why? For chrissake, why? Did my education tell me Jesus was white, even if it didn't tell me he was Sidney Poitier in *The Lilies of the Field*? Billy didn't. One day after school, when the Bible had been thumped with a vengeance we'd both found muscle-cramp boring he said to me, 'What color do you think Jesus was?' White, I thought, but I said, 'I don't know.' And Billy had said, 'I figure, being from the Middle East, he'd have to be kind of brown, I guess you could say he was tan-colored.' What jump from tan to just colored? The woman who'd just saved my skin dragged me back from this reverie.

'Y'OK?'

I looked up. She was sitting opposite me—row after row of stacking chairs—on the other side of the aisle, both of us a few rows down from the door. A small, beautiful woman, big eyes, wide mouth, I guessed to be about thirty-two or -three or so.

'I'll be fine, thank you. Till I have to go back out there.'

'They gone now. They won't be back.'

I sighed audibly, stared up at the ceiling. Stained, rusting tin sheet without a decorative splash of imaginative paint to it.

'I'm truly sorry about your brother, Miss Gore. But I didn't kill him.'

'He weren't my brother. Marcellus was my nephew. His momma, Messalina an' me, we sisters. I'm Claudia Arquette. An' nobody killt Gus. Gus killt hisself.'

Good God, was I going to arrive at every place too late? Not so much the harbinger of death as the guy with the long-handled broom come to push the mess around one more time.

'How did he die?'

'Gus been killin' hisself slowly for a year or more. Dyin' on the inside from somethin' only he could tell. Last week he took the quick way out.'

'How quick?'

'How quick? How quick can drivin' a motorcycle through a brick wall at a hundred miles an hour get? I'd say quick as lightnin'. Least I hope it was. Took off his head and both arms.'

I leant my head on my palms, elbows on my knees and hoped not to puke. God knows why, I found this a bloodier image than anything Mouse had told me.

'And there weren't no white man in no powder blue Chrysler chasin' him neither. Somebody made that up or put two an' two together an' got five. Gus killt hisself. I know that. Even his Momma know that. Only Lucius and Antony needs a white man in a blue car—and if they seen more of their brother since he got home, 'stead of struttin' their stuff up in Chicago all the time, they'd know Gus got reason aplenty to kill hisself.'

So. She knew. I was surprised. I thought it to be the kind of thing you never told your family. I unbent, stretched a little and rubbed at the swelling on the side of my mouth.

'I'm very sorry to have troubled you on a day like this of all days. There's nothing more to be said. I guess I'll just go now.'

I stood up. She waved me back in my seat, still clutching the gun she'd taken from Gus's brother.

'You ain't goin' nowhere till you tell me what you wanted of Gus.'

'You know. Please don't make me go over it again.'

'Know? What do I know? Boy, you start talkin' or I'll stand in that doorway and scream till Lucius and Antony get back here.'

'I don't get it. You said yourself. He had plenty of reason to kill himself.'

She cocked her head, one eye wide, like a reverse wink, and looked at me like she thought I was stupid.

'I know he had his reasons, 'cause I seen the way he was eaten up inside. But I don't know what they were. He wouldn't talk to nobody. All I know is somethin' happened. Somethin' out there in Vietnam. What I don't know is what.'

There it was, that phrase again—*something happened*. I didn't want to do this. I didn't want to have to tell this woman her nephew was a . . . what? . . . a murderer?

'Please, Miss Arquette. Don't make me do this.'

'Was you in 'Nam with him?'

'No. I never even met Gus.'

'Then how come you know where to find him?'

'He ever mention a sergeant called Mouse?'

She nodded. 'Sure. He loved Mouse. Nearest thing to a father he ever got. Wrote about him in every letter.'

'Mouse and me, we go back a long way.'

'Great. So you and Mouse is buddies. Now quit stallin' an' tell me what you know.'

I told her. I began with that heartbeat flutter that you get when you tell someone things you know can rip their little world to shreds. It soon dawned on me that I wasn't ripping her world to shreds. She was nodding, slowly, as if confirming what I was saying with her own assumptions. There were no tears, no wails. A calm I could not share seemed to surround her like river mist. And when I had finished, she sat, eyes down at the raggy carpet floor, legs crossed, one foot swinging almost carelessly, the gun held loosely in her hand. She had no questions. What I thought was a question turned out to be a statement.

'So Marcellus trained as a soldier, went to 'Nam and shot niggers? Well, I guess I knew that. Might have denied it in my time, but I knew it. But now you sayin' he killt niggers in a big way, a bigger way than we thought he would? New ways to kill niggers. Bigger ways. Ways we can't imagine.'

I wasn't about to use the N-word back to her. I just said no.

'Well, what else would you call it. Uncle Sam calls him up, sticks a rifle in his hand, trains him to use it, sends him t' th' other side of the world and then tells him to kill. And Vietnam bein' full o' colored he kills colored. Kills all the colored he can. Sounds to me like the white man got this down to a science. Gettin' colored to kill colored. You heard o' George Wallace? Don't answer that. Course you have, everybody heard o' George Wallace. Alabama's own bantam rooster of a governor. A few years back he was sayin' he didn't give a cuss what was bein' said about him by any leader of any new African country, 'cause "the average African don't know where Africa is let alone where Alabam' is." Well I bought myself an atlas an' a 'cyclopedia and I found out about Africa, an' Asia and you know what? I found out that most of the world is colored. Most folks on earth ain't white, they's colored. Abyssinia, India, China, Vietnam—they's all colored. An' I'll be damned if the sweetest trick whitey ever thought up in these United States of America ain't to round up our niggers and send 'em all to other countries to kill their niggers. Hell, at this rate there soon be no niggers left! Now . . . don't tell me that ain't the way it is. Don't tell me. Or I won't send for Lucius and Antony. I'll shoot you myself.'

She never raised her voice throughout that entire speech, but by the time she finished I had never felt so frightened of a woman in my life. She was head and shoulders shorter than me, but the power she packed into every syllable battered me harder than Lucius' fists. I felt as though she'd picked me up and splattered me across the floor.

'It wasn't his fault.'

'Don't apologise for him. You don't have that knowledge. Dammit, you don't have that right.'

The woman was exhausting me. I felt like I was bleating more than talking.

'What are you going to do now?'

'Do? What I gots to do that's what. I gotta tell Messalina soon as the boys go back north. Hell, woman's son kills hisself, don't you think she got a right to know why?'

I could think of half a dozen reasons not to tell a woman. I could think of a dozen lies to tell. I'd tell myself I was sparing her feelings. But Claudia Arquette didn't seem to see it that way. At least she hadn't insisted I be the one to tell Gus's mother. She leaned in close to me, her face inches from mine. Her voice a mezzo whisper.

'An' what are *you* goin' to do now?'

This was not a question I'd anticipated. She had not asked me why I had been looking for Gus. She had not even asked me my name.

'I don't know,' I lied.

'You must have had a reason to want to talk to Gus. You one o' them reporters?'

Ah, the easy option. Not to have to mention Mel. Not to have to explain the vague if not spurious nature of my occupation.

'Yes,' I lied.

'An' you was goin' ter come here, knock at my sister's front door and ask Marcellus how come he killt . . . goddam, how many did you say it was now?'

'A hundred and thirty-four.'

'A hundred an' thirty-four, a hundred an' thirty-four ole men, women an' kids. You was just gonna knock on the door and say, "Howdy, Gus, you don't know me but I hear you killt hundred an' thirty-four Vietnamese"?'

What had I been going to do? Had I even thought it through? I had walked up to a shanty house in shantytown, a lone white idiot, knocked on the man's front door, knowing what I knew, ready to say what for fuck's sake? What daydream of decency had led me to think I could cross the tracks in any other sense but the physical, cocooned in my rental, windshielded off from the world? What had my old man said, 'We never done nothin' to them'? And I had replied, 'But what have we done for them?' And this, this paying of my dues, those years in the Movement, they bought me rights, bought me immunity? Good God, was I crazy too?

I was floundering. What was the point in stumbling around for the answer. It wasn't blowing in the wind.

'I don't know,' I said.

'You don't know. But you a re-porter, ain't you?'

'Yes,' I lied.

'So sooner or later it will all come out? Everythin'?'

Head up now, back straight, her hands spread wide on the everythin'. I fumbled.

'It could. I mean. Most of it will. No. I'm sure it will. I'm sorry.'

'Don't be. Let it out. Let it bleed. It's a massacre. Who could ever expect somethin' like that to stay secret?'

It seemed to me to be the direct echo of words I had said to Mouse only a couple of days before. I had meant every word of them. Why did I find it so hard to believe that Claudia Arquette meant every word? Why should I have found rage and denial more acceptable than what I now faced? Why? Because I kidded myself I was a former journalist, a working private eye, that, the little guy's death notwithstanding, I was an impartial seeker of the truth and I would not believe in my own agenda except to be forced to recognize it in the distorting mirror of her own. I had stepped into a foreign country when I crossed the tracks, I'd known that. Claudia Arquette was the foreigner, that much ought to have been logical. What wasn't was the sense of a conspiracy between us. A massacre shared. A bloody, messy secret that we would race one another to lance like a swollen boil.

She led me outside. There was the merest breeze to wrap itself around me. Sitting in a tin hut at the end of July had not been much different from taking a Turkish bath. I emerged soaked in my own sweat, my hair plastered to my scalp, my shirt clinging to my chest. Claudia Arquette looked cool in her black, sleeveless dress, cool in the face of multiple murder. I had never met someone so seemingly calm and angry at the same time. Unless, of course, it was Althea Harris Burke. But, then, I hadn't seen Althea in six years.

'Y'know,' Claudia said to me. 'Gus was like a diver come up too fast. He got a bad case of the bends. We weren't expectin' him. He just turned up one day last year sayin' how he'd been discharged. Messalina wasn't even suspicious. She'd gotten her boy back. And that was all that mattered to her. But when Gus started acting crazy I took a look at his papers, expecting the worst—like a medically unfit or a dishonorable. I was wrong. They said "honorable discharge."'

'They would,' I said.

'After what you done told me in there ... why?'

My rental was where I'd left it. Both side windows and the rear windshield smashed. I swept the glass shards from the driver's seat. Claudia Arquette said, 'That'll cost you.' This whole trip would cost me. I'd known that from the day Nate Truegood had me pulled into the 5th to tell me Mel was dead.

'Don't come back,' were the last words Miss Arquette spoke to me.

§

I slipped the shift into drive and headed for the tracks, felt the suspension jolt as I crossed the line. A couple of blocks on I looked in the rear-view mirror to see if I was being followed. I was, but not by the Gore Brothers. These guys were white. Two white guys in suits.

Another, large tan car, same model as the one before. And if I had not been tired and stupid that fact might have told me something. Was a long time before it did. Only thing I managed to figure out was that I probably had lost them in Chicago, and that they'd found me again in New York, and had someone pick me up as I got into Jackson. Whoever they were. I'd not seen a sign of them around the Gore house, but then I hadn't been looking. But maybe two white guys in suits had thought better of something I'd no choice about—maybe they hadn't crossed the tracks. Maybe they just sat at the frontier and waited for me to re-emerge from a foreign country.

I drove back to the hotel. They were trying to be subtle about it, a car, sometimes two, between us, but it was definitely the same model of car I'd seen in Chicago, only now with Mississippi plates. Did they think I was stupid or something? I was.

There was no reason to stick around Jackson. I could just check out, but with the suits out front watching it required a little ingenuity. Up in my room I put on my spare clothes, three shirts, two pairs of Levi's, stuffed clean socks and underwear into my pockets. I'd seen this in an old Marx Brothers movie. How to skip out of a hotel without paying—wear everything and abandon your suitcase. I had every intention of paying, but I couldn't be seen carrying a case of any kind.

I waddled to the front desk, pockets bulging, feeling I must look like a New York street bum, swathed in everything he owned, suffering stinking heat some of the time in preference to the threat of cold anytime. I checked out, paid in cash and asked if I could leave my bag with them. No problem. The guy hefted it over, stuffed full of hotel towels to give it the right feel, and thought little of it.

'I'll be back,' I lied.

I made it to the car sweating like a pig and hoping for two things—that they'd neither of them seen Harpo's performance in *Room Service*, and that they'd stay together and follow me rather than split up.

I drove into downtown Jackson, cruised around with them sitting close behind, until I found what I was looking for—a department store with three or four entrances. I parked out front, left the keys in the ignition. If they got out and looked they might well think I was careless, but they might also conclude I was coming back and think better of the over-exposure of following me in on foot.

I didn't look back. I walked quickly through cosmetics and women's clothing, straight out the back and hailed a cab.

'Where to?'

'You know a used car lot?'

'If I know one I know ten. Which one you want?'

'Pick one a couple of miles out of town.'

The driver looked puzzled by this, twisted his lip and made a face, but did what I asked. I kept looking through the rear window, and I saw no one following. I could imagine the scenario. They'd sit there for maybe ten or twenty minutes, then one of them would case the store, while the other watched the car, then they'd give up and drive back to the hotel. If they were smart they'd ask immediately if I'd checked out, if they were dumb they'd do it only around midnight when it was pretty well obvious I wasn't coming back.

About fifteen minutes later the cab pulled up in front of a set of chain-link gates, behind which a German shepherd jumped and barked. The driver got out and yelled.

'Orvis! Brung yew a customer.'

I saw Orvis emerge from a portahut. A fat, grubby, unshaven old white guy in baggy pants and an undershirt.

'That you, Chester?'

Chester didn't answer the man. He looked at me and said, 'I gots to go now.'

I got the hint and tipped him a sawbuck for his trouble.

Orvis yanked on the dog's chain and pulled the gate open just enough for me to squeeze through. He gave me the once-over.

'Son, you a mite overdressed for the weather. Fact, you drippin' like a lathered up horse.'

But this time I was out of lies. I just shrugged and followed. Orvis shuffled a few paces, stopped and looked me over again.'

'Y'ain't sick, are you?'

'No, I'm fine. Just a little warm.'

He shuffled on muttering, 'Three shirts in summer. My, my. Still. S'a free country. Now, what kind o' car you lookin' fer?'

I looked at the towering piles of wrecks, stack upon stack as far as the eye could see, all rust and shattered glass. Wondered if he actually had a car that ran.

'Cheap would be good,' I said.

Paying bills in cash was a good way to avoid being traced, but it ran through folding money too quick for me to get profligate.

Orvis scratched his balls.

'Cheap. Ev'body wants cheap.' Another good scratch. 'But y'can have cheap if you don't mind old.'

'How old?'

'Nineteen hunnerd and fo'ty nine.'

'Just so long as it goes.'

He led off behind another stack of Detroit rust.

'Oh she goes right enough.'

And he pointed at a '49 Buick Roadmaster. A black-bodied, white-wheeled, twenty-year-old classic convertible.

'Sit in. Fire 'er up.'

I sat in the driver's seat. The springs were OK. Just as well I'd no idea how far I might be going next. I turned the engine over. A few farts and grunts at startup, but then a fairly satisfying engine turn-over once it came to life.

'How much?'

'Hundred.'

'How much for cash?'

'I don't deal no other way but cash.'

I talked him down to eighty-five.

Back in his portahut he took the money and said, 'Ain't no radio o' course.'

And I was curious to know where this was leading.

'But I got one o' them eight-track gadgets. I could let you have it for twenty. Came out of one of the wrecks. Some kid got killt out on the highway. I could fit it in a couple of minutes. Hell, I'll even throw in the tapes the kid left in the car.'

I bought it. Like I said, I'd no idea how far I was going. Soon found out. I gave him the twenty and an extra ten. Said I had a couple of phone calls I had to make, and he left me to it.

I stripped off a couple of layers, breathed in the reek of my own sweat and called the rental company out at the airport. Told them where they could pick up the powder blue nightmare.

The guy said, 'We charge for pickups.'

I said, 'You have my card number, bill me.'

'We will,' he said.

I didn't tell him about the windows and the rear screen. It'd all show up on my American Express bill I'd no doubt. Then I made the call that really mattered.

'Mouse?'

'Johnnie? Where are you, man?'

'Mississippi. Look, I don't have much time. You said you were in touch with another of the Nine. I need to know who.'

'What? Why? You were going to talk to Gus.'

What was the point in mincing words? Hit the man.

'Gus is dead.'

The line went quiet. I let Mouse work his way through it, listening to his breathing. Then he said 'How?', soft and tearful, and I told him.

At last he said, 'Why not stop now, Johnnie?'

'Can't do that, Mouse. Wish I could, but I can't.'

'So what you want?'

'An address. You said you heard from one of the others from time to time.'

'That would be Notley. I don't have an address for Notley.'

'I thought you knew where he was?'

'Rumor man. That's all I hear—rumors.'

'So what is the rumor?'

'Moondog.'

Moondog? This was not good news. I'd heard of the Moondogs. I'd even come within six feet of them. They were a bunch of out-of-it acid crazies from Arizona—'We are the people our parents warned us against'. They spent most of their time holed up in a ghost town they'd reclaimed in the Chiricahua mountains, over to Mexico way. Every so often they emerged on what they called 'mind-expanding gung-fu forays into the streets of straight'. That's where I'd come across them. Some of those streets of straight had been in Chicago. Rubin and his Yippies had shown up with the pig they'd christened Pigasus, and were hell bent on nominating him for president. How do you top that? No problem for a Moondog. You show up—all thirty of you—bare-ass nekkid, with Commanche headdresses and warpaint, igniting your farts with cigarette lighters and just daring anyone else to outcrazy you. The cops didn't even bother to lock 'em up. They bundled them all into a school bus, drove to a thrift store, fitted them out in cast-offs and dumped them over the state line into Indiana. The way I heard it, the cops told 'em they'd shoot on sight if they ever set foot in Chicago again. But—I had to be sure.

'You mean Notley's joined the Moondogs? Is that what you've heard?'

'No, man. What I've heard is Notley *is* Moondog.'

Oh shit.

§

I headed south, decided to cross the river at Natchez. There were closer bridges, but I figured however good the head start it would pay to avoid the obvious. I was a few miles into Louisiana, before I got bored enough with road to want to look at what I'd bought. I had a thousand-mile drive ahead of me to Arizona. What crap had a dead teenager willed me to pass the time? I flipped open the glove compartment.

Buffalo Springfield.

Streetfightin' stuff. Could I bear to listen to Stephen Stills singing 'For What It's Worth'?

Bob Dylan's second album, *Freewheelin'*.

Nostalgic stuff. Always liked the album.

Big Brother and the Holding Company, *Cheap Thrills*.

Loud stuff.

The Velvet Underground and Nico.

Decadent stuff. Waitin' for my man.

Simon and Garfunkel's *Bookends*.

Who was I to be different?

Two Sly Stone albums, including the new one, *Stand*.

So far, so good.

The Mothers of Invention, *We're Only In It For The Money*.

An acquired taste. OK. Maybe I could acquire it.

Rotary Connection. Who? Never heard of 'em.

Another Dylan, *John Wesley Harding*.

Lyrically baffling to the point where I had begun to wonder if the songs meant anything, but, all the same, compelling stuff.

Janis Ian, *For All The Seasons Of Your Mind*.

Pay Dirt. I loved Janis Ian. Maybe it wouldn't be such a bad trip after all. The kid had taste and he'd left me over twenty tapes, worth more than the player. God knows, they might even have been worth more than the car. I stuck *Buffalo Springfield* in the slot and settled down to cruise. I'd done this so often, but it had never felt like this before. I was beginning to feel dogged by death. I was beginning to feel like the angel of death. The body count was mounting. Mouse had a point. Why not stop now? The more blacktop slipped between the wheels, the further I was from Mississippi, the better I felt. Not happier, just better. I'd been right all along. Never should have gone back—but here I was heading back to Arizona. It was years since I'd been in Arizona. Nineteen years. Nineteen years since Billy upped and left.

I crossed into Texas in darkness. I'd driven all evening—the breadth of Louisiana. Over six hours—I dared not push the engine on that gas-guzzling monster, but I'd seen no sign of a tail in the rear-view, so a few miles over the Texas line, just outside of Jasper, I pulled off the road at the first cheap motel, checked in, and wished for dreamless sleep. Don't know why I felt I could sleep in Texas, why I would be safer than in Louisiana. Is the homing instinct vestigial even in the most lost of lost boys?

§

I'd not been on the road more than a couple of hours the next morning, 'Hot Fun in the Summertime' blasting out on the eight-track, when, I caught sight of a motorcycle cop in the rear-view. In those days—what? three or four years before the first oil crisis—you could drive across Texas with your foot on the floor. I wasn't. I didn't think the old car could hold up going much more than fifty-five, and I doubted I'd been doing much more than forty-five, though I was certainly burning a little oil. But the cop put on his siren, overtook me all the same and pulled up his Harley

Electra Glide thirty feet in front of me. I flicked off Sly Stone and sat tight. He strode towards me, sunlight glinting off mirrored sunglasses, like the cop who stops Janet Leigh in *Psycho*, one hand conveniently on his hip, close to what was certain to be a butt-side holster. It has always been my instinct to get out and stand. It seems like bad manners to stay put, but that's what they want, and they have ever been prone to misinterpret the move, especially if a man my size stands up in front of a shorter cop.

He leaned over the door. Looked at me.

'Git out,' he said.

I git. Waited for the run-through of the clichés. 'Assume the position.' 'Spread 'em.' Billy-club in the kidneys. 'We know how to handle hippies in Texas, boy.' Never happened. He left me standing, walked round the car, and came back to me by the open door.

'Mind if I sit in the driver's seat?'

'Sure.' I waited to see what this guy's game was. Was he going to go through the glove compartment hoping to turn up a lid of dope? Was he getting ready to plant a lid of dope?

'Your car?' he asked.

'Yeah. I got the papers right . . .'

He waved the idea away.

'Y'know. First car I ever owned was a '49 Buick Roadmaster. Last year in high school, 1956. Year Elvis went big. Boy this sure brings back memories. Riding along with the top down and 'Heartbreak Hotel' on the radio. Goin' t'the drive-in. Makin' out on the back seat. Hot damn, makes me feel like a teenager again. Y'don't have any Elvis for th' eight-track, do ya?'

I could scarcely believe it. He'd pulled me over for the nostalgia trip. I realized—Mississippi plates, my accent—he couldn't see me as I saw me at all. I'd never been quite so glad that I'd got that haircut before I set out for Chicago. I didn't look like a hippie, I looked like a . . . civilian. I wasn't a big city New Yorker, I was just another reb. Thank God for that. As every Southern cop knows, all New Yorkers are Comm'nists and the only reason a New Yorker would be driving across Texas would be for purposes of subversion.

'No. I'm sorry. I don't.'

'Weeeell—y' cain't have everythin'.'

'You want to try her out?'

'You mean that?'

'Sure.'

'How d'you know I'll bring her back?'

'Then I'll just keep your Harley.'

He roared with laughter, turned the key and pulled away faster than I would have dared, leaving me in a cloud of dust, the most reluctant and bewildered ambassador the Yippies ever sent South. He was back in less than ten minutes. Clapped me on the back, wished me well and said if anyone tried to give me ticket while I was still in the county I was just to tell 'em to call Ray Bigsby at Huntsville and things would be 'taken care of'. Don't you just love Texas?

§

I skirted Austin, cut a route through the Hill Country, aiming to pick up the interstate west of Fredericksburg. I ran through the tapes, played the ones I'd liked almost to death—*Buffalo Springfield* depressed the hell out of me, that damn song had turned into my generation's obituary—flirted with the new stuff—Rotary Connection turned out to be a psychedelic mess, but I kept reversing the tape and replaying just to hear Minnie Riperton hit the highs, wondering how a human being could produce such a sound—and had one untried album left. Simon and Garfunkel had always been a little too folksy for me. They left me craving electric guitars and a little bamalama bamaloo—they gave me parsley, sage, rosemary and thyme, when what I really wanted was liver and onions and a root beer. What the heck, I stuck *Bookends* into the eight-track. Big mistake, and by the time I realized it I could not turn off the memory it tapped. 'America'—not a song I'd heard before—two kids on the road hitchhiking their way out of New York. Can't remember where they were headed but it took the boy four days to get to New York from Saginaw—must have been doing something wrong—and then they stand on the New Jersey Turnpike, counting the cars, all come to look for America. Well, after a fashion I'd done that myself.

1961. While I lay in hospital in Washington, Bobby Kennedy asked representatives of SNCC to meet with him. Mel went, as one of our $10 a week legal eagles. Like might speak unto like. And Althea went too—I assumed as one of our leading theoreticians on non-violence her presence and argument were meant to reassure the little man. No way.

I heard about it from Mel. Kennedy made it plain that he and his brother considered the Freedom Rides to be a pain. They were doing all they could, and what we were doing wasn't helping—it was, inevitably, furthering the violence. This went down well with nobody. But it had to be Althea who flung the man's record in his face. Mel sat at my bedside almost choking on giggles as he told me how she'd rounded on him with 'Joe McCarthy's been dead more'n three years. How come you still got your head up his ass?'

It had, by his own admission, been Mel—a man I had spent most of my adult life restraining—who got between Kennedy ('the man yaps like a terrier') and Althea ('Turner, I'll swear her biceps are bigger than his') and steered the meeting back to the issues. The upshot of this was that we horse-traded. We'd switch our efforts to voter registration. In return we, an organization habitually broke, got tax-exempt status. We'd moved, said Mel, into the next phase.

'It's what we came to do,' I said. 'To get people registered and voting.'

'I know,' he said flatly.

As ever, he and Althea passed at the bedside, he leaving, she arriving, like two wooden figures in a German weatherhouse, as though they could not inhabit the same space at the same time.

Her version was the same as Mel's. And at the end of it, she added, 'Your li'l buddy is not a happy man.'

'It's what we joined to do,' I said again.

'T'ain't what will be done, it's what has been done. That is one troubled little white man.'

I suppose the blow to the head had fogged me. I certainly found I had double vision that came and went, and print could swim on the page like characters dancing in *Fantasia*. But it had fogged my judgment too. I had picked up on none of what she was pointing out to me. Maybe that's the effect of self-pity—you see only yourself?

About ten days later they discharged me. I found Mel and Althea outside, each with a cab waiting.

'Let's all go in one,' I said.

They looked at each other, a little like two women who've turned up at the party in identical dresses. Then Mel stuck his hand in his pocket, paid off his driver, and I found myself book-ended between the two of them in the back of a cramped cab.

At that time Mel and I shared a large apartment in Adams-Morgan. Two flights up. Mel lugged my stuff up the stairs. Althea extended an arm to me. An affectionate, if ludicrous gesture. Strong as she was I was head and shoulders taller and twice her weight. If I fell she'd never be able to hold me. As things turned out that became the metaphor. I fell, and I could not hold her. Mel made coffee, she strolled around, poking her nose into everything and at last said, 'You boys seem to be set up very nicely.' The meaning was not wasted on Mel. That night after she'd gone he said, 'Woman means to have you.'

'I know,' I said.

'You going to let her?'

'I can't figure out a way to stop her.'

'Is she what you want?'

Mel and I had told each other everything from about three weeks after we met at Georgetown. There wasn't a girlfriend I'd had in all that time that he hadn't met and expressed an opinion on and vice versa. I'd even been there when he'd lost his virginity. He wasn't for mine—that had happened when I was fifteen back in Texas. Mel was a late beginner, a virgin at twenty, and, truth to tell, not a hit with women. Whatever Althea Burke's intentions towards me, he would have his say. That was the way it had always been. House rules.

I answered honestly, 'Hell, I don't know. Everything's a blur. Last thing I remember is stepping off that bus in Mississippi . . . then wham . . . here I am.'

Did he wince at my mention of Mississippi? Did I imagine that tiny physical recoil from the memory I had prompted in him?

'Could be you need someone around.'

'What?'

'Maybe it'll all take longer than you think. You nearly died. Maybe getting back together is longer than they're all saying. Maybe somebody should be here.'

'Are you telling me to move this woman in?'

'No,' and he paused, for a second or two would not look me in the eye. 'No, I'm telling you I'm leaving.'

He woke me the next morning. I'd slept fitfully. He'd banged around all night, doing God knows what. He stuck a cup of strong black coffee in my hand, threw the cat on the bed.

'I'm packed. And all my stuff is in the large closet in the corridor. You can let the room if you want. Take care of Liberace.'

No—I did not know the piano player. Liberace was the cat's name. 'When will you be back?'

'I don't know.'

'Where are you going?'

'California, Mexico . . .'

'Why now? The Movement needs us more than ever. After what you told me yesterday it sounds to me like we're going to be at the heart of things.'

'We are. Or you are. It's what you wanted to do. But, I can't do it.'

'Is it money?' He shook his head. 'Is it Althea?'

'Hell no. The woman's battery acid on legs, but she may be what's good for you. You want her, you have her.'

I stopped arguing. He was not simply leaving, he was running away. Running away not from what had happened to him, but from what had happened to me. I could articulate it but I couldn't understand it.

He hoisted his backpack, kissed me on the top of the head, picked up his portable typewriter, and told me he'd be seeing me.

Later that day a banging on the door shook me out of a daydream and I opened up to see Althea, backpack strapped on, typewriter in hand. I had swapped a short, dark man with backpack and typewriter for a shorter, darker woman with backpack and typewriter. And I knew that the two of them had cooked this up between them. Somewhere in the natural hostility that served as communication they had found time and space to truss me up. I could have shut the door in her face then and there. I didn't. I fell. I fell and I could not hold her.

I made love to a woman well out of focus. Altheas swirled about me—two, now three, all grinning at me. I had to assume they were all happy Altheas. She clung to me so hard the muscles in my arms ached, she straddled me so hard I thought I'd break a rib before she was through.

I woke to find her looking me, big orb eyes like Dinah Washington, in that little face. One hand tracing patterns on my chest, the nail scoring a fine red line in my skin.

'Mr Raines.'

'Miss Burke.'

'You can call me Althea.'

'Althea.'

I rolled the word around a while. It was the first time I had called her by her Christian name.

'Althea. I know nothing about you.'

'What would you like to know?'

'Well . . . what do you do?'

'Do? I'm a student at Howard.'

Howard was the all-Black university in Washington.

'Aha. And what do you study?'

'Divinity.'

'Jesus!'

'That's the feller.'

In this fashion I pieced together a biography of the lover who had moved in on me. The conversations we might have had over coffee, after a movie, we had stark naked as she padded about the apartment looking into everything again, looking for a space to rest her typewriter.

She settled on Mel's room. Blew the dust off his desk and set her Olivetti down.

'You weren't really going to let the room, were you?'

Of course I wasn't. I was still expecting Mel to be back in a week or a month. Or more. In the meantime I found I had set up home with a twenty-two-year-old grad student, orphaned at twelve, native of Little Rock, who had been politicised in her last year in high school when Ike sent in the troops in an effort to stop open warfare between the state and its desegregationists.

'Had to be a better way,' she told me. 'That's when I learnt about civil disobedience and non-violence.'

And so for a while, a long while, well over a year, we lived. Exchanging snippets of our narratives. Althea moved in her books, box upon box, ancient Bible commentaries, tattered old hardbacks of Thoreau, *Walden, A Week on the Concord and Merrimack Rivers*, the paperbacked works of the latest thinkers, Sartre, *On Being and Nothingness*, Cruden's *Concordance* forever propped open on the desk. I went back to my work, turning over obscure state laws from the 1870s looking for cause to drag Alabama or Mississippi governments into their own courts, occasionally venturing out, into Georgia, down to Albany to campaign and to picket, to run the gauntlet of spit, abuse and billy clubs. Never, but never, to Mississippi—and no one ever suggested that I should. My head healed and my heart overflowed.

In the fall, the October of 1962, things changed forever. After Cuba the world was not the same place and Althea was not the same woman.

We were watching the Khrushchev–Kennedy stand-off on TV, just like Mostoftherestofamerica. It had reached the point, the only such I can honestly remember in my lifetime, when it seemed the world might just vanish in a nuclear puff. Those of the Restofamerica that had dug shelters took to them to spend nine days living off canned food, burning up flashlight batteries and pissing in chemical latrines—some that hadn't wept aloud, strangers spoke to each other in bars and diners for no better reason than that they were all damned together, and in Mississippi as the apocalypse dawned men prepared to die equal but separate and go to individual hells in individual hues—but mostly we watched TV. Dying as we had lived, in thrall to the tube.

A few minutes after yet another of JFK's addresses to the nation the phone rang. Althea picked it up.

'I think it's your old man.'

'Dad?'

'Johnnie, this is your daddy speakin'.'

I knew he was drunk. Drunk and miserable and pathetic. There was always that side to his character, the sublime sentimentality of a man who doesn't drink often enough to be an habitual, happy drunk. What better reason to get sentimental than the imminent apocalypse?

'Son, I think we should all be together at a time like this. Come on home.'

I had a court case in Atlanta less than ten days away.

'Dad, I can't just drop everything . . .'

'Son, drop everythin' afore everythin' drops on us! I'd like all my boys around me. C'mon home.'

'You've got Huey, Dad.'

'And I want you. I want all my boys here. You, Huey, Billy. All my boys. A family should be t'gether at the end of the world.'

He hadn't mentioned Billy by name in over ten years. Either he was more drunk than I had ever seen him or he really did think the world was about to end.

'Dad, is Lois there?'

Lois came on the line.

'You know. It would be good if you came. You and your young lady.'

'Even if the world doesn't end?'

'Especially if the world doesn't end.'

I stalled, got Atlanta out of the way and put it to Althea.

'Meet the folks, huh? What do you think they'll have to say about me?'

'They know about you.'

'It's one thing you tellin' 'em you're shacked up with a nigger. Another to meet miscegenation face to face.'

'My father never called anyone "nigger" in his life. And he'd probably think Miss Egenation was your name.'

'You telling me he's pleased about it? Wasn't him invited us as I recall. It was your stepmother.'

'Then come and meet her. She's great.'

'Do I press you to meet my family?'

'You have no family. You lost your family.'

'No—they lost me. And I don't see any reason to get mixed up with another.'

All the same, we got on the plane to Lubbock.

It seems to me that I have fewer recollections of Althea's reactions that first day than I do of my father's. He was overjoyed to see me. That was obvious. He'd driven out to the airport with Lois—a task he usually left her to do alone. He was still caught up in that 'we-ain't-dead-after-all' euphoria that gripped America, and for all I know the rest of the world as well, for days after the crisis. Althea was, more than a little, bog-eyed at everything she saw. Sam insisted on the tour, the whole shebang, with narrative, from Great-Granddaddy's log cabin—the wood stove tarnished now there was no adolescent to be set to polish it (Huey was not yet adolescent and rich kids don't polish stoves)—to the cotton fields—old, back home and so on—to the range, where buffalo had not roamed in my lifetime but where the old man's herd of longhorns placidly grazed with no thought of roaming, to the endless skyline of derricks that spelled out Raines wealth to the world. Cotton, oil and cattle—a world bound in leather and smelling of grease. Occasionally I got backslapped or one of those soft punches to the shoulder that carried the unspoken line that all this oil, all these cottonfields, all these Texas longhorns would one day be mine. Whereas yesterday they'd been set to be dust and ashes or Comm'nist, dead or red. Sam could say a lot with a punch.

We got through dinner. Beef, predictably. Althea ate about two ounces, predictably. My father, predictably, got sentimentally drunk and steered to an early bed by his wife. When Lois got back I said it had been a long day and that maybe Althea and I would just turn in too.

'Sure,' said Lois. 'You're in your old room. Miss Burke's in the end suite.'

I looked at Althea, Althea looked at me. Twenty-four years old and I'd never brought a girl home before. I'd not expected anything. I'd just assumed.

'Only kidding,' Lois said.

We settled into bed. Sheets pulled up, looking out across the plains through one of the great glass walls that wrapped around the house. Sex seemed impossible. I never had had sex in my father's house, and Althea seemed to understand this. For a while it seemed as though neither of us had anything to say. Two pretend virgins taking in the night landscape and the big sky.

Then she said, 'Your daddy's rich.'

'And my momma's good-lookin'.'

She giggled.

'Hush little baby, don't you . . .'

'I meant rich beyond.'

'Oh he's rich beyond my dreams or your dreams, and way beyond Lois's. She married him when he was flat broke. But he's not rich beyond his own dreams.'

'I never thought of you as a rich kid.'

'You knew I had money.'

'Sure . . . but you know . . . not a rich kid.'

'I didn't grow up with money. I wasn't raised a rich kid. I was almost growed before Sam hit it rich.'

'You almost growed, white boy?'

'Nope. I *just* growed.'

'Well, tank de lawd for that.'

And she exploded in peals of laughter.

We got through the second day. To my amazement Althea rode, and rode better than I did. We spent a long afternoon on the range. Me and Sam way ahead, because he set the pace and didn't seem much to care if he jolted me to pieces in the process, Lois, Althea and Huey trailing behind. I listened to his dreams, his new dreams, over here he was going to build a whatsit, over there a thingumajig, both of which would speed up something on the God-knows-what. He didn't ask me any questions. Not one. Now, he had never been much curious about my life back East but he'd usually rattle through a few of the formalities—he'd always asked about Mel, but could never remember his name, always 'that little feller'. It was as though he thought any question, anything at all to do with the life I led away from home, was to risk opening a can of worms. So I listened to him instead. And when the five of us met up again it seemed to me he wasn't looking Althea in the eyes. I say seemed. I mean seemed. I cannot be sure at all.

We almost got through dinner. We were past dessert and but a move away from hard booze.

I wasn't paying attention. Lois had put Huey to bed and was back and forth between the kitchen and the dining room. I followed. I gave scant notice to whatever it was Sam had decided to chew the fat about with Althea. Body language, like I said not a phrase we knew then, should have told me. He was stabbing the table with the tip of one finger—the 'fuck-you' digit rapping down. All I caught was the tail end of whatever. A phrase to stop me in my tracks.

'What is it with you people?'

'We people?' Althea said, big eyes popping.

'Yes. You people. I don't get it. What is it with you people?' I stuck my foot in the door.

'What people would that be exactly, Dad?'

Sam turned in his chair, clearly unaware that I'd heard any of what had been said.

'You. You two. The both of you.'

'Us?' I said with no real idea what he'd say next but fearing the worst.

'Dammit, son, you can say I've had too much to drink and that my brain's addled—but the only word I can think of is "pinkos".'

'Oh, we be pink alrighty,' said Althea in her corniest stepinfetchit. Then she slapped the table with the palms of her hands and hooted with laughter.

'Lawd, Lawdy Mass'Raines, we is pink!'

Sam went from pink to red. The poor bastard was blushing. I could not share the joke nor the laughter. It would have been so unlike my father to have 'you peopled' anyone just because they were black. We'd heard too many dumb Texan politicians do that. But I was amazed to hear the phrase on his lips even out of its habitual context. I found myself wondering whether Althea's was the laughter of relief or a poke in the eye for the old man.

'What were you talking about?'

'Cuba,' Sam said. 'What else is there to talk about?'

I felt the knot in me unwind a little. We'd stepped back from the brink to argue about brinkmanship. Had to be an improvement.

'Your Daddy was just reminding me that Cuba is only two hundred miles from Florida.'

'Actually,' I said, 'it's only ninety.'

Sam just nodded.

I took my seat and decided to pitch in. To argue was better than letting the situation slide.

'Dad? How close do you think Turkey is to Russia?'

Sam looked perplexed. I realized he didn't really know where Turkey was at all.

'What's Turkey got to do with anything?'

'It's closer than ninety miles. It has a common border with Russia.'

'So?'

'We have missiles stationed there. Far more than they ever got on to Cuba.'

'And that makes what Khrushchev did right?'

'No. It just makes it even.'

'Even? This is about getting even?'

'Sure—what else is the balance of power about? It means having as much blow away power as the next guy. Maybe getting equal is a better way of putting it. Equalising the threat. If you blow me away I'll blow you away before your missiles land. Mutually assured destruction. MAD for short.'

'You didn't make that up?'

'No, Dad. I didn't. It's in common use. That's what the Cold War is. That express certainty.'

Sam looked at Althea. She stopped laughing, got her breath back. I dearly wanted her to say something. She could antagonize the old man all she liked—just please don't laugh at him.

'That's why we can't win, Mr Raines. It's what you might call a bum's game.'

Sam looked from her to me. Still flushed from booze and embarrassment, his eyes shifting slowly between his son and this ball of fire he had brought home.

'But,' he said at last, 'we did win.'

I flipped a mental coin, decided it would be better for me to answer and got in first. Not that Althea was in any hurry.

'No, Dad. We didn't.'

Sam got up, muttered a soft 'Jeezus', left the table and came back with a bottle of his favorite Four Roses whiskey. I knew the sign. It meant he was hunkering down to get serious at almost the precise moment he would lose the ability to hold onto the serious.

'Tell it to me one more time, son. JFK went on the teevee and told us we'd won. That Khrushchev feller was moving his missiles out. I saw people dancing in the street down in Lubbock. Those guys that had took to their shelters came out stinking to high heaven and happy as hogs. Old Elmer Mitchell didn't get out till two days after, 'cause no one thought to tell him it was all over 'cause no one realized that pile of clods and old oil drums in his backyard was his shelter. I saw people on the news in Washington and New York, cheering. And you say we lost.'

I let him pour out three large shots of whiskey. Waited while he downed his, cradled my own and sniffed it and saw out of the corner of my eye that Althea wasn't touching hers.

'No one said we lost, Dad. We just didn't win. That's what the game is about. No one can win. We just evened up in a new way. All the same pieces are still on the board. We just shuffled them around.'

'How so?'

'We'll be moving some of our missiles out of Turkey too.'

'Like tit for tat?'

'Mr Raines, that just about sums up the last fifteen years of history.'

'Tit for tat? So our prowess, our pride got nothin' to do with it?'

'Not a damn thing,' I said.

'You don't have the . . . the . . . feeling that we might just have won this one? Whatever the fancy phrase or the hotshit theory . . . That JFK plain outsmarted that Khrushchev feller . . . That we kicked ass . . . That we kicked the Russians all the way back to Russia . . . That we did what we had to do to stem the . . . the tide of Comm'nism? . . . That it won't be Florida next after Cuba?'

It cost him a lot to say that. It was articulated slowly and shot full of hesitation, but I could not doubt the sincerity of it. The old man really felt this, and, as ever with Sam, what he felt he meant. He was not one to doubt the validity of his own emotions, be they love or rage. Personally I thought Jack Kennedy had sailed so close to the edge he had terrified himself, but this was not the moment to say so. Sam's version of things put me in mind of Ike's domino theory—the great nonsense idea of the Fifties—but it wasn't the time to mention that either.

Althea tipped her whiskey into my glass. Kissed me on the ear, smiled, let it be said, sweetly at Sam and bid us both goodnight.

I sat with him for an hour or more. He was working his way towards the fourth rose and he was going to have a stinker of a hangover the next morning, but someone had to hear him out, listen to him ramble through his history of the world since 1945, the view from his own briarpatch, America and the geopolitical crisis by a man whom I had hardly known to set foot outside his own state. I said as little as possible. I had no stomach to kick him when he was down, and too little intellect to sway him. Billy would have done that. Just when the old man is getting ready to say black is white, and there is a poorly chosen metaphor if ever I heard one, Billy could talk him out of it.

In bed that night. Two virgins once more, wrapped in satin sheets and moonlight. I said, 'You know, I really thought for a moment he was going to throw the race thing at us.'

'Me too. But he didn't. I guess it's bred in me to steel my muscles at the sound of "you people".'

'He thinks it though. I can feel it. What am I doing with you? He just isn't saying it.'

'What did you expect? And since when could we read minds?'

'I expected him to behave at home as he does in public. He'd never hire or fire a man on grounds of color. Why should he think twice about us?'

'For one thing you're his son, not some ranch hand. And for two things we fuck. Bring sex into any equation, you alter the whole damn shebang. If I were you I'd forget about what he thinks of us till he says it. You should be more worried about his Cold War politics than his race politics. You came late to the debate over Cuba. We'd been at it ten minutes before you noticed. Believe me your old man's a homespun cold warrior.'

'He's not as right-wing as he sounds.'

'You sure about that?'

'Well OK. He's right-wing. But . . .'

'But what? He's your old man . . . so that makes it OK . . . he's your old man so he doesn't count? . . . Turner, didn't you say to me once that what you and Mel had in common, what we all have in common, was that we ran away from Mom and Pop. That we're all of us runaways one way or another. Turner, Mom and Pop ain't some one-horse town in some mythical America. They're real people.'

'Sure. But . . .'

I'd no end to the sentence.

'That word again. But.'

'I know.'

There was a silence. We both stared out at the night sky. Then she turned to me and said, 'Turner, can we go now?'

Well, sock it to me one more time.

'If you like.'

'I like.'

'I'm sorry about the old man.'

'Don't. Do not apologize for him. Do not apologize for anyone. You do that too often. I am sick of you apologizing for the whole white race. It is not your father's unarticulated blunders into our relationship that bother me. So he struggles not to be offended and not to give offense. What else would you expect? How prepared do you think you can make a man for you turning up with a black woman?'

'I shouldn't have to prepare him . . .'

'But you do. Let it be. It doesn't matter. We live in the middle of the beast. I grew up knowing that. I grew up expecting the unintending worst from the well-meaning best. And it matters not a damn.'

'Then why are we leaving?'

'Because I have to go.'

'Go where?'

'Cuba.'

'Cuba? Why Cuba for Christ's sake?'

'Because it's what matters. It's what matters now. I thought we had come here in the wake of a world crisis. Your family wanted to see you one last time before we got blown to dust. Maybe to see you and meet your woman. We left it too late. We should have come when Sam asked or not at all. Because what I've seen is not the last hug of the nuclear family— what I've seen, and if you haven't too I'll be amazed, is the resumption of the norm. A reinforced normality. A triumphant normality. We won. We kicked ass. We showed them Cubans. We showed them Russkis. And the fact that we sailed that close to oblivion is quietly forgotten.'

Her fingers snapped in the air to make her point. That close to oblivion. A skeeter's wing away.

'Just do this for me, Johnnie.'

I did not make her ask again.

The next morning I made excuses to Sam and Lois. Told the lies Althea would have me tell, and we left.

As ever Lois drove me to the airport. As ever she said, part self-satire, wholly meant, 'Y'awl come back now.'

And Althea said, 'Of course I will.' But she never did.

§

It took her a month to get an itinerary worked out. But she cracked it. You could not fly directly to Cuba, but you could fly to Austria, cross over at Bratislava into Hungary, with the right paperwork, and, again with the right paperwork, cross into Czechoslovakia and from Prague fly to Havana.

'So you'll be away for Christmas?'

'I guess I will.'

'You really want to do this?'

'I really want to do this.'

'Why?'

'Why? Because it's the big picture, that's why.'

'I thought we were in the big picture—what makes you think it's suddenly out there?'

'Of course it's out there. Of course it's the big picture. What do you think we've been doing? We're going to give a man back his right to sit down at the department store soda fountain. Get served a milk shake. Then stroll on down to the voting booth and cast his vote for whomsoever. Johnnie, I've no doubts we'll win this one ... and when we do I want that man to have the price of a milk shake in his pocket.'

'The only equality is economic equality?'

She smiled at me—not sweet, not lovely, hard and shiny like Naughahyde.

'It's the first equality. All others stem from it. You see the big picture now?'

I saw it. Only an idiot would deny it.

Her first night back from Cuba, in late, late December of '62, is seared into my memory. Her room was just as she'd left it, books and notepad open on the desk, her Bible *Concordance* permanently propped on its little wooden lectern, some project for her Master's nearing completion, scribbled yellow legal pages spread out and covered in Liberace's pawprints. She walked in, coat still on, looking at everything as though she'd never seen it before. Pacing around as though undecided whether to stay or go, heels clicking on the floorboards, a stranger in her own home, shooting sharp, inquisitive glances at me. Then she cleared the desk, threw the whole damn lot to the floor with a single sweep of her arm, right down to the last damn paperclip. The crash sent the cat scooting, kept me hanging on. Waiting on her next move.

'Good,' she said to me. 'Good. That felt good. A fresh start.'

We talked about it. About Cuba. Talked about it for weeks. It was, she said, with not a trace of naiveté, a structured totalitarian state. Fidel was in charge, no doubt about that. He had created new freedoms—and stolen old ones. But all this she put in half a dozen articles in half a dozen journals. They're there for the record, but the remark that sticks in the memory is one she never used in print and I don't think any journal ever would have printed it—'They work like niggers over there.'

I did not doubt the truth of what she said. I doubted where it was taking her personally. Professionally it had taken her out of Divinity and into a Master's in Political Science. God got put back in his box. Marx, Marcuse and Wright Mills took pride of place on Mel's old desk. She was and wasn't the same woman. What could I expect? She was twenty-three, I was only a year older, and at that age expect change. The vehemence she had brought to SNCC and the Movement was simply looking around for a new outlet. She was the same woman in so many ways, sexy, affectionate, funny, always cutting me down to size with a one-liner or a put-down. As long as those things remained the same why should I care? I cared because I could not follow. The tangent she took was not, and I don't know why, open to me. Maybe I was still committed to all the things I'd believed in when I'd graduated . . . gradualism, the ultimate triumph of a non-violent ideology. Althea wasn't. And if I'd been less wrapped up in her and in my work I'd have seen that the Movement itself was shifting beneath my feet and I'd've asked myself the question I did not pose until it was way too late: How long can non-violence sustain itself under the hard rain of violence? A few weeks after she got back I dragged Althea out of a couple of public meetings because she'd hauled off and socked some guys who thought she was an easy target, and a month or so later I only prevented her arrest at a demonstration by sitting on her. When the cops came out wielding clubs she was all geared up to fight back. And I might have asked myself how long the Movement would have room and tolerance for white guys. How long before we became the enemy within?

But—as long as she was affectionate sexy, whatever . . . love dies slowly. Not with a bang but with a whimper. It drizzles out like a guttering candle. Me, like a besotted and blinded moth, seeing nothing but the fact of light so long as there is light. She left me so slowly. Slipped away from me an inch at a time.

The second time she went to Cuba, there was trouble. She'd polished up her Spanish, she met with Guevara, and she appeared on Cuban television, denouncing the American embargo, and hence she appeared in the logs of those spooks who have little else to do but sit around and watch Cuban TV all day. They arrested her at Dulles when she got back. Half a dozen burly feds to tackle one little black woman. Althea had tipped off the press. It was not an incident they were ever going to write up sympathetically, but the photographs said more than any commentary. It looked like what it was, a metaphor for the overwhelming use of force. Althea was Cuba, six two-hundred-pound Feds hustling her out of Dulles were Uncle Sam. It worked. If she'd done that in '66 or '67 it would have worked superbly, she would have found a press and a public at least halfway receptive to her message. As it was she was pioneering the exploitation of the media, way ahead of Rubin and Hoffman. When they stuck a mike in front of her all she had to say was, 'This is how America conducts itself, abroad as well as at home. It bullies the little people.'

My father phoned me a day or so later. He never mentioned Althea, but then he didn't have to. I knew why he'd called.

By the April of '63 I felt I was living with a caged tiger. Her anger came in waves and battered against whatever was there, me included. Her affection became ferocious, her attention negligent. I'd go days without seeing her, then she'd appear out of nowhere, fling herself at me, drain me and move on. I'd wake from post-coital sleep to find the bed empty, a light shining from Mel's old room and she'd be stuck over her books oblivious to my presence until the next time. I am not an inarticulate man but what I felt I could not utter, I could not find the words to create the confrontation I wanted and dreaded. I said nothing. I watched part of me die instead.

That spring I picked up the phone and got blown away.

'Hi, cowboy.'

'Mel?'

'Of course it's me, you fuckin' idiot.'

'Where are you?'

'New York. I been back about six months.'

'Back from where?'

'Mexico, Guatemala . . . you know . . . places.'

'Are you coming home?'

'What? With Little Miss Fireball still in residence? Are you kidding? Nah . . . what's home? I've lost the sense of that word. I guess home is New York. Maybe a bad habit rather than a home. Sometimes it feels like I never left. I have an apartment in the East Village and a job on the *Voice*.'

'I still have your stuff.'

'Keep what you want, put the rest out on the street. Let the bums help themselves. I'm kind of fixed up now. Which is also why I called. I can fix you up too.'

'I don't get it.'

'I mean there's a job on the *Voice* I could put your way. I could even find you a room.'

'I have both of those things here, Mel. And, as you put it, I also have Miss Fireball.'

He paused in his rattle.

'Yeah, but for how long? I watch TV. The woman's on fire. A moving violation on legs. Know your Emily Dickinson—"You cannot something something a fire", jeez I forget, but the next line is, "A flame that will ignite will burn without a spark upon the stillest night". That's your Miss Burke.'

'I'm so glad you shared that with me.'

'Fuck you, Turner.'

The next call was about six weeks later and went better. He didn't mention Althea.

'There's still a job for you here.'

'I'm not a reporter, Mel.'

'Neither was I.'

'I'll think about it.'

I wasn't lying. He'd put it in my head. How could I not think about it? But consider it? Never. Leave Althea? Never.

It was not long after that the Movement announced the big rally in Washington that summer, timed for August 28. Tolstoy's birthday—not that anyone knew—and the day W.E.B. du Bois would die—not that anyone knew. Principal speaker Martin Luther King, known to us in SNCC as 'de lawd'. I hardly ever heard Althea refer to him as anything else.

It was understood we would be there. A march of hundreds of thousands of people to demand civil rights and an end to segregation, to pressure Jack Kennedy into getting his Civil Rights Bill out of logjam, through the House and the Senate and into law, was something we'd both worked for and believed in. Then, it was decided that Althea should not speak. Althea was compromised, pink at the edges, a revolutionary would-be and pretty far from the image the Movement wanted to present. She was furious.

Mel called me again. I said no. I urged him to come south for the march. All he said was, 'Been there, done that.'

One day in early August I got home to find Althea packed. Packed as simply as she'd arrived. Backpack shouldered, typewriter in hand.

'Don't do this,' I said.

'I have to go now, Johnnie. If you love me you won't stand in my way.'

'Go where?'

'I don't know.'

'Will you be back?'

'Don't know that either.'

She kissed me. Not with the fire and flame of her old passion, but sisterly. On the cheek. She pulled open the door. I grabbed her hand in a pathetic gesture—symbolic, no force in my grip, just wanting to hold onto her. She smiled, that Naughahyde look again, and just as gently pulled her hand from mine. I watched our palms slide, our fingers part, my hand big and white, hers small and black and pink of palm.

I called Mel.

'No problemo. The job's gone, but there'll be another one up for grabs at the end of the month.'

'And the room? Would we be sharing an apartment again?'

'Nah . . . woman I work with needs a lodger. You'll love her. She's this real sassy Englishwoman called Rose. Has a place down by the Fulton Street fish market.'

It took me a week or two to pull out. Find a home for Liberace. Sell off what was worth selling. What wasn't I put out on the street along with Mel's stuff. It was all gone the next morning. All except a box of Althea's old divinity texts. I had never bothered to imagine the day I might leave my work, leave the home I'd had those last few years, but I now found I could do it almost on auto. Without Althea I'd lost that life, that way of life. Home, the work, the Movement—all that mattered. Stripped clean and tossed down. I'd lost me, and lost America with it. I knew now how Mel felt after Mississippi. I knew how much he'd lost. Lost himself, lost his place in the nation and its culture. I'd been on those same skids myself since Mississippi. I just hadn't known it. We were homeless. The well-educated, well-heeled Bums of America.

By chance, I did not so time it, I ended up catching a bus for New York on the morning of the big march. Washington was quiet—every congressman had found a good excuse to be out of the city that day, there were more cops standing around than regular citizens. As I stood in the bus depot a black guy came up, looked at my pack and bag and drew the obvious but wrong conclusion, and said, 'You just got in for the march? Then you'll need one of these.'

And he pinned a SNCC badge on me. A black hand and a white hand clasping each other. I still have it. Somewhere. It's all I have left of those long years of my life. Besides it reminds me of the last time I saw Althea in the flesh—my hand clasping hers.

On Saturday, August 28, 1963 I was the only passenger on a bus heading north, as bus after bus poured into the city southward. I tried counting and gave up. Years later Paul Simon captured that same bleak feeling I had that day when he sang about counting the cars on the New Jersey Turnpike—a line that still makes me want to weep. God knows, maybe the man thought he'd written a song of optimism. To me it has always spelt night and darkness, the glare of headlights in the rain, perfectly capturing the way I felt on a bright sunburst August morning. A quarter of a million people. 'All come to look for America'—just when I knew I'd lost it.

§

I have seen Althea many time since in the remoteness of mediation. Althea in the New York Times, Althea on the nightly news, Althea on the cover of Time, arguing the case for Labor, for Equality, whatever. She has never lacked a cause or a platform. She even flew to North Vietnam, but got totally eclipsed by Jane Fonda. Just as well. By '72 she was acceptable enough to run for Congress as a Democrat and get slaughtered in the Nixon landslide. I heard her challenged on her record on several occasions, the accusation of Communist sympathies flung in her face. And I heard her answer. It went roughly like this, a basic model even if the detail varied with every utterance: 'Do you have it on record anywhere that I was or ever claimed to be a Communist? I say now what I said in '62 and '63—it's as valid now as it was then—what are we trying to achieve by sanctions on Cuba? Have we improved the chances of democratic change in Cuba by these means? Have we made it less of a totalitarian state? Of course we haven't, we have simply gone on making an enemy in our own backyard. And if you still think I'm a Communist I'd remind you that HUAC came to the opposite conclusion.' It worked—revise, backtrack, rewrite. By '77 Carter thought enough of her rapport with the Unions to put her in charge of an off-cabinet Labor Relations committee, and in 1984

she finally made it in into Congress for one of the Georgia districts. I believe it is
now one of her missions to give Slick Willie a hard time.

§

1969. I had hoped to make El Paso that night, but there was no way I
was going to push that old Buick the way the traffic cop had done. I
have never much liked driving. That Jack Kerouac/Sam Shepard number of 'just-get-into-the-car-and-go' has never been me. I know, almost
unAmerican and one day it'll be a felony. But there I was, crawling along
the interstate in that broad flat nowhere of southwest Texas feeling more
bored than I had thought possible and determined to pull in at the next
motel even if it was run by Norman Bates, when, as Kerouac had put it,
God pointed his forefinger at me. I had brought it on myself—cruising
roads as straight as arrows, having played every tape at least five times, with
only the aftermath of harvest, endless fields of wheat-stubble and straw,
to look at I had come to welcome any distraction. Dead skunk—score
one. Live, scuttling armadillo—score three. The merest, the smallest, the
most shot-up roadsign (that's Texas for you, take out your boredom on
a harmless road sign) achieved the status of literature, the serial novel
of 'No Littering', 'Eat at Fred's—only 45 miles ahead' and 'Farm Road
1,000,001'. God pointed his forefinger at me. The clouds gathered, the
sky blackened, the thunder rolled and lightning zapped down all around
me. Great bolts of electricity, a summer tempest fit to fry me, set the
cornfields blazing. Talk about your burning bush, I felt my entire ass was
on fire. I floored the pedal, surrendered all my misgivings about the car
and tore out as fast as I could.

I found a motel, somewhere west of the Pecos is about as accurate as
I could be. And the guy who ran it looked nothing like Norman Bates.
Just as well. I had God and Kerouac to worry about. 'Off the Road',
'Don't go to Arizona' ran through my dreams like a mantra. But when
I woke in the morning it was gone. The storm had blown out, it was a
pleasant, summer morning, the last breath of cool in the long day. I sat

on a verandah, chair propped back on two legs like Henry Fonda in *My Darling Clementine*, drinking overcooked hotplate coffee from a plastic cup and eating a sticky, too-sweet blueberry muffin and finding both tolerable. Arizona here I come.

§

It was later than I thought. Isn't that always the way. I had turned off I-10 at Bowie and headed south along a gravel road into the furthest corner of Arizona. I hated to admit it, but I was beginning to think I was lost. All I had to go on was the knowledge that the Moondogs had holed up in a ghost town on the slopes of the Chiricahua mountains. I had thought I would ask. But I hadn't passed anyone to ask. It was the empty quarter. Arizona Deserta. I wasn't quite driving in circles, but I did have the feeling that I was going nowhere. Half the farmhouses I passed seemed to be abandoned, those that weren't had chain gates and big dogs—so I drove on. South. Closer to Mexico.

About fifty miles on I could see my first sign of life since I left the interstate. A horse and wagon were pulled up at the roadside, the horse grazing on the shoulder, and an old feller in dungarees and a straw hat was slowly whacking in a fence post. I pulled up.

'Afternoon, sir.'

'Almost evening,' he replied. 'But a good one to you all the same.'

'You wouldn't happen to know where . . . ?'

Where what? Dammit I hadn't worked this through. Again. Was I going to ask him where a drugged-up bunch of crazies were holed up?

'I'm looking for . . . a community.'

'Community,' he echoed. Didn't seem to be a question.

'Well—a commune more like. Somewheres hereabouts. Group of . . . young people. You might have seen them.'

'If you're looking for the hippies, why don't you just say so?'

Point blank range. Got me right between the eyes.

'I'm looking for the hippies.'

He took off his hat, wiped his brow on his sleeve, and used the hat to point.

'T'aint far. Carry on along Buzzard Creek Road. In about fifteen miles it swings south, you go east up a dirt road to the foot of the mountains. About six or seven miles beyond that the road twists into a canyon like a corkscrew. That's your whatdeyecallit commune. When I was a boy it was San Pedro. Nobody lived there since the Depression. Nobody 'cept ghosts. Till the hippies that is. You don't look like a hippie to me.'

'I guess not.'

'Well, some of them are decent folks.'

'Some of them?'

'Just like everybody else. Some are, and some ain't. Enjoy the sunset. Looks to be a good one tonight. See them little ribbons of cloud, them long wavy ones.'

I turned in my seat. Looked back westward.

'Just the kind of sky to glow of an evening, like fire on the horizon.'

He picked up his mallet and started pounding his fence post again. I drove on. Missed the turning and doubled back. The old guy was right—corkscrew described the road pretty well. It doubled back on itself a dozen times in a matter of a few miles. High above me were the bluffs of a narrowing canyon—the sort of rock formation you see in Westerns, Burt Lancaster leaping from one to another as though it were effortless.

I passed through the neck at the head of the trail and found myself in a wider, flat-bottomed canyon. If I had but known the term I'd've realized I'd blundered into what is called a micro-climate. Not desert, not mountain either—but a little of everything. Alligator juniper, man-zanita, Arizona oak, patches of prickly pear and ocatillo—all nestling under towering cliffs of green-tinged rhyolite columns looking like the ribcage of a long dead monster, and watered by a snow-fed cascade that leapt down between the columns to cut a path across the canyon floor. By comparison the town, or what was left of it, seemed tiny. A couple of dozen buildings, some patched up, some in complete decay. Here and there hens clucked around, goats strained against their tethers and pigs peered over the tops of pens. And in the middle of a big plot of tilled red earth a red-skinned woman stood hoeing the weeds from a bed of squashes.

It was like a Hollywood device I've seen in countless movies. After whatever ordeal, whatever rejection, the hero, and what's left of his family, suddenly stumbles across 'the place'—somewhere where things work, where the rent is affordable, where the guys with pickax handles are actually using them to dig not beat your brains out, and everything has a hint of paradise to it. It all smacks of New Deal propaganda and invariably the movie ends with, 'Can we stay here, mister? Can we really stay here?' and the bit player playing 'mister', always seemed to be Henry Travers or Arthur Hunnicutt or anyone who'd made the folksy benign his own, pulls on his pipe and smiles. Is that the way *The Grapes of Wrath* ends or have I just not seen it in a long time? A cinematic cliché? Absofuckinlutely, darling, as my late wife used to say.

I got out of the car and ambled over to the Indian woman. Before I could speak she said, 'We didn't know when to expect you. First it was yesterday evening, then lunchtime today, and it was only half an hour ago we really knew you were on your way. I suppose you'll want to see Notley right away?'

She pointed to an ochre-colored adobe chapel—the cross on its roof still intact, a few gaping holes in the walls, a door looking pitted with age and bullet holes.

'In there?'

'It's sort of his place. We all have our own place.'

'And he's expecting me?'

'Of course.'

Maybe Burt Lancaster had been leaping from rock to rock, flashing news of my arrival?

'In there?'

'How many times do you want me to say it?'

'Will my car be OK here?'

'Everything will be OK here. Nobody will steal a thing. You go on now.'

I stepped into the chapel and waited a second or two for my eyes to adjust to the light. There was a figure up a stepladder, painting something onto a huge image tacked to the wall. As my eyes resolved the image became clearer. The old woman from Village 77, staring blankly into Mouse's camera. It was the same blow-up I'd seen back in Lubbock at Mouse Photo.

The guy on the ladder didn't turn.

'Been expecting you,' was all he said.

I didn't think I'd made any noise, but, God knows, it was so quiet in there, maybe he could hear me breathe?

'Mouse?' I said.

'Yep.'

'He told me he didn't know where you were.'

He wiped his hands on his Levi's, leaned back to get a look at what he was doing. Still with his back to me. I could see clearly now. The old woman was still the old woman, but I'd swear the pink outfit she was wearing, somehow over-projected onto her, and delicately touched up with paint and gouache, was the same one Jackie Kennedy had been wearing that day in Dallas. There was even the dirty crimson of dried blood on the lapel. But instead of Jackie Kennedy's high cheekbones and numb grief, there was the vacant stare of a Vietnamese peasant. Beyond grief. Calmly fixing to die.

'Mouse didn't lie to you, Mr Raines. All I ever give him is a box number in Tucson.'

He came down the ladder, backing towards me, looking up at his handiwork. Wherever I went I seemed to see not the writing on the wall but the painting on the wall. Tsu-Lin, Huey, the anonymous painter of the Last Supper in Lazarus, now Notley. I began to feel I'd stumbled into a national obsession. Over to the left another gigantic blow-up. A shot I knew and I tended to think everyone in Amerika knew. The guy kneeling in the street in Saigon, who had his brains blown out by a Vietnamese Police Chief, in front of Eddie Adams' camera. Associated Press put that picture into half the newspapers on earth. Only in this version it wasn't Nguyen Ngoc Loan pulling the trigger, it was Elvis, Elvis as seen in one of his third rate movies, cowboy shirt and sixgun, Elvis as reworked in three overlapping frames and washes of primary colors by Warhol—and now, it would seem, by Notley.

He turned to me, took a few steps across the room, stuck out his hand and smiled. I knew him at once.

A little guy, shirtless, lean and slim. Clean-shaven, short-haired, looking nothing like Frank Zappa. A purple heart ribbon, profanely tacked onto the fly of his faded blue Levi's.

'I'm Notley. But you know that.'

I knew him at once. Not from any photo of the New Nineveh Nine, but from the streets of Chicago the year before. Add the war paint, the Commanche headdress and the bucket of shit. This was the Moondog I'd seen in my last few minutes in Chicago. I knew him. And he knew me.

'Chicago? Right?'

One finger tapping the side of his head as if to prompt memory to speak.

'The plaza, you were the guy with the pig. Right?'

'Right. Turner Raines. And you were the guy in the feathers. Why Commanche? I thought this was where Geronimo's Apaches hung out.'

'Apaches didn't go in much for fancy headdresses. Commanche's much prettier. And it was Cochise, by the way, not Geronimo. They say he's buried somewhere around here, but no one's ever found the grave.'

'You guys been here long?'

'I've been here since I got out of the army, but there are Moondogs who've been here since the beginning, since '64.'

'So there were Moondogs here while you were in Vietnam?'

He eyed me quizzically, discerning precisely what I'd meant.

'Point taken, Mr Raines. But if I really were Moondog, I wouldn't be Moondog—if you get my drift. It's kind of a moveable feast. And yes there were Moondogs here while I was in 'Nam, and there were Moondogs here while I was studying to be an architect at Santa Barbara in '64.'

'Is that how the army got you? You lose your graduate deferment?'

'No I got that. I got that. I was safe till they abolished it. But, as a matter of fact, I volunteered.'

'Good God. Why?'

He shrugged, waved a hand to show me we should sit down. Big cushions to sit cross-legged at a low table.

'Seemed like the place to be. At the time.'

'At the time?'

'I wasn't the only one, Marty Fawcett volunteered too. There are more of us than you might think.'

'His mother thinks he was drafted.'

'Well—that's probably what old Marty told her. Take it from me, the kid volunteered. He was itching for action. Maybe it was a way for a skinny guy with acne to show the world what he was made of.'

He sprang up again.

'Now—can I get you some tea?'

I said yes, and began to feel that this was a warm afternoon in the suburbs with an aunt, not the baking heat of the Arizona desert with the uncrowned king of the hippies.

He came back with a tray—more like the maiden aunt than ever—poured out green tea from an iron pot into wide bowls. He said nothing for a minute or two until his tea had cooled. Then he took it up, sipped at it and said, 'Try some. You might like it.'

It was fine by me, a little oily, faintly aromatic like the Earl Grey stuff Rose habitually served. I had gotten to like that, I could get to like this.

'You'll have a question or two I imagine,' he said.

I had. I just didn't know what they were.

'I guess I do. I suppose it comes down to asking if what Mouse said happened did happen, and I don't mean by that that I doubt Mouse's word. I just ...'

'That's OK. Why don't you tell me what Mouse told you.'

He was a good listener. I was a surprisingly good talker. I skipped the geography lesson—after all he'd been there, I hadn't—but it still seemed to take an age to get through even the gist of what Mouse had told me. Notley occasionally closed his eyes, but when he opened them never looked away. The man was focused. It was as though he were taking notes. He could not have been less like the out-of-it hippie Mouse had recalled for me.

I got to the point where Mouse is in his own backyard burning his uniform—I thought Notley would somehow want to know this—and I stopped.

'You known Mouse long?' he asked.

'All my life.'

'He's a great guy.'

'The best.'

'But not the brightest?'

I shrugged it off. 'Maybe not.'

'Mr Raines, there's nothing factually wrong in what Mouse told you. That, pretty well, is what happened. We killed a hundred and thirty-four unarmed Vietnamese women and children—and a few men. It's the interpretation and moreover the lack of interpretation that's wrong. Mouse was new to 'Nam. We all were, but Mouse more than the rest of us. Mouse just isn't asking the right questions.

'Let's begin with Jack Feaver. A Green Beret, a colonel who breezed into Mighty Joe Young waving his orders and recruiting us grunts. I never saw those orders, Mouse never did, and I don't know anyone that did.

Mouse saw rank and assumed authority. We all did. We were wrong. Jack wasn't on any mission with orders from Saigon. He was acting alone. If Mouse still thinks we were acting for the United States Army it's because he hasn't added it up, hasn't arrived at the big picture. We were unwitting renegades. Feaver chose us because we were greenhorns, even our officers were greenhorns. He knew we'd do what we were told.

'Think about it. If Feaver was acting officially all sorts of conditions apply that never came into play.'

He began to count off points on his fingers. All the precision of an academic from a shirtless hippie. I could not but be impressed by his powers of analysis—and I began to wonder if he'd run out of fingers.

'Why us? Why a bunch of new guys. We had "Lerps"—Long Range Reconnaissance Patrols—trained and equipped for the trip he put us through. There was no need to come recruiting.

'There were no Vietnamese along—now that's odd. We always worked with locals. A patrol of that length with no native guides or native speakers?

'There were no choppers in support. We could have been flown into that village, we could have been flown out. Didn't happen. At any one of half a dozen points on the way out Feaver could have summoned aerial support and he didn't. He could have whipped up a Huey with a single radio call—till we lost the radio that is.

'Radio silence? What was that about? Feaver just bullshitted Sputnik. There was no necessity for silence. It was Feaver's way of keeping it all quiet till he'd done what he came to do. Same reason he didn't call in the choppers.

'There were no Corpsmen—that is paramedics—why? One would have been virtually standard. None volunteered and he didn't ask for any. Why? The only reason I can come up with is that some of them—maybe most of them—were conscientious objectors and Feaver did not want any potential whistleblowers along.'

'But he got you.'

'Yeah—he guessed wrong.'

'He could have killed you.'

'I don't know why he didn't. If I'd moved I think he probably would have done.

'Now—Mouse wonders what the mission really was. I find it hard to believe he still doesn't know. The mission was to wipe out that village.

That's all. We weren't diverted by it, we didn't get lost, and it wasn't simple vengeance for Sputnik getting killed. In fact I'd say that if Sputnik hadn't gotten killed Feaver would have had to shoot him himself. He needed to motivate us. He needed a death. Stanley getting blown away was perfect. He could not have hoped for a better way of whipping us up to bloodlust. And when we got to it he headed straight for his target. Why else did he bypass that first village only to hit the second? We didn't stumble into Village 77, we followed a carefully mapped-out plan. We didn't know it but we were a bunch of renegades out to commit a massacre. That is about as plainly as I can put it.'

I knew it would sound stupid but I asked the obvious. 'Why?'

'Remember when it was. It was a matter of days after Tet '68. The VC had made it all the way to Saigon, even got into the grounds of our embassy and taken potshots at GIs. They'd taken Hué and held it the best part of a month. To a man like Feaver it made perfect sense to strike deep into VC-held territory. It was tit for tat for Tet.'

'But that village wasn't VC. Mouse said you found nothing.'

'Of course it was VC. When we first hit the ville there were no young men anywhere. And when a couple of dozen came off the fields I doubt there was anyone between sixteen and sixty among them. A ville with no young men, no teenagers? They'd all gone for soldiers. We just took 'em by surprise by coming at them from the wrong side. They regrouped soon enough—how else could they get so close to wiping us out at the Hershey Bar Stockade? No—it was VC, enemy territory, and I've never doubted it. That we found nothing says a lot about our lack of thoroughness and everything about the art of concealment. They were Cong. Feaver was right about that.'

'I don't get it,' was all I could say.

'That's OK. It took me a while. The motive is the hardest thing of all. Asking for reasons why a trained killer should kill is like pissing into the wind. Why are bears Catholic? Why does the pope shit in the woods? But, consider what Mouse said Feaver said to Gurvitz. "Let's take the war to them".'

'Mouse is certain he said it.'

'He did, I heard it too. Word for word that is what the man said. Now, Mouse is right about what Feaver said, but he has no sense of what the man was really saying. "Let's take the war to them" wasn't just his way of dismissing Gurvitz—it was his statement of policy, it was what he meant to do. And he said straight after, while Norman was still huffing and fluffing at him, he said, "Does it really matter if ten men violate the neutrality of Laos when our bombers do it three hundred times a day, when we send Lerps in there for weeks at a time?" Odd that Mouse should forget that. I couldn't. I knew we were bombing the Ho Chi Minh trail, zapping the shit out of a neutral country that was never going to fight back, but I'd no idea it was on that scale. In that light Feaver was right—what did it matter? But it remains—what Mouse missed was the key to the whole mission—"Let's take the war to them"?'

'It sounds almost . . . personal.'

'Maybe it was. The man is driven. There is no other word for it. It was something between him and his people back in Saigon. Of that I'm certain. You remember the part where Mouse said we torched the ville?'

I nodded.

'In war, in terms of combat, that deep into enemy territory, it made no sense, no sense at all. It alerted the VC to our presence as surely as if we'd hoisted the Stars and Stripes. But that wasn't its purpose, that was just a risk worth taking. Feaver did it to alert our people to what he'd done. He was sending a message home. Two messages. The first message was "Fuck you!" and the second was "Look at the map!"'

'Look at the map? For a village with no name?'

'Oh, it had a name all right. We just didn't know it. Norman dubbing it Village 77 was convenient, helped us to think of them as less than human. The fact that it wasn't named on his map doesn't mean it hasn't got a name. Everything in Vietnam's got a name. It's called Phuong. I know, I asked around when we got back to Joe Young. A couple of the Vietnamese knew the place, and they said it was called Phuong.'

'Does that mean something?'

'I'll get to that. The day after we got back we all got summoned to Da Nang and discharged. The cover-up was immediate. Can't blame anyone for not asking too many questions—it was a lifesaver. Saved my life, might even have saved Pete Chambers if it had been a tad quicker. Mouse told you I was out whoring the night Pete was killed? Such cynicism. I was trawling the bars in Saigon, looking for Green Berets. I found them, two guys with far too much booze inside them, two guys who'd worked with Jack Feaver, two guys who'd been part of the same operation. They called it Operation Phoenix. I'd never heard of it. They said it was a CIA-run hit squad—infiltration, assassination, slaughter. There's been next to nothing about in the press. I did some research—it exists. Oldest reference I found was a piece in the *New Yorker* about this time last year.'

Notley got up, rummaged around on his workbench, and came back with a bunch of newspaper clippings and a torn and battered hardback.

'I doubt there've been half a dozen mentions in the press all told.'

He flourished the clippings.

'*New Yorker*, *New York Times* and there's one only a couple of months old from the *Wall Street Journal*. You'd really have to be following foreign policy to know about Phoenix—and you'd have to be reading between the lines to know what it really is. But, then, these days I do both.

'Now, Mouse says he was shocked by what happened out there—maybe he should be, but when he says that sort of thing is almost commonplace—happens all the time—he doesn't know the half of it. These Green Berets had been on dozens of hits, worked in free-fire zones—did Mouse tell you what that is? It's the assumption that any Vietnamese in a designated area is Cong, and you kill 'em. But if you don't kill 'em . . . if you don't kill 'em at once you get inventive with torture . . . electrodes on the balls . . . well that's traditional isn't it? . . . but being forced to swallow white lime? And best of all . . . their favorite trick, blindfolding suspects, sticking them in a chopper hovering three feet off the ground and throwing them out. Until the time comes when the chopper is three thousand feet off the ground. There was a lot more. They were drunk and they were revelling in it. They loved telling me this. They weren't like Feaver, and they were like Feaver.

'I'd heard enough. I shook them off and went to find Pete. As you know, I got there too late. All I got of Pete was the book he'd been reading.'

He pushed the book across the table to me. I looked at it. *The Quiet American* by Graham Greene.

'I started to read it on the plane coming over. Turn to the first page. There's a woman character. Name of Phuong. Greene translates it for you. It was like an epiphany when I came across it.'

I opened the book. There were bloodstains spattered across the title page, seeping in from the cut edges. I found the word Phuong.

'Phoenix,' I said. 'He translates it as Phoenix.'

'You get the message?'

'I think so. As you said. He was sending a message to his own people, the massacre, the fire . . .'

'But you don't know why. And for a while neither did I. I've spent a lot of time on this. I've asked a lot of questions. This is what I think happened. Feaver was part of Operation Phoenix. They killed thousands of people—no arrests, no trials, just wiped out on suspicion. My source reckons that maybe as many as 20,000 people have been killed by the Phoenix program in the last two years. I say killed. My source said "neutralized". May not be the same thing.'

'Your source?'

'Guy at the Pentagon. Answered a lot of questions. Albeit some of his answers were couched in Penatagonese.'

'The Moondogs have sources in the Pentagon?'

'Don't sound so surprised. We're not a bunch of hicks. We're organized. Weren't you guys organized? Didn't you and Rubin and Hoffman plan to stitch up Chicago? But the best is yet to come. It's so simple it's brilliant. My source tells me that Operation Phoenix was suspended some time before Tet. Some internal conflict within the Company over its value. I shouldn't think for a second it was a moral issue. And there's your motive. Jack was telling the CIA in Saigon that it was time to start up again. Time to take the war to them. He picked Phuong because it was VC and because of the name. He could not have made the message bigger if he'd used a skywriter. We were just the tools he used. Could have been anybody. And that doesn't absolve us.'

'You didn't kill anyone.'

'Nor did Mouse. But we did nothing to stop it. Doesn't absolve us either.'

I let it sink in. He poured hot water over the tea leaves and brewed a second pot.

I said at last, 'That's your theory?'

'That's a fact.'

'A fact?'

'It ceased to be theory when I put it to Jack.'

'You talked to Feaver?'

'No—Feaver wrote to me. Not long after Chicago. He wrote to me. I wrote back.'

'Wrote back where?'

'Vermont. He's back home in Vermont.'

'Discharged?'

'Apparently not. Leave, a sort of semi-permanent leave. I don't quite understand I have to admit. But whatever he was hoping for, he didn't get. They got us all out of the army, broke us up, sent us home. It was the safe thing to do. Except Jack. Jack is still in the army. I'd say he didn't get what he wanted. Phoenix was revived. He won that one—he just isn't going to be part of it stuck out on the family farm in Vermont. Why they didn't just kick him out, I don't know.'

'I think perhaps I do. I studied some military law in college. If the army discharges Feaver, honorably or not, then he can't be indicted for anything he did as a soldier.'

'I think it's my turn to say I don't get it.'

'Why Chicago? Was he back for that?'

'Apparently.'

He got up again, pulled a piece of paper off a bulletin board above his bench.

What he had handed me was a torn piece of a broadsheet newspaper. I recognized it. Not from this paper, but from some other. It must have been syndicated. I was sure I'd seen it, read it somewhere. A punchy, bloody account of Chicago, and in the centre panel a photo of a naked man in Commanche head-dress and paint—still recognizably Notley. I looked for the byline. There wasn't one. It must have been on the torn corner. The whole piece was stapled to a legal sheet, on which was a handwritten note.

'How nice to see you again, Notley. I have followed your "career" with some interest.'

Then there was a line I couldn't read and a signature—Jack Feaver.

'What's the line at the bottom?' I asked. 'Is it Russian?'

'That's what I thought too. But it's Greek. Would you believe one of our Moondogs used to be an associate professor of classics?'

Of course I would.

'It's Sophocles. From *Oedipus at Colonus*. It reads something like, "It needs must be that transgression comes, but woe betide the hand by which . . ." I'm paraphrasing but anyway you get the gist.'

'Shit happens.'

'My professor was keen on the word transgression. The implied movement involved. That may be the only word I have right.'

I was drawn to look at the Elvis again—the three split images created the impression of freeze-frame movement towards the victim—*trans-gression* as Notley would insist. Where Warhol had merely intended the iconoclasm of repetition, Notley, by turning the figures edge on, had almost made me see the hand pull the gun from its holster and squeeze on the trigger. I was sure this had been moving footage too, that I had seen it on a newsreel. But this was the image that had stuck, the still, the permanent distorted face of the moment of death. The split second the line was crossed forever.

'To whom is he referring. You or himself?'

'Oh, to me. I doubt Jack Feaver thinks he transgressed for a second. There've been other notes and letters, but that was how he found me, that piece in the press. Just wrote to me care of The Moondogs, Chiricahua, AZ. The US Mail can be amazing. Finds me every time. Better than the CIA. Thing is, Jack actually approves of what I do. He thinks it has purpose.'

'Doesn't that worry you—Jack Feaver admiring you?'

'Of course it does.'

'And you admire him.'

'That's not the word I'd use. But . . . there are more things Mouse didn't tell you.'

He stood up. Pointed to the ribbon on his fly.

'You know what this is?

I nodded.

He pulled back the hair covering his forehead. There was a blue sort of ziggy-zag scar up near the hairline.

'I got that for this. One purple heart per wound. That's the way Uncle Sam does things. A measure and a stick. There was blood all over my face and in my eyes. I was in that kind of numb stage when all the body's morphins cut in and cut you off. The other guys were picking up the bits of Tod and Bob. Feaver wiped my face and checked the wound. "You'll live," he told me. "For how long?" I said. "Is it me next?" He said something like, "Hell no, when something like this happens you do it yourself." From that moment on he walked point. Alone. He led us through two more minefields, marked mines, led us around them, took two to pieces with his bare hands. And he did this until we were within sight of base. What Mouse didn't tell you was that we'd all be dead if

Jack Feaver hadn't led us out of there. Admire him. No. I don't admire him. I acknowledge him.'

'And what do you make of "woe betide the hand"?'

'I make "damned if you do, damned if you don't" out of it.'

So did I.

'You wanna eat?' he said.

§

I leaned in the chapel doorway and watched cars and vans and motorbikes pour into the darkening canyon. A couple of Ken Kesey-style psychedelic schoolbuses, and at least a dozen beaten up VW campers. The population had swollen from the handful of figures I'd seen dotted round on my arrival to nearer a hundred. Floodlights came on on the rock walls, speakers high up in the trees started to pound out a Canned Heat album. Bob the Bear, six foot what and two hundred and fifty pounds, singing that unexpected, mellifluous falsetto. It looked as though I'd turned up for the Moondogs' prom night.

Notley stood at the propane stove chopping vegetables, splashing oil around, and asking me a thousand questions. By the time the meal was ready he knew as much about me as I did about him. I disowned any involvement in organizing Chicago, even the word 'organized' seemed to me like a major overstatement.

'But that was a great stunt with the pig—wish I'd done it myself. I'd no idea you guys were going to do it. Last I heard was Wavy Gravy'd thought it up and then decided not to do it.'

Trust Rubin to think nothing of stealing an idea. Why not? Ours was a left-over culture found lying in the street.

I sat back down on the floor cushion. Notley set a Spanish omelet and a green salad in front of me.

'We grow the greens ourselves. For that matter we raised the bell peppers too. And you'll have seen the hens scratching around.'

'Almost self-sufficient?' I asked.

'Can't make gasoline and acid,' he said. 'Though we did have a guy tried making his own acid—never worked. Grass grows easy—all the home-grown maryjane a man could want.'

'Don't the cops . . .'

'What? Don't the cops what?'

'Don't they ever bother you?'

'No they don't—but I think that's pure laziness. They'd need to come in force to be effective and that means coming all the way from Tucson. They'd be out of do'nuts and coffee before they got halfway. There's not enough county cops between here and Tombstone to be worth worrying about. Besides, we're careful not to piss off the locals.'

'No music after ten p.m.?'

'Hardly,' he said.

The bell peppers were fine, the egg yellower and fresher than I'd had since I stopped living in Texas. The mushrooms were kind of bitter though. I must have pulled a face.

'An acquired taste,' Notley said. 'Stick with 'em. They grow on you.'

He was smiling as he said it. The smile turned to a grin. I bit into another bitter, hard, little mushroom and swallowed. Notley grinned some more. I looked down at the plate, ill-lit by candlelight, and fished out a whole mushroom. It wasn't a mushroom. It was a peyote cap. A moon button. The Moondog had fed me moon buttons. The bastard.

§

I drifted on a dream. A far from pleasant dream. The reality of what I was seeing might have been acceptable, tolerable in a state of sobriety. Goddammit, I'd been to orgies before. I'd smoked dope before. But I'd never taken an hallucinogenic before. Sex an' drugs an' rock an' roll were more cheap thrills than I would want in the course of a single day. I'd heard the Stones' *Satanic Majesties* before—it had just never occurred to me that it was plain evil. I'd watched people fuck before—I'd just never seen them turn to animals. A guy in the middle of a group grope who suddenly had the head of a wolf. I closed my eyes and shook my head. When I looked again he was human. But he transmogrified into wolf before my eyes. And once set on that path I could not stop—a repetitive lycanthropia. This woman was part pig, the guy whose cock she was sucking part buffalo. Watch out for those molars, feller.

'They'll grow on you,' he'd said. Everything grew on me. I wandered around, lost in rock 'n' roll's wilderness, feeling like a lone human stranded on the island of Dr Moreau, like Jack looking for the beanstalk. Everything grew—plant and animal erupted and enveloped me. And I hated every damn second of it.

The last human face I can recall seeing was the Indian woman I'd encountered first. She took me by the arm and spun me round, asking 'Are you OK? Are you OK?' but even as she said it she changed into a dog-woman and I could not answer.

I drifted on. The music merged into a cacophonous blur, filling the canyon, less like a huge hi-fi and a hundred yards of cable, than God's own jukebox booming down from heaven. And it seemed that God had a taste for John Lennon's 'Tomorrow Never Knows'. Maybe they had it on a loop? Maybe it was just that everything had that same insistent drum pattern to it? Maybe I imagined it? The Moondogs became one long chain of coitus, a sexual conga, a gang bang for a hundred heaving buttocks. One or two women—I could only tell that by looking at their bodies, the faces would be horses or tigers or God knows what—came on to me. Sheer hospitality and good manners I'm sure, but I was overwhelmed by nausea. The desire to puke became paramount. A surging tide inside of me that led nowhere and turned my legs to rubber.

Somehow I found my way to the edge of the stream, where the water calmed after cascading down the canyon wall. I fell down and puked. Puked until I strained and heaved on nothing. I dipped my head in the water and shook myself like a dog. John Lennon's Tibetan drums seemed to have stopped. I could hear . . . Minnie Riperton singing Dylan . . . 'how does it feel?' over and over again 'how does it fee-ee-ee-eeell?' way above soprano, like a cross between a boy treble, an angel and a dog-whistle—and I knew it was only in my head. That this was the 'trip'. And I was the one who'd thought psychedelia was pure hokum. It's pretty well the last thing I remember of a long night with the Moondogs—'how does it fee-ee-ee-eeell?' And, Minnie, I have an answer for you. Awful.

I woke face down in the stream. It was daylight. I felt like I'd been hit by a truck. I felt lucky I hadn't drowned. I raised my head and puked again. Tasted the acidity of bile and sucked in water from the stream. I was prising myself off the ground when a hand came down to grip one of mine and pulled. I was too heavy. I looked up at her. It was dog-woman, dog-woman with her own features once more, the flat little nose and the red tint of skin.

'Again,' she said, and I got to my feet feeling like Pinnochio on stilts. She stuck one shoulder under my arm and propped me up.

'You eat one of Notley's omelets?' she asked.

'Yes.'

'You know—he actually thinks that's funny.'

I didn't.

I looked straight ahead and tried to focus. The canyon seemed quiet, almost empty. A couple of mongrel dogs rolling in the dust, a couple of dozen hens scratching for worms.

'They've all gone?'

'Yep.'

'Notley too?'

'Be back tomorrow night. Can you wait that long?'

'Wait? I don't think I'll ever be able to move again.'

'I wouldn't worry none. You'll be fine.'

She sat me down in front of what I took to be some sort of domed teepee, a canvas and roadkillskin cross between the home on the prairie and Buckminster Fuller. She informed me, a little po-faced, that it was a sweat lodge.

'Just what you need,' she added. 'Sweat the junk out of your body.'

I sat and rested a good half hour before she came back to me.

'Give me a hand to finish the fire. Won't kill you to work a little.'

About fifty yards from the lodge she'd begun piling up timber and dry branches over a pile of large, smooth, round stones.

'If we finish this now, then you can sleep until it burns through.'

'How long does that take?'

'Hours.'

It took about another half hour to pile up enough wood, then she put a light to it. We watched it flare up. Another half hour and it settled down into a searing slow burn and she said, 'We can leave it now. High time you ate something.'

I dozed off by the lodge. She woke me and stuck a bowl of clear miso soup and a couple of corn dodgers in front of me. I managed about half of it.

'What's your name?'

'It's Ethel—Ethel Harvest Moon. And whatever you say next do not sing and do not even think of rhymes involving moon and June.'

'It's July.'

'It's damn near August.'

'You ... you don't look like an Apache. I mean you don't look like any Apache I've ever seen.'

'I'm not. I'm Oglala.'

'South Dakota?'

'I was born in Montana, but South Dakota's home. As much as you can call any place home. You got somewhere you call home?'

I thought about it. Then I thought about it some more. Then I fell asleep.

Ethel shook me awake. The sun had moved across the sky. I figured it to be about six in the evening.

'I need you to help me. The fire's burned down. Time to lift out the stones. I rolled them in, but they have to be lifted out. I can't do that without you.'

The stones were a stage beyond red hot, approaching the white—a kind of tangerine heat. I used an old manure fork to place five stones in a pit in the center of the lodge. Ethel splashed water over them and closed the flap. She began to strip off.

'Now—we'll be naked in there. But let's get this straight. It's a sacred place. You lay a finger on me and I'll break it. Savvy?'

She was naked already. All it took was one arm to hoist the dress over her head. She could have been the most desirable woman on earth. The state I was in, I would not have noticed.

I disrobed slowly and in utter self-consciousness.

'Tell me,' I said in the hope I could distract her from looking at me. 'Isn't this where you see visions and spirits of the ancestors come to visit you.'

'Oh, so you read a book on it? Big deal. You have a problem?'

'No. I don't think it's a problem. It's just that if spirits were to come to me . . .'

'Yeah?'

'If spirits were to come to me . . . I don't think there's anything I have to say to them right now.'

I pushed my Levi's down to my ankles and stepped out of them. I could swear she was grinning at something.

'Don't worry about that. You don't want to see spirits, you won't see spirits. God knows, Notley's done a sweat lodge every week for almost a year in the hope of seeing spirits—they haven't favored him yet. You have nothing to say to them. I don't think they have anything to say to him. Now get your skinny white butt inside and I'll close up.'

I have pleasant memories of it. One of the most terrifying experiences of my life. I had stepped into an oven for the roasting of human flesh. When Ethel climbed in after me and pulled the flap behind her we were in total darkness—not a chink to let in a single ray of light. I heard the hiss as she splashed more water on the stones, and then she began to chant in a language I had never heard before—my skin rolled with sweat and my blood ran cold. Maybe it was all those corny old Hollywood movies, Indians dancing in a circle while some white guy waits for the chop. After a couple of minutes she stopped. I was beginning to feel like I was suffocating, and with good timing she thrust back the flap and a blast of cool air rushed in. I gulped it in like water.

'How does it feel?' she asked.

I'd heard this somewhere before. I gave the same answer.

'Roll with it. It doesn't get any worse—and you'll get used to it.'

'What's with the chanting?'

'I am invoking the spirits. Mother Earth, Father Sky.'

'Is there a whole family we can't see out there?'

'Pretty much.'

And she sealed us in again. And she was right. I did get used to it. The sheer foreignness of her chanting in Oglala or Sioux or whatever diminished as I came to hear it as a kind of music, and when my body said it had had enough she seemed to know instinctively that it was time to take, literally, a breather.

After half a dozen chants I heard her say, 'Your turn.'

'Me? I said—I have nothing to say.'

'They'd appreciate a prayer. Even a selfish one. Just pretend you're phoning home. Your mother's just glad to hear from you. She doesn't mind that you've called to touch her for twenty bucks. Ask them for something.'

'Like what?'

'For Christ's sake . . . use your imagination!'

I was too hesitant. I mumbled and she said, 'Speak up. There may be some deaf gods out there.'

'O Mother Earth, O Father Sky . . .'

So far, so good.

'We have an election due in a little over three years. If you're listening up there and if there's anything you can do about it, please don't let it be won by another man in a suit.'

I heard the hiss of water on stone, then Ethel's voice.

'Are you taking this seriously?'

'Absolutely.'

'Suit yourself.'

Well—she got me to laugh. That was something.

We crawled out. I was feeling better already. I looked at Ethel. Buck naked and dusted in white powder. I looked down at me—the same effect. Salt. I was caked in salt.

'Now we dunk in the stream.'

'First I got to piss.'

I stood with my back to her, aiming at the base of a bush. I heard her flop down into the stream, and she said, 'I wouldn't worry about the color.'

The color? Good God, I was pissing pure Florida orange juice.

'That's because you lost so much liquid in sweat. It lasts a day or two. And don't worry about the size.'

The size? Good God, I was pissing through an acorn. What had happened to the damn thing?

'That's the dope Notley fed you. That passes too.'

I passed a night in Notley's bed. In the morning Ethel shook me awake. She was in shorts, T-shirt and hiking boots.

'Grab breakfast and meet me outside in twenty minutes.'

She stuck a straw hat on my head, handed me a little backpack and led me up the side of the canyon and out onto the mountainside. For about two hours we hiked upward in silence. I stopped countless times to let my lungs recover. When I started again I'd find her sitting on a rock around the next bend. The last time she was sprawled on the path in the blast of full southern sun, staring into the distance. I flopped down next to her.

'What are we looking at?'

'Mexico.'

'Is it still there?'

'Hasn't moved lately.'

She took the pack off me, unrolled a waxpaper parcel and laid out ham sandwiches for two—just when I'd been expecting hippie food.

'Eat up. It's good. We raise our own hogs too.'

I looked at Mexico till I got bored. Took about ten seconds. Then I ate.

Ethel said, 'What is it between you and Notley?'

I said nothing.

'Things the two of you did in Chicago?'

'Were you in Chicago?'

'No, but Notley told me you were. That was quite a stunt you pulled. Is that what this is about, some stunt of Notley's?'

'It isn't about Chicago. He's been places I never have.'

'Vietnam?'

'I wasn't talking geography.'

She didn't press the point.

'You know. The guy has qualities. A lot of him is pure asshole, but he has qualities. But he doesn't appreciate what we have here. He's out pulling another stunt now—he no longer tells me what. Are you two planning something?'

'No—we're not.'

'Because . . . these stunts don't work, do they?'

I said nothing.

'OK—then give me this—they don't work *anymore*.'

'That's probably true.'

'It feels like we're just nibbling at the edges.'

That I could not deny. I'd stopped nibbling a while back. Until very recently it had been one of Mel's roles to remind me of this.

'It's like we're Commanches whirling around the wagon train. When what she should really be doing is taking the fort.'

I said, 'Is that a metaphor?'

It was her turn to say nothing. To see if Mexico had moved lately.

Then, 'We could make it work here. So long as the man leaves us alone, we could make it work here. If Notley continues to pull stunts they'll come for us. I think that's one of the reasons I have to leave.'

'What's the other?'

'You can get too comfortable. You can get . . . too easy.'

§

Notley said, 'You stayed?'

I said, 'Seemed like the place to be. At the time.'

'So . . . now you know, are you going to publish?'

'Can things like this ever stay secret?'

'Who would tell?'

'How can I not tell? It's murder. You'd tell. You've already told me.'

'Yes—I'd tell. I was always going to tell, sooner or later. I was just waiting for the whole puzzle, rather than just a few pieces. And I've been thinking about the piece you brought me, what you said about the difference between military law and civil law. And I think they've got Feaver every which way. He's on a leash and they can jerk it anytime they want. To discharge him, honorably or not, puts him, as you say, beyond their reach. As long as he remains a soldier they're still controlling the issue, they're still controlling the fallout, they still hold the pieces. They have CYA.'

'CIA?'

'No. CYA. Cover Your Ass.'

'Then why let you go? Why let anyone go?'

'Who gives a fuck about a bunch of grunts and a black sergeant? I imagine they'll sit on him for another year or so, then pension him off. If it blows after that it's ancient history and, again, who cares?'

'Why doesn't Feaver just quit?'

'I don't know. But like I said the man is driven. I can only conclude there's still something he wants out of them—out of the system.'

I thought about it—to no purpose. To second guess him was pointless. I'd never met the man.

'You say he's in Vermont? Where in Vermont?'

'Roughly where New York and Vermont meet Massachusetts. Near Manchester. Place called Squab Hill, between Granville and Manchester. Why do you ask?'

'I think I have to talk to Colonel Feaver.'

'For Christ's sake—why?'

§

The Buick died on me, conveniently, on an access road approaching Tucson airport. I stuck the tapes in my bag, abandoned the car and walked into the terminal. I got myself on a flight to Houston with a connection to Kennedy. Time to go back to New York. The endless homecoming. Part of me wondered why I had not said New York when Ethel had asked what I might grace with the name of home. I seemed to be always arriving at New York. A place to which I constantly came. Less the long goodbye than the long hello.

§

1963. I got off the bus from Washington that summer's day and went in search of Mel's apartment. Everything I owned—or everything I had not disowned—was in a backpack, so I walked. A meandering route from the Port Authority to the East Village. I'd never set foot in New York City in my life. It was a little like walking into a movie. That lighter than air, eye-bedazzled feeling. I sat in Madison Square and stared up 5th Avenue. I dawdled on Lexington and watched the Chrysler gleam like diamonds in the sky.

I found myself outside Mel's building around mid-afternoon. A note was pinned to the door. 'Turner. Gone to work. God knows how long

I'll be.' And on the back was a scribbled map of how to find the office of the *Village Voice*. I found it. I found Mel, bent over an old typewriter, typing furiously with one finger of each hand, oblivious to his surroundings, oblivious to me.

'So you made it,' was all he said.

He'd changed his image. I'd lived so long with the old one I had long since thought it permanent. Mel had always been Beat—the 'nik' is derogatory—and his idea of Beat cool had been black. Black jeans. Black roll-neck sweater. Black, heavy-rimmed glasses. A neat black, mephisophelean, goatee beard. He could have played tambourine for Peter, Paul and Mary or polished the horn for Dizzy Gillespie. Now he seemed to have discovered color. He looked a little like the outside of an Italian restaurant, a dash of green, a dash of red. A ring in one ear, a multi-colored scarf at his neck. A T-shirt he'd done up with knotted string and then dyed. Round-lensed, brass-rimmed little spectacles. He was, had I but known another derogatory term, the prototype 'hippie'. The beard was growing. It was a couple of years before his face vanished altogether—down to eyes and nostrils—but I could see the way it was going. Pretty soon hair would take over—hair was here to stay.

'Take this.'

'What?'

'It's the address where you'll be staying.'

I looked at it.

'Don't take a cab, they'll hear your accent and mark you for a rube. You'll end up crossing the Tri-Borough bridge both ways. Take the subway to City Hall and walk from there. Down the side of the Brooklyn Bridge, cross Pearl, cross Water and you're there. Can't miss it.'

'You mean you're not coming?'

'I got work to do. What's your problem?'

'I mean. I never even met the woman.'

'You two will get along just fine. Rose is OK. A little off the wall maybe, but OK.'

He went back to two-fingered typing, hammering down fit to break the machine. I left. It was not the reunion I'd been expecting. But, then, what had I been expecting? He was right about Rose though. A little off the wall. But we got along fine.

I walked down Frankfort Street, under the roads leading to the bridge, wondering if the roar of traffic would stop at night and let me sleep, crossed the side streets, glimpsed the towers of Wall Street in the near distance and found myself in a part of town that looked bombed out. My first reaction was to re-read Mel's note, on the assumption he or I had got something wrong. I turned into Front Street. All the buildings were boarded up. They looked as old as the Republic, neglected, uninhabited, deserted. A smell of fish hung in the air. A guy in a bloody apron pushed a cartload of lobster along the cobbles. I looked for the right house. A five-story warehouse. Only the first floor had glass in its windows, and I took that to be my destination. I walked up the stairs and tapped gently on the door. A few seconds later it was yanked back and a turbaned woman stuck her head out.

'Yes?' An upper-class English accent.

'Turner Raines. Mel sent me. You must be Rose.'

The door was pulled wide. There stood a six-foot woman stark naked but for the turban, spattered from head to foot in half a dozen different shades of paint. She looked like an animated Jackson Pollock.

'Elizabeth Diment,' she said. 'Called Rose because of some unimaginative bastard's joke about an English rose. Not funny, but I live with it. After all, I'm not even blonde!'

I could see that. She led me into the apartment she was half-decorating —one wall started before the last was finished, colors tried out in streaks all over the place, what furniture there was tucked away under sheets. But—it was big. Looked across the way to the ruins of another warehouse opposite, but it was light and spacious.

Elizabeth/Rose showed no inclination to get dressed and no consciousness that she was undressed. I supposed it made some sort of sense. Paint the apartment and don't ruin your clothes. Skin is waterproof and almost anything washes off it.

'I'll put the kettle on, shall I? Why don't you take a look at your room. End of the hallway, on your left.'

The apartment was spacious. My room wasn't. It had nothing in it but a mattress. I lay down on it. An inch less and my head and feet would have touched opposing walls. I didn't care. I wasn't going back, I wasn't looking back. If anything it suited my mood. I wasn't about to be re-born, but a room the size of a womb could do no harm. I went back to Rose

and her paint and her very English cup of tea, and said, 'Fine.' She named
a low rent, less than I'd paid for my share of the Washington apartment,
and we shook on it. We drank tea. Me in my Levi's and Tony Lama's,
Rose in her nothings. She told me all about herself—I figured that was
one of the functions of tea—how she'd come to America in search of a
great-grandmother in Virginia who'd supplied General Hooker with the
commodity to which he has, ever since, lent his name—scratched bits of
paint off her boobs, munched on chocolate chip cookies and in the end
leapt up, pulled off her turban—red hair falling in giant ringlets halfway
down her back—and disappeared into the shower.

We spent the evening in some of her favorite bars. Several of her
favorite bars. We ended up in Pete's Tavern on Irving Place drinking
margaritas. Just before she got totally drunk, she stuck five dollars in my
hand and said, 'Make sure we get home OK.'

I rolled her into a cab, I rolled her out and I put her to bed.

'You know, Texsh, I think we're going to get along jush fine,' she said.

And so began a pattern of our lives that took up one and often three
nights of our weeks for the next few years. She would appear the next
morning, made-up, levelheaded and we'd go into work together. She
was given to steams of rage, and I could hear her anger roar out across
the entire floor of the office—'Can none of you dozy fuckers learn to
spell?' 'Good God, man, you'd forget the date of your own Revolution
if I hadn't tattooed it onto your arse!' One unfortunate freelancer got so
exasperated with her he uttered the near-fatal line, 'I wouldn't normally
even think of punching a woman . . .' and before he could finish the
sentence she had coldcocked him with a left jab and was dancing around
him doing the Cassius Clay shuffle, yelling, 'Get up, you spineless little
toad of a man!' If this sort of thing happened late enough in the day it
would inevitably end in what she called 'a bit of a crawl' and we'd hit the
bars again. I didn't mind. I didn't understand it, but I didn't mind. She
seemed to know what she was doing.

It was an odd relationship, but I quickly forgot to view it that way.
We had suspended gender. Sex did not rear its greedy little head. Her
indifference to flesh and gender could astound people. I'd get dragged to
clothes shops with her, yeaing or naying the stuff she swanned out of the
changing room wearing, more often than not dragged into the changing
room with her. After one expensive afternoon hitting the lingerie shops

of 5th Avenue, she tried on six different bras over dinner. We had guests. Mel did not know where to look—or to be precise he knew exactly where to look—and whichever girlfriend he had in tow never spoke to me or Rose again. I got used to it. It was like living with a six-year-old, permanently kicking off her clothes and running across the beach. It meant no more than that.

We finished the apartment between us. Gradually over the next five or six years the landlord—'that old skinflint, darling', never did get to meet the man—did up the rest of the building and we found ourselves with neighbors. Rather than go down further the neighborhood started to come up a tad. Down the street they started a Seaport Museum and parts of Fulton Street got, as Rose put it, 'a bit bloody posh', but the 'poshness' never reached our end of the street. We lived in an enclave of general neglect, modest improvement, modest rent and stinking fish. One day a scrawny tomcat appeared through the window with a chunk of cod in its jaws. It stayed. Rose, me and 'Neddy Seagoon'—don't ask why—an unholy and not wholly unhappy trinity.

Over the next three or four years we—Rose and me, two non-native New Yorkers (the cat after all was a native)—saw our city change around us, felt its center of gravity shift from around 52nd Street (all that jazz) to around the East Village, to Alphabet City—a movement generated by thousands, tens of thousands, of other non-native New Yorkers pouring in from Ohio, Iowa, Indiana (pick a nowhere place and take a guess). It was kids, kids disowning their family physically as we had metaphorically. New York filled with new huddled masses yearning to be free. They huddled around Tompkins Square, they slept a dozen to a room exactly as the last wave of immigrants had done, and I'd put their average age at sixteen or seventeen. By 1967 they were making the East Coast version of the summer of love. I remember walking across the square with Rose one August night, dope hanging on the air, *Sergeant Pepper's Lonely Hearts Club Band* booming out of a dozen different windows, feeling outnumbered, almost old and not much minding that we were, and Rose said, quoting quite unintentionally from the Beatles' previous album, 'Where do they all come from?'

§

1969. I got into the apartment. Neddy sat by his empty bowl and howled until I fed him. Rose was back—clothes scattered across her bed, the wardrobe door slid back, a waft of scent still hanging in the air, an open suitcase with two bottles of duty-free British gin—she just wasn't around. This was nothing unusual. Most of her relationships amounted to short-lived sexual frenzies, often no more than one night stands. I learnt early on that if she wasn't home for a night or two it didn't mean I'd find her at the bottom of the East River.

I slept late. Ate a lazy breakfast at lunchtime and weighed up the merits of my last conversation with Notley. He had a point. Why ask? I had a point, and I rather thought I would stick to it. I had to ask. The near-dormant part of my character crept to the surface. I had to ask, I had to give the guy a hearing. I'd heard Mouse's tale. I'd heard Notley's, and the two were not the same. Supposing the third was not the same as the second? Then another voice in the head said, 'But you saw the photographs—they are the constant in this, the photographs, as surely as $E=MC^2$.' And another voice said, 'Ask.' After all what were the chances he would shoot me? In cold blood? In Vermont?

When I set off for Hoboken late afternoon, Rose still hadn't shown up. I picked up my conspicuous yellow VW in the stacker and yet again drove north—it seemed like driving this route had become as imprinted on my flesh as a lifeline. I cheated fate. Just for the hell of it. Swung back across the George Washington bridge and up the east bank of the Hudson—Yonkers, Poughkeepsie and places north. Why not? I had criss-crossed America, turned it into a cat's cradle of tire tracks. What mattered one more bridge, one more stretch of highway?

Why did I leave it so late? Never did figure out why. Did I think of darkness as some kind of cover? Whatever—dusk was creeping down by the time I passed Hudson Falls. All the same I followed Notley's instructions and I found the place easily. Through Granville, across the state line a mile or so into Vermont, a mile or so down the road to Manchester, off at a graded road marked Squab Hill and follow the track. All it lacked was a sign saying 'mass-murderer this way'. Where the gravel turned to dirt there was a mailbox balanced on a skewed pole with 'Feaver' stenciled on the side. I parked the car by the side of a wood and set off on foot. It was past dusk and moonlit. There were fields of stubble all around me, chaff and grain scattered across the track. The aftermath of harvest. As I rounded the edge of the woods, a hill rose out of the stubble like a knob—a sharp hill, straight up, straight down, exaggerated like the illustration to a fairy tale. Atop this hill was a house . . . And in this house there lived a giant.

How to describe what I saw by the light of that silvery moon? Put simply, as simply as it hit me, Squab Hill was the log cabin, backwoods, Natty Bumppo version of my father's house. Where Sam had built in glass and steel and alloys this monstrosity on stilts was hewn from pine, the bark still on the logs. It crept up the hillside to tower over the fields at treetop height. It was the same principle at work, I felt, the boldness, the ugliness of fuck-you arrogance.

The first floor seemed to be garages, the retractable door of one was wide open and a greenish light—they've landed, they've landed, take me to your leader was my first thought—glared out across the yard. There were no lights on the second or third stories. I left the shelter of the trees, crept up to the house, trying for shadows, knowing that if I wanted a look inside I'd have to risk stepping into the light. Why? For fuck's sake why? Why was I behaving like . . . like what? A guerrilla? A boy scout? Or just a hammy gumshoe? I could have just walked up to the door and rung the bell.

Then I saw it—a trail of chocolate chip cookies leading from the cement apron right into the light. What was he up to? Trying to trap a squirrel or a racoon? I flipped one over with the toe of my boot—didn't look poisoned. Picked one up. Looked fresh to me. Tasted fine. What the hell was going on?

I stepped out of darkness, followed the trail. Wondering what trapped animal I'd find at the end of it. I'd got a few paces into the garage when a voice behind me said, 'Works every time', then a blow to the back of my head turned everything black and I fell into oblivion.

I woke. Oblivion had been dreamless. The green light was still on. The door was down. I couldn't tell whether it was day or night, or how long I'd been out. My watch was gone, so were my boots and belt. My head throbbed and my muscles ached. Why all of this hit me before the more immediate reality I do not know. But . . . I found myself in a cage, a bamboo cage, suspended from the high ceiling. There was a water bottle and tube taped to one bar, a mess of boiled rice in an old ice cream carton next to it and a hunk of stale coarse bread on the floor of the cage.

I rubbed at my chin. No real growth of beard. I'd been out hours or minutes not days.

'Does it hurt?'

I hadn't heard him come in—or had he been standing there for hours waiting for me to come round? I looked down at him, half hidden by the glare of the lights aimed at me and the sharpness of the angle. I knew the voice at once. I'd heard it one Mel's tape. '*Call me Broken Arrow*' . . . That's what he'd told Mel in the Port Authority a lifetime ago.

'Yes,' I said.

'Must be cramped in there. I built it for someone a lot shorter.'

'Mel?'

'You know the little guy?'

'Yes.'

'I guess he won't be joining us.'

Question or statement? I wasn't sure.

'Mel's dead.'

Feaver seemed to weigh this up a second, took his eyes off me and then locked them back on me.

'You kill him?'

'No. He was my oldest friend. Did you?'

'Kill him? Of course I didn't—I needed Mr Kissing alive. You a reporter too?'

'Private Eye. Mel and I went to school together.'

'How did he die?'

'Stabbed to death in my office in New York City.'

'So you took his place. Looking for me.'

'I was looking for the man who killed Mel.'

'Then you have a ways to go yet.'

He flicked out the light and I was in darkness. Overwhelming, total darkness, not a crack of light from anywhere.

I estimated it was another two days before he came back. I say estimate. The bread grew moldy in a matter of hours. The rice began to smell rancid. I ate both. And I eked out the water.

In darkness this absolute, your eyes do not adapt—there is nothing to adapt to. I learnt about my prison with my fingertips. The bamboo struts were about an inch and a half thick. No amount of pressure or kicking would break or dislodge them. They were tied together with leather thongs—bound over and over, tied with multiple knots, and, worse, put on wet, so they'd shrunk tight to the wood.

For a day or so I lived with it. I could not quite sit upright, either my back or my neck had to bend. I could not stretch my legs full length. I think I began to get cramps after about thirty minutes. After a day I sacrificed some of the water, splashed a little on two of the thongs and tried to ease the bars in the floor apart. Took me an age, and I gained less than two inches, but it was enough to let me lower one leg at a time almost full length, dangling below the cage—feeling the circulation return to the leg, the pain almost delicious. That was when it hit me. This wasn't just a prison. It was a device for torture. Mel might have got off lighter than me—he was five foot seven to my six two—but the principle remained. Confinement was torture, relief was torture.

I tried holding in my piss, but then I thought what was the point? The point was my own inhibition—childhood memories of all the dogs I'd trained to piss outside not in a corner in the house. I broke the taboo. I unzipped and pissed through the bars. A few hours later I felt the need of a crap. I held out again. One more taboo. One more battle lost or won. I couldn't get a good angle. Pants around my knees. I ended up hugging those knees, drawing them up to the chest and merely hoping for an approximation of aim. Not good. Shit on the bars, and the impossibility of ever wiping my ass. To this end, I ripped up my shirt, tore it into strips just like they did on *Wagon Train* when the Indians attacked.

I also found I could flip upside down and dangle an arm or lie with my face pressed to the bars, the smell of my own shit and piss wafting up from the cement floor below—worse, far worse, but just as evocative as the bucket of shit Notley had spattered me with in Chicago. When W. H. Auden said that everyone secretly likes the smell of their own farts, I figure he didn't have this situation in mind.

I was sleeping when Feaver came back. The lights flickered on, and I heard the squeak of a pulley wheel. A battered and scorched tin pot of rice and bean shoots, mold already growing on them, was hauled up within my reach—a pint of brownish-looking water in a plastic bottle propped up in a corner of the can.

I didn't move. Just stared down at him, almost blinded by the light. 'Take it,' he said. I took it.

The heat was up—when that summer had it not been up?—it had to be high nineties in that garage—the food rotted almost as quickly as my shit. I soon ceased to mind either. I ate rancid rice, I picked bugs out of pond water, and hunkered down and shat whenever the urge took me—waiting for the splat below became one of my few entertainments. I began to see why cons would bet on anything, the race between two bedbugs, how long it takes a turd to drop fifteen feet.

It is one of childhood's games. Put yourself in an imaginary situation. Captured by the Japs (well—I'm that generation), fleeing from the Apache, interrogated by the SS . . . what kid doesn't imagine their own response in extremis? What kid did not have his own sense of heroism nurtured by Hollywood? Surprisingly some of what you imagine can be pretty accurate, but mostly it's the mental stuff. Nothing can prepare you for pain you have imagined but not experienced. I mean what are the limits? How can you even guess? The mental stuff . . . well, everything distorts just like the movies and your games tell you it will. I tried to keep track of time and lost it, although it would be better put that I had no way of measuring it to begin with. I heard things—any bump or scratch magnified by singularity—I saw things—in total darkness I imagined I could see shapes and colors, and I dreamt things. In spades I dreamt. I had only to close my eyes to be anywhere but where I was. The old trick with the morning blues and the alarm clock. You imagine you've gotten up and are going through the daily routine with numbing ordinariness . . . meanwhile the body sleeps. The body gets what it wants. I got the opposite. My mind needed escape, so my body slept. And while it slept I walked to the corner deli for coffee, opened my mail and read the morning paper.

I was out of everything but water. I figured I had not seen Feaver in about three days. I was in real pain. Real pain produced my one spark of inspiration. I wriggled out of my Levi's, screamed out loud as my left leg locked up in the calf and I had to force it down with my hands—God knows what damage I was doing to my own muscles—and found the metal tag that you use to zip up the fly. The one piece of metal in all I had been wearing that Feaver had left me. I scraped away at a thong—spent all of an afternoon (or was it a morning or a night? whatever) until it parted. I then found I hadn't got the strength to kick the bar I'd freed up until it snapped. I took a long breather, then let my weight prise it down and out. I figure I had created a five- or six-inch gap. I could get my legs down the gap almost to the top of the thigh. I could stretch fully—and it hurt like hell. I rested up, one leg dangling one folded, and worked on a second thong. Another two and I would be able to drop out of the cage altogether.

The light came on. Bounced around in my skull.

Feaver was standing there, holding the biggest Bowie knife I'd ever seen.

'Pull your leg in.'

'What?'

'I won't ask you again.'

He swung the blade at the rope holding my cage. I yanked in my leg as the rope parted. The cage crashed to the concrete floor. The impact jolted every bone in my body, and a broken spar took a piece out of my left arm. I lay in the wreckage—a pile of broken bamboo and rancid shit with me in the middle of it.

Feaver said, 'When you're ready, I'll be upstairs.'

He walked up the stairs to a door high in the wall. Looked down at me as I picked my way out of the remains of my prison. I got clear, tried to stand and found I couldn't. My muscles simply wouldn't do what I told them.

'I can't walk!' I yelled up at him.

'Then crawl,' was all he said.

I did just that. I picked my way up the staircase, dragging my legs and feet. Must have taken me ten minutes. In the room above a bare pine table sat in the center of a bare pine room. I hauled myself up into the chair opposite Feaver, my breath tearing in and out of my lungs, needles and pins stabbing every inch of my body.

For the first time I got a good look at him. My size, more or less, more muscle—well, he would, wouldn't he—and a look of James Coburn about him, that is the way Coburn looked then. I'd put him at about thirty-five.

He'd set out a meal. No more rice specked with mold. Freshly-squeezed orange juice, toast, scrambled eggs, crispy bacon. A breakfast fit for my old man. Breakfast? Good God—was it morning?

I asked the question.

'No. It's 1700 hours,' Feaver replied. 'At least, it was when I came to get you. You were in there just over six and a half days. Call this a late late brunch if you like.'

I always thought sensory deprivation would extend the sense of time. Hollywood talking again. My guess, that's all it was, was five days—out by a day and a half.

He walked over to the stove, came back with a pot of coffee, poured me a cup and I let the smell assault my senses. I forked egg onto a slice of toast—Feaver had waited till he heard me at the door before dishing up, they were moist and fresh—and he'd chopped scallions, red pepper and a little jalapeño into the mixture. I gulped a good half-pint of juice and held out my glass for more. That phrase from the newspapers surfaced in my mind—the condemned man ate a hearty breakfast. We both ate. He asked me my name. I told him, then he said nothing for a while. Looked at me from time to time, topped up my coffee, made me more toast.

At last, when I'd finished he said, 'I hope you haven't suffered too much, but I thought a taste of 'Nam would be educative for you.'

'Educative?'

'So you don't have to imagine what you can't possibly imagine anyway.'

'I see. So that's what you guys do to the Cong?'

'No, Mr Raines—it's what they do to us. I spent twelve weeks in a cage scarcely bigger than yours.'

'You escaped?'

'Obviously.'

'Why aren't you a cripple? Twelve weeks and your muscles would never work again.'

'I developed a program of exercises. I kept my muscle tone by working out.'

'In that space?'

'It was all I had. It was that or, as you say, end up a cripple. In fact it would do you good.'

'Right now a shower would do me good.'

'Afterwards. Follow me.'

I could limp along now. Needed a wall to support me, but at least I was off the floor. I bumbled after him into the next room. Another bad taste nightmare in glossy pine, but this one had carpets—the shaggy kind that you can never get clean. It all reinforced the sense of being in a cheap motel out West.

Feaver lay on the floor. I all but fell down next to him.

'Now—sit upright—spine straight—grip your right ankle with your left hand . . .'

He noticed the gash in my left arm.

'OK, let's make it the other way round. Now—twist—then stretch the leg. No—further. Stretch. Good. You got it.'

It was, and I cannot think of a better word, almost paternal. He put me through a forty-minute workout. On my back, on my front, on one side and then the other. When we'd finished I felt better, and I had an inkling of how he'd survived. I'd worked out on the shagpile—if I stretched an inch or a foot too far what was to stop me?—he'd worked out in the cage, back against the bars, straining every muscle for every inch of space. He led me to a bedroom—I was hobbling now, unaided by walls or floors, still in pain, but confident I would not go through life encumbered by the gait of Charles Laughton in *Notre Dame*. He flicked on a light in the bathroom, threw me a towel and told me he'd lay out some clean clothes for me. I sat under the shower for ages. Days rolled off me. I could have sat there all day, but that wasn't the point. He'd gotten me there for a reason. I had, like it or not, an appointment.

When I stepped back into the bedroom I found clothes, pretty much my size—he was my height but a lot broader—laid out on the bed. Not, I was delighted to see, army fatigues, but pretty well what I would have chosen myself. Blue jeans, white shirt—he'd even ironed the shirt. As I was pulling on the jeans Feaver appeared, took my left arm in one hand.

'You could use a stitch or two, but I figure that's more than you want, right?'

'Right.'

He tore the back off a huge Band-Aid and slapped it across the wound.

'Your choice,' he said.

When I'd dressed I hobbled back into his sitting room. No sign of him, nor in his kitchen. I found him in what he probably called his den. I braced myself for whatever he might be doing, a mural, a photograph, a vast canvas—God knows everyone else had their vision of America, their American dream writ large upon the wall. But Feaver's were blank. Plain pine walls. He was seated at his desk—an old newsroom-style rolltop—a rack of guns padlocked to his right, and just a small cork bulletin board to his left. I looked at the sole item he'd pinned up there with a thumbtack—not a laundry list or reminder to buy milk—just that same syndicated piece Notley had shown me. Only this was the original not a photocopy and the by-line wasn't missing—it read 'Mel Kissing'. I should have known. Under my nose, socking me right in the puss and still I missed it. Mel wrote the piece while we were in Chicago, Feaver saw it and through it found both Mel and Notley. I should have added up the names—Cochise, Broken Arrow. How could I have missed that? It's so . . . so . . . so fuckin' obvious. How dumb could I get? Answer? Dumber.

'So now you know,' Feaver said, reading my mind, not looking at me, just intent on what he was doing—going through the contents of my bag. He'd broken into my car—after what I'd just been through it scarcely seemed worth protest.

'Freud speaking,' I said.

'What?'

'That day in the Port Authority, when Mel asked what he should call you. You said Broken Arrow—you had no expectation of the question and no prepared answer. You said the first thing that came into your head. What was on your mind was Notley—you thought of Notley, you thought of Cochise.'

'Actually, I was thinking of Mouse. I already knew where to find Notley. It was Mouse I needed to find—but I see you did.'

He fanned out Mouse's photographs, like a cardsharp showing a flush—I looked away. He folded and stacked.

'I knew he'd taken a second camera. There were bound to be photographs. I had to see for myself.'

'So now you have it all.'

'No—but I have enough.'

'And?'

'And I'm sorry to hear Marty died. Sorrier too about Gus.'

'Are you?'

'Of course.'

'You sorry about Mel Kissing too? Or was he disposable?'

'As I said, I needed Mr Kissing. I'm more sorry about his death than anyone's. There was nothing I could do about Marty or Gus—but I rather think I led Mr Kissing's killer right to him. They watch me—you know—not all the time. I don't think they can afford that. And the day I went down to the city I felt certain, as certain as I could be, that I wasn't followed. I was wrong. Kissing died for my mistake. I'm sorry about that.'

I pointed to the envelope containing Mouse's photos.

'They all die for your mistake too?'

He didn't answer. Got up out of his chair. Unlocked his gun rack.

He hefted out a bolt action rifle. Racked it once and took a bead on me. A wee small voice in my head said, 'This is not it. He did not get you all this way to kill you now.' My body heard it just in time, and I managed not to piss myself.

He swung the rifle parallel to his chest in one of those well-honed parade ground maneuvers, yelled 'catch' and threw it to me. I caught it and gasped. The damn thing seemed to weigh a ton.

'Lesson number two,' he said. 'The VC is a little guy. Average height under five four, weight around a hundred and five. He totes a gun like this all day . . .'

I took a good look. This wasn't state of the art Russian made. It looked years old.

'Took this off a VC I killed in '63—it's French made, dates from the 1930s. Most of them have AK47s now, but those that don't are still using the stuff the French left behind after Dien Bien Phu. It weighs three times what an AK47 weighs. He can march all day on a handful of rice, lug this damn thing and aim it with an accuracy that makes our guys with semi-automatics look like kids at a county fair. You know much about Dien Bien Phu?'

I knew nothing and told him so. When Dien Bien Phu had happened I'd been more into girls and Little Richard than international politics in faraway countries no one had ever heard of.

'They moved artillery across a mountain range. Stripped it down, strapped it on to bicycles, pushed it, put it back together. Took the French completely by surprise. They were expecting coolies in pointed hats to rush at them with machetés. Vietnamese blew them to hell. They can still do it. Stuff gets moved across territory you'd think twice about taking a mule into. They can appear out of nowhere, behind your own lines, armed with equipment we'd need a chopper to shift. Now—do you get my point?'

I didn't.

'This—this is what we're up against. A rice-fed killing machine who doesn't need Hershey bars, Coca Cola and visits from Bob Hope. Given the nature—that is what it is—of our enemy, I try not to make mistakes.'

'Ah—I was wondering when we'd get to that.'

'Mouse told you about the dynamite kid he killed?'

'Yes.'

'I'd heard about them. Till then I'd never seen one. Used 'em a lot against the French. One guy straps on as much high explosive as he can run with, charges an otherwise impregnable line and blows a hole in it with his own body. The kamikaze for our times. Mr Raines—we don't have time for mistakes.'

I threw the rifle back at him. He caught it one-handed.

'Fine,' I said. 'The little guy with the rifle in Vietnam is invincible—so you slaughter his unarmed women and children instead.'

Feaver locked the gun back in the rack.

'Are you even listening to me, Mr Raines?'

'Of course, Mr Feaver. Sole purpose of visit.'

I could see from his eyes that he knew the quotation in full. 'Is it your intention to in any way subvert or overthrow the Government of the United States?' was a question on the old immigration form and some English joker—God knows, Wilde, Waugh—had written 'sole purpose of visit' as his answer. The way I heard it, they still let him in. But . . . there was not a flicker of a smile.

Feaver muttered 'Jesus Christ' and stormed off. I followed. It was the first time I'd managed to unnerve him. Best chance yet to get more out of him than he was getting out of me.

I found him in yet another room, rough pine and spartan, hardly a speck of dust but hardly a human imprint either. Like all his rooms it looked unlived in or lived in by a man who lived between his ears. This one was a west-facing sun trap—huge glass wraparound windows, a view down the valley—it was almost like home. I'd be summoned to a room like this by Sam to receive a catalogue of my sins or, in sentimental mood, to get a version of his 'one day, my boy all this will be yours' lecture.

He turned on me, back to the window, angry but holding it in.

'Mr Raines, do you have any idea what's happening out there?' The left arm sweeping across the vista, demonstrative, possessive, whatever. I stuck my neck out.

'Yes. If you ask a question as dumb as that I'll give you an answer just as dumb. You've been to Vietnam, I haven't. You've blown away women and kids. I haven't. You sat in the cage for twelve weeks. I didn't. You've already convinced me that imagination is not enough. But do I know what's happening in Vietnam? Are we talking about the big picture? Then yes. I think a lot of Americans know what's happening in Vietnam. I think most sentient beings in America *should* know what's happening in Vietnam. I spent the last six weeks talking to people back from 'Nam. And that's all America needs to do—just to listen to the kids who're fighting the war in Vietnam for them.'

'I wasn't talking about Vietnam. I was talking about America!'

Damn—wrong again.

'But—you're right about one thing. Every American should know what is being done in Vietnam for them. Every American should grasp where this war stands in . . . in America's . . .'

He was fumbling for words for the first time, chopping at the air with his hands.

'The word you're searching for is destiny,' I said.

'Fine—destiny it is. I'm not crazy about the word, but let's use it. What is the war's place in our destiny? And don't answer. I'll tell you. It's a watershed as big as 1776. As big as 1861. It's a war we have to win, but it's a war we're losing.'

'Bullshit,' I said.

I had him on the hop—just. He was nowhere near as cool as he tried to pretend. I stood stock still looking down the valley, he paced up and down in front of the window, a small figure in a landscape rendered up as Cinemascope.

'Did you watch Chicago on the nightly news, Mr Raines?'

'No, Mr Feaver. I was there. I was part of Chicago.'

Feaver paused and nodded. It is the only time in my life I have ever stated my involvement in that bloodbath with anything approaching pride.

'Fine, that's good, saves a lot of time. You'll know that Notley was there?'

'Sure—I read your clipping. That's how you found Notley, that's how you found Mel. It's also how you got him killed.'

He didn't rise to that.

'What is the slogan that your generation trucks out so lightly?'

Jeez—pick any one of two dozen.

'How about,' he went on, 'Bring the War Home?'

I shrugged. Fine by me. I'd heard Rubin use it a lot.

'What do you think it means, Mr Raines?'

'What it says. Give civil Amerika a taste of what's going down.'

'Good—we agree. That is what Notley did. That is why I wrote to him. That is why I admire him, he has his place. He told America what it did not wish to know. That if the war in Vietnam is not won it will surely come home. Notley kicked off the first battle in the Vietnam war to be fought on American soil. It was a timely reminder. Because if we do not pursue the war, if we do not win the war, then we will end up bringing it all back home. It will be fought out in our streets and on our campuses for the rest of our lives.'

'You know,' I said slowly, somewhat chilled by his vision of my future, 'You and Notley seem like the most unholy alliance I can imagine. You want opposing ends, but your means seem identical. We can't win another Chicago. We didn't even win the last one. But we can stop you winning in Vietnam all the same. If "Bring the War Home" won't work, if "By Any Means Necessary" won't work, there's always "Hell No We Won't Go". We can stop you.'

'And if you do . . . the history of America will be marred for a generation or more . . . the culture will be . . . crippled . . . the national psyche . . . permanently damaged . . . the last quarter of this century will make the ten years after the Civil War look like a national holiday. We could not reconstruct the South. We will have hell on earth trying to reconstruct America.'

(Was he preaching at me? Absofuckinlutely, as my late wife would say.)

I guess I'm giving you the gist of what the bastard said. Because I know that by the time I'd argued back and he'd argued back some more night was falling again, and a haze of sunset glimmered behind him in the window, blotting out his features, making it seem as though his voice spoke to me from a silhouette framed in a red-rimmed halo—a total eclipse of the man.

I'd had enough of his theory. I hauled him back.

'So for the soul of a nation you slaughter one hundred and thirty-four Vietnamese women, kids and old men.'

'The dead are dead.'

'And you pile 'em up.'

'And I pile 'em up. And people like you count 'em . . . you know, you're the first person to tell me how many died at Phuong. I never counted and I never asked. That's what's wrong with the way we are fighting the war. Too many clerks, too many statisticians, too many hacks. Too few warriors. Instead what we have are figures, ream upon ream of figures— percentages for this, percentages for that. Cost of a dead GI to the VC? 27 cents. Cost of a dead VC to us? $10,000. Payments made in compensation to the Vietnamese? $20 for a wound, $33.99 for a dead relative. Took a shoe salesman to work out that last figure. How many dead are VC? How many dead are civilian? . . . and everyone invents and everyone lies . . . when what matters, all that matters, is that the dead are dead.'

I thought for a split second that his tone might be sadness or regret, but I concluded it was just matter-of-fact. And he wasn't through yet.

'We can win this war. What we need is a General Sherman—someone who'll cut a swathe the length of Vietnam through every living thing like marching through Georgia.'

Hurrah, hurrah. The flag that sets you free.

Right.

It was a good time to tell him he was nuts. I didn't bother. I did what any self-respecting coward would do, I changed the subject. There were things I still had to know and I felt time running out.

'Why did you set Mel to find the Nine? You had all Mouse's 35mm? Were you just mopping up?'

'No—nothing so simple. I gave the 35mm films to Phoenix. I needed what Mouse had. Notley wouldn't put me in touch with Mouse. That's where your friend came in.'

'What concerns me is where he went out.'

'Like I said. You have a ways to go yet. Get your gear together. You're leaving.'

Orders are orders. I did as I was told. Which consisted of finding my boots and my belt—the only items of clothing six days in the cage hadn't ruined—and my bag. My notes were in it, my car keys weren't and neither were the photographs. That didn't surprise me. I didn't think anyone would ever see them again. They'd be buried along with Mouse's 35 mm shots. Without them my notes were uncorroborated. Just the word of two discharged grunts, albeit purple-hearted grunts, versus a serving colonel. Which is to say . . . next to useless. I figured to keep his clothes. It would be so unlike your average mass-murderer to send a guy out buck naked.

Feaver reappeared. A change of outfit. Combat boots. One of those vests of a thousand pockets that hunters wear to house cartridges and fishing flies. And he had an M16 over his shoulder.

'Come on,' was all he said.

I followed him down to the garage again. He flicked a lot of switches, the lights came on, the doors swung open and I saw the night cut up by floodlights, sweeping out across the ridges of a freshly plowed field all the way to my car. Stuck out on the side, looking, as it inevitably had to, like a fat little bug at the perimeter of light.

'You moved my car?'

He ignored this. Reached into his inside pocket and stuck the envelope containing Mouse's photos in my hand.

'I don't get it,' I said in all honesty.

'Take 'em.'

'What?'

'Take 'em. They're yours. Write it all up. Publish what you can.'

'Mel Kissing died to get you these.'

'Mel Kissing died to get at the truth. The truth is in your hand now. Finish the job, Mr Raines. Publish them.'

I finally got the message.

I stuffed the photos in my bag.

I felt I'd earned them. O hubris, O fuckin' hubris.

Feaver said, 'I suppose you think you've earned them?'

'Something like that,' I said wondering about the man's power of perception.

'Not yet, but you will.'

'Eh?'

'Your car is about two hundred yards off. The keys are in the ignition. You could be out of here in less than two minutes. Between you and the car are thirty land mines. Maybe a couple more. I wasn't counting. You get across without tripping one, and the whole story is yours. You'll be home free. You could even end up a hero.'

'You're kidding?'

'No—I never kid. Start running.'

I laughed. He swung the gun off his shoulder, racked up and said, 'Run.'

I didn't move. He put a bullet into the ground right between my feet. I stared him out. I'd seen this Western too. He slipped the gun onto rock 'n' roll and cut up the ground around my feet, nicked a piece out of my boots and I ran. Right across that damn field. In a straight line for my car, with bullets zipping up behind me. And a voice that just screamed. I think it was me. I know it was me. I ran until my lungs burned, and then I still ran—on and on as straight as a die. What was the point in bobbing and weaving? I was as likely to hit a mine that way as this way, so I just ran. I fell on my face, sprawled full length on the ground. I waited for the earth to move. It didn't. Then Feaver's voice boomed out across the field.

'Get up!'

I turned my head. Nothing but the glare of floodlights.

'Get-up-you-son-of-a-bitch!' Every single syllable word rattled off with metrical emphasis.

I couldn't move—I was glued to the ground with terror.

Feaver put a spread all around me. Another bullet nicked into my boots. I leapt up. Screamed. I ran. Still screaming.

I collapsed against the side of the car. A last volley of bullets tore into the ploughed strip a yard from my feet. The muscles in my legs twitched and jerked with a life of their own. I couldn't see Feaver—he could surely see me, lit up like the Statue of Liberty. The light was blinding. Why then do I have the lasting impression that he had waved at me? Just once, but he waved. And then I knew. There were no mines. He wanted me alive. He needed me alive. He always had. There was still something I could do for him, he could not do for himself. This was endgame—he'd just moved his last piece. Me.

I got to my feet, legs like jelly, sucked all the air I could into my lungs. He wasn't going to shoot me now.

'Fuck you, Jack. Fuck you, Jack!'

I don't know how long I yelled or how many times I said it. Twenty, fifty, a hundred? Fuck you, Jack. I was hoarse when I gave up. And answer came there none. The lights went out. I was alone in the sugary pinewood darkness of summer. After the roar of Feaver's M16, an almost deathly quiet. No rustling in the grass, no hoot of an owl, no fervent ticking of night insects, no booming bass of frogs—between the two of us we'd silenced every other life form. I felt like Ishmael—the last living man, bobbing to the surface on Queequeg's coffin. For a few minutes, till I came to my senses, got in the car and drove off, I felt as though I'd survived a unique ordeal, been washed up as the sole survivor, alive when Mel and Marty and Gus and half a squad of grunts and a hundred and thirty-four Vietnamese were not. But I hadn't and I wasn't. That was Feaver's point. To save me imagining what I could not imagine. Call me Idiot.

§

I drove carefully. I did not trust myself at speed. Just over the state line, a few yards into New York, someone came up behind me at sixty, pushed me off the road and into the ditch. My head bounced off the steering wheel, and when I looked up whoever it was had swung around to fix me in his headlights. He walked out between them, face hidden by the glare as Feaver's had been by the sunset, but it wasn't Feaver. He was too short—that much I could see—and he was aiming a pump action shotgun right at me.

'Get out!'

I stood at the side of the car. Put my hands in the air. Gangling idiot that I was.

He blew the hood off the VW, and levelled the gun at me again before I could even blink. The hood slammed into the windshield and shattered it. I found myself wondering, almost idly in the face of possessive terror, if he might actually not know the engine is in the rear on a VW.

He came right up to me.

'Where is it?'

'Where's what?'

He slammed the gun into my face. I went down and as I did he put the boot into my ribs. I watched from the ground as he walked to the back of the car and pumped two shots into the engine, saw a trail of gray-black smoke start up out of the grill.

He came back to me.

'Where is it?'

He dragged me half upright with one hand.

'Where is it?'

'I don't know what you're talking about.'

'What did he give you?'

'He didn't give me anything.'

'You got one chance, sucker.'

I was on my knees now. He placed the barrel of the gun against my forehead and said, 'You got one chance. Where is it?'

'Where's what, for Chrissake?'

He pressed the barrel into my skin. I heard the explosion, felt the force of it, felt blood and brain slide across my face, saw him bounce off the side of the car with half his head blown away and fall at my feet like a rag doll. I didn't even have time to scream.

Three guys came out of the darkness. The first one turned back to a guy with a rifle and said, 'Clear the car now. It's going to blow any minute.'

Then he and a third guy took an armpit apiece and dragged me away. I'd got as articulate as 'whaaa?' when I heard the gas tank blow and twisted round to see my little yellow Bug go up in flames. The second guy caught up with us, my bag in one hand, his rifle in the other.

'Got it,' was all he said.

They hauled me to a gravel road. A tan Ford was parked just off the highway. They helped me into the back and I remember noting the cop gesture as one of them put his hand on my head and steered me into the seat.

I found myself seated between two guys, with the one giving the orders up front next to the driver. He turned round to me and said, 'You know, if you'd not tried so hard to lose us in Chicago and then in Jackson, none of this need have happened.' Then he turned back and the driver started up.

I must have passed out. When I came to it had begun to rain. Another of those short torrential summer downpours, pounding onto the roof, the wipers clicking rhythmically back and forth. Nobody spoke. We were on a deserted two-lane blacktop, and pretty soon we pulled up at a cheap-looking motel.

My legs gave and I sat on the edge of the bed with my head in my hands.

'Clean yourself up,' the man said. 'Go to the bathroom. Take all the time you want.'

I took more than he wanted. I'd barfed up breakfast, stripped off, wiped the gore from my face and was examining the wound to my cheek—not too bad, I'd have a nasty bruise rather than a scar; he'd biffed me with the barrel not the butt or I'd be out some teeth as well—when the man came in and sat on the can.

He said nothing. I spat blood and rinsed, then said, 'Who was he?'

'CIA. We figure he killed Kissing.'

Fine—so did I.

'And who are you guys?'

'They're CIA.'

'So,' I muttered through swollen cheeks, 'I just leapt from the frying pan to the frying pan.'

'*They're CIA.* I'm not. And I'm in charge.'

'Let me guess . . . the Andrew Carnegie Foundation for Repatriation and Reconciliation of Wayward Hippies?'

'Close. I'm with that five-sided building down by the Potomac you hippies tried to levitate a couple of years back. I was inside while you tried. Name's Hammond.'

I stopped looking in the mirror and turned to him. Neat-looking guy, about forty or so, good suit, button-down shirt, thick-set, tan, healthy—looked a damn sight better than I did.

'You're with the Pentagon?'

He nodded.

'Don't tell me,' I said. 'Notley?'

'I've been of some assistance to Mr Chapin. And he to us.'

'He tell you I was coming?'

'No. Maybe he felt you'd made your bed . . .'

'Dug my grave would be more apt.'

'You're alive—the other guy isn't. That's what matters.'

'I know. The dead are dead. That's all that matters. How long did you know I was up there?'

'We found out yesterday.'

'Yeah . . . well thanks.'

'Raines. We saved your life.'

'I needed it saving yesterday too.'

I turned my back on him and stepped into the shower. Let him talk to my ass. I saw the door open through the scummy nylon curtain. I let the water stream over me for minutes, I didn't move, I didn't scrub, I just re-baptised myself in this motel Jordan. A hand came through the door and laid a clean white terrycloth robe on the lid of the can. I took it, slicked back my hair and stepped into the bedroom.

Hammond was going through my bag—the notes, the photographs— just as Feaver had. He fanned out the photographs, made a face, said, 'I sent out for food. Won't be anything special, there's just a diner down the road.'

'Well, as I already lost breakfast and seeing as how the soft shell crab season is over I'll join you in brownies and a burger.'

'I know you're pissed, kid, but we have things to do. Let's just cool it now. It could be a long night.'

Who was I to argue?

My savior, the guy who'd fired the rifle with the telescopic sights, came in with coffee, French toast, fries and overcooked sausage for three.

Hammond let me eat my fill without any questions. I was on the last bite of greasy French toast when he said, 'Tell me about it.'

'No. You tell me. You expect me to talk to the CIA, you better give me a good reason. And don't tell me how you just saved my life. I heard it already.'

Hammond, sitting on the bed, turned to the other guy, upright on a chair right by the door, and said, 'Wallace?'

Wallace swallowed, coughed into his hand.

'Mr Raines. I'm Wallace Craig. I'm with the Agency. I appreciate you might not want to believe this, but it is as factional an organisation as any other. There are some of us who know this war cannot be won and are anxious to prevent it being pursued further. It is not in the national interest.'

'We've got common cause, huh?'

Hammond said, 'You'll find you have more in common with us than with the people running Phoenix. You know who William Colby is?'

I shook my head.

'He runs the Phoenix Program in Saigon. Or he did until a matter of weeks ago. But now the agency's in retreat from stuff like Phoenix. Every time the press mentions it they take a step back from it. If Colby can whitewash Phoenix then one day soon he'll come back and run the CIA—it will be like Caesar crossing the Rubicon. I'd rather that didn't happen. If Phoenix isn't blown soon . . . then it's conceivable it never will be. Exposing Jack Feaver is a good place to start.'

'So, what do you want from me?'

'I want to deny them their deniability.'

I had the feeling that it was a phrase he'd worked out well in advance. Polished it like haiku. I gave him what he wanted as neatly as I could.

'It's a circle jerk. What goes around comes around. Feaver set Mel Kissing to find him. If Mel had completed the circle and found him he'd have picked up all the evidence Feaver wanted along the way—or he probably wouldn't have found him. Feaver didn't know Mel was dead. He was still expecting Mel when I showed up. When I realized what I'd blundered into I expected him to destroy the evidence, and half-expected him to kill me too. I could not have been more wrong. He's fighting a one-man campaign against the way the war is run. Unlike you he thinks it can be won. He'd given all his photographs of the massacre to the Phoenix Program. I don't know what he expected. Maybe he got what he expected. He shook 'em up and the program was kicked back into life. Maybe he thought his own fate was a price worth paying.'

'What changed his mind?'

'Chicago—people like Notley, people like Abbie Hoffman and Jerry Rubin. He decided he needed a platform. Wasn't enough to warn his own people anymore, he had to warn America. But, like I said, he'd given the photographs to Phoenix. He needed the roll Mouse had kept. He couldn't leave Vermont without a tail, so . . . I found it for him. And then he threw it all back at me and said "publish." '

'Why?'

'Took me a minute or two to work that one out myself. But it's obvious. He wants his day in court.'

Hammond seemed to want to take this in for a while, then he said, 'Let's give it to him.'

'Sure,' I said, sarcastic as a teenager, 'I'll send the photos to the *Voice* if I'm ever in New York again.'

'Nah,' Hammond replied. 'Think big. Send 'em to the *New York Times*.'

Wallace yawned. Just the cue I needed.

'Could I get some sleep now?'

Hammond said, 'Why not?'

Wallace prised himself put of his chair, shook himself like a waking dog, and said, 'There'll be someone outside all night, Mr Raines. You can sleep easy.'

Right.

§

I spent most of the next day going over it again. It is what I believe is called a de-brief. I annoyed the shit out of Hammond, but then I was trying very hard to do that, and at the end of a long, deeply dull afternoon, he seemed to feel he'd had enough and I hit him with the question that bugged me the most.

'How long have you known?'

He didn't bat an eyelid.

'There were rumors. Almost at once there were rumors. But it was well-contained. They didn't just discharge the squad that Feaver led, they buried their records. It was impossible to find them. I didn't have that kind of clearance. In the end they came to me in the shape of Notley and that was only at the end of March this year. Of course he knew the names of everyone involved, but Notley tells you only what he feels he has to to get what he wants, and short of knocking on the door of every Puckett in Kentucky . . . well we never had the man power for that.'

'Mouse. Notley could have told you where Mouse was.'

'Could but wouldn't. He's protective of Mouse. Everybody seems to be. And can you see Mouse talking to us?'

'Probably not. So what you're saying is you waited for a sucker like me to come along?'

'We waited. That much is true. For a couple of months we just regarded it as a watching brief. We knew where Jack was—for a while that had to be enough. To have made direct contact with him might have been to blow it all—they were watching him, and who knows what his reaction would be if we got to him. But, no, the sucker we were waiting for turned out to be Mel Kissing.'

'How did you get to know about Mel? Mel wouldn't even tell the *Voice* what he was working on.'

Hammond looked at me, kind of quizzical, as though he thought I could guess. I did. I traced it out in the air as much for myself as him. 'Fulton. Barclay Fulton works at the Pentagon. Mel phoned him. The old pals act. I know. I called him myself. Fulton found Marty Fawcett for him. He must have "clearance" as you put it, and either Fulton told you or he let it slip or you spied on the guy.'

'He told me. In confidence and in panic. A secret that burst inside him and just had to be spewed up. Kissing's death really shook him. Once I knew there was someone looking for the New Nineveh Nine—someone with more chance than we had . . . well, we put a tail on you, didn't we?'

'And I lost it.'

'Like I said, kid. You never knew when you were well off.'

§

I'd managed to ruin another set of clothes. The blood and the brain would never wash off my jeans and shirt. Hammond asked me my size and went to a store. 'I can hardly turn you loose looking like that, can I? You look worse than a Moondog.' The only convenient store had hunting as its specialty. I got kitted out in a baseball cap advertising engine lube, a heavy, red-check shirt and blue jeans cut so big in the ass they hung off me like empty potato sacks. All I needed was a furry waistcoat clipped from roadkill and rabbit and I'd of looked like Elmer Fudd. I felt like Elmer Fudd. He drove me to Rennselaer and put me on a train for New York.

'You OK with this, kid?'

'You mean I have a choice?'

'No.'

The conductor nudged me awake at Penn Station. I hailed a cab and went home to Front Street. It was just getting dark. Another hot August evening. I let myself in. The kitchen was fragrant, a hum of spice and action. Rose was at the stove clearly in one of her rare, much-hyped domestic moods. A voluminous blue dress, a big wooden spoon and her hair up. If the hair went up I always knew she was serious about something.

'Good bloody grief! What do you look like?'

Then she noticed the bruise on my left cheek.

'Been in the wars, eh? Mummy kiss it better.'

Even the kiss hurt. I stood rigid for the embrace. More than perfunctory. I had to conclude she'd missed me.

'Now, darling, are you hungry?'

What had I eaten in the last two days? Diner breakfast and diner lunch. Coffee so thin you could see through it. I could eat Rhode Island.

'You doing something special?'

'Chicken and chickpea tagine.'

'What's a tagine?'

'Stew. Moroccan stew with lots of spices. My sister was home for Wimbledon week too. I must have told you about Lucy—you know, inveterate traveler, lives out of a backpack. Just back from Morocco. She insisted on showing me some of the local nosh. Trust me, it's divine.'

'I'll trust you. Just let me change first. I don't feel right like this.'

'You look like . . '

'Yeah?'

'A good ole boy.'

'I was born a good ole boy, Rose. Come a long way from Bubba.'

I found Levi's that fit me like a holster, a clean white shirt. My Tony Lama's were spattered with blood and crud—but they'd clean up with a little saddle soap—besides I had eight more pairs in the bottom of the closet.

I fell into the couch. Rose set a feast out on the coffee table. Stuck Jefferson Airplane on the turntable—the new one, kind of raucous for my taste, 'up against the wall, motherfucker!' I was not one of America's 'Volunteers', I'd just been coerced. By the time I'd muttered my compliments on her cooking and listened to all the gossip of two weeks in London— 'Biba's has opened a much bigger shop . . . I spent the earth . . . the Arts Lab was a bit of a washout . . . everybody's too stoned these days . . .' she had worked back to the second album, *Surrealistic Pillow*—I'd always liked that. It had, still has, an elegiac feel that suited my mood—Marty Balin lost in melancholy on 'Comin' Back to Me', Grace utterly lost in the craziness of 'White Rabbit'. It hit the note.

Rose didn't ask me any questions—she was on one of her London highs. I was glad. I really didn't want to talk about it. Any of it.

She cleared away—I wasn't moving, and she wasn't complaining—put a plate of what looked to be fudge on the table.

'Have an Alice B, darling.'

'A what?'

I ate one before she answered, about the size of a walnut, sort of nutty, buttery and spicey.

'Something else from Morocco?'

'You don't know what an Alice B is? Good Lord, Turner, perhaps you'd better put your Elmer Fudd outfit back on and ne'er call yourself hippie again. An Alice B is named for the late Alice B. Toklas, cook, companion and, for all I know, lover of Gertrude Stein, and author of *The Alice B. Toklas Cook Book.*'

'So?' I ate another, they were delicious. Coriander and cinnamon.

Rose got up and took a cookbook from the shelf of cookbooks she kept handy between the kitchen and the living room and read to me.

'Haschich Fudge—note the odd spelling, lots of Cs like a German surname—Haschich Fudge, which anyone could whip up on a rainy day. This is the food of Paradise, of Baudelaire's Artificial Paradise . . . euphoria and brilliant storms of laughter, ecstatic reveries and extensions of one's personality on several simultaneous planes are to be expected. Almost anything Saint Teresa did, you can do better if you can bear to be ravished by *un évanouissement réveillé.*'

'You mean it's a hash brownie?'

'Absofuckinlutely, darling, a brownie with knobs on . . . but so much more than a hash brownie. Stronger, sweeter . . . cures the munchies as soon as it starts them. Alice advises not to eat more than two.'

I'd already had two. I had a momentary flashback to that lunatic Notley springing his culinary surprise on me and then I thought what the heck, it's only smokey the dope and I needed the release, I needed *un évanouissement réveillé.* Rose ate two, then we both ate thirds. And the storms of laughter, hers far more than mine, followed, along with the euphoria and the ecstatic reverie. She ran through half her record collection, a thousand hours of chatter, and as an unnameable record—they'd achieved a seamless blur and hum to me—spun idly in the final groove, she peeled off her dress and took me to bed. In all the years we'd known each other we'd never done that. I had thought of it as a house rule, a way of surviving together in that apartment—no sex. I began to wonder what exactly it was Saint Theresa got up to.

§

A hammering at the door woke me. Rose stirred but didn't wake, one huge, brown-nippled breast breaking cover as I slipped from the bed and pulled a blanket around me instead of a robe. I stumbled down the stairs, that feeling of too much dope and too much sex making me weak and benign all at the same time.

It was Nate Truegood. He knocked the benign out of me with a single blow. Suckerpunched me, straight left to the jaw and I sat down on the raised stoop, my ass bumping on the wooden boards, wide-eyed and legless.

'What was that for?'

'That's for lying to me, hiding things from me and the next one'll be for the visit I got from the Company this morning at seven fuckin' thirty!'

If he was going to hit me again I wasn't going to stop him. He was a big man but he was slow and he was pudgy and his punch lacked the weight of his shoulder behind it.

'What company?'

Nate seized an edge of the blanket and spun me off the stoop like a kid's top. I found myself sitting on the cobblestones bare-ass nekkid with Nate still up on the stoop looming over me.

'*The* Company. That's what! The CI fuckin' A. How come I get the Langley spooks calling on me at Sunday breakfast, givin' my wife a case of the jitters and tellin' me Mel Kissing is a closed case? I'll tell you why, one reason. You, motherfucker! That's who.'

'Yeah. Right. It was me. I was wondering how to tell you.'

He swung at me with his foot, missed by a yard, lost his balance and sat down with a thump far harder than the one I'd made. He howled out loud.

'Jesus Christ!'

'Nate, can we stop this now?'

'Who's gonna hear? It's Sunday. The fishmarket guys are off work, your neighbors are probably all upstate or out at the beach. Nobody'd hear if I was to beat your brains out with my bare hands.'

He picked up the blanket and threw it to me.

'Cover yourself up. I seen bigger cocks on a roach.'

He was spent. I'd seen this moment too often not to recognize it. I wrapped myself in the blanket and sat down next to him.

'So,' he said. 'You found the guy who offed your buddy.'

'Yes.'

'And?'

'And he's dead.'

'You kill him?'

'No—that was your friends from the Company.'

Nate weighed this up a little.

'Should I close the case?'

'I don't know. Is that legal? Is their word enough?'

'No, it's not. I don't like spooks. They lie for a living. You tell me I can close it, maybe I can. I figure you're not likely to quit on your little buddy just because the suits tell you.'

How little he knew me.

'Then close it, Nate. Mel's killer got iced by the spooks. I saw it happen.'

'You're sure?'

'Sure, I'm sure.'

'Motive?'

'Something Mel was working on. A story one bunch of spooks wanted suppressed and another didn't. Mel just got in the middle.'

Nate didn't ask me what—I'd already passed the bounds of what interested him.

'I'm not happy.'

'You're not happy? I'm totally bummed out. I been pistol-whipped, shot at, kicked about and now I got you thumping the shit out of me.'

'No apologies for that, Raines. And you ever pull a stunt like this on me again I'll beat the bejasus out of you.'

He got up, headed for his car, skewed across the end of the street, door open.

'Nate,' I called. 'Does this mean I get to keep my license?'

'What do you think, dummy? All I can say is you might like to consider a less dangerous line of work.'

I climbed the stairs back to the apartment. Watched Nate drive off from the living-room window. I felt two hands creep up my chest, two breasts pressed into my back.

'Were you telling him the truth? It's over?'

'Yes. It's over. I'm not a good liar.'

She squeezed me tight.

'Don't tell me anymore. I don't want to know.'

Tighter. Then she turned me in her arms, pulled away the blanket, stripped me naked as she was herself, kissed me deep and long. I had a split second to wonder, to work out that this might not be the one-night stand I had assumed it to be, before my cock came up and she took me by the hand, pulled me back into the bed and said, 'Do it to me one more time.' Sunday was sweet.

§

It was a couple of days before we rolled out of bed and back to some passing semblance of reality. I had priorities, just.

I typed up all my notes, packaged everything I'd collected since the end of June, stuck it all in a padded envelope and posted it to the *New York Times*. I signed the accompanying note 'Mel Kissing'.

Then I went in search of a car. Not liking driving is not the same thing as not liking cars. Whilst I never much felt I needed a car in New York, the Texan in me hated the idea of being without one. And I could not face another Bug. It had been like watching an old friend blown to pieces. I've no idea why, but all my instincts told me to buy American. And I did. An act of faith in Detroit perhaps? I could scarcely believe Amerika deserved any.

I got lucky. Guy over in Queens sold me a 1963 Studebaker. Lots of fins and a silly shade of pink, but a good price. Mileage a little high, and a few dents in the front end, but a good price for the year all the same. I drove over to New Jersey, stuck it in the same high rise stacker in Hoboken. It would probably be weeks before I had any use for it, but it was strangely reassuring to know it was there.

I caught the PATH train back to Manhattan, cut across Broadway and Nassau to Fulton, dropped by the market and picked up a couple of live lobsters. I got back to Front Street to find a backpack, complete with tent and bedroll, dumped in the hallway.

'Raines?'

Rose calling to me from inside the apartment.

'You'll never guess who's here.'

All I could see was some guy's head across the back of the couch. Short-cropped hair, a ring through one ear, the shoulders of a crazily embroidered Levi's jacket—and I was none the wiser. The head turned. It was my little brother Huey. Huey with short hair. Huey in New York. Huey where he'd never been before—ripped right out of context.

'You didn't tell me you were coming.'

'Not a lot of time,' he said. 'Just sort of . . . y'know . . . did it.'

'Why d'you get your hair cut?'

Rose intervened. 'Turner, for fuck's sake. Does he need an invitation? He's your kid brother. Just say hello and stop asking silly fucking questions.'

Huey got up and clapped me in both arms. Felt fake. The little bastard was up to something and I knew it.

Over dinner he produced a flier for a rock festival upstate—place called Woodstock. Near where Bob Dylan had lived as some kind of recluse ever since his motorbike accident.

'You wanna come?'

He was looking at both of us. From me to Rose and back again.

'Dylan's gonna be there.'

Right.

Rose said, 'I can't. I've had half of July off as it is. It's really nice of you, Huey but . . .'

Huey fixed his attention on me.

'It's gonna be big. Maybe 20,000 people. Janis Joplin, Hendrix, The Who . . .'

'It doesn't sound like me,' I said.

Rose said, 'Well, there's nothing to stop you. You like Janis Joplin, don't you? And you haven't any work at the moment, have you?'

Hadn't any work? For all I knew it was piling up behind my office door. I hadn't been there in weeks.

'Why don't you go with Huey? A day out. It'll do you good.'

'Er . . . it's more like four days,' Huey said.

I said nothing. Rose said, 'Don't you worry, Huey. The old grouch will go with you.'

The old grouch pointed out that he knew nothing about any damned festival in Woodstock. Rose picked up last week's *Voice* and found the music ads.

'So? It's been all over the *Voice* for weeks. Masses of publicity. Here it is. And it's not in Woodstock anymore, it's in Bethel. They had to move it. No idea why. But it's now at a place called . . . hang on . . . Yasgur's Farm. Silly bloody name. Who the fuck has a name like Yasgur?'

She folded the paper open at the ad and stuck it in front of me.

'Go with your brother, Turner . . . stop being a total prick and go with him.'

I tried procrastinating a little longer. I didn't have a sleeping bag. I'd left that somewhere in Lincoln Park last year. Rose went to the closet, pulled hers off the top shelf and threw it at me.

Was I being a prick? Absofuckinlutely, darling, as my late wife used to say.

§

So it was, Huey and I joined a human tide slouching towards Bethel. Here I was driving upstate, along the banks of the Hudson yet again, only days after I swore I never wanted to see these hills again. I might reiterate that it wasn't me, exactly, that I did it for the kid, but truth to tell I almost enjoyed it. It was a small step back into the recent past. Abbie Hoffman buzzed around, seemed to be in a dozen places at once. I got 'Hey man, haven't see you since—' and he was gone. Wavy Gravy appeared to be playing court jester for the whole week—big, floppy hat, no front teeth, and what seemed to be a pig's bladder on a stick. He was greeting anyone that passed like he was Woodstock's host. Wavy always struck me as the gentle, practical side of the hippies. Brown rice and stuff like that. He was someone I thought Huey should meet. I'd just got it lined up and I looked back to find Huey had drifted off and when I looked back the other way Wavy was greeting a bunch of kids who looked pretty much like the runaways I'd met in Chicago—the universal American girl-waif.

God knows how I ever found Huey again.

It began to rain on the first night. Richie Havens was a few bars into I forget what song and the rains came down. I don't recall it stopping for long. I'd've given up and gone home. Huey would not hear of it and nor, it seemed, would hundreds of thousands of other kids. They stayed, had to admire them for that. Wavy Gravy's Hog Farmers fed as many as they could and looked after the bum trips. It worked. A gathering of—what was it?—400,000 people camped in the shadow of Chicago '68 and it worked. I have since heard Woodstock referred to as the 'birth of a generation'. I doubt that. Chicago was the funeral. Woodstock the wake.

It was the third day. Early evening, we were drifting. Slithering from nowhere to nowhere on a sheet of mud. A bunch of freaks had made the most of the weather and started a mud slide—running at full tilt to the crest of a slope and ass-surfing down it for as long as mud and momentum would carry them. Huey just had to try. I passed.

'What's to lose?' he said. 'We're soaked already.'

I watched him skid down that slope whooping his head off. We have all kinds of crazies now, I thought, and if I have to choose between the acid-tripping, mud-caked, brown rice-eating freaks and the Kill-for-Peace Crazies I last saw Mel lost in then there's no contest. All kinds of crazies—hippies, yippies, hogfarmers—but nothing, nothing I'd seen in three days in the Woodstock Nation or three months in the imploding politics of New York had prepared me for what I saw next.

A guy resembling Mr Natural, spiraling hair, bushy beard, Moses' staff, all in white—dirty, mudded white—not so much a robe as a gigantic, outsize XXXL shirt—but skinny, painfully skinny, where Mr Natural was plump and round—got up on the stump to speak. A real stump, a sawn-off tree not thirty yards from where Huey was slippin' an' a slidin'.

'I have seen the face of God.'

He wasn't shouting. All the same his voice rang out. Seemed to cut through the hullaballoo. Half a dozen freaks turned to look.

'I have looked to the heavens and I have seen the face of God.'

Now, anyone could draw a crowd for a while. I'd seen that a dozen times in the last few days. No one could keep one—at best the best were sideshows unable to compete with the endorphin surge of being one in quarter of a million—like minds among like bodies, the endless, infinite curiosity of the other—or the direct appeal of Janis Joplin, or the fanciful anticipation that Dylan might still appear out of nowhere like Jeanie from the lamp. But they got heard. I saw no one booed off—at worst a gentle mockery of folly. This guy quickly drew about two dozen of us.

'Bad trip,' said a short kid in front of me.

'Nah,' said the girl he was with. 'Every guy with a bad trip thinks he's seen the devil. You ever heard one say he's seen God? This'll make a change.'

'I am a seeker,' Natural said.

'Score ten to me,' whispered the kid in front. 'For sheer cliché.'

'I have been a seeker after truth since I was as young as you are now.'

It was hard to make him out, but I'd've put him at sixty-ish. Forty years of seeking.

'I left my home, I left my family in search of truth.'

Someone with freshman English under his belt now yelled back, 'Truth is beauty, man, beauty is truth!'

I had not thought Natural was wholly aware of us, his audience. His eyes were locked onto those same heavens in which he had seen God. But he looked down at the boy, said, 'This is all ye know on earth.' Uttered more as though it were our limitation than our simple necessity. The kid had no comeback line, so I figured he'd shot his bolt with one line of Keats. And for the first time I could see Natural's face clearly. One eye glittered bright and blue—the kind of clarity you might think could see into your heart. One eye was scarred and vacant like egg-white. Cut from brow to cheek in a savage line that had split the lid and healed into a ridge years ago for want of proper sutures.

'I have seen the face of God, and I am come to tell you there is no God.'

'You still think he's not tripping?' I heard the short kid say.

His girlfriend shrugged and walked away. 'I read this already. It's Flannery O'Connor. *Wise Blood*. The Church of Christ without Christ.' The short kid followed and I stepped forward. Slipped to the second row. Closer to that hideous face.

'God was our dream. God was our mainstay and our anchor in another age than this. When that age died our God died with it. I have seen the face of God. There is no God. God is dead. I looked to the firmament, to the stars in the furthest heaven, and I found no light that would not one day go out. I found no God, I saw the face of God and God was gone.'

A few dozen had dwindled rapidly to about six of us. This line was probably going nowhere. This amount of self-contradiction wouldn't keep anyone's attention. Just mine.

'It is four light years to Alpha Centauri. A distance so great as to defy numerical calculation. Four years at the speed of light. A speed unattainable for at the speed of light mass becomes infinite.'

Just when I thought he might have got himself back on the rails of a good argument, the word seemed to stop him in his tracks—'Infinite . . . infinite . . .'—he pondered it as though another voice had said it to him, shaking the straggly white hair, head down, then head up. A momentary stare into the nothingness of his heaven and he was off again.

'And I looked beyond Alpha Centauri . . . I looked to the end of space and time. I looked to life. And I found none. In the arc of heaven there shines only this blue light of earth. A billion galaxies, twisting in space. Half a billion stars in our galaxy. Burning rock, cold rock. The rocks keep their secret, because they have none. The stars burn out only to burn again. We are life, there is no other. The earth spins alone in darkness. We live in darkness. We die in darkness. We die alone. The stars burn out. We are Man. And Man is all. In the midst of infinite space are stars so dense they devour their own light. Time and space invert. And another universe is born. The same as this. The same black vault of night. The same blinding nothingness of endless night. New stars burn. New gods abdicate meaning. New stars burn to dust. There is no God among the stars. We are life. We are all. We are everything. We are the dust of a thousand suns, a million stars, a billion universes drained of light. Turned inside out. Burned to dust. Alone in the vast canopy of space. The same old sheepshead pattern scrawled out into eternity. The world created, cracked, blown apart and re-created a thousand times. How do we not know that this is so? The stars go out. They burn to dust. We are stardust. There is no God. I have seen the face of God. God is dead. The age of God has gone. We are stardust. We are carbon.'

By the time he got to this we were alone. He was just another crazy. Kids had drifted off. What's another crazy? He rambled on—I've no idea how long. It just went round in the same half dozen loops over and over again. I felt a hand tugging at my shirt. Huey plastered with mud, looking like he'd just scrambled loose from some aboriginal initiation rite.

'Johnnie, Johnnie. Country Joe's up next. You know? "Feel Like I'm Fixin' To Die".'

'You go. I have to hear this guy out.'

'Jesus, Johnnie, you think we'd ever find each other again in all this if we split up? C'mon man. He's just another crazy.'

But he wasn't just another crazy. He was my brother Billy.

'I have seen the face of God!' he boomed out. Yelling with the full force of his lungs now.

Huey let go, as though this was more than he could take.

'Five minutes, man. I'll be over there.' Huey pointed to the nearest tree and walked away. Billy got down off the stump and came closer to me. He was shorter than me. I'd outgrown him. His good eye scanned my face. I found myself fixed on the poached-egg eye. Wondering how this had come to be. How Billy had come to this.

He spoke. The mouth opened. He had fewer teeth than Wavy Gravy and what he had were blackened stumps. His breath foul upon my face.

'In a trench of the Atlantic ocean beyond the light of any sun, there lives a mollusc in darkness so dense, in pressure so great the oxygen in the water is unbreathable. So the mollusc has learnt to live in darkness and in cold without oxygen, to respire anaerobically. And at the bottom of this trench, where perpetual night reigns, where God's creature has learnt to live without light or oxygen, there lives another of his creatures that has learnt to live without light or air and to eat the shit of this mollusc. We are stardust, we are carbon, we are mollusc shit.'

I glanced at Huey, back against the tree putting a match to yet another joint. I was still not sure how much Billy was aware of me, close as he was. Was I animate or inanimate to him? Real or a made up necessity, as the recipient of his rant? I had thought he might have gone on talking if I walked off, but in the second it took to look back he had thrust his face into mine, an inch or so away from me, talking to me and me only.

'You see this eye?'

He brought up a bent, scabbed, near-nailless finger to point at his poached egg.

'With this eye I looked beyond Alpha Centauri. With this eye I saw God. I saw the truth that God is dead. The eye offended. Matthew 18:9. "If thine eye offend thee, pluck it out"!'

He might as well have stuck a hand through my ribs and wrapped it around my heart. I could scarcely believe it. He had done this to himself. Taken a knife to his own eye.

'I had sought truth my whole life. And when my eye showed me that there was no truth, no beauty, no God—I plucked out that eye!'

He roared. Blasting me. The good eye roved. God knows what he was looking at, what he was seeing. He didn't know me from Adam.

His voice dropped, his shoulders hunched. I had never seen the man look so small. He was thirty-seven, doubled up into a blind, toothless sixty-year old. He seemed to vanish before my eyes. Bent over his stick, creeping away from me at a snail's pace. I could hear him muttering for minutes after he left me.

'Stardust, carbon, mollusc shit.'

Creeping away in search of the next transfixed fool who would listen to his revelation of the banality of life on earth and for a brief span of eternity lift the albatross from his neck. I wanted to weep. I could not. Rain provided tears enough for me. I wanted to run after him. I could not. He left me. Again. I felt as though twenty years of my life had risen up to fall on me like a weight. Billy made a great Mr Natural. He'd got his message home to me with the accuracy of a sharpshooter. I had never felt my life so hollow. I had never felt the years so hollow. Truth and beauty had shrivelled up and died in an instant. There I stood, nothing more than this temporarily animate lump of carbon, stripped of meaning, and wanting to die. I felt as though someone had taken all that had been good and great in my childhood and trashed it. I didn't have a dream left. The dreamer had left me. History repeats. The dreamer would always leave me.

He'd be about seventy-five feet away from me when he turned to look back at me with that cockeyed look.

'I had a dream,' he said in a voice almost lost in its own hoarseness, less than a yell, louder than speech, as though it swelled up from deep within and never quite surfaced. 'I had a dream.'

And I still say he did not know me from Adam.

§

Do I need to say that I did not, could not, would not sleep? No matter. I got kicked out of the tent anyway. Huey had picked up two girls,
two more runaway waifs, one for him and two for him. They had kept
his place in the human sea for him. He had dragged me back to them,
him ripped up with energy, me the walking dream, to hear Country Joe
McDonald belt out his anti-war anthem one last time. I sat through the
Band and Crosby, Stills and that other guy and I don't think I heard a
word or a note of any of them. And at the end of the day, as a thousand
private frenzies thrashed out around us, Huey zipped up the tent and
told me he wouldn't be long.

'Get him,' said the first girl to the second. 'Won't be long. Who does
he think he is, Johnny Come Quickly?'

I heard sotto voce placation from Huey, no words, just a sort of sexual
susurrus. Then, 'Who is he, your old man?' Huey laughed. 'My father?
Good fuckin' grief no—he's my big brother. He's just a tad uptight
tonight.'

So I was uptight. Nice to have the definition. Then the girls broke out
into giggles and giggles turned to moans, and I turned off to it. I wrapped
Huey's poncho around my head and shoulders. It was still raining. No
matter. It was raining on earth, somewhere upstate New York in the
summer of '69. I was somewhere else entirely. I was uptight not upstate.

I felt like the town fool in an ass-kicking contest. How many times
could I kick my own ass? Why had I not stopped Billy in his rant and
said 'Look, Billy, it's me, little Johnnie.' Why had I let Huey lead me by
the hand back into the musical oblivion, why had I sat cocooned in it
and done and said nothing? Why? Because he did not know me, and the
half of me that wanted to scream 'Biiiilllllyyyyy!' was in thrall to the half
that said he still wouldn't know me after I'd done it. But there was more.
Oh yes, there was more. Beyond, beneath, whatever, down to the belly
of the beast . . . beyond the broken heart there was the broken dream.
Billy had been . . . what? . . . the best of me . . . no, more than that, the
best of us, the best of my generation. What was it Ginsberg wrote about
the best minds of his generation? That he'd seen them rot? No . . . it was

something about madness . . . being destroyed by madness. Billy had been
the kid who'd put on the seven league boots and strode past us kids and
Mom and Pop Amerika as well. Billy had dreamed, as he'd put it himself
to me all those years ago, he had dared to dream. And was this how the
dream ended? A half-blind, half-naked, bumbling, shabby, scabby mad-
man? A Mr Natural of doom and despair?

Well, know thyself—as some fool in Hamlet put it, be true to thyself.
Well, truth is the bigger part of me has always been a coward. I've known
that since I was a kid. The coward would never have faced Billy, would
never have sought him out among the shards of his dream. So who was
that guy who girded up his poncho and set off through the fields of
Woodstock that night in search of his long-lost brother?

I came across a group of dopeheads sitting around, passing a joint the
size of a Havana cigar between them.

'I'm looking for someone. I'm looking for my brother.'

They were too stoned to understand a word I said. One of them just
pointed off a ways to where a fat guy was humping some girl by lantern
light. They were watching like it was TV. I bumbled over. The fat guy
had fallen asleep on her. He was snoring. She smiled up at me—a sweet,
friendly smile. An unselfconscious smile. She didn't mind the fat guy, lying
there buzzing in her ear while his cock slackened off inside her—she
didn't seem to mind me.

'Excuse me.'

'Sure thing, man.'

'I was looking for someone.'

'You found her. Just get Sluggo off me and you can have sloppy seconds.'

'No. I mean I was looking for a guy.'

'Really isn't my night, is it? Those heads are too stoned to do more
than look on and giggle, Sluggo's fast asleep and you're looking for a
guy. God, if I'd known it was just a spectator sport I'd of stayed a virgin.'

I gently rolled Sluggo off her.

'Actually I was looking for my brother.'

She held out a hand. I pulled her to her feet. She turned her back on
me. Picked up a wraparound skirt, twisted it on and turned to face me. I
could see now. She wasn't some horny teenager, she was my age. Another
'50s leftover deciding, in the words of J. Joplin, to get it while she can.
She tilted her head a little and looked up at me. Topless, pretty, inviting.

'You sure? You not lookin' for me?'

'He's a big guy. Shorter than me. But big. About forty but he looks older.'

'Tell me, do the words needle and haystack have any meaning for you? There must be hundreds of thousands of people here.'

'This guy looks like Mr Natural. He gets up on the stump and preaches.'

'Oh him. Gahd—everybody's seen him. And you say he's your brother?'

'Yes.'

'Weird.'

She came with me all the same. A posse of two picking our way through the sleeping bodies, the thrashing bodies, through the far from silent night.

She thought she'd seen Mr Natural camped out over here. I relied on her for 'here'. God knows how I'd find my way back to my own tent. There was no landmark to go by, just an inner compass of some sort. It led us to a lone, hairy freak, gently strumming a dobro and singing some sort of Hindu mantra over and over again in Donald Duck's voice—'Hawe Kwishna, Hawe Wama, Kwishna Kwishna, Wama Wama, quack, quack, quack' and so on. He too had seen Mr Natural. But not over here, over there. And so it went on. Hours, I guess. Not far off dawn. Pillar to post. Camp to camp. And freak to freak.

And by the dawn's early light I could see a great white T-shirt up ahead of us, on the stump of a tree, back to us, flapping gently in the breeze like a dirty white flag.

'That's him,' she said softly.

Maybe it was. Up on the stump ready for the first sermon of the day. But as we drew closer I could see. It wasn't him. It wasn't Billy. It was just his shirt. His shirt fixed up on two poles tied like a crucifix. A hollow symbol of the hollow man.

'Well,' she said. 'Maybe he'll come back for it.'

'No,' I said. 'He won't.'

Because I knew he wouldn't. He'd gone naked into the world, dragging himself 'through negro streets at dawn' looking for ...?

She led me back to where I'd found her. I stood and turned a full circle. Lost again. Then her inner compass kicked in, she took me by the hand, led me back to my own tent. I could hear Huey snore twenty feet off.

'So, are we going in?'

'We can't. My brother's in there with two girls.'

'So—maybe we could share your poncho. It's kinda cold out here. I'm freezing my tits off.'

We sat facing the tent, wrapped up like two Cherokee Indians on the Trail of Tears. Me and a half-naked woman I had met two or three hours ago and did not know.

'If your brother's in there how come we spent half the night looking for him?'

'Not him. My other brother.'

'You have two brothers?'

Well. No. I didn't.

I said, 'What's your name?'

'Grace.'

'No, Grace. I don't have two brothers. The kid in the tent is really my nephew. He just thinks he's my brother. Mr Natural's my brother. Mr Natural's the kid's father.'

'Weird,' she said, and weird it was. So I told her the whole story. The whole unholy trinity of Billy and Lois . . . and me. And she fell asleep. I'm damn certain she fell asleep before I was halfway through. So I told my secrets to a sleeping Grace. The perfect stranger. Just when I needed one.

A few hours later, one of Huey's girls emerged from the tent. Buck naked. Pulled on her clothes. Smiled at me without a hint of embarrassment— hippie kids seemed to do that all the time—and said, 'Your brother's quite something.'

I said, 'I'm sure he is.'

Because I knew he had been.

Naked into the world . . . dragging himself . . . brain bared to heaven.

§

Bob Dylan didn't show—which disappointed Huey, but then I'd never thought he would. I didn't think Dylan would ever perform live again. What did I know?

I was rolling up Rose's sleeping bag. Three days of me unwashed and still it smelt of Rose. Huey had packed his tent and his gear and stood like a grunt, overloaded and anxious, watching the human tide, slouching back. I wondered if he'd ever tell me, whatever it was.

'You know that bumper sticker you see sometimes?'

'What bumper sticker?'

'America—Love it or Leave it.'

'Oh—that one.'

'I'm leaving it.'

'You're not going home?'

'I'm not going back to Texas. If I go back I get drafted. They already sent for Gabe.'

'So you're skipping out?'

'I guess so. I mean. What choices do I have?'

The kid could make me spit fire sometimes.

'I tried to tell you what the choices were more than a month ago in Lubbock. You didn't want to know. Told me I talked like a lawyer.'

'Maybe it's now I need you to talk like a lawyer.'

'Then maybe it's time to hightail it to Canada, 'cause you used up most of your options. College, National Guard, C.O.—you wasted more'n a month when you could have done something. Though I'll tell you now it was late even then.'

'So what else is left? Why are you giving me a hard time about Canada?'

'I'm not. It may well be the right thing for you to do. There is only one alternative.'

'So?'

'You don't want to hear it. Really you don't.'

'Try me.'

'You report when they send for you. At which point you are still technically a civilian. They cannot give you a binding order. So when they ask you to step forward it is a request not an order. Don't do it. Don't step forward. Stay where you are.'

'And? What next?'

'Well, if enough of you do it, you'll have started a revolution.'

'And if it's just me?'

'You'll go to jail.'

'Jeezus, Johnnie. I might have known you were leading up to the catch.'

'Time to talk like a lawyer. You said so yourself. But . . . as you will still be a civilian it's civil disobedience not insubordination—it will be jail not the stockade.'

'That is the best you can come up with?'

'Huey—it's all I can come up with. Now, I suggest you take the car and go to Canada.'

'You mean like, just drive across?'

'What the fuck did you expect? Checkpoint Charlie?'

'No . . . I guess I expected something like the underground railroad. Like slaves being smuggled to the north. I don't know.'

'You don't know because you haven't thought about it. This whole draft issue has been one long rant between you and the old man. You never really thought it would happen though, did you? No—nobody will stop you. You're not a wanted man. Not yet. In a few weeks when it's obvious you've skipped out the draft board will tell the FBI, and from then on I strongly advise you not to try and cross back. They'll be watching. They even read the death notices in local papers just to see who might make a break for home to bury Mom or Pop. Whatever—don't do it.'

I zipped up my backpack, reached into my pocket.

'You'll need these.'

I tossed down the car keys. He bent down for them and I grabbed his hand.

'I see you already tried to chop off a finger.'

He pulled the hand back, rubbed at a reddish scar on the fourth finger of his left hand. Suddenly he was sheepish, shy and my little brother again, not the hard-assed brat.

'Chop would not be the word. Saw more like. Took a blunt knife to it one night when I was tripping. Couldn't even make a good job of that, eh?'

I said nothing. I could not have done it either. Huey scooped up the keys and said 'Canada' softly, more to himself than to me, as though the prospect were at last a reality and not another verbal weapon in his private battle with family and country.

'You wouldn't happen to know anyone in Canada, would you, Johnnie?'

We'd finally reached a kind of pragmatism. Maybe now I could talk to the boy without getting chewed out. I rattled it all off like catechism. It was second nature to me. Some guys up in Toronto had written a Dodger's Handbook. Could have written it myself. Huey listened and nodded a lot. He even wrote down Mike Koscuiscko's address. But I didn't want him being a leech on Mike.

I asked if he had any money.

"Bout five hundred in cash, but I got my bankbook too. Must be close to twenty-five grand in there.'

He hiked up his T-shirt, showed me a money belt wrapped tightly around his waist. Such foresight from a kid who up to now had struck me as having none. Twenty-five grand? Maybe I should make him pay me for the car?

'Whatever else there is to say about the old man, he's no tightwad. Johnnie, you're the only one says no to his money.'

'Maybe that's because I never was a rich kid.'

'What the fuck is that supposed to mean?'

"Zackly what it says. Now how good's your French? That could count with the Canadians.'

'OK. OK to good I'd say. Mom made me learn, her mom was from New Orleans. French gets sort of passed down.'

Jeez—the things I did not know about my own family.

'Then I think you'll be fine. Don't mess around. Ask to become a landed immigrant as soon as the Canadians look at your passport. "Landed Immigrant" is the term—get it right.'

'Sure—supposing they ask about the draft.'

'Won't happen—they're not allowed to.'

'And if I don't do the landed immigrant thing?'

The kid would drive me nuts.

'Aw shit, Huey—then buy a goddam fishing rod and tell 'em you're on a fishing trip!'

I'll be damned—the kid was actually thinking about it. I never should have given him the choice.

§

Thinking about it, I never should have given him the car. But it was traditional. A brother walks out on you—he gets to keep the car. How many cars did I have to lose this trip?—the Buick, my old VW, now the Studebaker. I'd lost more cars than brothers lately.

I found myself walking. It felt stupid, and I hadn't done it in years, but I stuck out my thumb. First car to pass me with a spare seat pulled up. Three zonked out guys heading back to Boston. Dropped me in Palenville. How . . . how handy. I hadn't seen Tsu-Lin in weeks, hadn't spoken to her since the day I phoned up to tell her Mel was dead. I owed Tsu-Lin Shin $229. Courtesy of Joey DiMarco. I'd've paid that for a shower and a shave.

I handed the money over. I got the shower and the shave. As it happens I got lunch too. Another hand-made Chinese flurry of herbs and . . . well . . . rice . . . and stuff . . . whatever it was Chinese people ate.

After lunch Tsu-Lin took me into her studio.

The little canvas of Bosch-ish faces had given way to an eight- by twelve-foot monster. And it had lost the touch of Bosch. It reminded me of nothing quite so much as a latter day *Guernica*. The central image was a pig rather than a bull, and the backdrop wasn't a cubist rendition of the Basque town, was all made up of bits of the USA. I thought I saw the sweep of the Golden Gate Bridge—I knew damn well I was seeing a panorama of Chicago—and wasn't that composite skyscraper made up of bits of the Empire State building and bits of Wall Street? Whatever it was it was gruesome, it was bloody, and if this had been three or more years in the evolution I hoped she thought it was worth it.

She stood beside me, looking at me as I looked at 'Chicagonica'.

'Year of the pig,' she said.

'Is that like something in the Chinese calendar?'

'No—stupid. It's the painting's title. Don't you think last year was the year of the pig?'

'Oh,' I said feeling bewildered rather than stupid. 'It's last year?'

'Gimme a break.'

We sat on that flaking verandah. It seemed symbolic. If Tsu-Lin had ever bothered to top out the trees that had grown up we'd have been

looking right down at the Hudson Valley—the view that drew all those
Vanderbilts and Rockefellers up here a couple of generations ago in the
glory days of the first American Empire. Now, we sat here in the wan-
ing days of the last. Tsu-Lin served up tea—the green stuff so favored
by Notley Chapin. I made tea-time conversation, something as banal as
'What a summer it's been'—and I was referring to nothing more than
the weather by it—and unleashed a small tornado. Maybe I'd annoyed her
by having so little to say about her magnum opus. Maybe it was another
bee in her bonnet just waiting for me to poke it with a stick.

'The summer Mel died,' she said.

'The summer we went to the moon,' I said.

'What?'

'I said the summer we went—'

'I heard what you said. I meant what is that supposed to mean?'

'Just what—'

'What a waste of fuckin' time that was.'

'What?'

'Moon shot, cum shot, it's all just one big jerkoff! We've gone to the
moon for nothing. It's a total waste of money.'

'Could be. What's out there?'

'Not my point. I meant. If I were a poor American—if I were a
black woman scraping a living skivvying in Alabama or Mississippi I'd
be thinking, "Whitey's on the moon now. So fuckin' what?" And I bet
that's exactly what the Blacks are thinking.'

'Never thought of it that way.'

I wasn't lying. I had not thought about it that way. Uttered by my punk
brother it hadn't been a notion worth thinking about.

'Whitey on the moon. I guess it is.'

'And if I were a little yellow woman with slope eyes who can go all
day on a bowl of rice and still tow a tank uphill with my bicycle—I'd
say it was the act of a nation that had lost its way.'

If this was irony, it was lost on me. Lost our way? It had been the dream
of a nation—Jack Kennedy had committed us to this years ago, and by the
time it happened it was smeared in the gore of a foreign war we could
neither win nor lose and dusted in the shards of the Great Society. But
it was still our dream. I had not dreamt this dream in an age—but before
all that, before Russian Sputniks, before Kennedy's knee-jerk reaction,

it had been Billy's dream and I was hearing Billy far louder than I was hearing Tsu-Lin. Perhaps if I had communicated a little of Billy's dream to Huey I might not have got the shit kicked out of me outside Sweet Chucky's bar back home. But what could I say about Billy to Huey—how do you tell a solipsistic brat about a father he never knew he'd never had?

'My brother Billy used to be fascinated by the possibilities of what might be out there.'

'Now there's a name I haven't heard in a while. When we were in college you used to talk about Billy as though you'd seen him yesterday.'

Had I so written the man out of my daily deliberations? Had there been no room for him in my conversation? Of course Tsu-Lin was right. Memory like an elephant. But once set on a course she was unshakeable— if I asked her again what she thought was out there she'd tell me all over again about waste and poverty, and if I told her I had seen Billy only yesterday ... well ... what? That there was nothing more, no further spark in heaven just because brother Billy had said so?

Tsu-Lin drove me down to the road about five in the afternoon, and put me on a bus back to New York. One more homecoming.

When I got into the apartment there was a note taped to the TV screen. Dated today.

'Gone to Baltimore. Back tomorrow aft. luv R.'

Fine. Mañana.

§

Came the mañana I decided to take reality by the shirtfront and go into the office.

Once I'd opened the door, shoving aside a pile of flyers and bills, I was hit by the smell of stale air. The place had been shut up for a month, in a heat wave. I'd never bothered with air-conditioning. I threw open all the windows. Didn't make much difference. The stale air of New York in summer—rotting garbage, blocked drains—wafted in. I sat at my desk, flipped the lid off a cup of deli coffee, and wondered where to start.

I sifted bills from flyers, tossed the junk mail, and put off the obvious
first task as long as I could. What the place needed was the spring clean
it never got last spring. And there was only one place to start.

I went down to the basement. Got a bucket and mop off the janitor,
scrubbed up the last of Mel—a brown, crispy melstain on the floor—and
poured him down the sink. So long little buddy. And once started, once
over the sentimental hump of flushing my best friend into the New York
sewers I found it easy to get to work. I dusted, I sorted, I junked, and I
rearranged. I hoped the phone might ring. I hoped someone might call
with an offer of work. I hoped some forlorn parent might walk in off
the street and I could pick up life exactly where I left it. No one did.

It left time for one of the heavy things in life. Move the refrigerator
and clean up whatever gunk has congealed behind it. Sort of thing you
do once every ten years if at all.

I gripped it in my arms and tugged, trying to break the seal of sticky
crud that glued it to the floor. It came free with a jerk that sent me back
a step, still clutching a six-foot refrigerator in my arms, and there was a
clunk as something landed on the floorboards.

I parked the refrigerator and looked to see what had been wedged
between it and the filing cabinet. There, point down, sticking in the floor,
was a small, black-handled ice pick. Just like the one I used to have, the
one that killed Mel Kissing, the one now gathering dust in the evidence
room down at the 5th Precinct.

Would you recognize your own fingerprints? I don't mean do you
know every whorl and swirl, but would you know your own thumb or
forefinger by a scar or a mark in the same way you'd know your own
teethmarks in the flesh of an apple? So happens I would. That big scar
on the forefinger of my right hand, from when I got it trapped in the
door of that old Fairblast wood stove of Great-Granpappy Raines when
I was about six.

I rooted around in my desk—found my Junior Detective Kit and dusted
off the handle of the ice pick. Played Sherlock Holmes with a magnifying
glass. No doubt about it—I'd handled it. It was mine. And if it was mine
how did my prints get on the one Nate Truegood had slapped in front
of me in June? I regret to say there was a very simple answer.

I locked up. Caught a cab back to Front Street. Still no Rose—thank
God. I turned out the kitchen drawers, rattled through cutlery and

implements until I found it. A small black-handled ice pick. Identical to the one I'd found an hour earlier, identical to the one that had killed Mel. It had always been one of my chores to hack out the icebox. 'Bloke stuff,' Rose would say. We'd had it for years. Only it was new.

I began to feel my heartbeat rise. I felt a new world begin to tear itself apart just as the old one had done the day Nate told me Mel was dead.

Rose was nothing if not methodical. A place for everything and everything in its place. There were two drawers in the top of her bedroom chest—one she called her knickers drawer, the other housed bills and receipts. I had never known her to throw anything away. In a matter of seconds I was clutching two receipts that threatened to self-combust and take me with them. One, dated mid June, was from an Upper East Side clinic that most in-the-know New Yorkers knew was a cover for an illegal abortion practice—$1,000. The other, dated the day after Mel died, was from a hardware store on East 8th, one ice pick—$2.98.

Oh no. Oh Jesus.

What did Mel say when I asked him who his new woman was, the last time I saw him? He said, 'Nobody you know.' What does 'Nobody you know' mean? It means somebody you do know. In all the years of cat and dog battles I'd seen the two of them have I never thought for a second that they had been or could be lovers. They were too much alike. But they had been. He'd gotten her pregnant sometime before I went to Toronto. Clumsy little prick. And he'd what? Ignored her, refused to acknowledge it was his, just stiffed her for the money? What? What? And what had Rose done? Put on her tight little English pigskin gloves, picked up the household ice pick, gone into my office and iced Mel? Iced Mel and left my prints all over the murder weapon?

Oh no. Oh Jesus. Not Mel.

It didn't bear thinking about.

I thought about it.

Rose had spent over two weeks in England this summer—putting herself beyond reach, beyond suspicion? When I came back from Vermont did she ask me any questions about Mel, about all I'd been doing? No—she tumbled me into bed to smother any suspicion I might have had with sex. And when she'd heard me and Nate wrap up the case that Sunday morning, she asked me, 'Is it over?' And to seal it up she'd taken me back to bed.

How dumb could I get?

I put the receipts back, shoved the drawer back. Stood in the sitting room.

Freeze framed.

Stopped in time and space.

Carbon and mollusc shit once more.

Who was it wrote, 'My life closed twice before its close'?

And Mel's voice came into my head once more, mangling Emily Dickinson's verse with his forgetful something somethings . . . not sure which was heaven and which was hell. I don't think he even knew the words to 'Blowin' in the Wind'.

It's no doubt a cliché, and a big one, that the dying man sees his whole life flash before him. As a kid, when I first heard the phrase, I had this idea of *Pathé* News or *The March of Time,* all speeded up but still with the rooster crowing and that portentous voice telling you how important it all was. Like the first time I got a *Reader's Digest* letter telling me I'd won a major prize, it takes a while before you realize the insignificance of your own life. I was wrong, it isn't a movie—I can tell you, the twice dying man sees his life as a second rate slideshow, a series of clattering transparencies jerking round in an endless loop on a shaky carousel, lit by a flickering projector. As your enfeebled brain searches desperately for meaning it discards most of the restofyerlife and just gives you the snapshots.

Mel, that last night in the Village . . . beardless and angry—well, when wasn't he angry? Cut to Mel on the slab, the day Nate Truegood showed me his corpse, leached of life—who knows if the dead feel anger?

Rose, hair up in a turban, spattered with paint as she had been the first time I set eyes on her. Cut to Rose, hysterical with grief the night I got back from Canada to find out Mel was dead. How does anyone fake something like that?

Althea, backpack on, typewriter in hand, leaving me. Why now? Why think of Althea Harris Burke now? But Althea cut to Rose. Rose peeling off her dress to take me to bed, and Rose cut to the guy up in New England pressing the barrel of his shotgun to my head. I had not thought about him since I saw him blown away by Hammond's sharpshooter. It was a memory I could readily erase. I had never wanted to see that image, re-live that moment again—but the carousel juddered back and forth.

Rose peeled off her dress again and again and the guy's head exploded right in front of me, over and over again.

For the first time I was curious about him. Up till now I'd merely been grateful that he was dead and not me. And I'd taken it for granted that he had followed Jack Feaver into New York, and killed Mel. But he hadn't, and I think I'd only been able to wrap the issue in my mind by concluding that he had. He'd followed Mel—of course he had, why else had Mel bothered to mail me his notes?—but he hadn't killed him. He never got the chance. Rose had killed Mel. Rose had killed Mel.

Cut to Rose. Peeling off her dress. Cut to Rose, hysterical with grief. How does anyone fake something like that? What was it Nate had said? 'One blow, pierced his skull and buried the blade almost to the hilt in his brain. That took some strength.' Good God, had she been that angry? Had her whole body turned to rage? And rage to superwoman strength?

Cut to Rose, hair up in a turban, spattered with paint as she had been the first time I set eyes on her. Cut to Rose, hysterical with grief. Cut to Rose. Peeling off her dress. To take me to bed. How does anyone fake something like that?

I heard the door bang open. Rose breezed in, dress billowing around her, hair bouncing, eyes bright, a smile on her lips, a brown paper bag of groceries in each arm. She dropped the bags and kissed me. A wet smackeroo, packed with feeling, her tongue prising my stubborn lips apart.

She must have bought pasta sauce, lots of it. When she pulled off to draw breath I looked down to see burst bags and broken glass and a bloody tide lapping at my feet.

'Johnnie,' she said. 'Johnnie.'

She kissed me again . . . and I knew I was damned.

§

Who would ever know?
Who would ever tell?

§

There are times listening to Americans that you'd think we were roast alive on the grid of Vietnam. That faux-Texan George Herbert Walker Bush, a man whose stake in the state was a vacant plot of building land, summed it up neatly when he put both arms in the air at the end of the Gulf War and told the nation, 'We have finally lain the ghost of Vietnam.' Vietnam does not matter. Not in the way Bush thought it ever did. 'We got our ass kicked'—I've never believed that, I've never believed America was defeated by the Viet Cong. America was defeated by the processes of Democracy, by a million kids in the streets exercising the right of free speech to say, 'Hell no we won't go.' The Founding Fathers gave us that right when they dreamt up America. No foreign war has been quite as powerful as the First Amendment. Some of America, God knows maybe the larger part of America, has never grasped this. It sees humiliation in every minor incident—a boat hijacked by Cambodia, an embassy seized by fundamentalists—as down to giving way in Vietnam. We have a memorial—a much contested memorial, the least glorious memorial the dead of any nation ever had—to our fifty-seven thousand and some dead. Do we even have a statistic that's any better than a guess for the Vietnamese dead? And Jimmy Carter said we owe them nothing.

§

Amerika tore itself to rags and ribbons even as we kissed, before I could free myself from that permanent, all-enveloping embrace just to draw breath. Days of Rage. The Crazies set off a bomb in a Marine Midland bank, brought the war home to Manhattan—another on one of the import piers—let's kill fruit for peace. And the Weathermen put bombs in toilets in the Capitol—let's blow the pants off women in Congress and put an end to global capitalism. And then, for good measure, they trashed Chicago one more time and blew themselves to heaven or hell on West 11th. And the Motherfuckers? Well you can't keep track of everyone—

maybe they just became one more neon explosion in the neon oven.
But by then we were all up against the wall. Tricky Dicky blew away
some campus bums at Kent State, and did more to bring the war home
than Notley and Feaver could between them, told a thousand lies and
got kicked out of office. That was '74—by then I found it impossible to
take any pleasure in his resignation. 'So we got Tricky' was overwhelmed
by 'who didn't we get?'

She kissed me one more time. This time for ever. This time.

Time passes. We live like squirrels in our nest, and Amerika tore itself
to rags and ribbons even as we kissed.

Time passes. Rose and I kept Sunday sweet for twenty-four years. We'd
turn off the cooker and the radio, unplug the phone, read the Sunday
papers, which in New York, you can always get on Saturday, walk in the
park, talk, and end a blissfully peaceful day with an early night like a
couple of horny teenagers. Once every ten years it would be fulsome in
the way I, and maybe Mailer, had imagined it. When New York suffers a
heavy snowfall, flakes floating down outside your window the size of old
JFK half-dollars, the traffic seems only too willing to give up. I have seen
it like this on Thanksgiving and on a few Sundays. To wake to a blanket
of white that quiets the city and to see not a tire mark on it. To walk up
an Avenue and hear only the crunch of your own feet on virgin snow.
Sweet Sunday. It is the most enduring fragment of the sixties. Perhaps the
only one of the many I have kept that I still believed in. Sweet Sunday.

Time passes. Rose died last year. She wanted her ashes scattered in Fish
Bridge Park, a couple of blocks from the apartment, down by the side of
the Brooklyn Bridge where the traffic roars by at rooftop level. It's the
smallest park in the city—a thin strip of reclaimed vacant lot that looks
like the last hippie enclave in Manhattan, cherry trees, honeysuckle, wis-
teria and dusty vegetables growing in the shadow of the bridge, yearning
sunflowers and scarlet tulips bending in the breeze off the East River. She
planted the tulips herself. The city said no, so I did it anyway. I have lived
alone in her apartment ever since. Her apartment. When the will was read
it turned out she'd owned the whole damn building since 1962. Never
told me. Kept up the fiction of the skinflint landlord for over thirty years.

Mouse? Mouse found no one in West Texas much wanted their family
portrait taken by a black man, and after his Village 77 photos went syndicated only psychos wanted their photograph taken by this black man

so he sold up and put the money into a gas station franchise. He told me, 'I look more acceptable in dirty overalls, it confuses whitey less—'sides I make five times what I did.' The Justice Department sent federal marshals and attorneys to take his statement. He wasn't charged with anything, but they picked up the life he was trying to make and shook it. He was famous, if not infamous for a while—and he never blamed me. I still hear from him time to time.

Cousin Gabe, no matter how much pizza he forced down, gained no weight. According to Mouse he was as skinny the day they drafted him as he had been the last time I'd seen him. He disappeared in combat, down on the Mekong Delta, in December 1970. The army listed him as M.I.A.—Missing in Action—but Mouse would have no truck with this and told me so.

'Kid ain't M.I.A. He's N.D. double N.'

The army made an acronym out of everything, but this was not one I'd heard. I had to ask.

'N.D. double N. 'Nother Dead Nigger in 'Nam.'

Notley Chapin joined the Weathermen—perhaps the craziest of the crazies—and he was believed killed in the explosion that tore through their bomb 'factory' on West 11th in the spring of 1970. But then someone reported seeing him in Missoula, and then Des Moines, and then Pierre, South Dakota, and it became clear that either Notley was alive or we were in the grip of a potent urban myth in which Notley was reincarnated in all the two-horse towns of America. I waited for a report of him glimpsed talking to Elvis in a midwestern diner on some boulevard of broken dreams. But—he was alive. Turned himself in in 1984, only to find the case against him so tissue thin it was thrown out of court. He too was famous for a few months, wrote his memoirs and then went back to Arizona. Runs a vegetarian restaurant in Tucson. About once in every five years some journalist of limited imagination turns up to write a 'where-are-they-now' piece on Notley, chats to him over the tofu special and delights in publishing the fatuous truism that man mellows, thereby missing the equally fatuous truism that man also lies to journalists. I will never eat another meal cooked by Notley Chapin.

Ethel Harvest Moon was one of a group of Indians who occupied the old prison on Alcatraz a couple of months after Woodstock, claiming that under the Constitution of the United States redundant federal land reverted to them, the indigenous people. They were still there, arguing the case well into 1970.

Jack Feaver stood trial. The only one who did. As much of America was for him as against him, a fact on which he surely gambled. He became a cause célèbre. Said his piece, got a derisory two-year sentence and was out in ten months. His name remains a symbol. A by-word for mindless slaughter, a mnemonic for the shabby way we failed to back our boys in 'Nam. I, and the nation, have not heard from him since.

A few weeks after it opened I went down to that cold, cobalt wall that is our monument to the Vietnam war, still clutching my snapshot of the New Nineveh Nine. The Quick—Notley, Al Braga, Lee Puckett—looking for the Dead—Stanley Mishkoff, Tod Foster, Bob Connor, Pete Chambers, Gus Gore, Marty Fawcett. I suppose I hadn't really expected to find the last two there—they'd died at home. The other four I had, but they weren't there either. It was as though they'd been erased from history. I stood by as guys of Huey's generation traced out the names of the dead with fingertips outstretched and tears in their eyes and I looked in vain.

William Colby returned from the field, crossed his Rubicon and became, exactly as Hammond had told me, Director of the CIA. There followed a much-vaunted cleansing of the agency stables in which few outside the CIA could believe.

Abbie Hoffman killed himself five years ago. And I heard just the other day Jerry Rubin got hit by a car crossing Wilshire Boulevard—he died twelve hours later.

My brother Huey never came home. Six weeks after he failed to show for induction two grey-suited FBI agents drove out to Bald Eagle and called on the old man.

'We're looking for Samuel Houston Raines.'

'You found him.'

'No, sir—we're looking for a much younger man.'

Sam reached for the phone, pulled a string for the first time since I'd got my head kicked in on the Freedom Rides, called his old pal in the Texas Hills, and fucked up his retirement—writing his memoirs, waiting for death, whatever.

'Lyndon, get these pieces of shit off of my porch.'

We none of us ever heard from the feds again.

Lois paid for Huey's college time in Toronto, and when Carter am-
nestied the draft dodgers in '77 she begged him to come back and make
his peace with Sam. He wouldn't. Sam died without ever seeing Huey
again. In his seventies the old man had planted vineyards and reaped a
second fortune with his 'Never Raines Texas Cabernet'—slogan on the
bottle, 'Never Raines But It Pours'. Still embarrasses the hell out of me
every time I see it.

Lois will be sixty-five this year. Her hair has dulled. Not much else
has. When Rose died she urged me to come 'home'. Two widows in
that great glass mausoleum. I couldn't do it, though for a while I seriously considered going back to live in the cabin—but then the Plains
Historical Association, Society, Museum, whatever, approached Lois and
asked if they could adopt it as some sort of state monument to open to
the public at $5 a head on summer weekends. Lois passed the request
on to me. I said OK.

My brother Billy? God knows. A white-frocked saintly hobo of the
backroads come to tell you life is meaningless?

Me? Like I said, I live alone now. But then from this vantage point
it seems to me I always have. I sit in Fish Bridge Park and listen to the
rumble of the traffic on the Brooklyn Bridge, and once a week I will
walk to the other side and gaze at Liberty from the Heights. No one
whispers sweet heresies in my ear. The sound and the fury gone silent. A
stream of white noise in the head that just seemed to turn off. And what
would I not give to hear those whispers again? For a voice that would
simply tell me where the next battle is to be found—a voice that would
avert the inevitability of loss and make me feel that life need not always
come to down to this—the emptiness of ease, the comfort of inaction.
Oh Sweet Jesus, just whisper to me one more time.

Geographical Note

Occasionally I get accused of playing fast and loose with history. Whatever. With this novel, I'll own up to having played slow and loose with geography, geology and time. I've compressed all three. The main story is strung out over about five months. If you add up the days and weeks my hero spends here or there, it'll never make five months. Vietnam is a composite. The march undertaken by the New Nineveh Nine passes through a 'sampling' of most of the terrain Vietnam has to offer. Arizona—well, you'll search the Chiricahuas for anything quite like Notley's hideout. I threw in bits of geology and flora from New Mexico and Texas as well. Lubbock is Lubbock and Texas is pretty much Texas—but I wanted Mt Bald Eagle, a vast shale tower sitting on the plains. There isn't one, so I made one up. A couple of years after, I was pleasantly surprised when, heading north to Amarillo, I found a tower actually existed, not on the Texas plains—I should be so lucky—but at the bottom of Palo Duro Canyon a few miles outside Amarillo. I call this vindication—of a sort—a touch of 'build it and he will come.'

Acknowledgements

There are plenty ...

Gordon Chaplin
Marcia Gamble Hadley
Patty Ewald
Sue Freathy
Ion Trewin
Clare Alexander
Rachel Leyshon
Victoria Webb
Mike Cochran
Ray Robertson
Phil Marchand
Alexandra Anderson
John Armour
Sarah Teale
Zoe Sharp
Jerry Kearns
Rex Weiner
Dwight Hobart
Zette Emmons
Peter Blackstock
Deb Seager
Morgan Entrekin
Sam Redman
Frances Owen
Allison Malecha
&
Arthur Cantor ... who spent a lifetime in the hip hooray and ballyhoo, who housed me and argued the toss and made dreadful jokes while I wrote several novels up on West 72nd. Arthur died a few weeks before I finished this one. No one in the history of New York had a wittier, more literate landlord.

Read on for an excerpt from John Lawton's next novel,
The Unfortunate Englishman.

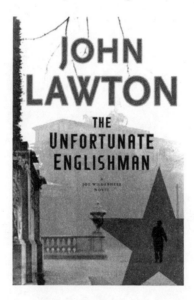

Praise for John Lawton:

"John Lawton is so captivating a storyteller that I'd
happily hear him out on any subject."
—Marilyn Stasio, *New York Times Book Review*, on
Second Violin

"Lawton's gift for atmosphere, memorable characters
and intelligent plotting has been compared to John le
Carré, but his dry humor also invokes the late Ross
Thomas . . . Never mind the comparisons—Lawton
can stand up on his own."
—*Seattle Times*, on *Then We Take Berlin*

§1

West Berlin: June 28, 1963

He took Berlin.

Wilderness had done stupid things in his time. Stupid things. Unforgivable things. The only person who would not forgive him this time was Wilderness himself.

He took Berlin.

Why, after all this time, had he got involved with Frank Spoleto again? Was once not enough? Had he not learnt the lesson? You can lead a horse to water but you'll never make him trust anyone called Frank?

He took Berlin.

It was a ludicrous scheme from the start . . . to smuggle a nuclear physicist, a veteran of the Manhattan Project, out of East Berlin using the same tunnel they had used to smuggle coffee, sugar, and God-knew-what during the airlift in '48. Ludicrous? Crazy. Just asking to get caught.

He took Berlin . . . Berlin took him . . . Wilderness was in the Charlottenburg nick, on the Ku'damm. He'd denied everything. He wasn't at all sure how long he could keep this up.

Shooting Marte Mayerling had been a mistake. She'd slipped behind him dressed as a rubble lady, a *Trümmerfrau*, and he'd shot on instinct, shot on memory. For a moment, too long a moment, he and Nell Burkhardt had stood riveted to the spot, unbelieving, her hand wrapped around his. Then the mirror cracked and he had ripped up his shirt to stuff a finger in the dam wall and stanch the flow of blood. Nell had got rid of the gun. Surely she had? With any luck it was gone for good. He'd never see the gun again. He'd never see Nell again.

Berlin took him.

A squad car. An ambulance. A vanload of coppers. Then the slow crawl, hand on horn, honking a way through the surging crowds of Kennedy supporters back to the Ku'damm. A grey cell and black coffee.

As coppers went, this lot were civilised. No one had hit him, no one had so much as raised their voice to him. He had not asked for a lawyer; he had simply asked, repeatedly, that they charge him or let him go. For all his time in Berlin he still had no idea how long they could hold him. Only when the shift had changed and a day copper, a burly sergeant in his forties, had recognised him from the old days just after the war—"You used to sell me black-market NAAFI coffee. You *und* liddle Eddie. *Im* Tiergarten"—did it begin to seem inevitable that a chain of connection and causality would be set off that would lead him to this moment. The moment Burne-Jones walked in.

"You should have sent for me at once."

"I resigned two years ago. You surely haven't forgotten?"

"You know, Joe, when I have your balls in my fist, sarcasm is really rather ill advised."

"Alec, I would never have sent for you. It's all too . . ."

"Too what? Too bloody familiar?"

Wilderness could not deny that.

It wasn't just familiar; it was almost a carbon copy. Tempelhof, or thereabouts, that cold autumn of 1948, the height (or was it depths?) of the blockade. Lying in a makeshift, prefab hospital in the American Sector with a Russian bullet in his side. Rescued, promoted to a rank he'd never surpass, and thoroughly bollocked.

"Sign here."

"Eh?"

"Sign on the dotted, Joe, and all this will just go away."

Wilderness read the page in front of him.

"So . . . I'm re-enlisting?"

Burne-Jones said nothing. Just stared back at him, accepting no contradiction.

Wilderness turned the page around to show him.

"There's a typo. The date's wrong. You've typed 1961 instead of 1963."

"Just sign."

"If I sign this, it's as though I never left. It's dated the same day I resigned."

"Quite."

"Quite my arse. It means all the time I've been here I have technically been working for you."

"And how else do you think I could get you out? The West Berliners want your guts for garters. You were found with a half-dead woman clutching a smoking gun."

"No, Alec, that is not the case. There was no gun."

"Oh. Got rid of it did you?"

Wilderness said nothing.

"Well . . . it will put in a ghostly appearance when these dozy buggers get around to testing your clothes for powder residue, so I suggest we get out now. They won't like it; after all it's a stark reminder that they don't run their own city and that what we and the Americans say counts for a damn sight more than what the chief of the West Berlin Police says. Sign, and it, whatever it is, becomes an Intelligence matter. Sign and walk, or keep up this nonsensical surliness and get charged with attempted murder."

Wilderness signed.

The sense that once again Alec Burne-Jones had him by the balls was palpable. A tightening in the groin demanding all the flippancy he could muster.

As they stepped out into the summer sunshine on the Kurfürstendamm, Wilderness blinked, looked at Burne-Jones and said, "You owe me two years' back pay."

And Burne-Jones said, "Joe, how exactly did you get rid of the gun?"

§2

The zoo, West Berlin: June 26

Marte Mayerling might well die. Wilderness dropped the gun, threw off his jacket and tore at the tails of his shirt to stanch the flow of blood from the wound in her side.

Nell seemed frozen, standing over him in silent shock.

Marte Mayerling was far from silent.

"So, he shoots me . . ." over and over again, a mantra of delirium, the deathly high that is blood loss.

"Nell . . ."

"Joe?"

"Take the gun. Take my passport and go."

Nell snapped out of her trance and rummaged in his jacket for the passport.

Wilderness took his hands off Mayerling for a moment, the blood surging up again, slipped out of his shoulder holster and threw it to Nell.

"Get to the zoo station, call an ambulance and then disappear."

"Disappear?"

"Nell, vanish . . . you were never here."

He pressed down on the wound. Mayerling's insane chant grew softer and softer. She might die on him any minute and the only plus to that scenario would be her silence. She might die before the ambulance arrived. She might die just to spite him.

Time melted at his fingertips. He had no idea how long he leaned on her. His hands went numb. Fifteen minutes? An hour? It seemed to him an age since she had spoken. He heard the sound of sirens approaching, and Mayerling stirred again, one last croaking complaint of "He shoots me . . . so he shoots me . . . " Then they were there, a white-suited ambulance crew, a huge Daimler ambulance and seconds behind them West Berlin coppers in their tiny Opel, guns at the ready.